THE SNOW KILLER

A DI BARTON INVESTIGATION

ROSS GREENWOOD

B

Boldwood

First published in Great Britain in 2019 by Boldwood Books Ltd.

Paperback ISBN 978-1-83889-447-4

Ebook ISBN 978-1-83889-442-9

Kindle ISBN 978-1-83889-443-6

Audio CD ISBN 978-1-83889-448-1

MP3 CD ISBN 978-1-83889-446-7

Digital audio download ISBN 978-1-83889-441-2

Boldwood Books Ltd
23 Bowerdean Street
London SW6 3TN
www.boldwoodbooks.com

To my children, Isla and Aiden, even if you do keep interrupting me

'I never killed anybody that didn't deserve it.'

— FRANK WHITE: THE KING OF NEW YORK

PART I

WINTER

50 YEARS AGO

1

I must have been ten years old when I first tidied up his drug paraphernalia. I didn't want my sister crawling over it. We called her Special – a take on Michelle – because she was an enigma. Special was a term of endearment for us, funny how nowadays it could be considered an insult. She never spoke a single word and seemed more of a peaceful spirit than a physical entity. Give her a crayon or pencil and a piece of paper, though, and her smile filled the room.

I monitored my father's habit through his mood swings or by how much time he spent in bed. The foil and needles increased rapidly just before we escaped London a few years back. I cried because both my parents left evidence of their addiction.

In many ways, my mother was as simple as Special. Swayed by my dominant father, she did everything he said, even though she had more common sense. Joining him in his heroin habit was inevitable.

Until the night we left, we took holidays and ate out in restaurants. I didn't know where the money came from because I had no idea what my father did.

The evening we fled London, we packed our suitcases at ten

at night and caught the last train to Peterborough, arriving at two in the morning. I recall beaming at my parents, especially when we checked into a huge hotel on the first night. My mum's brother, Ronnie, lived nearby. When we eventually found him, he helped us move into a cottage in rural Lincolnshire, which was cheap for obvious reasons. The single storey building had five rooms and no internal doors. You could hear everything from any room – even the toilet.

Six months after we settled in our new home, I lay in the damp bed with my sister's warm breath on my neck and heard my father casually say he'd shot the wrong man. The fact my mother wasn't surprised shocked me more.

Life carried on. My parents continued to avoid reality. We ate a lot of sandwiches. Lincolnshire is only two hours north of London but it felt like the edge of the world after the hustle and bustle of the capital city. I walked the three miles to school. Special stayed at home where she painted and coloured. My mum sold Special's pictures. She drew people and animals in a childish way, but they captivated people as the eyes in the pictures haunted the viewer.

One freezing night, my sister and I cuddled in bed and listened to another argument raging in the lounge. We had our own beds but only ever slept apart in the hot summer months. At six years old, she didn't take up much room.

'You did what?' my mother shouted.

'I saw an opportunity,' my father replied.

'What were you thinking?'

'We're broke. We needed the money.'

'What you've done is put our family in danger. They'll find us.'

'They won't think I took it.'

I might have been only fifteen years old, but I had eyes and ears. My parents constantly talked about money and drugs. By then, that was all they were interested in. That said, I don't recall being unhappy, despite their problems. Normal life just wasn't for them.

My mother's voice became a loud, worried whisper. 'What if they come for the money? The children are here.'

'They won't hurt them,' my father said.

A hand slammed on the kitchen table. 'We need to leave.'

'It's three in the morning and snowing. No one will look now. Besides, where would we go?'

'We're rich! We can stay where we like.'

Crazily, they laughed. I suppose that's why they loved each other. They were both the same kind of mad.

That was the sixties and a different time. Not everyone spent their lives within earshot of a busy road. In fact, few people owned their own car. If you've ever lived deep in the countryside, you'll know how quiet the long nights are. So it makes sense that I could hear the approaching vehicle for miles before it arrived. The put-put-put we gradually heard in unison that night sounded too regular for it to be my uncle's ancient van. And anyway, good news doesn't arrive in the middle of the night.

Mum understood and her bellow filled the cottage. 'Grab everyone's coats and shoes. I'll wake the kids. Move!'

We slept more or less fully clothed due to the draughty windows and non-existent central heating. The warmth from the fire failed to reach the bedrooms. I rammed my boots on in seconds, and I slid Special's warm feet into her little red wellies. Even at that time of night, my mother wore full make-up, but her beauty couldn't disguise her wild eyes and trembling jaw. She hustled us kids to the back door where our jackets hung.

I held my hands out to my father. 'Come on, Dad. Please, let's go.'

My father peered through the window. Judging by the volume of the car's engine ticking over, they had arrived. Then, a heavy silence. He glanced past me at my mother.

'I'll stay and talk to them. Get the children safe.'

Until that point, the extreme danger hadn't registered. The expression of grim acceptance and resignation on my father's face told me what I needed to know. I grabbed his wrist and pulled him away from the window.

'Please, Dad!'

'Go. Don't worry about me. See you at Uncle Ronnie's when I get there.'

I frowned at him. If it was going to be all right, we wouldn't need to go to my uncle's. The loud, hard double knock on the front door jolted us from our inertia and my sister, mum and I fled through the back door.

We waited at the side of the house. Even the clouds seemed to hold their breath. The inches of settled snow cast an eerie light over the fields. I peeped around the corner at our visitors and recognised three men: a gaunt man, a fat man, and a man with weird sticking-out teeth. They'd been to our place on numerous occasions. Goofy, as I'd secretly nicknamed him, watched Special in a manner that gave me goosebumps. I always took her to our room if they arrived and we hadn't gone to bed yet. I called the other two Laurel and Hardy for their different sizes.

Perhaps, it would be okay after all. Even though they talked down to my father, I thought they were friends. They joked that they all worked in the same line of business. Our front door opened. With the fire long dead and no electricity, the interior showed black and solid. Out of this darkness came my father's outstretched hand holding an envelope.

A flash startled me, followed by a deafening, frightening bang. It lit my father up like a photograph. Terrified like rabbits, we panicked and left our hiding spot. Stupid, really. The cottage sat on a straight track. There wasn't another house for miles. We ran in a line up the snowy lane towards the wood. If you run like that, holding hands, you can only go at the pace of the slowest runner. Special's little boots slipped and skidded across the surface. She rarely went outside.

The first trees and only cover remained distant. I stole a glance back, knowing if they came after us, we would never make it. They stood in a line in the centre of the road, unmoving. Weirdly, considering the weather, they wore similar blue suits. Each had a raised hand. They were colour on a blank canvas, and clear as if it were daylight. We were sitting ducks. This time, multiple booms crashed around our ears.

Incredibly, we carried on running. A sound not dissimilar to a whip cracking whistled by my right ear. A lone crow in front of us launching into flight seemed to be the only consequence of the volley of bullets until my mother stumbled. She dragged herself up with gritted teeth and spat on the floor. Her eyes fixed on the distant tree line, and we continued to move forward. I heard the men laughing. Another torrent of cracks echoed from behind, and my mother hit the ground face first with a sickening thump.

I crouched and scraped the bloody hair from her cheek. Blood poured from her mouth. The snow devoured the liquid even though it gushed out. Her eyes lost focus and, with her dying breath, she gasped, 'Run.'

The men's footwear crunched closer. I swung Special onto my back. She adored that: playing horses. She weighed nothing but could hang on like the finest jockey. I set off much faster, terror loaning speed and strength to my legs. I reached the wood and burst in. Branches rustled and scratched my face. But just the trees at the edge were thick conifers, the ones beyond only skeletons. I prayed that our hunters would give up if I put enough distance between us.

It wasn't a forest by any means, and soon I reached the edge. A large expanse of white opened up before me. The voices behind me echoed louder and closer. Special's soft, slow breath warmed my ear. I clung to that fact. She didn't understand. I had no choice and fled into the snow field. Beneath the covering of white, rutted uneven ground unbalanced me. I managed twenty stodgy paces when I heard chuckling again.

Special's grip loosened after the next succession of shots boomed out. I grabbed her little arms to stop her sliding off my back. Another bang shattered the silence, and a stabbing pain seared my right thigh. After lurching a few more paces, my leg gave way. I collapsed onto my side and Special rolled off. She stared at me. She wasn't sad or frightened. Her face only displayed kindness. Special had never uttered a word, but she tried that night.

'Sorry,' she mouthed. And then the light inside her died. My beautiful sister faded. My sister who gave the best hugs in the world.

A few seconds later, a man appeared in my vision. It was Goofy. He reached down and put his hand towards Special's neck. I didn't want him touching her. Energy coursed through me and I pushed up with my arms. The agony in my leg stole my power as I attempted to stand, and I crumpled backwards.

The killer shrugged and removed his hand from Special. His fingers came away dripping with blood. He ran a parched tongue over misshapen teeth and put a finger in his mouth. He regretted that she'd died, but only because it prevented him from having her.

A voice in the distance barked out, 'Finish them off.'

Goofy leaned over me. I smelled the whisky my father drank when he couldn't get what he needed. His eyes narrowed. I'd often been called Junior at school. A smattering of freckles below cautious green eyes hinted at an age beneath my years. My parents didn't waste money on haircuts any more, and my mother was no hairdresser. One of the other kids in my class called me Oliver Twist. Perhaps my innocence made Goofy pause.

The wrinkles between his eyebrows deepened, and a cheek twitched. The snow fell again and flurried behind him. Maybe he thought twice, but he remained ruthless at heart. I stared at his eyes as he leaned back. I kept my gaze on him and implored for mercy until I peered into the barrel of his gun.

The next retort and flash were muffled as though the weather had taken the brunt. And darkness fell.

They left us in that bleak field in the depths of winter without a care. The papers would be full of the news for weeks. They called them the snow killings.

2

A veterinarian on his way to a morning call at a nearby farm found me covered in blood and lying in the middle of the road. I was two miles from where they discovered my mother, and a mile from my sister. I'd tied my belt around the injured leg and crawled and dragged Special, even when hope was gone. A drunken Goofy had aimed for my face, but his wavering hand meant he hit the top of my head. The strong skull bone broke, but it deflected the bullet away leaving me only with an extremely bad concussion.

They said I should feel lucky to be alive, but it doesn't feel that way when you're alone in the world. They mentioned the possibility of a Traumatic Brain Injury, but they hoped for no permanent damage. I would never be the same after that, anyway. I don't think that's surprising. Any hopes of a normal future perished in that field.

They removed the bullet from my thigh, and the leg healed fine. Curing a mind was a different matter. Bruised and battered, it vanished to a distant place and left me a vacant creature who responded to little.

I tried to talk to the police. I stuttered about three men, but when I attempted to describe the murders, it finished with me choking and crying. They'd nod at each other and exchange meaningful glances. I assumed they would do their jobs and catch the killers. The visits from the detectives upset me for the rest of the day though, and I'd forgotten about Uncle Ronnie.

As my only living relative, he became my legal guardian. Arriving a week after the deaths, he said he'd overheard someone talking about the shootings. Lucky really, because he didn't read newspapers. The cottage still had a patrol car outside when he arrived. The police found him cautious and evasive when questioned, but he wasn't a suspect, and they soon left him alone. The police had determined a clear line of events by examining the murder scenes, and I assumed they had suspects.

My screaming ruined the funeral for the few present. In fact, more police and gawkers attended than mourners. I wondered who paid for the family graves, three in a line, until I caught a subtle glance from the vicar to my uncle. The church was in Peterborough, Orton Longueville. I asked why that particular one and Ronnie told me that he'd saved the vicar's life once. He gave no further explanation.

After three weeks of little change in my mental state, I managed to describe the man I called Goofy to the police. Uncle Ronnie stayed throughout the chat with them. Afterwards, he tutted and shook his head. All he said was, 'No good.' He arrived the next day and told the nurses he wanted to take me for a walk. Fresh air would help waken me up. He borrowed a wheelchair and trundled me to his car. I never returned to hospital and didn't see the authorities again.

It turned out that Ronnie existed off the grid. Eccentric and crazed, he lived a solitary existence without rules. He slept in a touring caravan pulled by his old van, and had five spots where he would camp for a month at a time. He later told me that was the only way my mother found him. She visited each spot in turn. Some considered him a kind of gypsy, but he said he just didn't want to live with other people.

To his credit, he took me in. The cramped caravan unsettled

me at first. Despite owning little, he'd hung old photos on the wall. He removed them after I mentioned they scared me. I had nothing. Ronnie asked me if I wanted to go back to school. He smiled when I said, 'No, thank you.'

Ronnie disappeared often in those early months. When I asked where he went, he simply replied, 'Putting affairs in order.'

Ronnie could best be summed up as 'the son of a poacher'. His father taught him all he knew, but it wasn't only animals that Ronnie stole. Pretty much anything not nailed down was fair game. Even securely fastened things were loosened and quickly sold on. In the end, I became his partner in crime. He didn't speak a great deal, but I think he began to enjoy having me around. There was great value in another pair of eyes in his line of work.

The only thing he'd kept of his father's was a hand grenade. The story behind it was the only tale of any note that he ever told me. The first time he spoke of it, he stood me up next to the fire and leaned in. This is what he said:

'The Japanese overran my father's position at the fall of Singapore in the Second World War. The regiment knew well the enemy's cruelty to prisoners. With his ammo used and the enemy just feet away, he clutched his last grenade. He couldn't bring himself to pull the pin and, even though he survived, he left his health and sanity on the Death Railway. After being rescued at the end of the war, he acquired another grenade. He kept it as a souvenir to remind him of his decision.

'Back in England, he found his son, me, staying with an aunt after an air raid had buried his wife. He took me to the woods and we lived an isolated life. He said he'd never be taken alive again, but died of a heart attack in his sleep, so he never had to make that drastic choice. He raised me to feel the same way.'

I heard that story often. And that belief grew in me too.

We visited the vicar on numerous occasions. He was partial to game, hare being a favourite of his, although he received a TV once. He often gave me a few pennies and a wink. To my astonishment, Ronnie knew nearly everyone. They cheered his arrival. Backhanders and deals filtered through every office and factory.

I put the murders to the back of my mind. Tears wouldn't help my predicament. We only made one visit to the family graves in Peterborough. When we arrived, fresh flowers lay on the stone. Ronnie had left instructions and money for them to be placed there regularly.

I existed as Ronnie did; a hand-to-mouth life with brief flashes of danger. He taught me how to shoot and lay traps. We relieved washing lines of their contents when we needed new clothes.

Ronnie instilled in me a desire to keep fit. His twenty-minute exercise regime most mornings also became mine. It stilled my mind. We would run together, sometimes by choice, other times when people chased us.

Gradually, I emerged from the shadow of that terrible night. I read anything from books to the magazines and newspapers we'd find. Mainly to relieve the boredom. Ronnie only needed cigarettes to achieve the same goal. When we were out, I'd notice other young men and women in brightly coloured clothes and striking hairstyles. By contrast, my own clothes reminded me of vagrants I'd seen in London. I also remembered the cinema trips of my youth. I wanted to see movies again and mentioned this to my uncle.

That was when we finally talked. I should have known something was wrong because he'd lost weight when he had few pounds to spare. There were places where he hid his money, and we visited them. He also had a leather bag of jewellery, which he kept behind a panel in the caravan. I asked him if he knew who killed my family. He refused to answer, insisting that they'd still be searching for me. He said I should never trust the police. That was why he removed me from the hospital. Besides, revenge wouldn't bring my sister back.

It turned out he was quite a few years older than my mother

and, even though they were both called Smith, he was only a half-brother. I never really knew who my mother was, and Ronnie didn't enlighten me.

A little later, he took me out for a drive. He wanted to take deer from one of the royal estates in Norfolk. It was a rare venture because the rich have the best gamekeepers. I think he just hoped to feel the rawness of the hunt one final time. His carelessness on that last day shocked me. His laboured gait betrayed any reassurances of being okay.

He crouched and shot a target from a good distance and gave me a melancholic smile. His lack of urgency surprised me. I stepped from foot to foot as he struggled to rise. A big deer is incredibly heavy. We gutted it on the spot to make it lighter and left the innards for the foxes, but it still took some dragging. It was slow going, made worse by Ronnie's obvious weakness. Human voices whispered nearby. Ronnie fired in their general direction. My pulse quickened as he'd never done anything like that. He wobbled and lurched as he ran.

It's strange to think that all those close to me have been killed by guns. The bullet that arrived as we got in the van pierced Ronnie's back and zipped out the front of his stomach. Must have been a powerful rifle as I later found the bullet embedded in the passenger seat. He managed to pull the door shut, and I drove us away. He'd shot his last deer, but he wouldn't get to taste it. I headed for the hospital but Ronnie stopped me with a final request. He declared himself ready.

'Take me home,' he insisted. The caravan had always been his sanctuary.

'Come on, Ronnie. They'll be able to fix you if we go now.' I didn't know if that was true, but it had to be worth trying.

He placed his hand on my leg and left it there. I gently covered it with my own, not recalling him deliberately touching me before.

'I've been bleeding.' He focused on the distance and swallowed. 'From the back passage.'

I returned to the campsite and helped him into a deckchair. He pushed me away when I tried to check the wound.

'Do you want a drink?' I asked.

'Yes. Some water, please.'

'Anything else?'

'Just quiet.' His head tilted backwards.

At that point, I decided I had to know and there wouldn't be another chance to ask him.

'Who murdered my family?'

He didn't reply, but his Adam's apple bobbed up and down.

'Come on, Ronnie. Where can I find them?'

His lips remained shut. His breathing slowed, and I assumed the worst. Suddenly, he whispered the words I needed to hear. 'The Boy's Head, Oundle Road.'

I sat next to him in silence because that was all he wanted. I thought about the killers, and guessed that if they weren't in prison then they'd got away with it. A plan hadn't formed at that point, but I understood the life I lived would expire when Ronnie did. He took an hour to die.

I know Ronnie believed that retribution would not bring my sister back, and he worried that the men were still searching for the only living witness to the crimes.

I disagreed. I was sure they would have forgotten me, but I would always remember them. And the need for revenge consumed me.

3

I collected the valuables that Uncle Ronnie had hidden and found his money. There was a lot. More than I understood the value of. I'd seen pound notes before and knew it would be a while before I needed more.

I dragged Ronnie into the caravan according to his wishes then placed the rest of his things with him. A man's whole life barely covered the floor. I squeezed his hand. He would never have made old bones, but he lived how he wanted. He always said it was better to go down in flames, so I watched him burn.

Despite his violent pursuits, he remained at heart a peaceful man. If someone bettered him or ripped him off, he would take it on the chin with a wry smile, almost as if he was pleased to be tested. No bitterness or rancour darkened his life, no spite or the urge for retaliation kept him up at night. But I was different.

I drove to Peterborough, bought new clothes from large, confusing shops and got a proper haircut. Smartly dressed women examined my money closely with suspicion. I looked in the window of the newsagent's near The Boy's Head and noticed a card looking for a lodger in Black Ermine Street, Orton Longueville – a small village a mile away. That was the same village where they buried my family. It would make my life simpler because I intended to maintain their graves.

It was as easy as that. My ancient landlady had few concerns as long as I didn't have more than one bath a week. I told her to call me Ronnie Smith. My uncle would have liked that. She put me upstairs in the loft conversion of her bungalow, while she slept downstairs.

The first Saturday there, I walked into the pub at lunchtime. Incredibly, all three killers lined the bar, as if they were waiting for me in a cowboy film. Laurel looked smaller, perhaps because Hardy had expanded. Goofy stared hard for a few seconds and then laughed. I thought at first they recognised me, but they were just sniggering at seeing a nervous youngster in their drinking hole. Empty eyes appraised me, and I backed out on trembling legs.

I found a job on the till at the local newsagent's. Fortuitous really, as I had only popped in for the paper and discovered him sacking the thief he currently employed. Brutal early starts and long hours for what seemed small change drained my enthusiasm. However, with no friends or family, I had little else with which to occupy my time. So I persevered.

I served the men regularly. They came for drinks and smokes almost on a daily basis. As time passed, I caught them coming out of houses nearby, so I soon knew where they lived. Laurel and Hardy had families and mistresses and Goofy lived alone. They enjoyed the high life, though, driving flash cars and wearing sharp outfits.

Ronnie always told me that thoughts of vengeance would stop me healing. He was right – I sickened further as I listened to their bragging. They took what they wanted. People avoided their stares and feared their tread. Seemingly, nobody challenged them.

I asked the owner of the shop why the police didn't arrest them as they were clearly criminals. He said that terrified families said nothing, and the men always had concrete alibis. The suspicion was that they had friends in high places and were therefore untouchable. They even had a tab at the newsagent's; one which they never settled. My minuscule remaining faith in the police and justice diminished further.

I festered with the need for payback and planned my revenge. There would be three men and three murders. I had the tools and the nous to do it, but that wouldn't be enough. I needed them to feel hunted. They would die frozen and alone. They should suffer the terror my mother, my sister and I experienced. They must know it was me.

They ended my family's lives. I would do the same to theirs. I had no doubt of my father's guilt and probably my mother's too, but Special was special, and I was innocent. Neither of us deserved to die. I needed to walk free after I had balanced the scales, so I was still alive to remember our family and tend to their final resting place. And then when the time came, I wished to be buried with them.

When decision time arrived, I woke from a bloody nightmare full of inspiration. I wrote each of them a note, which I hand-delivered in the dead of night. It said:

Fear the north wind. Because no one will hear you scream.

And I waited for it to snow.

PART II

———

WINTER

PRESENT DAY

4

DI BARTON

Detective Inspector John Barton watched the weather forecast and smiled at the upcoming snowstorm. Crime levels plummeted when it froze, and his job would get easier. People stayed in, so the poor little hoodlums had fewer victims to rob in the street, and there were fewer empty houses to burgle. Only car thefts rose. He shook his head as he thought of the countless individuals who were shocked when they left their engine running to defrost the windscreen only to return to find it had been irresistible to an opportunistic thief.

However, all that would be none of his concern because he had two days off. He wasn't even on call. Tonight, he could turn off the phone. His plans consisted of a cold beer in his hand, a pizza in the oven, and a decent film on the box. He leaned back in the cosy armchair as the programme returned to the breakfast news headlines. Another mass shooting shocked America. The gun situation over there fascinated him. How different would his job be if 40 per cent of UK homes contained a loaded weapon? Would he still have the balls to do it?

His son wandered into the lounge sporting a rueful expression. Even though Barton's wife had said to stop calling him Baby Luke, Barton had struggled to get out of the habit. He occasionally whispered the words when he checked on him last thing at night. He knew, seeing as Luke turned four years old a while back and had just started in reception class, that it should be plain old Luke.

'School for you, my boy. Time to get dressed.'

'I didn't make it to the toilet quick enough, Daddy.'

News like that always registered slowly and Barton couldn't resist trying his luck.

'Best you go and tell your mother.'

'She said to say it was your turn.'

'Hmm.'

Barton gritted his teeth and pressed pause on the remote so he wouldn't miss anything. He helped with these tasks when home. That seemed fair, as he put in long hours, and his wife did all the dirty jobs while he worked. Nevertheless, mucking out was firmly at the bottom of his list of favourite parenting jobs Without a word, he picked Luke up under the arms and carried him to the bathroom and, with trepidation, hooked the top of his pyjama bottoms back.

'There's nothing there.'

'Oh, it must have been a trump.'

It was going to be a good day, Barton decided. 'Now you're in the right place, let's see if we can coax something out.'

'What does coax mean?'

'Encourage.'

'What does encourage mean?'

'It means don't get off the toilet until you've done a poo.'

He kissed his son on the head and returned to the lounge. His nine year old daughter, Layla, had developed an unusual fascination with old quiz shows. His paused Sky news programme had turned into blaring *Supermarket Sweep*. Layla had inherited 99 per cent Holly, 1 per cent Barton. The same azure eyes as his wife drilled into him. They challenged him as he walked into the room and frowned at the TV.

'Are you responsible for that stench?' she asked.

'No, Luke's guilty of that.'

'Nice. What kind of man blames a little boy?'

Where did this attitude come from? The teenage years loomed ahead like driving towards a towering tornado. Barton decided a psychological argument over who owned the TV before 9:00 a.m. could only be a bad idea. He never won, so settled for something he could control.

'Get ready soon. We're walking today.'

Layla squinted at him as he left the room but already understood the game they played. She blamed him for not letting her walk to school on her own. Perhaps he was over-cautious, but he had investigated a kid snatched on the school run. Besides, they had to accompany Luke there, anyway.

'I'd like porridge for breakfast, please, Daddy.'

He trudged to the kitchen. She got her own cereal, but if she wanted porridge, he had to make it. He could say 'have cornflakes or nothing', but porridge was healthier. Layla knew this and won again. His wife, Holly, gave him an appraising look.

'Are the kids dressed and ready, John?'

Barton laughed despite himself. She had guessed they wouldn't be but liked to pull his leg. He'd told her to relax this morning. Strange how he managed complicated investigations for Peterborough's Major Crimes unit, with multiple lines of enquiries and clashing personalities, yet parenting remained a constant struggle. Three kids shouldn't be hard to handle, but his pounding head indicated otherwise.

'Layla wants porridge.'

'In the cupboard, red box, instructions on the side.'

He placed his best puppy face on. 'Where's Team Barton today?'

'I'll have a cup of tea when you're ready too. Can you do pancakes?' She failed to stop herself laughing and stood to help. 'I'll wake Teen Wolf.' That was their nickname for her fourteen year old son from a previous relationship. Barton regarded him as his own flesh and blood. His actual name was Lawrence.

Holly had insisted the children's names all began with an L so they felt a sense of kinship. She took his surname when they got married, even though she reckoned Holly Barton sounded like the name of a female lorry driver who delivered Christmas trees.

While he filled the kettle, he pondered on whether waking Lawrence was a worse job than wiping Luke's bottom. His wife returned as his phone rang from where he'd left it on the table.

'Can you get that, Holly?'

'I'm the cleaner, nanny, nurse, agony aunt and, at times, sex goddess. One thing I am not is your secretary. Answer it yourself.'

An early morning call on his mobile wouldn't be positive. She understood that. His day off already looked precarious. Detective Sergeant Zander's name showed on the screen when Barton picked up the phone.

'Hey, Zander, good to hear from you.'

'John, I don't think I can take any more.'

5

DI BARTON

Barton slowly put the phone down.

'What is it? What's wrong?' asked Holly.

'It's Zander. He sounds suicidal.'

'Oh my God, talk to him.'

'He's hung up.' He cringed at his poor choice of words.

'What?'

'He hung the phone up. The line went dead.'

She shook her head at him. 'John. He must be at home. Drive over there.'

Barton turned to the lounge. 'What about the kids?'

Holly rolled her eyes. 'I think I'll be able to cope. Now get out of here, you huge lunk.'

He raced to the kitchen, snatched his car keys from the hook, and stepped out of the front door. A sagging tyre stared back at him from underneath his blue Land Rover. Job number three that day involved another garage visit. A big man needed a large vehicle, but lately he always seemed to be getting flats, however when he had taken the car to be repaired, they couldn't find any damage. He suspected a local comedian, probably a kid, deflating them as a joke.

Cursing, he returned to the house.

'Did you forget your puncture? You'll have to take mine.'
Holly beamed at him. 'Let me get my camera out of the boot.
Luke brought the reception class teddy home yesterday and I
need to take some photos for his homework.'

He plucked the keys from her hand with a frown and hustled
outside. His wife owned a Fiat 500. She loved it, but he did not.

Barton's dad drew inspiration from the song 'Big Bad John'
when his only boy arrived in the world forty-five years ago
weighing in at ten pounds, and named him after it. Barton
hadn't quite reached six foot six, but his dad used to sing the
chorus to him when they met. Barton missed that now. It had
been more than a decade. He missed having a thirty-two-inch
waist too, but the years flew by. Beefy Tired John might be more
appropriate.

He yanked the frost cover off Holly's car and rang Shawn
Zander one more time, to no avail. He left a message saying he
was on his way then put the front seat back as far as it would go.
A flash from Holly's camera lit up the gloomy morning. Winding
down the window, he couldn't help laughing. 'Happy now?'

Holly gave him a kiss. 'You're so cute. It's like having my own
clown car. Even your nose looks a little red. Now off you go. I
know he's threatened to commit suicide before, but this time he
might mean it. No fast food either, okay?'

He waved her off and almost reversed her car into an old
man walking across the drive. When the man had shuffled past,
he moved again and had to slam the brakes on for a second time
as another pensioner walked behind his vehicle. Neither
acknowledged their close escape.

When the Bartons had first moved into Black Ermine Street,
they had brought the average age in the road down by about
thirty years. It was actually a cul-de-sac of twenty-five properties.
Barton lived at the top in one of the few houses. He had a nice
view of the green opposite and could see who came in and out of
the street as they had to pass his house. A large hedge kept
prying eyes out of his front rooms.

The rest had been bungalows on nice plots, full of retired folk. It was a peaceful place, but gradually death took its toll and fresh faces arrived. The area's popularity soared and so did the prices. Rich people moved in and demolished the bungalows to build huge mansions on the plots, or they extended upwards and outwards.

The two people that he'd almost flattened were a few of the remaining oldies who lived down at the bottom. Many of them still had the old metal windows and weird-coloured doors. They were quiet people, and he didn't even know their names, but he liked that. As soon as anyone found out you worked for the police, they would knock on your door for anything from rowdy trick-or-treaters to missing pets.

Everyone left him alone apart from the ancient git who lived on the other side of the green. His house was slightly raised and pointed straight at Barton's front door. From there, he monitored Barton's comings and goings and annoyed him almost daily. He seemed to think that Barton was his private security guard. Luckily, he wasn't about this morning and Barton edged the tiny car out of the end of the road before waving to Holly, who gave him a thumbs-up at the window.

* * *

DS Zander lived in Orton Waterville, the next village along and only a few minutes by car. He was pushing forty years old and had been looking for a more specialised role so he could spend more time with his family, when the unthinkable happened. One night, he popped in to look at his boy sleeping, something he often did. He found a dead body. The neighbour's ancient boiler had leaked carbon monoxide through the wall. The poor lad had died quietly in his sleep.

How do you cope with that? Carbon monoxide victims can have a red hue to their faces on death. Zander performed CPR for ten minutes before the ambulance turned up. Later, the post-mortem showed the boy had passed over two hours beforehand. Barton refused to ponder that fact. He suspected Zander thought about it all the time.

His work colleagues had sorely missed his presence around the office. He was an athletic black guy with a smile that disarmed everyone; people talked to him without hesitation. No one used his first name. He was Zander to all; friend or foe.

That grin understandably struggled to break free these days even though it'd been a year since Zander's son had died. There were signs of late that he might get through it, and he'd returned to work, but Barton hadn't seen his wife, Diana, since the funeral, where her weeping ripped at everyone's souls.

The first few flakes of snow fell as he arrived at Zander's terraced cottage. It was a peaceful location for a successful couple. He knocked on the door and peeked through the letter box. He heard the TV, which pleased him. In his experience, people generally took their own lives in the quiet. Those serious about committing suicide didn't inform anyone beforehand either. The phone number still went straight to voicemail.

As he unlocked the back gate, Barton prepared himself for an unpleasant sight. No sounds came from the garden. The rear door hung open. For a moment, he felt like he did on a drug bust. Realising his purpose, he charged into the front room and found DS Zander sitting on the sofa cuddling a teddy bear.

Barton sat next to him and waited. The pair used to enjoy each other's company and laugh together. They had often joked about being dinosaurs even though Barton himself was only in his mid-forties. They were promoted to sergeant at the same time, and Zander had been genuinely pleased when Barton moved up again to inspector. Guilt sneaked up on Barton when he remembered his visits tailing off as Zander's absence from work continued. They had all thought he'd never come back. To do so took real inner strength.

Their eyes met and Barton detected a tired smile, so he pointed his fingers at Zander's lap.

'Step away from the bear.'

After a pause, Zander put his fingers under the bear's chin and replied, 'Get me a helicopter and a million pounds, or Paddington eats lead. And I want that Kylie Minogue too, dressed like she's ready to do the can-can.'

Barton grinned. It was a game they often played, so he hoped his friend and colleague was okay.

'Are you all right?' Barton asked.

'Yeah. I spotted the previous neighbour entering next door. I thought he was moving back in.'

'Shit. He can't have been?'

Barton suspected he would want to kill the person responsible for his child's death. Zander had only had one child too, which must have made it worse. Sometimes a surviving sibling pulled the family through and let the parents know they had something to live for.

'No, he was grabbing the last of his things. I went out to him and shook his hand.'

'Eh?'

'It wasn't his fault. He rented the place, which makes it the owner's responsibility. The landlord provided a safety certificate from eleven months ago, so he's covered. Carbon monoxide alarms are only compulsory if you're burning solid fuel, not gas. It's just a tragic accident. After I spoke to him, the grief hit me again. I have a number to ring to talk to someone, but I couldn't get through, so I rang you. Then I remembered the memory bear.'

He half smiled at Barton's clouding gaze.

'You send some of the dead person's clothes off to this company, and they make a bear of their clothes.'

Barton's mouth fell open.

'That's what I thought. Morbid! Diana thought of it. I couldn't stand to be near it at first. I hid from the pain, but it meant I didn't get better. Holding this bear means I know I can carry on. When I see it, I remember him, and, even though I'm sometimes sad, the gut-wrenching agony that kept me in bed has gone. There is a future, and I will be part of it.'

'Kind of makes sense,' said Barton, although the speech sounded a little rehearsed. 'So, you aren't going to... you know... why you called me?'

'No. I'm really sorry. My grief comes in waves. Diana moving out a while ago, and the neighbour thing, meant I had a bad few minutes. Don't tell anyone. I needed someone to listen, and you're good at that. I guessed you'd come over. Being back at work is helping, too. I need it.'

Poor man, Barton thought. Sadly, he knew most relationships broke up after losing a child and Zander's marriage had been no different. Nothing Barton could say would solve anything. Experience had taught him that listening and being there were the only things needed.

'Shall we get out of here, grab breakfast?'

'I don't feel like being around people.'

'McD's drive-thru? I'm supposed to be on a diet, so it will taste like heaven on earth.'

'Ah, I don't know.'

'Come on, my treat.'

Zander relented and stood. He wiped a trickle from his eye and sniffed.

Barton's wife, Holly, always said what you really need if you're upset is a Barton bear hug. It worked on her and the kids, and something told him to use its power right then. He stepped towards Zander and enveloped him in his huge arms. They stayed that way for thirty seconds before Zander pulled away. He nodded and squeezed Barton's shoulder while avoiding eye contact.

'Thanks,' said Zander.

'Let's go.'

'Don't tell anyone about the bear, will you?'

'Of course not.'

Zander cocked his head to one side and added, 'And definitely don't mention the hug.'

7

THE SNOW KILLER

The carriage clock ticks along as I stare at the phone. The doctor said he'd call this morning. It's nearly 9:00 now, so any time soon. I'm not confident of a positive diagnosis, although the pills he gave me are helping. He wanted me to attend the surgery for his verdict, but I said I'd rather not have to take the bus.

I turn on the TV and catch the back end of the news. It's all crime nowadays. There are few upbeat stories. The wind whistling through the windows makes me shiver even though it's warm with the radiators on full blast. The property is glazed, but I had that done twenty years ago. Nothing lasts forever.

My health is deteriorating now, and I venture out less often. The past is becoming strangely vivid, while the present eludes me. The doctor mentioned that I'm lucky I've stayed in such good shape. I kept up the exercise routine that Ronnie taught me, and most days feel as strong as I did back then. That would slow the progression and help maintain my faculties longer. The ringer on the phone startles me, and I take a deep breath.

I concentrate on the tone of the doctor's voice to try to detect the news before he gives it. He asks after the tablets and if they've been of any benefit. With hope, I confirm they have, and then I identify a soft but audible sigh. Apparently, that confirms his suspicions. If the medication has been helping, then his prognosis was right. Along with all the other factors, it means the worst. I ask a few more questions, thank him and end the call.

It's strange to be told what will probably kill you. Actually, not kill me in my case. This thing doesn't strike the deadly blow but instead wears you away until something else does. My days will be different now. The shadow of advancing illness will blacken each new dawn.

It's unlikely that I will become one of those who finds a joy in knowing the end is in sight and can therefore appreciate every single precious second. I have few pleasures nowadays. The dominant emotion I feel is regret. What did I do with my time? Not much. In many respects, I avoided living. I could have raised a family and children. I never built a home with someone I loved.

Perhaps what's worse is receiving such terrible news and having no one to tell. Shrugging, I acknowledge that sharing was never my style. Burdens are for carrying. I immediately decide that nature won't be allowed to take her course. I've seen the slow end, and that's not for me. In a way, there's also relief. It's been obvious for a while something wasn't right.

I flick on the lounge lights even though it's daytime. The black nights and silent mornings of winter are upon us. That is a positive thing. It's my favourite season by far. I casually wonder whether it will be my last. The speed of my decline is unknown. It could be years, the doctor brightly replied when asked. His enthusiasm paled when I asked how long remained until the bad days outnumbered the good.

Never mind, the medication is helping for now. They can adjust it as necessary, and the doctor said he'd see me in a few weeks unless I found the side effects intolerable. But my generation doesn't complain, we endure. I survived, didn't I?

And there are still things I enjoy. The clock on the wall indicates the approaching arrival of one of them. With a cup of fresh tea and a bar of my favourite chocolate, I settle in front of the TV. This ritual started when I checked the weather to avenge the slaughter of my family. Although I tuned into the radio back then.

I stare blankly at the local news. Images of torn vehicles on motorway hard shoulders darken my mood once more.

What am I proud of? Will the world know I was here? Did I enjoy myself? Coach trips were superb for fleeting relationships and idle chatter to go along with some sightseeing. I never dared apply for a passport because of concerns that my name might register somewhere – overly cautious as always.

I managed to get a new NI number by saying my birth was never registered. They were more forgiving in those days. I remained Ronnie Smith with a different date of birth than before. The only real footprint I've left on this world is the assassination of three murderers. I sometimes wonder if the final killing was the last moment I truly felt alive.

That is a distant memory now but, if I concentrate, I can recall every detail. The aftermath remains clear despite the passing of time. I swore not to repeat those terrible acts, although the reasons have dimmed of late. I think about it more and more.

Is the ability to kill an inherited trait? Was it a gift from my father? Since the invention of the Internet I've read around the subject to an obsessive degree. Serial killers detach themselves from their crimes while 'normal' people struggle to cope with the taking of another's life. Those with no conscience feel no guilt, but I have regret – whether solely for myself rather than my victims though, I'm not sure. I wasn't a killer before that terrible day, that I do know; I was only a child.

But committing those crimes is the thing of which I'm most proud. Revenge is a powerful motivator. The anger I channelled to provoke the desire to get even still remains. It hasn't dimmed, but as I've aged I have learned to ignore its demands. We all feel rage and wrath. We occasionally want to murder. It's a normal human reaction, and virtually everyone dampens those desires because they know it's wrong. Or at least the fact that a life in jail is the likely outcome, and by the time they have formed a decent plan, they realise it's not worth it.

I smile ruefully and think of the idiots I've felt like topping over the years. Those calls were sometimes hard to ignore. Alcoholics Anonymous says that if an alcoholic resists drinking for any period without treatment, they are a dry drunk using willpower to stay clean, often white-knuckling and hanging on by their fingertips. Perhaps that's me and inevitably, at some point, I will lose my grip.

I watch Sky news now. The presenters are more glamorous than on the other channels. It's a peek into a glitzy world that I've never known. Hopefully, the woman with the carroty hair and fantastic eyes will be on. I grin when I see her come into view, and my mood lifts because it's patently ridiculous to present in a sunflower-yellow dress.

It won't be long before the PC crowd stop that sort of thing. They'll have to do it in unisex dungarees in the future. It wouldn't matter though; I'd still watch it.

I recorded the programme for years. Since they invented pause, rewind and catch-up, that isn't necessary. Modern technology helps with some things. With a big bite of a Milky Way, my eyes widen as it begins and I see the map of Britain.

'Hello there, it's turned into a rather chilly morning. Ice has become a problem for commuters and, to our surprise, for those in the east of the country, snow could be an issue through the course of the afternoon.

'You can see this area of low pressure moving in and expanding. Some places will experience extremely heavy snow. By this evening, there should be a couple of inches. The worst of it will occur tonight when an increasing northerly wind could cause drifts. Cities like Peterborough and Cambridge, which don't usually get much snow at this time of year, will be hard hit.

'The good news is that milder weather will push in by

tomorrow morning and the snow should melt rapidly. We'll then have a spell with warmer than usual temperatures before another cold front hits us in approximately two weeks' time.

'If you don't need to leave the house this evening, I'd stay in. This is dangerous weather, so if you are going out, please take care.'

My right eye twitches, and I spit the contents of a dry mouth into my teacup. With a trembling hand, I place the drink back on the coffee table and finally breathe.

A snowstorm is coming. Usually, I feel wary. This time though, energy courses through my veins. Even the fog of my illness is beaten back. Is this a sign? I don't often venture out in such conditions. Memories or urges may resurface. I shudder at the recollection of the things I've done. Normally, I'd have a day of white-knuckling ahead of me, but now is the time to look back. I will venture out in the snow when it arrives.

The sensation is almost sexual. I haven't been interested in serious relationships since the nurse all those years ago. That's another thing they took from me. Only snow claims my affection. Once, I considered moving to Scotland where bad weather is guaranteed. I dismissed that quickly; it would have been a bloodbath. I press rewind with a smile and let my mind wander back to the men I punished half a century ago.

I'd noticed a change in all three men shortly after I warned them. A nervousness that hadn't been present before invaded their lives. Spring flowers had burst through by then though, so perhaps it didn't seem real. Maybe they showed the notes to each other and thought it was a joke.

Goofy seemed the most unsettled so I decided he'd be first. If the police caught me after him, at least that devil would have suffered.

Six long months passed before it snowed. My life changed in the meantime. I dated a few people who came in the shop but kept it light-hearted. I made friends with one of the older paper boys. He loved the movies, and we'd often go together. The more violent the film, the better. He liked gore, and I wanted ideas although I already knew how to kill.

On a Friday night at closing time after winter finally arrived, I followed my three targets as they left the pub. Goofy's drinking had noticeably worsened since the note. I hoped that was the reason, anyway. The other two staggered back with him to his house and burst into riotous laughter as he fell through the front gate. The gently falling snow gave the perfect cover. A white coat with a hood, a hat, and tightly wound scarf disguised me. A person scuffing through the powder dressed like that could be anyone of any age.

The others faded from view through the flakes within a few moments of leaving. I removed the sharpened weapon from my pocket and waited until Goofy pulled himself up. He shuffled to his front door. The key scratched at his lock as I stood behind him. I'd seen many a stray shot from distance tear the spinal column and disable but not kill its target. With years of built-up rage, I plunged the screwdriver into his back. Once, twice, three, four times. A thrust for each of my family.

He screamed, sharp and short. More a fox's yelp than a human cry. Twisting to one side, he slumped against the door and scowled through teared vision. The flurries hid us from the road, so I revealed my face.

'You? Why?'

'You shot my parents.'

'What?' His words came out with a gurgle, and he spat blood down his chin. 'You work at the newsagent's.'

'Yes, and you murdered my little sister.'

His expression widened in an instant. Few forget shooting a child. He spluttered a reply, which tailed off to a wheeze. 'I killed you, too.'

'No, you shot me. There's a difference.'

I removed the Stanley knife from my coat and placed it on one side of his neck. Our eyes met for the final time.

'I'm going to kill every one of you.'

He had the same strange expression on his face that my father had. Clearly, if you live a life like theirs, being murdered isn't such a surprise.

I pushed his head down so the spray wouldn't cover me and pulled the blade hard across his throat. I enjoyed a few seconds watching the blood pour out and darken the front of his jacket, and then I left him to die.

8

I've drunk little alcohol over the years as it upsets my sleep but I've struggled with insomnia since I retired. Crosswords and word games don't tire you like a full day at the office. However, if ever news called for a few sherries, it's today's diagnosis. There's a nip in the air, which signals the approaching cold weather.

I enjoy the walk to the local shops. It's strange how when I had work to do, I rarely left the house. Now, I have so little company, a trip to the newsagent's or supermarket, and perhaps some conversation, is most welcome. The checkout boys and girls work hard, but they often chat to me if the line is small. I try to time it so I get to the till when there's no queue.

I occupy myself by looking at the prices while I wait. It all seems so expensive nowadays. Imagine paying so much for a single apple. In my day, they virtually gave them away. Having said that, when my TV broke, I discovered I could get a new one for about the same price as a pair of good quality shoes. It's a strange world I find myself in. It won't sadden me to leave it.

There isn't a great deal for me to do before the end. I'll make an appointment with the solicitor soon. My will is almost ready. I had an enjoyable week deciding which charities deserved my money. Turns out, I'm pretty rich. I had a pleasant time a few years back when I sold all of Uncle Ronnie's heirlooms. I struggled to find somewhere to sell them, but eventually I found an auction house who had a look at my possessions.

I worried there'd be a stolen property list somewhere and an item would flash up on it, leading to an investigation. Of course, there wasn't, and I had the most exciting day at the auction. I prepared a story for if they arrested me on the spot, but I didn't really care about being caught. At times, I yearned for people to hear my story. It's been an ever-present aspect of my life for years but the itch is becoming intolerable these days. Maybe I could confess in my will and have a letter sent to the press.

The best objects fetched ten thousand pounds each. That's not a fortune, but Ronnie had been busy and there were plenty of them. Ironic that he should die having spent none of his ill-gotten gains, and I will too. At least this way, someone can put the money to good use. There's no chance the bloody government is having it.

The shops aren't far. I breathe the air in and the world has sharp edges. I evade the meathead policeman who tries to run me over in his Noddy car. He seems a decent man who acknowledges his neighbours. His house used to be a convenience store. A strange place that sold almost everything except anything you might actually want. That's probably why it closed. I can still make out the front door but there's a huge established hedge around the property now which reminds me of the passing of time.

I arrive safe and sound. Outside the off-licence, I spot the Chapman sisters. They are scum personified, in my humble opinion. I've known them since they were two grubby faced mixed-race kids struggling to get by on the rough housing estate their father dragged them up on.

Not any more. The eldest is a tall, willowy creature now in her mid-twenties. She reminds me of the strange, beautiful creatures from that film *Avatar*. It's probably the weird clothes she and her block-headed brute of a boyfriend wear. They make their legs look too long.

She is the brains of the operation, he the muscle. I've seen them dealing drugs for years. That big detective lives five minutes' walk away and can't see what's under his nose. The eldest Chapman is a supervising force. She sits in an enormous SUV and annoys everyone with her awful, loud music. Have the police given up? It's one of the few things that still makes me cross. Drugs caused our family's problems, too.

The younger sister, little Chapman, wasn't so lucky in the height department, but she is pure evil. The twisted devil got caught climbing out of houses all over the place, but never ended up in jail. She must be eighteen or nineteen now. She's the one who scoots about on a ridiculous tiny BMX, organising younger kids to cycle and flit around like annoying bees delivering their illicit goods.

I've seen her slap the kids' faces and push them about. They always come back though. I suppose they have no choice. The Chapmans and Block-Head are the alphas. The smaller ones can't survive out of the pride. Little Chapman spat on my shoe once. I'm sure she did it on purpose. It took a lot of willpower not to go home and get a weapon.

Once I'm at the shop there's a wide range of drinks and I ponder my choice. My landlady's favourite tipple springs to my mind. The past really does want to be heard today. I select a bottle of the best sherry, Harveys, and find a reduced pack of four steak burgers while I prowl the aisles. They're out of date after today, but I can freeze them individually, and they'll keep for ages. I've got a piece of cheese that needs eating up too, and with a bag of Doritos I found on offer, I'll be having a right party. While I stick around for the last person to be served, I ponder whether it would be nice to share these things with someone else.

'Morning, it's going to snow.' I grin at the boy. He often has a pink streak through his hair, which isn't quite my bag, but he smiles back.

'You be careful out there. Don't want to break a hip.'

Cheeky sod, I think as he rings up the items. I could break more than his hip. There it is again: a real flash of rage. I haven't experienced such violent thoughts so strongly and suddenly for many years. Where are they coming from?

Checking out always seems to take ages with price-reduced products and I hear a colossal tut echoing over my left shoulder. Pink Mohican boy rings a bell, and another louder tut sounds behind me. I start to perspire underneath my collar despite the chill in the shop. I pour the change into my hand from my purse as the total will be just over twenty pounds, so I can give him the correct money.

The manager arrives, presses some buttons, and the boy tells me the price. I stare at the coins, but I don't seem to be able to engage my brain to select the right ones. Panicking, I hand over a bundle of notes and receive an exasperated glance in exchange. I've forgotten to bring a bag too, but it's too late to ask for one now they charge for them.

I step to the side and put my money away. The queue behind me is large. 'Jesus,' the first person in line states as she barges past me. It's little Chapman.

'You might have nothing better to do, fossil, but I do!'

I frown at her. What an awful girl.

Grabbing the burgers and sherry, I hurry from the shop. There's a poorly maintained cobbled path, Baggswell Lane, between my street and the centre, and I'm forced to slow down. The melting snow has made the surface slippery and anyone, let alone a geriatric, could easily fall. Footsteps approach behind me, which I ignore.

A hand grabs the bottle I'm carrying and spins me around. Of course, it's her.

'Don't you ever shame me with a bad look like that, old timer.'

She attempts to rip the bottle away from me, but my body is feeling strong today. When she can't pull the sherry from my grip, the surprised expression on her face amuses me. Young people think they know everything. Suddenly, Little Chapman thumps my wrist hard with a closed fist. The bottle drops and smashes at my feet. She likes that. Finally, she shoves me in the shoulder, and I fall to the wet ground. It's not weakness that made me an easy target. It's shock that someone could be so brazen in broad daylight.

'This is my manor. Don't forget it.'

She leaves with a lopsided grin. I clench my fists. A surly youth walks by but doesn't look over, never mind help. It takes a minute to crawl to my feet on the sharp stones, and I start to shuffle back to my bungalow. I decide I am pleased that I can't have that drink, because I'll need a clear head for my plans. The Chapmans will soon discover that I don't just get mad. I also get even.

I limp back down the lane. The pain fades as I move, but my mind returns to the others I killed. They underestimated me, too.

Back then, Goofy's demise shocked nobody. The local press called it a gangland hit. Within a few days, the drama faded. Even with all the people that came in and out of the newsagent's, I heard little talk of it. The ones affected most by it were Laurel and Hardy. I served them less than usual and nearly always together. Safety in numbers, I suppose. Despite their forced bravado, they became shadows of the past.

The woman I lived with inherited a fat spaniel from a dying relative. She presented it to me with the words, 'I'm too old for a dog.' It pined for a week. I guess she missed her previous owner. But animals live in the present. The hound was called Angel, and when she realised that she'd still be fed and there were walks to enjoy, she settled in fine. I tried to give her a different name but she responded to nothing else. After ten years, only Angel worked. I marched her all over, but her stubborn excess weight puzzled me until I caught the landlady sharing her corned-beef sandwich.

Once a week, late at night, I visited my family's grave and left fresh flowers. In the summer, I took them from people's gardens on the walk there. In the winter, I borrowed them from other plots. I continued to go every Sunday and, even when I could afford to buy my own, I still filled the vase in the same way. I'm not sure why. Perhaps I did it to remember Uncle Ronnie.

On one of these walks, I spotted Laurel arriving at Orton Longueville church. I kept out of sight and noted that the grave he visited belonged to a lady who'd died recently aged fifty-nine. That made her about the right age to be his mother. Her plot lay in the left-hand corner because that area had the few remaining spaces. Ironically, the gravestones of my parents and sister stood nearby.

When the snow next fell, I decided to act. Since the winter weather had returned, Laurel's nervousness had increased. I hated him. His breath stunned you from the other side of the counter. He hawked up phlegm and spat it between his shoes, and I couldn't think of a person the world would miss less. Even so, I didn't relish the thought of killing again and wondered if the dog was making me soft. But if I reminded myself of Special, my resolve hardened.

The following Sunday came. The weather forecasters failed again and a clear day arrived. The snow lay thinly on the ground and melted fast. I felt I had to strike. Leaving Angel at home, I fetched the .22 rifle from the van. I'd kept Ronnie's weapons just in case I needed them. That morning, I wiped the gun and rounds of fingerprints, and found the thin leather gloves that would help keep my aim true and my fingers warm.

Orton Longueville church can trace its history back to 1240 AD. It's a small but pretty building. Tombs and memorials surround it. Most of the occupants residing in the cold earth died long ago. Over the years, their descendants perished, so there were few visitors, and likely none on a bitter Sunday morning. It's sad those graves grow over but, in the end, we're all forgotten. I never let my family's final resting place fall to ruin.

The rear of the churchyard backs onto a road that leads to a hotel. There was a hole in the fence in the far corner that's still there today. A large rhododendron hides two missing panels. I discovered that when Angel escaped through it once, and I chased her. She thought it a game afterwards.

That morning, I found a white gravestone to hide behind and waited. Sure enough, half an hour before the church service started, Laurel arrived.

From fifty metres away, a bullet may not have pierced his thick coat, as .22 Rifles are not assault rifles. They are quieter and less deadly. With all the skill that Ronnie taught me, I plugged Laurel in the thigh, around about the spot where those men shot me. Then, with crinkling eyes, I put another one in there for good measure.

I checked to see if the sound had alerted anyone and ran over. He made a lot of noise for a little man. Such terrible language as well. Luckily, there was nobody nearby to listen to his screams. I had a trapper hat on, which I removed. His howling stopped. Eyes widened and his mouth gulped with questions. Why was the newsagent's assistant trying to kill him?

He solved the conundrum faster than Goofy though and connected the dots. He tried to sneak his pistol into view, but I tutted and shot him in the chest. The velocity of a .22 round is such that after it punches through the outer layer of its target, the bullet often lacks the energy to come out of the rear. It ricochets around the body cavity instead, tearing through organs and blood vessels. Laurel didn't have long. He knew that, but still wanted to blame someone else. His desperate claims rang false.

'It was Big Eddie's idea. I didn't want to kill that family, and definitely not the kids. Goof fired at them. Get me an ambulance.'

It's funny that I was almost right to call his friend Goofy, although, considering his teeth, maybe it wasn't such a coincidence. I pointed the gun at him and spoke the last words he would hear.

'You failed. Unfortunately for you, I survived. I'm going to your house now to wipe out your family and your Labrador.'

He blinked with pain and snarled a reply. 'You'll die like this, too.'

From observing him pet his dog, I could tell he clearly loved it more than his wife. I lied, because I shot neither, but I wanted him entering Hell believing that. I rammed the rifle into his neck and blasted him in the throat. The blood pooled beneath him. I had no qualms about desecrating holy ground. If there was a God, he watched as they murdered my family. I didn't need friends like Him.

9

Little Chapman's assault is front and centre in my mind when I get back to my house. I drag out the toolbox from under the stairs and empty it out in front of me. Looking through the implements, I smile at each one as my youth returns. Vehicles weren't so reliable then. A bulky wrench with old imperial measurements on it reminds me of fixing a flat tyre with Ronnie on a rare day out to the coast. A thick, flat-head screwdriver triggers the memory of when I loosened a screw and received a mouth full of oil after breaking down on the way back. For a few seconds, I taste the bitter-sweet liquid again. Yet, I struggle to recall what I did last week. What did I eat yesterday? Did I have anything?

That tool had another purpose. I grab it and feel its heft. Its weight is reassuring but perhaps it's too heavy for me to use now. Although I recall thinking at the time that a human body wasn't designed to resist sharp, pointed objects. Another smaller Phillips screwdriver catches my eye. Its shank is still long but thin. The tip is keen. I place it to one side next to a file. That will do. I'll sharpen it later.

There's a newish Stanley knife, which I place next to it.

Finally, wrapped in newspaper from the 1970s, is the hammer. I open it out with care. It seems bulkier now. Well, we all weaken as we age. To kill with something like that needs technique *and* strength: a big swing and follow-through. I drop it back in the box.

The paper crumples and dissolves in my hand, but parts are readable. There are footballers with long hair and tight shorts. One proudly sports a moustache much the same as Burt Reynolds had. My eyes flick to a picture of me on the wall taken around that time. Ronnie had stolen a camera, and we fired off a few shots. I got them developed after he died. We'd taken a selfie. I bet the kids think they invented them. Only our mouths smile, and I can't recall if I was ever happy.

I sense, rather than see, the falling snow thickening outside. It must be a change in the light. My shoulder aches from earlier, and I massage it with the other arm. I might as well have one of those burgers while I wait. It could be my last meal. I place my food on a tray and sit in my landlady's old chair and recall my last act of violence.

A fresh breeze had brought evil weather from the north. The forecast dry night disappeared with darkening clouds. It proved an ill wind for Hardy, the final man who murdered my family.

Earlier that day, my landlady had received sad news. After a spell of weakness, they explained, her heart was failing. We had a strange relationship – polite and respectful, but distant and quiet. She spent most of her time in the kitchen, often staring out of the window with a glass of sherry, while I read in the lounge.

I had seen little of her of late and a nurse had visited. The nurse called for me to visit my landlady's room and gave me a gentle smile. She was a short, slim creature, much like myself. We both had the same way of smiling with one side of our mouths raised as if life couldn't allow us complete joy.

I edged into the room expecting the stench of death, but I

smelled flowers. I saw none so assumed it was chemical. The nurse perched on the bed and held her hand and my landlady coughed to clear her throat.

'Ronnie. Thank you for coming.'

'That's okay. I'm sorry.'

'Don't be. I'm old and ill. All my happiness is behind me. My path on this earth contains only loneliness and pain. There's only one thing I want.'

She peered at me over dirty spectacles. I sensed it was no small thing she was preparing to ask. But for some reason, I knew that whatever she requested, I would agree to. I nodded for her to continue.

'I want to die at home.'

I glanced at the nurse and raised an eyebrow.

'Community nurses like me and doctors can visit, but she will need someone present throughout the night at least.'

I smiled at her and stared dispassionately at the old woman. She'd hardly made me feel welcome. There had been no pleasant meals together or an offer to take me into the city. We'd lived around one another, not with each other.

'Will your family be helping?' I asked.

She laughed with a childish titter I'd never heard before, even when she giggled at the strange shows she listened to on the radio. After wiping the dribble from her chin, she explained.

'Three of my children didn't reach adulthood, and my other sons moved to Canada. Have you seen any visitors?'

I considered making her beg, and then immediately cringed at my cruelty. Had killing people damaged me? Besides, she looked as ill as Ronnie did when he died.

'Okay.'

Maybe that was why I said yes. It wouldn't be a long promise. The nurse left but my landlady and I smiled at each other until her eyelids drooped and closed.

I took Angel out that night to think about things. When I

stepped from my house, I couldn't believe my eyes. The owner of the property opposite came out at the same time. He was one of the policemen who questioned me at the hospital after the shooting. Many men wore hats in the sixties; he tipped his and stared right through me.

When I recovered my poise, I realised that in the hospital I'd have looked considerably younger, and a huge bandage had covered half of my face. At the time, he spoke fast, kept crossing his legs, and ignored my answers. He rarely held eye contact. I remembered his name – Inspector Griffin – because of the mythical winged creature with the body of a lion and the head and wings of an eagle. Like his namesake, Griffin's cruel glint framed a pointed beak.

I followed him at a distance. He strolled straight down Oundle Road towards The Boy's Head. When he was almost there, Hardy walked into my line of vision. He also headed towards The Boy's Head. Hardy had vanished after the demise of his second friend, I'd presumed for good, but instead he must have been busy eating at home because he waddled across the field that separated his house from the pub.

His sly, wary expression slackened with relief when he recognised me from the paper shop. He said nothing though. Inspector Griffin held the pub door open for him. They nodded to each other jovially as the first proper flakes fell.

Returning to my house, I gave Angel a bone the butcher had kept for me, and put on my white coat. My life had been on hold. I could see that now. The finale beckoned, and then I could move on. I grabbed the items I needed, drove the van to the edge of the field near the pub, and waited.

The flakes, little more than sleet, stroked my face that night, yet the cold seeped into my bones. My teeth chattered. A grim evening like that prevented most from venturing out and it kept Hardy inside the pub until closing time. On leaving, he checked the road both ways for non-existent traffic and pulled up his collar. He stopped at the snowy field and contemplated going around it on the path. I let myself out of the van as he chanced it.

With normal shoes on, he shortened his steps to prevent himself slipping. His head jerked up when my door slammed. My walking boots cut through the slush with ease, and I strode towards him. He knew he couldn't run. If he had a weapon, he didn't grab it.

I stopped a metre away with Laurel's gun pointed at him. He actually smiled. I kept my other hand behind my back. Hammers make nice surprises.

'It was you all along. You sent those cards.'

'Yes.'

'Back then, I read that you hadn't died. I thought you'd want revenge, but the others laughed. What could a kid do?'

'Kids grow up. Keep walking.'

I followed him towards his house until the heavy sleet blocked the sight of the paths and roads. A blurry pair of head-lights blinked in the distance and disappeared from view. We were alone. The street lights failed to master the pervading gloom.

'Is this it? Are you planning to kill me? Leave me in the snow like an animal?'

'I have questions, then we'll see.'

He nodded. I couldn't tell if sweat or melting sleet trickled from under the trilby hat above his fat face. His breath came in short gasps. Up close, I understood why he scared people. He must have weighed three times what I did even though we were a similar height.

'Did you tell the police about the notes I sent?'

'No. Goof said to destroy them. He reckoned they'd link us to the other deaths.'

'I think you mean the other murders, not deaths. What kind of sick monster shoots children?'

'We couldn't risk anyone talking.'

'My sister was deaf and dumb. She couldn't speak even if she wanted to.'

'How could we have known that?' I noted the distance between us close slightly.

'The others said you made the decision.'

He took the chance and lunged for me. I stepped back as he slipped to his knees and grasped at thin air. I checked around at an empty night and brought the hammer down. His meaty forearm jerked up, staying the painful blow, and he howled into the dark. I swung harder. The second strike broke a bone in the same arm. He glared up at me with defiance. His mouth twisted into a cold sneer. Even at the end, his need to hurt won out. He spat his final words towards me.

'Your father was a hitman. He killed whoever they told him to. Men, women, children. Then he made a mistake and stole from the wrong people. You all had to die. Blame him.'

I swung my weapon in a huge furious arc; the blunt point hammering down onto the crown of his head as he bellowed, 'The Colonel ordered me to do it.'

Too little, too late. The metal thudded through the thin fabric of his hat and crunched into his forehead. He keeled over with a resounding whoosh of breath and remained silent. The wind and snow strengthened as I checked his pulse. It seemed there were others guilty, but I didn't know or care who the Colonel was. I was finished. These men killed my family; I saw them do it. I had settled the score.

I think if I hadn't seen Hardy that evening, the events afterwards might have made me forget about pursuing him. Still, you get the luck you deserve. That's always been the way for everyone but the innocent.

I decided to choose life from then on, not death. To my detriment, I suspected I might miss what I'd become. Was it the power I would yearn for? Perhaps it would be the blood in the snow? I read the news afterwards. They called my work assassinations. The police released a note that Hardy tucked behind a mirror in his house.

Fear the north wind. Because no one will hear you scream.

A city quaked during the next winter storm. They feared the Snow Killer. But I had retired.

10

DI BARTON

Barton persuaded Zander to go for a game of ten-pin bowling, and then a bar snack at a local pub once he'd messaged Holly to say all was fine. Zander seemed in reasonable form when he left him afterwards, and wanted to have a nap before his overtime night shift. The two of them had had a good laugh at the people staring at two such large men in Holly's little car. Zander kept waving at pedestrians, especially kids, and the tension in Barton's shoulders eased.

Barton knew part of the enjoyment he got from the job was that it made him feel alive. Awful things happened daily to ordinary lives and he helped with the fallout. It also made him thankful for everything he had. Perhaps that was why he didn't worry too much about the strain on his belt buckle. What was being a bit chubby compared to losing a child? Seeing his happy, healthy family tonight would be a pleasure and a relief.

Even though he wasn't on duty, he drove past the police station on his way home and couldn't resist dropping into work. Thorpe Wood station depressed everyone. Squat brown buildings failed to inspire, although the authorities paid lip service to complaints by regularly painting the hand railings light-blue. He nodded at a few faces he knew and proceeded to the detectives' office.

As it was a Saturday, only Detective Constable Alan Rodgers, an uninspiring constable with the nickname of Ginger, sat at his desk. He did have red hair, but his moniker came from the fact he had an unusual walk, almost a dance. Hence, Ginger Rodgers. He had joined the department when Barton had, but lacked the same ambition. Ginger scrambled something out of sight as his boss approached. 'Afternoon, Guv.'

Barton nodded at him. They all knew the lazy git wasted half an hour a day doing the *Daily Mail* crossword. Nice work on overtime. Still, he took his nickname with good grace. You wouldn't get away with that sort of thing with new recruits. Many a time Barton opened his mouth to make a joke and stifled it. Careers ended with throwaway comments these days.

He missed the simplicity of his earlier career. Nostalgic was never a word he'd thought he would use to describe himself, but lately he daydreamed about the past. He acknowledged they weren't the good old days. It'd been madness at times. There was also a fine line between banter and bullying. Modern policing was considerably more efficient, although modern complicated crime took more man hours.

Ginger offered to make him a coffee, which he accepted. Barton smiled fondly at the Nespresso machine resting on a cabinet. They'd bought it from a small lottery win, and it had been great to start with. It must be responsible for at least one of his love handles. Turned out the pod things were expensive, so few replaced them. Instant Nescafé would do as he logged onto a computer and scanned his emails. Deleting most, he only read the full details of one; a nasty rape.

DI Sarah Cox had been allocated the case. She had also applied for the next Chief Inspector position and, sadly, Barton had to acknowledge that she was the favourite. Time flew as it often did when he tackled his inbox, but he left happy that he wouldn't face an avalanche of correspondence when he returned on Monday.

At 20:00, Barton drove home. So much for a day off. The snow wafted down, settling on all but the busiest roads. The forecast was right for once. He stepped from the car. It wasn't a night to be out and about.

Holly gave him an exhausted look when he found her with a glass of wine in the kitchen. 'Thanks for texting me earlier. I'm glad Zander's okay. We should get him over for tea soon. Let me guess. You popped into the office?'

He held his hands up, crossed the room, and kissed the top of her head. Due to the big difference in height between them, he did that often as he'd have to lift her to kiss her on the mouth.

'Sorry. I'm back now. I'll ring for a takeaway if you like?'

'Come on, John. That's not going to do us any favours. Let's just have a few drinks and that veggie pizza I bought. We'll feel better for it in the morning as opposed to gorging on a Chinese.'

Barton took a cold bottle of Becks from her hand and prised the lid off with the opener.

'Shall I put the baby to bed?' he said.

She delivered a remonstrating glance. 'All done. Luke actually asked if it was night-time. Layla's ready too. She wants me to read to her.'

They shared a look. Both knew it wouldn't be long before her bedroom became a no-go zone. Well, definitely for him at least. He took another beer from the fridge.

'Don't have too many of those—I've bought some racy new underwear.'

'Excellent, mine are getting a little frayed. Do you still know my size?'

'Yuck!'

They turned in unison to see Lawrence behind them looking as though he'd caught his stepfather sucking his mother's toes.

He wore a thick hoodie with the hood up, gloves, and a

disgusted sneer. Dressed like that, he was tall enough to pass for an adult.

'That's horrible to hear. Keep your paws off my mum.'

'Surely you aren't going out?' asked Holly.

'Yep, I'm meeting a friend.'

'Which friend?' probed Barton.

'What's with the heavy-handed police interrogation? Am I under arrest?'

With a cheeky frown at Barton, Lawrence kissed his mother, and just before he slammed the front door a few seconds later, Barton shouted out, 'Be careful and be back by ten.'

'My, what has got into that boy?' Holly commented.

'Hormones. A lot of lads go through a rebellious stage at fourteen. Maybe I should take him down the cells, whack him around for a while. Straighten him out.'

That grabbed her attention. The one unbreakable rule in her house was that no one hit the children. It was what had caused the end of her relationship with Lawrence's father. She enjoyed a joke though and loved to be teased. Her reply was her all over, delivered in her best New York drawl. 'You touch him, and I touch you.'

'Oh yeah? I got some place needs touching.' His accent wasn't as good.

'What's in it for me?'

'Afterwards I'll fall asleep. My snoring is like whale song. Very peaceful.'

Holly laughed loudly. 'That's not the word I would use.'

A few minutes later, the girls left him alone in the lounge. He started a movie and pulled the lever to recline his armchair. He pressed the off button on his phone but then he remembered the scary call from Zander earlier. Missing one of those was not a risk worth taking.

Barton thought back to the last time Holly and he had sex. There had been around seven seconds of action one morning four weeks back until Luke came in demanding his breakfast. Perhaps that was what coitus interruptus meant.

With that in mind, he decided to keep his phone silent for an hour or two. He'd turn it back on after he'd seen the new lingerie on display.

11

THE SNOW KILLER

It's nearly ten at night. I pull back the lounge curtains. In the window's reflection, I can just make out my pupils dilating at the thick covering of snow. The wind whips the swirling flakes. I can't see the end of my front garden due to the flurries. Perfect. I'll take it as a sign I'm doing the right thing.

My oversized white parka is waiting on the bannister. I slide a weapon into each side pocket. The scarf fits snugly around my neck, covering my face from the nose down. I bought a thin ski beanie recently, so I could wear it and pull the hood up at the same time. That's going to be handy because it's a chilly evening. In the mirror, I'm just a pair of rheumy eyes.

Having lived in this quiet cul-de-sac most of my life, I know there's rarely anyone about at night in the winter. In fact, it's unusual to see anyone whatever time of year it is except in the safety of their cars.

I'm still in the same dormer bungalow in Orton Longueville that the landlady left me after she died. I wondered why she didn't leave it to her two sons in Canada, but it became clearer when they failed to attend the funeral. Caring for her in those last days saved me. I found a quality I never knew I had. She stubbornly hung on and took nearly three months to die so I quit the newsagent's and assumed the role of full-time carer. Thinking back, maybe I wanted the chance to look after someone. After all, I had failed Special and should have done more.

The community nurse and I became friendly, even lovers for a while but it wasn't to be. Her history was more traumatic than mine in some ways, and we never allowed each other to get close.

In the end, watching a person die naturally was more harrowing than observing a violent death. For weeks, continuous pain wracked her body and many a time I considered offering my services. Eventually, a more peaceful stage arrived. She slept a lot, or perhaps she had lost consciousness as she was non-responsive. The nurse recommended I talk to her, so I described my upbringing. I left nothing out. I think she listened and didn't judge.

The experience became cathartic for me. I felt that the circle was complete, and I could move on with my life. After she'd gone, I knew I didn't want to be around death any more, of any type.

College and finishing my education tempted me into training as an accountant and so I spent fifty years at peace in numbers and enjoyed the shallowness of work relationships. My office contained enough company to keep me sane, but I'm happiest on my own. I last used my gun when Angel's health failed. She was seventeen, and it was time. I decided I should be the one to do it. Her plot is at the corner of the garden and gives me comfort.

The memories fade, but you don't forget. For a while, I waited for a knock at the door, but no one suspected an eighteen year old. I joined clubs when I retired, new hobbies and pursuits opening up to me, yet I remain distant from those who reach out for friendship. It's too late for me to change now.

My new green wellington boots from the sale at Shoe Zone grip the pavement nicely. It is perfect snow: the kind that crunches as you walk on it; the stuff that sticks together like glue and would roll into the biggest snowmen.

The village is peaceful. The individual stone houses and cottages look beautiful sticking out of the white background. This area used to almost be a separate entity to the centre but, in 1967, Peterborough was made a new town to house London's overspill population. The pace of development was incredible. Thousands of homes spread out and surrounded picturesque areas like mine with faceless houses that all looked the same.

A short walk away, the Herlington shopping parade's brutal architecture wouldn't look out of place in Russia. Only the mini-mart is open. As usual, numerous young kids hang around outside when they should be in bed. The temperature can only be a few degrees below zero, and I perspire in my layers. I can't spot either of the Chapman sisters, and there are too many people about. Although I'm not worried that anyone will remember me. No one ever does.

A man with a growling Staffie lurches past. Shouted voices and herbal smoke from the wide open window of a flat above the shops drifts into the street. I imagine quite a few here lead criminal lives. There are always those who choose to break the law. This is the moment to decide if I should act.

I could go back home, turn the computer on and resist. That's what I've done for all these years if I felt the stirrings of anger at the world's injustices. It's easy to find relief now just by typing the words into Google. That reminds me of putting things straight back then and that's enough. I used to think everything should be left in the past.

I read that self-harmers in prisons are given red pens to draw lines on their legs or arms. It signifies the bloody cuts and gives them the same sense of release without causing any damage. I would type red snow into the search engine and it always calmed me down.

But today for some reason that control has disintegrated. Now I'm sure I will kill again.

I think back to the lives I took before. They were different times then. There were no forensics as such and there didn't seem to be much interest in solving the crimes either. I read an article later showing offences in the city dropped after my murders. Perhaps I did the police a favour. I should do so again.

I saunter through the streets behind the shops. This part of Orton Goldhay, a suburb of Peterborough, is mostly pedestrianised. The wind swirls through the alleyways that were supposed to make everywhere accessible but ended up as a maze into which the crooks could escape. Unless the helicopter they share with two other forces is nearby, the police have no chance.

There's no one else about, just the crunch crunch crunch of my footsteps. I find my way to the edge of the field behind the school and pause to catch my breath. The view is magnificent. A huge expanse of snow unsoiled by humankind stretches out into the distance.

Did guilt retire me from killing all those years ago? Didn't I choose life? I'm beginning to feel that I haven't lived one. I've changed these last few weeks. I'm starting to think that the deeds I did back then are my only achievements of any note. If I'm to start again, it will need to be tonight as, according to the weather forecast, the snow will have melted by midday tomorrow.

I was patient in the past, waiting months for the right conditions. Now, time is not on my side. Besides, it doesn't matter if I get caught at this stage. I want the world to know. If my family's deaths are remembered due to my notoriety, then so be it.

Two tall youths walk towards me, both wearing thick, dark hoodies. I stare at their faces through the flakes, and I'm pretty sure one is Big Chapman's block-headed boyfriend. The men don't notice me. One has trainers on, the other slip-on black shoes, and they slither and slide on the pavement, focusing on where they place their feet. It's crazy footwear for a night like this. They stop to light cigarettes and throw the matches over a fence.

I follow behind, close enough to hear their swearing, grinding my teeth.

I'm too old to attack two youngsters, unless I'd brought a gun, of course, but one of these losers will do if I get the chance. At the kids' BMX track, where the snow-covered humps resemble mini-Himalayas, the men bump fists, and one darts down an alleyway. The other has a furtive look around, but doesn't glance behind him. He heads to the metal container that they use as a café when the busy meets are on.

Ironic that the boys who raced around here on their bikes are using the same bicycles to deliver drugs. This man is part of it. He stands at the corner and urinates on the floor. The splashing hides my approach. The snow is ruined, soiled by a worthless yob. Sometimes they make it too easy.

I know what to do, even after all this time. The padding on my special gloves gives me extra grip. With a snarl, I stab the sharpened screwdriver into the middle of the target's back. Its brilliant point slips in with no resistance and I ram it home. The worry of not being strong enough was unnecessary. I think it enters the spinal column, which will instantly incapacitate him. If my aim was out, I might have speared the heart or a kidney, or maybe the liver. Any of them will do.

The youngster arches his back. His scream bursts out, loud and shrill, long and clear, but is swallowed by the night. I resist plunging the sharpened end in again and again. I was younger and angrier all those years ago. Family motivated me. That's not the same drive as wanting to rid the world of worthless drug dealers. He falls to his knees, his head turning in agony. I ignore the man's pain-filled, snarling threat. It's over for him. I'm shocked though. It's not Block-head, but he has the look of a criminal.

I crouch over my victim and do the world a favour. The blood in the snow can be my reward.

12

DI BARTON

Barton's eyes opened slowly, and he stared at a colossal violet-blue sun. It took a few moments for him to realise that he was looking at the TV. The film had clearly finished a while back. He didn't bother with a watch these days, so hunted for his phone, which had slipped onto the floor. The screen flashed notifications as it turned on. Worryingly, there were two missed calls from DS Zander and one from Detective Chief Inspector Naeem, his immediate superior. He jerked upright.

Climbing from the recliner, he stretched his back out, and realised he felt refreshed, apart from the wet patch on his bum. The phone told him 6:00. He hoped the empty beer bottle lying on its side explained his damp rear. Eight hours' uninterrupted sleep though was a distant memory and might even be worth an accident.

Two of the missed calls occurred two hours ago, the other just a few minutes ago. He rang DCI Naeem, the last one.

'Hi, John. Sorry to call you early when you're off, but we've found a body on your patch.'

'Murder?'

'Yes, it looks that way. Young male and a violent death.'

'How recent?'

'No rush to get here. The doctor confirmed life extinct an hour ago. It's like something from a horror film. The pathologist has just arrived, but the remains are solid, so the culprit will be long gone. I know it's your day off, but I thought you'd want the option to be involved. DS Zander was first officer attending around 3:00. I told him not to ring you. I wanted you getting your rest because we'll need refreshed officers to solve this as fast as possible.'

'I'll be there within the hour. Where is it?'

'The BMX track behind Steve Woolley Court. You can't miss it, everyone's here.'

'Make that thirty minutes.' Barton disconnected the call.

Barton's brain whirred and he thought of Lawrence. He hadn't heard him come back in last night. Cursing as he stood on a plastic dinosaur in the gloom, he shuffled his feet along the laminate floor so he didn't repeat the incident. Ears strained as he moved from the lounge. The boiler kicking in was the only sound.

Terrible thoughts gathered in his head but the years on the job enabled him to put them to one side. There was always time for fear later. He bounded up the stairs and opened Lawrence's bedroom door. A crumpled, seemingly unslept-in duvet covered the bed. Barton's heart raced.

A slim foot slid out of the covers. He crept as lightly as he could to the headboard. Lawrence didn't look so gobby when he slept. Barton kissed his fingertips and placed them on the lad's forehead. And breathed.

He jumped as he shut the door when a shout came from Layla's bedroom.

'John, is that you? If not, who the hell let a rhino in the house?'

Barton popped his head into his daughter's room. A peaceful looking Holly cuddled up with Layla. She waved at him.

'Did you fall asleep in here again?' Barton asked. Holly often succumbed to the *cuddle for a bit* ploy of Layla after she had her story.

'Sorry, John. I'll make it up to you. Did you wait up for me long?'

'I was buttered up and ready to go for hours.' He gave her a wink. 'Look, they've discovered a body over at the BMX track. I'm going over there. You know the score. I'll grab a quick shower, and ring you when I have more details.'

The light remained on in his younger son's room as usual. Barton's weight on the bare floorboards made an almighty creak as he stepped across them and when he peered in, Luke's eyes opened.

'Daddy, you told me bacon comes from pigs.'

He sat on the edge of the bed and ruffled the boy's hair. 'That's right.'

'Does it come out of the pig like milk comes out of a cow?'

At four years old, Luke was a proper boy and he preferred his facts grisly.

'It is the pig, so it's really a pig's bottom sandwich, not a bacon sandwich.'

'I want a pig's bottom sandwich now.'

'Okay, ask your mum when it's time to get up. Go back to sleep.'

Grinning, and knowing Luke would be up within a few minutes, Barton crept into his own bedroom and smiled at the matching bra and thong on his pillow. Next time. His freshly washed fleece hung on the door, so he took that, clean clothes and thick socks, and showered in two minutes. While brushing his teeth, he stared at his reflection in the mirror.

The hair he had left, he kept short. His forehead was getting higher and soon he would want to shave his head, but that made him look thuggish. When he played with the kids in the pool on last year's summer holiday, Luke shouted, 'Monster, monster', and Lawrence, watching, had called out, 'No, I think it's human.' That was a bit how he felt, like a hairy backed, great white beast. Ten years had raced by since he'd joined CID. Had his department aged him or life itself?

Holly arrived and peed behind him; the mystery long gone. She slapped him on the bottom.

'Oi! You fell asleep downstairs.'

'No, I did not. I was limbering up and poised for a marathon session.'

'You never came to bed. Our duvet is as I left it.' At his open mouth, she laughed and said, 'I should be the detective.' She kissed him, and he didn't mind her morning breath.

Barton tiptoed downstairs as best he could and checked his watch. Fifteen minutes: not bad. With the kettle boiling, he delved into the cupboard under the stairs and pulled his walking boots out and one of the big flasks he kept there. As he laced his footwear up, his brain clicked into gear.

People thought of Peterborough as a London-commuter town but it was closer to Birmingham than the capital. Most people had heard of it but weren't really sure where it was. A high-speed train exported people to London in fifty minutes but hadn't imported the deadly crimes. Peterborough had few murders and most of them were domestics or involved alcohol so were easily solvable.

He wondered what type this would be. Professionally, he looked forward to the challenge, but he also appreciated that whoever had died last night would have a mother and others who cared. It wouldn't be one person's life ruined.

He shouted up the stairs that he was leaving and thought back to his comment to Holly earlier that she knew the score. She worked as a teaching assistant, which fitted around the children's lives perfectly. That was how they rolled. His job came first, and she never complained. Strange how he had never considered that before. Was it fair? Maybe he'd surprise her later by putting her naked-lady apron on and doing the vacuuming. That always made her laugh.

Outside, he entered a winter wonderland. Three inches of snow had buried all the vehicles, but he didn't worry about clearing the windows or his car starting. A murderer had struck less than a five minute walk from his house.

13

DI BARTON

When he arrived at the field at the edge of which sat the BMX track, there was no mistaking the crime scene. Even though clouds hid the moon, glare from the emergency vehicles' lights lit up the gloom, reflecting light off the snow. It could have been daylight. The fierce wind from earlier had blown itself out. He strode across the snow covered grass and could tell the temperature was edging above freezing as the snow turned to slush under his feet.

An unexplained death grabbed officers' attentions. Any personnel out on the road attended if they had nothing better to do. Barton nodded at a traffic officer leaving the scene and the man pulled a grim face.

Cambridgeshire constabulary was an average sized force with an average sized budget. They suffered under the financial cuts, as had most, but the previous year crime increased by a shocking 25 per cent. The most damning stat was that seventy-eight crimes were committed for every thousand people. With who knew how many offences going unreported, the actual figures were likely to be much worse.

Not only London commuters flocked to the city for its inexpensive housing, but many immigrants also arrived for the plentiful jobs. Peterborough sat on the transport crossroads between the capital and the north. Being on the edge of the fens, the city was surrounded by flat, cheap land. Warehouses and distribution centres abounded. Ikea and Amazon gave thousands of people a chance, even if they didn't speak English, as they stepped off the buses from Eastern Europe and the police budget hadn't increased in line with the rising population.

Thankfully, murders were rare. This wasn't London, and it certainly wasn't America. The homicide rate was a measly twelve per million people but Barton never thought about that side of things. His attitude had always been to crack on with it. Do his best. And that started by putting his brain in fact mode.

Female murder victims usually get killed by their current or previous partners but as this victim was a man, probably a friend or an acquaintance had murdered him. When they found out who victims were, it usually pointed in an obvious direction towards likely suspects. There was over a 30 per cent chance he would have been killed by a sharp instrument. Most likely a knife.

The outer cordon was manned by a uniformed officer who Barton didn't know, so he showed his warrant card when challenged. After checking her name badge, he watched PC Zelensky fill in the scene log before she raised the tape for him. The increase in crime meant they had finally started recruiting again.

This new recruit looked about nineteen and eight stone. She was in for a steep learning curve, but she'd had the balls to challenge him, so kudos to her. Officers, often the higher ranks, would try to barge in and peek at gory scenes when there was no need for them to be there. The scene guarders were not just present to stop the public.

The first person he recognised next to the tent and inner cordon was Detective Chief Inspector Navneet Naeem, his immediate superior. She would be the Senior Investigating Officer. Barton loved her name. She kept her relationship with her inspectors and sergeants formal, but she and Barton had known each other for years. She'd introduced herself to him all that time ago when they were both beat constables by joking that he wouldn't forget her name because it sounded like a character from *Star Wars*.

She was fifty-five and retiring in six months. Peterborough had always been a multicultural place, and ethnic minorities were well represented in every department. She broke the mould though. Her parents had come over from India in the fifties, and she'd had a normal education and an arranged marriage at twenty. At forty, when the children could just about look after themselves, she decided she wanted to be in the police. It was almost unheard of back then, a woman of her background and age.

The whole department loved the story. She said at the interview, 'I want to work in CID.' The expression on her face meant no one smiled.

When Barton joined CID ten years ago, she was already a Detective Sergeant. When she attained DI, he made DS, and when they promoted her to DCI, he made DI. She often joked that his sticky doughnut fingers had got stuck on her coat-tails. Now he wanted her final position, but worried it might be a step too far for him.

Despite what he'd read in many detective novels, Detective Chief Inspector remained primarily a desk job. The DCI ran the investigation, but wouldn't be out knocking on doors or grilling suspects and witnesses. That was Barton and his team's task and he was a natural at it. His paperwork, on the other hand, could be improved, and he wondered how he'd feel doing more of it.

He also lacked confidence in dealing with the top brass. When he first arrived in uniform two decades ago, the management rubbed their hands at his size. He couldn't even count the number of football matches he'd attended for crowd control. If a disturbance broke out in a pub, they called Big John Barton. Send in the battering ram.

Although, he still smiled at the memories. When he barged through the door with his shirt sleeves rolled up, all six feet four of him, brandishing his truncheon, with a face that said, 'Who's first?', the colour drained from everyone except the drunkest fighters, and they were no bother. Nowadays, they taught you not to enter that way. If you go in with a weapon and anger, you raise the game. It's a shame because Zander and he often reminisced about the crazy buzz.

The upper management all remembered him from those days. His history was well known throughout the county and John now got the impression some of them would never see him as much more than a handy brute.

'Morning, Boss,' he said.

DCI Naeem smiled at him. For years, she'd said to use her first name. For him, though, using her title was a sign of the respect he held for her. It was therefore always Boss, or ma'am if any higher ranks than her were about. He passed over the flask of coffee that he'd made before he left the house.

'Creep.' She grinned, but it had become one of the things she'd brought in. A freezing officer wishing he had a warm drink focused less on an investigation than an officer who'd just had one. Five minutes' effort with the kettle on a case where a little bit of speed was immaterial became time well spent.

She poured a large coffee into the lid, took a few sips, and passed it to him.

'I take it you want to run the case for me?'

'Of course,' Barton replied immediately.

'Your regular team can move their shifts around. DS Zander and DS Strange are a strong core and, with you, our best chance of a quick result. Pull any constables you like to get the legwork done. As usual, we should attempt to solve this fast. The bad news is the victim has no ID on him: no wallet, no cash cards, no money apart from a twenty-pound note, and no mobile phone. There's no weapon in the immediate vicinity.

'The dog-walking couple who found him compromised the

crime scene. They attended a party and afterwards decided to take the pooch for a leak as they'd been out for so long. She's a nurse and uncovered the snow from the victim's face and body to help him. As you are about to see, assistance was futile. The heavy snow, which is melting, is also hampering our efforts on footprints. The CSIs are doing their best.'

'Any positives?'

'That John Barton's on the job.' She grinned at him. 'And Mortis is here. You can question him yourself. I know you'll want the minutiae. You're in charge now. I'll go back to the station and set up the incident room. We'll get the local radio and news involved. I'll allocate resources and let *those who must be obeyed* hear the gritty details. Someone will be missing a man in fairly good health.'

'Do I need to suit up?'

'They're almost finished in the immediate area, but you better had. Follow that path to the body.'

John smiled at her as she left. He would miss her gentle encouragement. She removed her forensic outfit, revealing a long blue coat, black suit and white shirt. All she'd ever worn since he'd known her. As he pulled a Tyvek suit on, he idly considered how many of each she'd been through over the years until her last comment registered. What did fairly good health mean?

He strode over to the pathologist. Dr Simon Menteith was famous for his lack of humour over the previous forty years. An immensely bright Scotsman, he had no interest in making friends. His stare could unsettle even the most confident of types. No one knew if he had a family. When Barton first started as a policeman, an older sergeant told him that Menteith wished to be referred to as Mortis. Not Mr Mortis, just Mortis.

In the early days of the job, your head spins with all the rules and procedures. You're easy meat for practical jokers. Barton's first words to him were, 'Excuse me, Mortis, will you be finished soon?'

People working with Mortis found him a distant type, and he always started his informal explanation on the stages of death, which sometimes seemed irrelevant: pallor mortis, algor mortis, rigor mortis, livor mortis, putrefaction, decomposition, skeletonisation, fossilisation. Hence the nickname stuck, but nobody actually said it to his face. No one dared.

Still, he was no fool. Barton had backed away under his glare, but then Mortis looked beyond him at the sergeant and smiled. After ten long seconds, he said, 'Not bad. You may call me that.'

Tentatively at first, Barton had. Now they maintained a friendly, efficient relationship. Mortis held a keen interest in all aspects of pathology. He would come out at any hour to inspect a scene, even when there was no urgency. He'd also proved to have a dry wit when you got to really know him.

'Evening, Mortis.'

The grey-haired man turned around. He stepped to the side with a magician's flourish and revealed the corpse.

Barton managed only one word. 'Jesus.'

14

DI BARTON

Mortis didn't need prompting and brought him up to speed.

'First, algor mortis, which is the second stage of death. It's been a cold night but not freezing. Upon my arrival, the body had matched the ambient temperature.'

Barton concentrated as he always had to when Mortis spoke. He knew the rectal thermometer would have been used and, based on the body's loss of heat through conduction, Mortis would give him an estimated time of death.

'Time of death guess on that is six hours. Tricky with this weather. A covering of snow insulates, but the cold could speed it up. Rigor mortis, though, is established, and therefore six hours will be in my report.'

Barton listened, but struggled not to focus solely on the throat of the victim, or the lack of one. The man lay on his side a metre away from a caravan-sized metal container, which he assumed was used for storage. The splatter of blood over that would be a new decoration. The snow resembled red slush in patches, with large, darker stains near the body. Perhaps because of how lit up the scene was, it didn't seem real.

'And then we have the cause of death. Slight damage to the neck.'

Mortis smiled at Barton, who grimaced. Mortis beckoned over one of the CSI team as he talked. 'This is Sirena. Crime Scene Manager. Possible reasons could be a vampire, an escaped lion, or an ogre. You'll note the small footprints in the snow. Sirena and I reckon they're from a fox.'

Barton shook his head. 'It would have to be a bloody big one.'

'Yes,' Mortis continued. 'Even urban foxes wouldn't attack prey of this size. I've seen nothing like this in forty years. So, we can assume that this neck savagery happened post-mortem. However, the deceased also has a deep stab wound to the back. Trauma such as that to the spine would have incapacitated the victim. It could have caused death, but if you look here...'

The jacket had been removed. Mortis crouched down and lifted the back of the man's T-shirt. 'There's blood escape here from this small hole but not as much as you would expect if blood loss from the back wound ended life.'

The woman, Sirena, removed her mask and took over. 'It looks to me as if there were quite a few foxes here. We see this sort of thing around bins usually. Even so, I'm still surprised by foxes eating a dead human body. The weather may well have made them ravenous, but it's hard to imagine one tearing a man's throat out. There are bird prints here, too. Possibly a crow or something similar. Again, they eat anything dead but wouldn't kill a human and would probably only go near one if it had been opened up.

'My guess is that whatever was used to stab the back also damaged the throat. Numerous times, I would have thought. That would have caused the spray of blood, too. The victim would have bled out quickly if the carotid or jugular tore in any way. An open neck wound on a deceased person may have been irresistible to a large, hungry fox. If urban foxes forage here, they won't be as scared of the smell. Don't you live near here, John?'

Barton raised an eyebrow at her. He wasn't sure they'd met before. He supposed she could know about him. She was foreign with olive skin, Greek maybe, but it was tricky to place her accent because her English flowed. She had massive eyes, either that or her glasses magnified them. And on reflection he assumed the latter. Barton remembered the CSI in charge of his first dead body. The man had offered him whisky within a minute of being introduced. He smiled at the memory and hoped this woman also excelled at her job.

'Yes, I do. There are loads of foxes first thing in the morning. An unusual old woman a few houses down from me feeds them. I've seen four in the same street at once, so that makes sense. Occasionally, you hear them fighting. Mortis, will you be able to do the post-mortem by the end of today?'

'Yes, I've nothing else that's urgent. I'll ring you as soon as it's done. I have a friend who's interested in blood splatters too, so I can send him a picture of that informally for a quick answer.'

Barton turned to the CSM. 'I don't suppose any more clues have been found in the area? Wallet? Phone? Axe?'

'No, not yet. With the weather last night, they may well be covered. I think this snow will be gone by midday, so we'll see if anything has been discarded nearby.'

'Okay, thanks.' Sirena did a mock salute and left them.

To Mortis, Barton asked, 'The boss said fairly healthy. Why?'

'The body has track marks up each arm, although only a few are recent. He's painfully thin as well. Look at the face; death won't have helped, but he would have been a gaunt individual. And we found a small bag of brown powder on him.'

Barton knew brown powder was likely to be heroin. You could get white heroin, but it was expensive due to its purity. This guy didn't seem like a connoisseur. Barton stooped down and took a photo on his phone of the individual's head. He took a full-length image of him too. The clothes were certainly non-designer, but they weren't dirty. The shoes, one of which had come off, had been polished recently. He looked about six feet tall with a well-groomed goatee.

Barton's instant explanation was an unpaid drug debt

leading to punishment of the worst kind. The fox thing was weird though. As his boss had said, identification of the deceased would be the first step, but he couldn't help feeling unsettled.

15

DI BARTON

Sirena, the CSM, was right: most of the snow melted by midday. Barton collared some constables to do another search of the area for anything incriminating, but they found nothing except an enormous pair of white knickers, which broke up the tedium. DS Zander admitted they might be his, but would wait for DNA confirmation before admitting his guilt.

DS Kelly Strange came on duty at 8:00. She, Zander and a couple of DCs door-knocked the closest houses to no avail. The surrounding area was heavily populated, and they'd need a bigger team if they were to rely on that.

The press turned up late-morning, luckily after the corpse had been removed. Barton analysed the scene now the body was gone and found it hard to imagine someone had died in this innocuous place.

DCI Navneet Naeem had called for a meeting at 13:00, so Barton got a lift back in the pool car with Zander and Strange. The boss had given him the heads up that the Chief Super would be sitting in and having a word, and Barton's hands perspired at the thought.

Twenty people filled the incident room perfectly. Not only was the Chief Super present but so was the Chief Inspector of

Operations. DCI Naeem had the floor. The initial break they hoped for had just happened.

'A woman living in the area called in to say her partner went out and didn't return last night. DI Barton, I would like you and DS Strange to attend immediately and report back. She's waiting at home for you. Night shift, you are released. Get plenty of rest, we'll need you later. The partner hasn't seen the local news yet about a body being found, so give her the description and, if she's up to it, take her to identify him. Call me straight after your initial interview.'

Barton nodded. 'Yes, ma'am.'

She continued. 'Five constables, you know who you are, are ready for the spade work. Murders occur infrequently here, especially in these circumstances. Speed is of the essence. Someone out there will be very nervous. And very guilty. Let's get to them before they disappear or concoct convincing stories. DI Barton, uniform are prepared to knock down doors if the drugs angle is realised. Chief Superintendent Jones would like a few words. Sir!'

A short, trim man in an immaculate uniform and shoes strode to the front.

'Thank you, Nav. Fortuitous that my colleague and I are here today. We may need the press to assist in this one, but let's keep them at arm's length for the moment until we get the result of the post-mortem and DI Barton's meeting. There's nothing that scares the public, or sells papers, more than a brutal homicide. I'll be interested to see your handling of the case, DI Barton. Please be about your work.'

He gave Barton an enquiring look and returned to the back of the room.

'Will all necessary resources be made available, sir?' DCI Naeem asked with a wry grin as she stood once more.

He smiled back at her and nodded. 'I am here to provide what's necessary. Get to it, team. I'm confident of a speedy result on this one.'

* * *

Barton and DS Kelly Strange got into the same car. He watched her manoeuvre smoothly out of the tight underground car park. She was a thin, blonde woman who had already put a few backs up. She arrived three months ago, having been recently promoted and transferred from the Metropolitan Police. Not that she'd given it the billy big balls about working in the capital, but he recognised a cool customer when he met one.

She had a slightly amused air, but also kept a hint of melancholy behind her smile. When Barton asked her why she transferred, all she said was that there were family reasons. No one else knew much more about her apart from the fact she lived alone.

Barton didn't care. She'd proven reliable and conscientious, which beat some of the others in the meeting earlier. When he thought of the dead wood in the department, a lot of them were the time-served coppers nearing the end of their careers. There was banter about the snowflake generation, but he'd found most of the youngsters keen and professional. Ginger joked that when he started, they didn't wear underwear never mind stab vests, and that he spent his days off cleaning the station windows.

In fact, someone had caught the man Strange replaced using the Police National Computer (PNC) for personal use, namely checking out his previous girlfriend's new partner. He'd also been reported for showing his Police ID to gain entry to football matches and concerts. It was sad. The guy had been in the job over two decades and said he did it because of anger over pension changes.

Barton had overheard a young recruit in the locker room comment that Strange had a cracking arse. That sort of thing used to be widespread. His old Detective Super would request a 'scribe' to take notes for him at meetings and deliberately pick the hottest WPC. Barton had poked his head around the corner and given the lad a stern look.

'Do you admire everyone's arses?'

'No, sir?'

'Do you like mine?'

'Sorry, sir.'

'Would it be okay if I judged you by your posterior?'

'No, sir.'

'Would you want to be suspended over making those observations?'

'No, sir.'

'Excellent. Carry on.'

Some reminisced about the wonderful old days, but Barton had worked with alcoholics and misogynists who wouldn't last five minutes nowadays. Physical arguments occurred back then. He couldn't remember seeing a fist fight in the office for years. The only issue that he detected was tension between Zander and Strange. They performed well together, but he felt as if he was intruding at times, or as if he'd just missed them arguing at others. Maybe they were shagging. He shrugged. It would probably do them both good.

16

It's midday before I wake. I recall the morning after all those years ago; a fire raged inside me then, too. The memories of last night are fresh, even the smell lingers in my nostrils. The bright new images stir something in my soul.

After pulling my creaking legs out of bed, I stare in the full length wardrobe mirror. A nondescript person leans forward and examines himself. I don't look like a devil, but I'm certainly hellbound. At least I'll know people when I arrive. My knees groan as I step down the stairs. The lights are off. Flicking the switch, I'm a little surprised not to find bloody footprints on the carpet.

I can't quite recall the immediate aftermath. It's as though my brain short-circuited as the blood sprayed. It still worked though, because I parked my wellington boots at the door, showing I took my time. After my first kill, I scoured the news, but that can wait. In the past, my body trembled with the fear of getting caught. This morning, I know that they'll capture me at some point. I will tell my story.

The sunshine through the windows warms my skin. The only snow I see is a pocket of white next to the far fence. That's good. The evidence is melting before their eyes. I'm not ready to be caught just yet. Let's find out if the police have improved, although I doubt they'll solve it without any help.

I pick my favourite mug out of the cupboard as the first tendrils of guilt embrace me. The smash of the porcelain on the floor doesn't widen my eyes. It's the whisper of *murderer* at the back of my mind. The burning embers inside are instantly doused. It's worse this time as I know nothing about my victim. He could be a father and husband: a decent man.

I carefully take down a glass next and swallow the day's pills in steady succession. Everything is becoming hazy. I clench a feeble fist and place it to my mouth. Why have I killed again? The reason seemed clear before, but not now. Then, I remember, I'm dying. Yesterday, I felt fine, but suddenly I feel a thousand years old. I can't recall what day it is. Perhaps this is the end. It's swifter than I imagined but no tragedy.

Why did I take that particular person's life? The glass slips from my hand, too. I blink at the pieces. Why am I crying?

17

DI BARTON

DS Strange nipped along with the traffic to the address. There was no need for gung-ho driving because as the city expanded in the seventies the planners built a network of dual carriageways, called the parkways, around and through the city. Peterborough boasted the fastest rush-hour traffic in the country, twice the speed of London. Established trees and bushes on the verges gave the impression of being in the country even though you could be minutes from the town centre.

Barton wasn't focusing on any of that. He couldn't help spending the journey contemplating his boss's easy rapport with the Chief. Did that come with experience or were you born with it? One thing he was sure of, he needed this case solved asap.

Barton resisted the computer age initially, but his tablet PC proved useful. He did still use paper where possible though, as it seemed to help his thought processes. He scanned all the notes and printouts on the way and checked the address. Mrs Evelyn Sax, thirty-one, waited for them. She was the wife of Terry Sax, twenty-eight, who had gone out last night at 22:00 and not returned. DC Ginger Rodgers had done a good job and pulled up some interesting information from the PNC before the HOLMES room was set up with allocated staff. HOLMES 2 (Home Office Large Major Enquiry

System) was the IT system used by the police for the investigation of major incidents. He read aloud pertinent parts for Strange's benefit.

'Terry Sax, multiple previous convictions, initially minor: shoplifting, criminal damage, then progressively worse: a Taking Without Owner's Consent when he was nineteen, and then two prison sentences, one at twenty-one for possession with intent to supply, six months served in HMP Peterborough, and then two years served starting the following year for the same offence. Again, in Peterborough, and later they transferred him to High-point. Nothing new for four years.'

'Maybe he saw the light.'

'More like he didn't enjoy the dark. They tend to get the message in the end.'

'Where's HMP Highpoint?'

'HMP Knifepoint, as the cons affectionately call it, is in Suffolk. Two years there would have blunted his enthusiasm for more custodial time.'

Terry Sax's rap sheet was common for a petty criminal. It read like a misspent youth that advanced to more serious offences and probably a drug addiction financed by crime. Drug addicts often progressed to dealing as it was the easiest way to fund their habits.

In the early afternoon brightness, it was hard to fathom the grim acts in the snow that morning. Barton's dad always said not to buy anything in sunshine as everything looked different when it rained. Sure enough, even though he'd nicked people from many of the properties nearby and knew otherwise, the area seemed a pleasant place to live as they drove through it.

There was no need for satnav. Barton read out the house numbers as they arrived. Patches of decent housing huddled amongst neglected spots, and the Saxes' was one of the nicest. The home in question had a large porch, immaculate front lawn and a better car than Barton owned.

'Strange,' Barton drawled.

He glanced at DS Strange and couldn't prevent a smile sneaking onto his face. She frowned and got out of the car. At the door, she knocked and turned to him.

'Remind me to chat about that when we leave.'

Barton didn't have time to comment. His eyes widened further when a lean woman who reminded him of his doctor, with trendy glasses and scraped-back hair, came to the door. She introduced herself as Evelyn Sax. Barton asked if they could come in. She examined their warrant cards and guided them into a spotless lounge. The functional furniture and flat-screen TV had seen better days, but it didn't resemble the disorderly home of a committed drug addict.

Barton went to sit in one seat and then chose another; a common ploy of his to enable him to check out the photographs. Some old pictures with people in seventies' flares and wild hair-styles hung on the walls, but the majority were of the lady in front of him in a variety of holiday spots with the dead man they discovered this morning.

She perched on the sofa, looking small and lost.

'Is it him? I just heard on the news there was a body found near here. I rushed down there but no one would tell me anything.'

'Evelyn, can you describe your husband for me, please?' Strange got her notebook out.

'Terry's tall and thin. He has a goatee and a shaved head. He needs glasses but rarely wears them.' Her eyes searched theirs for clues. 'Last night, he was wearing a black hoody, jeans, and black slip-on shoes.'

'I'm afraid that matches the description of the man found,' said Barton. There was no easy way to deliver information like that so Barton always gave it to them straight.

She seemed to shrink into the sofa and placed her head in her hands. Her shoulders shuddered for a while. Barton expected that to be the end of the usefulness of the conversation but, instead, she wiped her eyes and took a deep breath. The gaze she returned didn't waver.

'I assume he overdosed?'

'Actually, no. We suspect foul play.'

'Someone killed him? No way. He didn't have any enemies. Do you mean suicide?'

Barton noticed the woman directing her answers to Strange. He reached over and took Strange's notepad and let his partner take over. 'No, we don't think he committed suicide. Would you like a glass of water? A cup of tea?'

'No, I'm fine.' Evelyn's shaking shoulders said otherwise as she tried to maintain control. 'I won't be when you've gone, but part of me has always expected a knock at the door.'

'Can you explain a bit more, please?' asked Strange.

Evelyn took a moment to compose herself. 'We met because we were both addicts. You tend to know the others like you in the same town. It was over ten years ago when we first became friends. I'm sure you've heard similar tales. We became co-dependent and endured a shitty existence. I came from a normal upbringing, but an ex-boyfriend became hooked, and he gradually got me on it as well.

'I left that relationship and slept rough for a few days. Terry and I had each other's backs, but you know how these stories end. Terry's habit was brutal, and the only way to fund it was by dealing. He wouldn't let me get involved in that side of things, even though I suppose I benefitted from his crimes.

'Anyway, he got nicked and did two spells in prison. He received support at Highpoint and came out focused on changing. He helped me get clean at the same time. We found jobs, we bought this house, and we dreamed of starting a family.'

She paused as tears slid down her face. With another long exhale, she continued.

'Terry hurt his back and lost his job two years ago. You can guess how addicts cope with bad news and pain. He relapsed for a week, just disappeared, and then sorted himself out again. He does gardening work when his back lets him. Every now and again, he goes off for a few hours or even several days and uses again.'

'Was that where he went last night?'

'Yes, he said he was popping out, and he'd be back when he felt better. It was his code for using.'

'Why did you ring to say he was missing if he often went walkabout?'

'He said he'd be back by breakfast so I could open my presents with him. It's my birthday today.'

Strange scrunched her eyes as she thought about the questions that needed asking. Evelyn understood the process.

'You may think me hard by being like this, but I've seen friends die before. I know the real grief comes later. Ask whatever you want.'

'Why did you stay with him?'

'Loyalty, I guess. He helped me to get off the junk. I know how it takes a hold over some people. It's evil stuff. But the main reason was that I enjoyed his company. He made me laugh and put me first. Is it definitely him?'

Strange got up and sat next to Evelyn on the sofa. 'He fits the description, even down to his clothing. I'm sorry. We can arrange someone to pick you up to take you to identify the body. It doesn't have to be today.'

'I'd like to get it out of the way. But I still don't get it. Who would want to kill Terry?'

'Do you have someone to be with? Perhaps you could stay with some friends.'

'I'll be okay.'

'What about his family and friends? Who else needs to know?'

'He hasn't got any friends. He only had a mum, and she died when he was young. That's probably why he got in this mess.'

'He must have some acquaintances. People he texted, that sort of thing?'

'No, he hated mobile phones. Said the only person he wanted to talk to was me. That's not because he wasn't likeable. Men are just shit at keeping in touch, aren't they? He did occasionally have a guy call around for him. Thickset bloke. Terry called him Brick, which I assume isn't his real name.'

Barton considered the unfairness of life. It sounded like a depressing existence. He smiled slowly with respect at the woman's composure. The first few hours of any investigation were the most important so he decided to go for broke.

'The most likely explanation is a drug debt. Where does he buy his drugs?'

Evelyn barked a hollow laugh and shook her head. 'Good try. I'm not getting involved in any of that. I gave him twenty pounds to score. If he wanted more, I'd have given him it. We don't have secrets. When you've been us, you can't. You know who sells the drugs around here, Detective Barton, but keep me out of it.'

'He didn't have any enemies at all?'

'No, none. Not any more. He was a good man.'

18

DI BARTON

The two officers shook Mrs Sax's hand when they left. There were no words. Barton noticed her expression sink to the floor after the door closed. Halfway down the path, Barton put his phone to his ear and connected to Naeem and updated her. When he was out of hearing range from the house, he summarised his thoughts.

'Poor Evelyn Sax probably doesn't know the half of it. Terry Sax most likely found himself in debt with his supplier. Things got out of hand, and they took him out.'

'Do you know how many dealers are likely to operate in that area?' asked Naeem.

'Only two people control the drug trade around here – the Chapman sisters.'

'I feared as much.'

They spoke for a few minutes more before hanging up. Strange started the car as Barton climbed in. He took a deep breath.

'Come on, let's grab a sandwich. McDonald's?'

'Do you own shares in the yellow arches? Or have they presented you with your own seat? I'm bored with Maccy D's. I fancy Subway. They do a great tuna salad.'

Barton rolled his yes. However, the rule was that whoever drove got to choose.

'Excellent work back there. You handled that well.'

'Thanks, Guv. That must be the weirdest death message I've had to deliver.'

'I know. Maybe Mortis will tell us that it was suicide by fox.'

They both chuckled. Gallows humour was sometimes the only thing that kept you from sinking into ineffective gloom.

'That's got to be the shittiest part of the job. Giving someone news like that,' she said.

'Yeah, although remember being in uniform? No one tells you that you're going to spend most of your time dealing with people who are off their faces. I still have nightmares about them crapping themselves in my patrol car. I swear the stench would linger for weeks.' Barton grimaced at the memories.

'Nasty shit, indeed. So, what did the boss say?'

'The canvassing team will go out tonight and see if anyone's seen anything. No further intel has come in, which is a little odd. Usually a few nutters ring and confess.'

'Clever time to commit a crime.'

'Yeah. That has me worried. We rarely see professional hits around here. Our murders are impulsive, not planned.'

'Any ideas for this afternoon?'

'You get the pleasure of meeting the Chapman sisters.'

'Excellent. They have quite the reputation. It's a shame we can't just send in the SAS and be done with it.'

'As lawless scum go, they aren't too bad.'

'Really?'

'They rule with an iron fist. Everyone knows it and stays in line. That means we actually have less trouble. Turf wars are the biggest cause of serious violence.'

Strange nodded. 'I suppose that's the truth the world over. New guys turn up with a cheaper product to steal the clients, who are more than happy to take a bargain. The original guys don't like it, and next thing the ambulances are picking up people with machete and gunshot wounds. If the latest merchandise is too strong, it ends with overdoses. Get rid of the Chapmans and someone would quickly take their place.'

'That's right. It can be better the devil you know. Especially with these two. I'll extract some info from them today. They might not even be aware they've given me any. Best bit is, I have a good idea exactly where they'll be.'

'What's their story?'

Barton blew out his cheeks. 'It's kind of sad. The Chapmans are a product of modern society. I nicked them both a ridiculous amount of times when they were minors. To be fair to them, if nurture wins over nature, they had little chance. Their mother hailed from the Caribbean. She'd been a committed user before her inevitable early death. I was still in uniform when I discovered the body of that once beautiful girl in a bedsit in the town centre; fat, raddled, glassy-eyed, alone, and dead for three days.

'Their father, who originally came from Ireland, was actually a decent guy. He made me laugh and did a great impression of Father Ted. But he was really dangerous for women. He charmed the ladies with his easy patter and good looks, while running a team of builders out of a unit at the Herlington shops. He was blessed, as some men are, with a slim, defined body with minimal effort. Numerous spells using the prison gym kept him in tip-top shape.

'The problem being that when he had more than a few drinks, he liked a little cocaine. Like every addict, all promises were null and void after a hit. An evening's entertainment could turn into two or three day violent benders. Zander and I often got called because few could handle him. Everyone suffered under his fists, including the girls, who lived with him after their mother's downfall. His life ended in his flat through overdosing just after the older girl, Celine, hit eighteen. It seemed to have been the first time he had ever injected the drug.'

'Shame.'

'Yep, not many grieved for him. Hard drugs change people.

The kids lived under his mad rule for a long time. Afterwards, Celine discovered a surprising aptitude for business. She'd been doing her dad's books and rotas over the years whenever he was inside or went missing. After his excesses, he would lie on the sofa and tell her what to do while nursing his evil comedowns. Chapman Building Services still thrives today.'

'The sisters still run the business?'

'Incredibly, yes. After he died, Celine got custody of her younger sister, Britney. Their mother must have loved her music, and the five year age gap is reflected in their names. It makes it easy to remember as Britney Spears is younger than Celine Dion.'

'Nice tip!' said Strange.

'After their dad's demise, the sisters' petty crime stopped. The authorities trapped the dealer and his friends, the ones who supplied Daddy Chapman, in a police sting with information from an anonymous source shortly after. The drug squad cracked the conspiracy above, and they all went down. If Celine was involved, she was lucky as her name didn't come up in the investigation.

'The streets stayed quiet for a while, but then the number of overdoses and violent attacks picked up. A sure sign that a new dealer wanted the market. It took a long while for us to suspect the young Chapman sisters might be responsible. We're positive the girls run the show now and we're trying to build a case. Getting strong evidence that holds up in court is proving tricky though. We haven't found anything concrete to pin on them for years.'

Strange tutted. 'Sounds familiar. Wealthy drug dealers have money to hire alibis and pay grasses.'

'Spot on. We've been fed more disinformation than fact sometimes. The best barristers are on speed dial even for the minions. Celine runs the respectable business as a cover but, more importantly, they use the characters they grew up with as mules and street dealers. That way, the Chapmans are never near the product. They employ local kids on push-bikes and skateboards, and their workers' allegiance is not to the police.'

'What sort of people are the sisters?'

'Celine's a mixed bag. Her upbringing has made her calm, organised, uncaring and ruthless. She knows how to handle the most violent of men. I always suspected she killed her dad. Despite that, she inherited his charm and humour, and instils loyalty with her generosity.'

'She doesn't sound like someone to be underestimated.'

'Nope, not at all. Britney, on the other hand, reminds me of The Joker from the *Batman* films. She gets her kicks from hurting other people. The only law in the land that matters to Britney is her sister's. She manages the street kids, many of whom attended her school, and they all look up to her.'

'So, she runs it with fear?'

Barton tapped his chin with his index finger. 'In a way, but the kids love her and the drama. It's as though they think they're in their own dramatic TV show. Too many rap videos and shoot 'em up video games, I reckon. Violence and death mean nothing if you're surrounded by it on a daily basis.'

'Guns?'

'No. That's the one positive. Although beatings are unreported and people vanish. It's hard to keep track as users and street dealers are transient and flit from town to town. They upset people along the way and are rarely missed. Who knows if they've left the city or been buried? One thing we do know is nobody snitches on the Chapmans.'

'That sounds like the gangs down south. They aren't afraid of the police.'

'In a way. London has a population forty times bigger than Peterborough. I've worked these streets for years. Not only have I arrested and questioned most of the criminals, I've done the same to their parents. Celine seems out of our grip though. I'm sure I don't need to tell you that the worst part of our job is building a case on those who break the law, only to see them released from court when the judges give them another chance.'

Strange nodded her head three times. 'Or watch them get out of jail after they've served their meagre sentences just to carry on regardless. Have any charges stuck to Celine?'

'We've never arrested her, and nothing has stuck to Britney the few times we hauled her in since she became an adult. That's why with these two the case has to be built slowly. The evidence must be watertight and undeniable. Only on a conspiracy charge can these girls be given twenty years.'

'Or murder?'

'Yep, or murder. The thing is, this murder looks too sloppy for them. Why leave a body for a homicide investigation? All the necessary personnel and resources pour in. A big bright light shines on the area. The Chapmans won't want that at all.'

'They could have made a mistake.'

'True. Many years of a Teflon existence can make you cocky and lead you to believe the police are stupid. That said, I don't like them for this.'

Barton closed his eyes to think but spoke aloud. 'Britney goads the police at times, but little goes on in the Chapmans' world without them knowing about it. It's a source of pride between them.'

'They'll be on high alert if this wasn't their work, then,' said Strange.

'Celine knows the police are far from dumb. However, she's aware the authorities are bound by the rules.'

'We follow the law. It isn't a fair playing field when the other side don't.'

'No, but Celine will want this to go away fast.'

They drove in silence. Barton unclenched his teeth. The reason DCI Naeem respected him so much was his ability to read people and his commitment to fairness. Even the crooks recognised an honest man, and they'd speak to him with respect. The Chapmans hid in plain sight and would be easy to find.

Barton had agreed it with the boss. As soon as the post-mortem results arrived, he would pay them a little visit.

He also grinned at his new sergeant's performance today. With that kind of questioning, confidence and knowledge, she would be quite an asset.

Strange broke the quiet.

'By the way, you lot are really starting to piss me off.'

19

DI BARTON

Strange blurted out what had clearly been on her mind.

'I know I can trust you, John. You're *the* man in the department. Don't think I don't. I like a laugh, but the *Strange* thing gets me down. Even you did it back there. It's the easiest joke in the world, and it is funny. But to me, it's old. I've had it my entire life. The reason I left London was because it became relentless after I received promotion. The ones who were passed over said it because they knew it annoyed me. Even my DI mentioned it in meetings, and everyone would say "Strange" in an Inspector Clouseau voice. I spoke to him but he didn't care. In the end, it got to me, and I asked for a transfer.'

'Did you tell anyone here that when you arrived?'

'No, I mentioned I have family in the area, but my parents moved away a while back. I love the police and hope for further promotion, but how can I achieve that if I'm a joke? I don't want to mention the *B* word because I'd hate people getting into trouble. I'd also end up with a reputation as a grass. Zander, for one, loves saying it, but I suspect that's his way of flirting.'

Any accusation of bullying nowadays was dealt with swiftly. The guilty got demotion if they were lucky. He pondered his reply, leading her to interrupt.

'Do you think I should take it on the chin, maybe change my name?' The look on her face said she was only half joking.

'Hell, no. That's not a solution. We're nearly all decent guys here, you know. I'll put the word out and have a quiet chat in the right places. Zander would be gutted that it bothers you. There might be the odd joke while they get used to it, but I'm sure it'll stop. Do you want us to call you Kelly from now on? How's that?'

'Not good enough. I want to be respected.'

'You could assume a cool nickname, like Kickass?'

'Kelly Kickass? I'd sound like a wrestler.'

'Good point. Strange it is. Don't worry, consider everyone told.'

They parked in the Asda car park and wandered to Subway. Barton ordered for them both, while she chose a booth. He was contemplating probing about how she and Zander were working together, when their food arrived. Barton eyed his choice with suspicion. His arteries hardened with each bite of the chipotle cheesesteak on sunflower crunch bread, but stopping seemed impossible. He was relieved when Mortis' call came through.

'Afternoon, John. Have you got a moment?'

'Fire away. I can't believe I wish I'd ordered a tasty tuna salad.'

'I find that unlikely. Anyway, I've completed the preliminary checks, and it's almost as we suspected. A sharp implement into the spinal column would have caused paralysis as it was severed at T5. That's about the middle of the back. The victim may have passed out. Let's hope for his benefit he did. It's reasonable to assume that our man was surprised from behind. By the direction of the damage, the person thrust upwards, so I'm guessing someone shorter than the deceased, although they could have crouched for extra leverage.

'There's nothing to show what kind of implement was used for the stab. A boning knife or a sharpened screwdriver are reasonable guesses, but it could have been anything metal in that shape.'

'This injury didn't cause the death, as I stated. A second weapon was used. On checking the neck tissue, it's clear that the culprit sliced open the victim's neck with a keen blade. Livor mortis shows that they died on their front. So, stabbed in the back, fell forward, possibly onto the knees, then a person from behind reached round and opened the carotid and jugular with something flat and sharp. They would have died fast; unconscious in less than ten seconds. The nurse found the body facedown, but she moved him to check his vitals.

'The sides of the cut are clear and show signs of inflammation, meaning he was alive when the cut started. Further damage to the neck was most likely done by smallish animals as the cells here are not inflamed, showing us it was post-mortem. The sharp teeth of a fox look possible. Obviously, it's a bit of a mess.

'Further inspection shows mild liver and heart disease; probable cause is the history of intravenous injections over the body. Only a few of these marks are recent. Many appear to be years old, which indicates a reformed addict who relapses.

'My friend had a quick glance at the splatter photograph and confirmed it looks like what might be seen after a neck has been opened up with one long cut. Not repeated stabs as we thought with the pointed weapon. He'll have another look when he has more time.

'The evidence from the injury to the vertebrae and ligaments in the neck is more compelling. A T-shaped incision indicates use of a non-serrated blade, as does the lack of a curve to the tail of the incision in the triangular region of depressed bone. We can test for fragments of the weapon left in the bone, as some skill would be needed.'

Barton interrupted him. 'Hold on, that last bit flew way over my head. What are you saying?'

'My guess is that someone cut his neck from behind with an extremely sharp knife. Your victim wasn't killed. He was executed.'

20

Sure enough, when DS Strange pulled into the car park at the Herlington shops, the Chapman sisters' monstrous Porsche SUV shone in its usual spot.

'Wow, that's quite a machine,' said Strange.

'Bricklaying must pay well.'

'How do you want to play this, John?'

'If they start shooting, stand in front of me.'

'Which part of you?'

Barton laughed out loud. Perhaps they would get along famously after all. 'Let me do the talking. If they're both there, the short one will shoot her mouth off. Just ignore her.'

They parked in the far corner and walked up to the seemingly empty car. A door was open, and soft rock reached their ears. They found the younger Chapman basking in the winter sun. She lay in a reclined seat with a baseball cap over her face.

'Afternoon, Britney. Hard at it, I see.'

She didn't lift her hat, but her body tensed.

'I thought I could smell bacon. Can you move along? You're blocking the sun.'

'Is Celine about?'

She pushed a button, and her seat resumed its normal position. With a quick leap, she jumped out of the car towards them. She was dressed boyishly as usual. She had a habit of getting in people's personal space when she spoke to them. Barton inhaled the aroma of her shampoo.

'Corporal Barton, always a pleasure. Looking for something for the weekend? Little bit of Viagra so you can keep up with your girlfriend here?'

'I don't know what you mean. I need stuff to slow me down, stop me breaking people.'

'Amusing as ever. Now, if you want information out of me, you're going to require a warrant or a gun. Neither of which you seem to have.'

'I've got a copy of the *Daily Mail*. I could rough you up with that for a bit if you like?'

A voice distracted them from behind. It belonged to a tall, slim, elegant woman in a stylish suit. The contrast between the two sisters couldn't have been greater.

'Are you chatting my sister up again, John?' Her face held no emotion.

'She just gave me today's menu.'

'Shit, you got me. Put the cuffs on.' Celine handed a can of Coke to her sister and turned back to them. 'Let me guess, you're here to accuse us of stabbing that guy to death. Now, you know that's not our style. We run a peaceful construction business, you see. What do you really want? You need a nice conservatory up at your place? I can send a crew around. Just imagine, you and Mrs Barton sweating like two suckling pigs in an oven.'

'Murders scare people, Celine,' Barton said. 'I'd place bets on you knowing the guy. Owe you money, did he?'

She grinned back at him but without warmth. 'No one owes me money.'

She took a swig out of a bottle of water. Barton admired her long neck.

'We can have a little chat over behind that van. Doesn't do my rep any good to be seen talking to the likes of you.'

Barton set off and Strange followed.

'Not you, young lady. I don't know you. Stay here, keep an eye on my sister. If she spills any of that sticky poison on my beautiful motor vehicle, give her some old-fashioned police justice.'

When they got behind a large Transit and out of sight and earshot of the others, her facade slipped.

'Yeah, I remember Terry. Small-time junkie. Hardly knew the guy. He occasionally hung out with Brick. Pair of idiots sat up for days playing Grand Theft Auto. Think they're a couple of badasses shooting paper boys and shit.'

'New competitor in town. Made you nervous?'

'That guy had nothing to do with anything. He worked for us, years ago. That's how Brick met him. They have the same IQ and got on like a house on fire. Terry hurt his back and couldn't cope with bricklaying any more, so we let him go. I don't think I've spoken to him since. Brick sees him occasionally.'

'Where is your delightful boyfriend, Brick?'

'He's not my boyfriend, just someone I allow to have sex with me. No idea where he is. Give me your card. I understand you'll want to speak to him, so I'll get him to get in touch with you this evening.'

Barton detected a tightness in her mouth and around her eyes. Her sister seemed on edge, too. He would know for sure if he kept quiet, and she kept talking. After a few seconds, she proved him right.

'Things like this are bad for everyone here. Who knows why someone did a hit on him? Don't you worry, I'll be demanding answers. It'd be unwise to leave it up to your corrupt brother-hood, don't you think, Officer Barton?'

'We both want the same thing. We'll catch whoever did it.'

'Really? You wouldn't be wasting your time talking to me if you had the first clue.'

She strode off on her high heels. Brains and beauty are a deadly combo, thought Barton. She was right though. At the moment, they had hardly a thing to go on.

21

Barton rang DCI Naeem again when he got back in the car and brought her up to date. She sounded under pressure. Anyone not busy was out knocking on doors that afternoon and there was a wash-up planned at 18:00 to discuss their progress. It would be a short one if the canvassers drew a blank.

Strange queried the secret conversation Barton had with Celine. 'She didn't confess, then?'

'Sadly not. Said it had nothing to do with her.'

'She could be lying?'

'Maybe. I don't trust anything anyone tells me completely. We all have our secrets. When I first joined up, my sergeant told me to interview a suspected burglar. This guy trembled so much I was convinced he was guilty. He'd been seen leaving the house, too. I informed the sergeant it was definitely him. He laughed his head off.'

'It wasn't?'

'No. He lived next door, which I didn't know, and had gone to feed the cat. I learned a good lesson. Nearly everyone is jumpy when they get taken to the station. Most of the people we nick are young with unmet mental health needs. They're anxious all the time. In the Chapmans' case, they'd probably be more relaxed if they were responsible. So, I'm inclined to believe her, which doesn't leave us with much.'

'They could have stabbed him and been disturbed.'

'True. But she's smart enough not to do it there in the first place.'

'You said the little sister was nuts. Maybe she lost her temper?'

'That's the thing with those two. They don't lose control. The picture we're building up of the victim is of him being a slightly dim, gentle loner. He doesn't appear to be the type to get into a heat-of-the-moment fight. I reckon her boyfriend, Brick, will shed light on the matter. She said he'll be in touch later today. That means he knows something, although I'd put money on it not being incriminating. She'll have him hidden, and she'll tell him exactly what he needs to say when he speaks to us.'

'Brick sounds like the name of a guy who could do some damage.'

Barton chuckled all the way back to the station.

22

They arrived at the station and sat at their desks to fill in their paperwork. DCI Naeem was efficient as always, and the HOLMES room was set up and staffed. All information and evidence would be handed to a trained HOLMES operator, and they'd input it. In theory, the program helped with leads and solutions but the poor thing would be struggling at the moment with scraps to go on. There used to be a murder book, which everything ended up in, but in this day and age it went online.

The staff that handled that side of operations were generally now civvies. You filled in the forms; they recorded it. You handed them the evidence; they stored it. If it was paper, it would be scanned onto the system. If you wanted it back, they signed it out to you or gave you a printout. The civvies were much less expensive and a damn sight more organised. It left the officers more time to do proper policing. In the past, stuff got lost, and obviously that always occurred at the most inconvenient moment. It was good to see the police in the twenty-first century.

Kind of. A murder always caused an avalanche of paper-work: vehicle logs, statements, your own pocket notebook, completion paperwork, ethnicity paperwork, you name it. Barton accepted it had to be done or your arse would be swinging in the breeze. It must have been brilliant being a copper when paperwork was just your notebook. Rock up with your truncheon, say, 'You're nicked,' and be back home in time for *The Munsters*.

Barton picked up a ringing phone in the incident room at 17:55 to be told that a Sandy Janes had arrived to give a statement. Typical. Sandy Janes suited as a name. Brick did not, even though he was a bricklayer by trade.

At that point, DCI Naeem returned.

'Settle down, please. I'll be quick as we don't have much at the moment. What we do know is that an unemployed man called Terry Sax was...' she paused while she checked her notes '... executed is the word the pathologist used. It occurred last night while the snow fell, maybe 23:00. Our victim has prior convictions in the drug world but no recent police contact. His wife says he had no enemies.

'We all know the Chapman sisters. Obviously, they deny any knowledge and DI Barton and I agree this doesn't feel like their MO. At the moment, it really could be anyone. This afternoon, the house-to-house team have found nothing. We have no useful CCTV in the area, and we're unlikely to get more evidence from the crime scene. That means it's hard-work time.

'Who could it be? Why kill Mr Sax? HOLMES is giving us TIEs as we speak. That is our mantra: Trace, Investigate, Eliminate. What was Sax doing this week, earlier that day? Was he happy? Did he gamble? Do they know him in the bookies? We'll need to find out who he hung out with, and who he served his time with in prison. Talk to the shopkeepers, his neighbours, the paper boy. Yes, John.'

'Apparently, he only had one friend, and he's just come in for an interview. I have a suspicion he knows something.'

'In that case think out of the box. Unearth his old friends and past work colleagues. Okay, John, anything else you'd like to add?'

'No.'

'Well, what are you waiting for?'

Barton gave Strange a nod, and they left together. They stopped outside the interview room.

'When he arrives, you lead so I can concentrate on watching him. He will be very nervous, so go easy on him,' said Barton.

Ten minutes later, they had Brick in the room with them and Strange began the interview, only just managing to keep a straight face.

'This interview is being recorded and may be given in evidence if the case is brought to trial. We are in an interview room at Thorpe Wood Police Station. The date is twentieth October and the time by my watch is 18:15. I am DS Kelly Strange. The other police officer present is DI John Barton. Please state your full name and date of birth.'

'Sandy Janes, 1-11-88.'

Barton struggled to hear his quiet voice, focusing instead on the fascinating whiteness of Brick's teeth. It was hard to concentrate on anything else. The room quickly filled up with a fantastic scent. He'd been in the car all day with Strange and knew it wasn't her perfume.

'Do you agree that there are no other persons present?'

'Yes.' It was more of a sob.

'Before the start of this interview, I must remind you that you are entitled to free and independent legal advice either in person or by telephone at any stage.'

Barton also read him the police caution.

Brick's eyebrows raised. 'Am I being arrested?'

'No. You are assisting us with enquiries. Do you wish to speak to a legal advisor now or have one present during the interview?'

'No, I don't need a solicitor. I haven't done anything wrong.' And then he cried. Barton passed over the tissues box that he'd brought with him. It was always the same with Brick.

Barton had met thousands of people over the years, but Brick was unique. He contradicted all the rules. His features were chiselled like a movie hard man, although close up he was groomed to the point of being effeminate. He was softly spoken, yet he had the body of a seasoned heavyweight boxer and the wit of one who'd taken a few blows too many. The veneers looked new; probably a present from Celine. The phrase gentle giant was invented for him. He had been pulled in before for questioning because he moved in the same circles as the Chapmans.

As far as Barton knew, he was squeaky clean. Too dim-witted to be a boss and too much of a liability to trust to do a job. He and Celine made an attractive couple. Maybe it was just mutual attraction. Perhaps their relationship only had room for one personality.

Years ago, Brick had caught Barton looking at Brick's fingernails in amazement when they'd interviewed him. He told Barton that he always wore gloves when he worked and took great care of his hands. Once the crying stopped, Barton knew Brick would be quite jolly and get his story out almost like a performance. Barton found it more exhausting than trying to pin down an evasive criminal. Finally Brick started talking.

'I go for a jog most nights around nine thirty and often finish at the shops to pick up a snack. I was walking back from the centre last night a bit after ten – they close at eleven, you see – and bumped into Terry. He announced he was popping around mine on the off chance to check if I wanted to play computer games. I said, sure. I'm better than he is, but I still enjoy it. We were going to walk over the field by the BMX track, as it's a bit of a shortcut, when he decided he would nip and get a couple of beers. I told him I'd meet him at my flat, and he never showed up. That's it. Next thing I hear, he's been killed. Isn't it terrible?'

'Did you ring him to see where he was?'

Barton admired the sneakiness of Strange's question, but the ruse failed.

'No, he doesn't have a phone. Said they were the scourge of society, whatever that means.'

'How close were you?'

'We met up, probably once a month, and hung out. I don't know a lot about him. We didn't talk much. We'd play for hours. Sometimes we'd both fall asleep in our seats, and then wake up and carry on playing.' Brick's laugh was almost a titter. Barton massaged his temples.

'Did you know he took drugs?'

'Of course. So what? He didn't use in front of me. I used to tell him that stuff is toxic. But we all need a little help in life at points. Come to the gym with me, I'd say, but he never would.'

'Did he drink a lot?'

'No, he only ever bought a four pack, and he often left a few.'

'Have you any idea why anyone would want to kill him?'

'Terry? No. He wouldn't hurt a fly.'

Once they'd returned Brick to Reception, they wandered back to the interview room to chat undisturbed.

'I see what you mean about him not being the sort. Unusual dude, that's for sure. Hot too.'

'Ring your bell, does he?'

'With a body and a face like that, I don't care what his personality type is.'

Barton drummed his fingers on the desk. 'You don't talk much about your out-of-the-station life.'

'I wasn't aware I was allowed one.' She gave him a smile to say she wasn't about to either.

'Okay, at least he confirmed our timeline. It would help if we could discover who Terry scored from.'

'I thought you said it would be the Chapmans.'

'They will pull the strings but won't get involved in street selling for twenty pounds a bag. We'd be lucky to find that out considering the dealers are unlikely to fess up. Another thing that came to mind is that there are a few arseholes that ride trail bikes over that field. Shitty things making a massive noise, back-firing and spewing smoke out. Maybe one of them saw something.'

'Maybe one of them did it.'

Barton would sleep on all these facts. His brain worked in a similar way to the HOLMES program. He poured information in, processed it, and solutions came out. Right now, he kept coming back to the method of killing. It didn't make sense. He shrugged as he went to update the boss, assuming she hadn't left for the day. Many cases seemed strange at first, but perseverance paid off.

23

THREE DAYS LATER

I read the article for the fourth time. I had begun to think I'd made a mistake. The local news wrote what a great guy the man I killed was. No one seemed to have a bad word to say about him. They hinted at problems in the past but said he'd turned his life around. Trust it to be the tabloids, *The Sun* in this case, to dig up the truth. It turns out Terry Sax had always been in and out of trouble and served two prison sentences for drug dealing.

Leopards don't change their spots. He will have been involved with those awful Chapmans. I've been considering my next move even though my head feels fuzzy. I revisited the doctor to see if he could adjust my prescription, but he said if he went any lower it wouldn't treat my condition. There were other drugs I could try, but they had worse side effects.

That made me laugh. He must have thought I was crazy, and I didn't even tell him about seeing my mother at the sink yesterday. Clear as day, too. I think about my family all the time now. Mostly the unfairness of their deaths, but also, I think of the people who ordered them killed. I dream of *their* blood in the snow. It sickens me they got away with it. They'll probably be long dead, but I want to lash out.

Why do the authorities put up with these drug dealers? If I

know who they are, surely so must the police, but they never prosecuted those guilty of the crimes against my family, and they failed to solve the murders I committed. Such a useless bunch. Perhaps I should knock a few of them off their perches. That would focus their minds.

The female Chief Inspector with the weird name who was on TV asking for witnesses to come forward was right when she hinted that the murder was likely to be drug related, but she sounded worried about a turf war. As always, they won't be looking for me. That will be their and the Chapmans' downfall. I'll send a message to drug dealers everywhere that ordinary citizens can help where the authorities can't. I contemplate for a moment whether it's my medication that has brought on this moral crusade or if, now my life is nearly over, I'm just enjoying going out with a bang.

I will take from them what they took from me. And that is everything.

24

DI BARTON

Barton turned his car into the cul-de-sac and nearly ran over the old man he almost hit before. This time he was just standing in the way of Barton's driveway and staring into the distance. It'd been a long, fruitless day, so Barton wound his window down. He opened his mouth to give the guy a sarcastic comment, but something stopped him. Instead, he parked at the kerb and got out of the car.

'Are you all right?'

'Yes, yes, I'm fine.'

Barton did a once-up-and-down of his attire and noticed he was wearing one brown and one black shoe. There was also a slight far-off gawp to the man.

'Are you off for a walk?'

He stared blankly at Barton for a few seconds before his vacant eyes refocused.

'Damnedest thing. I forgot what I'd left the house to do. Don't get old, my boy. It's no fun at all. I do now recall I wanted a paper, and suddenly I couldn't remember the way.'

Barton pointed towards Baggswell Lane. 'It's down there if that's any help.' By the look on the man's face, it didn't seem to be.

An older lady who lived a few homes from where the disorientated man did walked past. At first, Barton thought she wasn't going to stop but eventually she did and gave them a cautious look.

'Hi, this gentleman is on his way to the shops and is a bit confused. Do you know him well?' said Barton.

Sharp eyes analysed him. 'No, not really. You understand what it's like in our street. No one talks much. He's been here years, before even I moved in.'

'Okay. What's his name?' asked Barton.

'Hmm. I forget.'

'How come? Isn't he your neighbour?' Barton asked with a frown.

'He lives a few doors away. Do you know your neighbours' names?'

Barton opened his mouth and then closed it. He looked around and his silence confirmed she was right. His shoulders slumped. He came across a lot of loneliness in his life, mostly old people. Men especially could be poor at maintaining relationships. If they never married, or their wife left for some reason, they often found themselves isolated and unhappy. He didn't know what the solution was.

Most lives started out with hope and possibility, but that wasn't how they finished. He hated to think of an inevitable end filled with despair.

Who were his own real friends? A working parent's life left little free time for social activities. He had drinking buddies, but when they left the force, they seemed to slip away. Part of that was having a young family. Even Zander, who he counted as his closest friend, he'd seen little of when he wasn't working with him every day. If he had one night free a week, he'd rather spend it with Holly.

The woman cleared her throat. 'And you're our friendly neighbourhood policeman,' she added to drive her point home.

Barton took a deep breath and was contemplating if he'd

have been better just running the fellow over, when the lady surprised him.

'I'll take him to the shop. He lives on his own and has always been a little off. Keeps himself to himself, this one.'

Barton decided it was a good thing that the man wasn't concentrating with the pair of them discussing him as if he weren't there. On closer inspection, he only had a vest on under his coat. 'Okay, that's great. You sure you'll be all right?'

'I think I can manage, assuming I don't have to carry him. I often see him buying milk and the paper.'

At that moment, raucous laughter carried from the green next to Barton's house. They all stared over at Britney Chapman and a group of friends standing under a tree, drinking and smoking. With fabulous timing, the Colonel came out of his house on the other side. He glared at the youths and limped over. Barton had seen him slumped on an electric scooter yesterday, but clearly the chance for a good moan had invigorated him.

'Can't you nick them?' asked the Colonel when he arrived.

'For having a picnic?'

'That's anti-social behaviour. I bet they're doing drugs.'

'It's just young people letting off steam. We can't arrest them for that.'

'That's the problem nowadays. These youngsters have no respect. You should go over and beat some into them.'

Barton stared at the Colonel. Then at the other two. The woman nodded her head. Even the bewildered gentleman scowled in agreement. His patience worn out, Barton uttered a goodnight and turned on his heel. His car could be moved later, perhaps under the cover of darkness. You've got to love old people, he thought.

He recalled being young himself and having nowhere to go with his friends. He imagined they used to go to the BMX track but weren't so keen now. As he arrived at his front door, an easily recognisable whiff of marijuana enveloped him. Maybe the Colonel had a point.

25

Barton opened the front door and slipped into his house. A cup of tea and a few quiet moments were required. Holly came down the stairs with an exhausted expression that mirrored his.

'Tough day?' he asked her.

'I feel like a prison officer. I'm tempted to beat the inmates, but the rules prevent me.'

'Sounds familiar. What's for dinner?'

'There are four chicken nuggets left on the oven tray and a few beans in the microwave. That rhubarb yoghurt went out of date yesterday, so you can have that for dessert.'

'Lucky me.'

She came over and put her arm around him. She still looked happy despite the kids giving her the run-around. 'You are fortunate to have me, Detective Barton. You just caught me at a low ebb and then trapped me.'

It was a familiar joke of hers that they only got together because she was vulnerable after the nasty break-up with Lawrence's biological father. He pulled her into a cuddle. A marmoset compared to his silverback; she was right. Blessed was how he felt when he met her all those years ago, and that feeling had never changed. When she'd wanted to get married for security, he couldn't agree quicker. Not once had he considered cheating on her.

He thought about events earlier at the station. DS Strange had worn a white blouse with an unreliable top button. She had searched online for the deceased's social media profile, which turned out to be absent, so spent much of the afternoon with her arms crossed and leaning over her keyboard. The only time the detectives' department had been as popular was when the previous Super retired and brought Krispy Kreme doughnuts in on his last day. Today, he'd had to threaten Zander with filing to get him out of the office. Then he'd caught Strange checking Zander out as he left the room.

Strange suited her tumbling hair framing her face. But Barton admired her in the same way he would a car. He could smile at the bodywork without needing a ride. Perhaps having three kids had drained his ardour as well as his bank account. Zander sent him a joke birthday card once that had the symptoms of low testosterone on the front. Worryingly, Barton had the weight gain, hair loss, decreasing muscle mass, mood swings, fatigue and diminishing sex drive. If his morning glory went, he'd have the full set.

Truthfully, Holly and Barton only needed a weekend together without the kids for it all to come back. Amazing what a bit of sleep can do.

Holly reached up and whispered in his ear. 'If you're really lucky, Luke might have left some chips on his plate.' Smiling now, she added, 'I take it that you haven't had a break on the murder?'

'No, not yet. It's only been three days but the whole case feels very cold. The victim had no friends or enemies and led a quiet life. There's no DNA recovered of any immediate use, no witnesses, no evidence, no murder weapon and no confessions. No further clues from the post-mortem. We cross-checked the footprints, nothing there. A wellington boot comes up repeatedly in the area, but it could have happened at any time. There were fingerprints everywhere which is as you'd expect seeing as they hold BMX meets there. He's not on Facebook or any other social media. All in all, no nothing, and probably no promotion because of it. The most concerning aspect is that we're struggling to see a motive.'

'What's going on with the promotion?'

'It won't be long before the DCI leaves. Application deadline is the end of the month, and then the process starts, so there's a couple of months' handover if we're lucky. As with all things police, it will drag on and be painfully slow and then rushed at the finish. Navneet's also not happy with this case because she doesn't want to go out on a final failure.'

'Why is no motive bad?'

'The easiest way to solve a murder is to find out why someone might want to kill them. It's money or sex, usually. This man's footprint on the world was virtually non-existent. I don't see who would want him dead, so I haven't got any suspects. It could be that he had an argument with someone, but unlikely. Everyone we talk to says the same thing: quiet bloke. That means he might have been murdered for no reason other than somebody wanting to take another's life.'

'Which means?'

'That it could be virtually anyone, and that person could be a psychopath. We'll struggle to solve it quickly unless something terrible happens.'

'Which is?'

'They kill again.'

26

FOUR MONTHS LATER

When I pushed my bin out for the collection this morning, I sensed the change in the weather at once. The air promised imminent snow and, luckily, it's been a good few days and I feel strong and capable. Christmas was a bleak time. I spent most of it in bed after a fall. Nothing broken, but I became easily tired and struggled to balance when I walked. I don't know what I would have done without supermarket deliveries.

The doctor visited on the premise of slightly adjusting my medicine but didn't fool me. He asked about family and friends. My vague answers didn't fool him. He said at some point soon it wouldn't be safe for me to live on my own. I later found brochures for care homes that he'd left on the kitchen table. I hope I have the mental strength not to let it get that far.

I had begun to think it would never snow again and contemplated finishing the job regardless because the bad days are now outnumbering the good. But I want to be remembered as the Snow Killer. It will be that which strikes terror into the hearts of people. Then my family and I won't be forgotten.

It wasn't unusual how quickly the Chapmans forgot to be careful though. Most people are the same. If danger's not staring them in the face, they soon return to normal. I was looking right at them, but they chose not to see me. There's a point in your life where you'll become invisible to the young. They are interested in power, beauty, fame and money, none of which they think I have. I wonder if that's always been the way. That will be their ruin.

Little Chapman has a new lover. I couldn't tell if it was a boy or girl at first. I must be getting old. When I spotted them pushing a pram, it gave the game away, and I followed them. She lives a few streets from me in a council building where they put single mothers with problems. The pair walk along the lane near my house without the child, laughing and clinging to each other. God knows where the baby is, or who the father is. They must have a curfew at eleven because I occasionally see Little Chapman walking back on her own at that time, although it's not like her to abide by the rules.

The snow billowed down this afternoon and I have to act. I've wrapped up warm as it's a bitter night. The clouds have gone now, leaving a clear sky. Brilliant moonlight bathes the streets; it's not a great night for stealth. I put my white coat on and walk the rear way to the field. Hopefully, I won't have to wait too long for my target to arrive.

There is a mean north wind that the houses had protected me from. Now I'm out in the open, it's brutal when it blows. Icy fingers successfully search for gaps in my clothing. I brought a huge shopping bag with me to hold the hammer and now gusts repeatedly wrench at it. A lone dog walker enters the small wood on my right, no doubt looking for shelter as he hastens back to the housing estate and out of the cruel wind.

The copse lies in the middle of a large expanse of grass that's covered in thick snow. I struggle through the drifts at the edge of the trees, slip through a dense bush and find the spot. It's quiet; even the owls are silent. I've been watching on three Thursdays now, and I could set my watch by him. I have an old towel, washed to death, for me to lie on, and I try to get comfortable. All is calm and peaceful, and then an ominous breeze rattles the empty branches above me. It warns of foul play. I shove the damp leaves off the canvas case that I hid earlier and remove Ronnie's 0.22 rifle. It's the weapon he used to teach me to shoot pheasants and partridge, deer and rabbits. Americans appropriately use .22 calibre for pest control. It's also the same gun that I used to kill Laurel.

The freezing metal pulls heat from my fingers. I tested the rifle a while back to ensure it still worked. I have cleaned it though. Oiling the parts to keep the rust at bay makes me feel young again. There's nothing quite like the feel of a gun. It's the ultimate equaliser. Whoever invented them changed the world. It doesn't matter if my strength fades, I'm sure I can find a few pounds of trigger pressure for the good of the community.

My watch shows I have less than five minutes to wait. The magazine clicks into place, and I try to relax. My knees ache and my coat arches at my shoulders to expose the lower part of my back but I push personal discomfort to one side. Ten minutes pass and I'm ready to quit. My fingers respond slowly to my brain's requests. I flex them as I hear approaching whistling.

The boyfriend of Big Chapman walks five metres from my hidden spot. The clear night means I can see the expanse of white beyond him is empty. I'm confident we're alone. I can't handle a brute such as him safely on my own. He needs to be nearly dead before I finish him off. I aim for the right-hand side of the centre of his back and squeeze. The crack echoes through the branches, but it doesn't sound like the boom from a higher-powered weapon. I quickly reload. He staggers towards the copse on the right as his hand reaches for the wound. I shoot him in the knee on that side. He collapses to his right, facing me. I put a bullet in his chest. That should do it.

He doesn't look like a thug close up. He looks only lost and scared. There's no sneer of defiance as his ruined lung causes him to spray red phlegm into the snow. A chill enters my heart and I start to doubt myself. Our eyes meet, and I want to leave him. Or should I save him? He's seen me though, and I have a job to do. I return to my bag and pull out the hammer.

When I go back to him, the sucking breaths have stopped. One of the bullets must have hit something important. That makes what I'm going to do easier, and I crush his skull with two of the firmest blows I can manage, the second of which sends a jolt up my arm that turns it to jelly. The head of the hammer remains stuck in the broken bone. In exhaustion, I drop to my knees. It takes everything I have to get up again.

I look around, and I'm relieved to find I'm still alone. I frantically kick snow over the body. My right arm shakes uncontrollably, and I struggle to put the gun in the case. It finally slides in, and I place it in the big shopping bag. I'd leave the rifle but I might need it again. I cross the field to the trees behind me and enter the wood. It's much darker with the towering pines but I know the way. I scuff along a slippery path, breath rasping from my lungs, barely able to lift my feet.

Orton Longueville church is up ahead. Someone left the rear gate open, so I needn't climb over the wall or through the hole behind the rhododendron. The lights inside highlight the stained-glass windows, which is unusual at this hour. Music, or perhaps a choir, reaches me. I must be quick. There's a small tomb from two hundred years ago that time has eroded. A loose stone panel can be pushed inwards. I slide the rifle in and hook my gloved fingers around the stone edge to pull it back into place.

I cower behind a gravestone near the church exit as I hear the crack of a heavy metal latch being lifted. People assemble in the doorway. The breeze blows their laughter over me, and I'm forced to crouch as they stand chatting in a huddle. The cold numbs my extremities further, but I force myself to stay until the last voice fades into the distance. Would it be so bad to die here now?

The night darkens as snow clouds gather above me. With gritted teeth, I creep from my spot to the front graveyard exit. The sensation of being watched drags my gaze backwards. A gowned figure steps back into the entrance of the church. Did he see me? I hurry away to the quiet village road and the cul-de-sac. I hope he didn't see me because more people must die.

27

DI BARTON

DCI Naeem had invited Barton out for a farewell meal for the two of them at the Ramblewood Inn near where he lived. It was a short walk for him as it was next to Orton Longueville church. In true Navneet style, she had a 50 per cent off voucher, but they had to spend sixty pounds to use it, so now they were both stuffed to the gills. Every time a space opened up in Barton's stomach, he took a sip of coffee and filled it back up again. They'd talked about the lack of progress on the case and the dearth of evidence. However, she hadn't mentioned his failure to get her job, but he knew it was coming.

'John, I haven't asked you properly how you feel about not getting promoted. I wasn't involved in the decision, you know, because I'm leaving soon. I heard you didn't bother attending the meeting to discuss your future development.'

'I suspected DI Sarah Cox would get the promotion before we even started the process. I wasted my time.'

'Is DI Cox a bad officer?'

Barton sneered sleepily at the question. He was too full to cope with the shrewd mind opposite him. 'No, she's great.'

'Better than you?'

'No way. Even Morse isn't fit to clean my shoes.'

'That's probably pushing it, but I would agree you are marginally better than Cox at the detective side of things. But her communication and organisational skills are excellent. Before you say anything, I know that we can always find people to fill out a form properly and not everyone has a nose for this kind of work, but she's good at that as well.'

'That's why I didn't get it, then? I suppose not solving the Terry Sax murder won't have helped my application.'

'A quick result might have made a difference, but the powers that be know it takes months to solve this sort of thing, and then it's often a stroke of luck further down the line. John, I'm saying this as a friend, but you're behaving differently of late. That's why you didn't get it.'

'What do you mean? In what way?'

'Have you had a recent bereavement or other bad news?'

'My wife's mother passed away recently.'

'Were you close?'

'Not at all. I overheard her calling me a fat yob when Holly and I first started dating. And that was the pinnacle of our relationship. She and Holly weren't that chummy either, but it still hit us hard as she was only in her early sixties.'

'Look, I won't have been the only one to notice, but you've been sort of morose lately. It feels like you're retiring, not me. It reminds me of when a career cop leaves with nothing to go home to.'

Barton finished his coffee and didn't deny it. That was exactly how he felt, even though it was irrational. He hadn't spoken to his wife about it and wondered if she'd noticed too. He suspected she would have. DCI Naeem was a good person for an officer to open their heart to. She had experienced most things.

She took over. 'Come on, John. I'll buy you a whisky. Let's get it all out.'

They walked through to the bar from the dining room and

found a cosy booth where they wouldn't be disturbed. Barton waited while she bought the drinks and returned with a grin.

'The barmaid reckons you gave her a speeding ticket fifteen years ago. I watched her like a hawk to make sure she didn't spit in your drink.'

'Great.' Barton had a sip of it and grimaced. 'Can you take it back and tell her to go for it? Might improve it.'

'Heathen. That's single malt.'

Barton didn't comment. It all tasted pretty similar to him. But he still took a big gulp and appreciated the warm glow. 'I don't know what it is, Nav. For some reason, I just feel a bit low. I'm not too far off the age my father was when he died, so I have a sense of doom. I am fatter, balder and uglier with each passing second.'

'Do you think not getting the job has made you feel worse?'

'Not really. Feeling like this has kind of crept up on me over years. Things that didn't bother me before now linger in my mind. Perhaps I can't handle any more sad experiences.'

'You should be pleased they passed over you for the job, then. Twelve hour days aren't going to improve your well-being.'

'It isn't just that. I should be happy. We've got no money worries, I love my wife, my kids are healthy, and I have a great team at work. I must be mad.'

Nav smiled and took his hand across the table. 'It sounds like mid-life blues to me. There's a stage all men go through where they are no longer *the man*. They see younger, fitter, faster, more handsome blokes about. These upstarts have more energy, too. You're bogged down with ailing parents and demanding children. Your sex-life isn't what it used to be and your partner has changed as well. It's what happens. It's a natural process we all follow, if we're lucky.'

'The alternative being an early death?'

'Correct.'

'What do I do?'

'You have two options. One is to fight it. Go mad, wear a too-tight suit, shag that barmaid, buy a Porsche, and wreck your family. I can definitely see you in a toupee.' She choked a bit on her drink. 'I see it nestled on your head like a dead squirrel, actually, perhaps a little askance as you type on your computer.'

'Very amusing. And option two?'

'It's just a stage. You'll get used to it. Your wife could be thinking something similar, but women tend to be better at handling it. They know not to throw everything away. In a way, they are lucky as they often have the children around them more.'

'How do a destructive boy, diva daughter and bolshie, disobedient teenager help?'

'At the moment, you're resisting the natural progression of life, John. You're focusing on the negatives. Enjoy the boy's creativity and innocence, ignore the mess. Watch your daughter flower into a beautiful woman, forget the insults. And try to keep Lawrence out of the juvenile prison system.'

'Did you feel like that with your kids?'

'A little, but I'd been a housewife for years. I loved getting out and stuck into a police job. My husband went through it though. He's still a moaning old git now. Don't resist it. If you focus on the family and the children, you will live in the present and look to the future. That's all they're interested in, and they drag you along. The past has gone, and most of it needs to be forgotten.'

'How are your boys?'

'They're both still at home, which in some respects is nice, but two lads in their mid-twenties bring new problems. Mo finished university and is training to be a GP. He's kind, caring, helpful around the house, and remembers our birthdays. He's never had a girlfriend, though, and doesn't want introducing to anyone he might like. I'm worried he could be gay.'

'You wouldn't like him being gay?'

'Sorry, I didn't quite word that right. My husband and I don't care if he wants to marry a sheep as long as he's happy, but there are others in our circle who are less tolerant of people's differences. I want to help if he's struggling. I hate it that he can't talk to me.'

'Maybe he hasn't decided yet. It's not clear-cut for everyone.'

'Should I ask him?'

'You mean show him a picture of Brad Pitt and Jennifer Aniston and ask which one's nicer?'

'Silly. Get me another coffee. You're finally making some sense.'

When he sat back down again, she told him to continue.

'You don't do anything. Create an environment where he feels he can talk to you if he wants. Take him out for a meal, just you and him, if you think your husband's attitude is worrying him.'

'That's good advice, John. Now, what do I do about Aryan? He's the reverse. You wouldn't believe the number of sobbing girls we've had at our door, saying the same thing: why hasn't he rung me? He said he loved me. It's disgraceful behaviour. What is Tinder? I keep catching him staring at it on his screen.'

'Ah, that's easier. Tinder is the modern method of hanging around in pubs and staring at people. Some young men have the itch to sleep with as many women as possible. Good-looking men get to do just that, and nice girls learn a valuable lesson.'

'Ah, so he'll grow out of it.'

'Eventually the fire in his loins will dampen. He'll meet someone he really likes and mess it up with his weasel ways, and he'll begin to grow up. The urge to start a family and have something deeper than a quickie might win the battle.'

Barton tailed off as he realised those words applied to his own life. It was a stage he'd experienced, and now he was at another. His boss's eyes softened as she realised her words were sinking in. She appreciated his comments too. He hoped they would stay in touch when she left work for good.

'Shall I call a taxi for you, Nav?' Barton asked as the bell for closing time rang.

'No, I'll walk from here. Come on, we'll go together.'

They put their scarves, coats and hats on in relaxed silence. When they stepped out, they both marvelled at the thick falling snow.

'Are you in tomorrow?' she asked.

'Yeah. Unfortunately, I need to have a word with DS Strange.'

'Really? She's a great officer. I love her get-on-with-it attitude.'

'She snapped at someone in the intel room yesterday, and DC Rodgers said she shouted at him to pull his fucking finger out over something else.'

'Ginger Rodgers does need to pull his finger out. Did he complain, then?'

'No, he knows that's the truth more than most, and he wouldn't grass anyone up either. He told me in confidence, as others have commented on her non-existent fuse of late. He was just concerned for her.'

'Okay, good. Keep me posted if you want any help, and thank you for your advice, John.'

'Ditto, Boss.'

She pecked him on the cheek and strode off in some very sensible walking boots.

Barton left in the opposite direction with the snow soaking his socks and trainers in seconds. He passed the vicar locking the gates of the churchyard and he nodded at Barton and turned away. Barton pondered how different people's lives were. He also realised that Nav had never held his hand or kissed him before. Everything had been kept at a certain distance. But now, she only had a few weeks left, and she was smart enough to understand when it was time to let go and move on. His mood lifted, and he looked forward to getting home.

28

THE NEXT DAY

I've caught a chill, and I've still got the shakes. It's an effort to get out of bed, and I don't manage it until noon. I wanted to take the next victim down today before they found the boyfriend, but there's no way I can function properly. I haven't slept, thinking about that boy's expression as he died. His was a handsome face of innocence more than mayhem. That said, they all look like that when they realise it's over. Big boys become mummy's boys. Well, they shouldn't break the law.

I turn the computer on and bring up the bulletins. There's nothing new at all. I check the local newspaper website, Peterborough Today, and there's no mention of a body on there either. It's only then that I notice how bright it is outside for mid-February. I pull the curtains back and stare out onto a featureless garden. Judging by the height of the snow on the bird table, there must be a foot of it. It's no wonder they haven't found him yet.

The weather forecast is on my side. Today will be bitter and icy. There's no risk of a thaw and probably even more snow tonight. I should still have time.

Both sides are stiff now, and I decide a bed day is best. I can't have taken my medicine, so I'd better start with that and then have something to eat. I don't want to lose my strength. There are more messages to send.

29

Barton reversed his Land Rover off the drive. His wheels spun momentarily in the thick snow before regaining traction as he edged through the village. He wished he'd just walked as Oundle Road was backed up with traffic. An icy blast raced in as he wound down the window to try to demist the car windows, so he quickly wound it back up and put the heater on full blast. When he could see and the car was cosy, he decided to take Nav's advice and go with the tide. He emptied his mind and let the information on the case flow through it.

There was still nothing much to go on. Police intel had checked the modus operandi of other violent cases and murders in the county. Worryingly, there had been quite a few matches, many of them recent. Stabbings were by far the most likely cause of death or injury.

Zander and Strange had worked through them and put most to bed. Maybe that was what was annoying Strange, because the lack of progress irritated him, too. The only similar case with someone found stabbed and with their throat cut was fifty years old. That would make it most unlikely to be a copycat and even harder to imagine a bloke in his seventies running around executing people. They'd had to ask crime Records for the file on that one and, as always, there had been a delay. The file would have been copied onto microfiche in the eighties and Barton wasn't holding out a great deal of hope on the quality of the information he'd receive.

Soon, resources would be directed elsewhere, and the chance of solving the murder would drop to negligible. Each case had a budget, and they'd gone through theirs already. With so much human traffic in the area, discarded bottles and cans littered the place. The BMX track masqueraded as a meeting point in the summer months for young lovers with nowhere else to go. A battered sofa was found under the trees and Barton wondered if it was worn out before or after it was dumped. DNA tests burned through the budget, and a lack of momentum wouldn't generate more money. Elsewhere, it looked as if there was the possibility of a local paedophile ring, so focus naturally moved towards that instead.

It was nearly 11:00 by the time Barton got to a desk in the incident room. Zander and Strange were the only two others in there, and Barton sensed trouble the moment he stepped inside. His head throbbed from last night's whiskies, and he wasn't keen on doing any peace making until he'd had more coffee.

Zander fidgeted behind a desk; Barton checked his expression. Then he focused on Strange's face. Tears dripped off her chin. She gazed at the screen in front of her but didn't seem to be reading anything. Another drop trickled down her cheek. Barton walked towards her. She would hate them seeing her like this.

'You all right, Kelly?'

Her jaw trembled, but she didn't speak.

'I'm just about to have a coffee. Do you want one?'

A howl arose from the back of her throat then the floodgates opened. Barton squinted at Zander, who beckoned at the floor near the coffee machine where there were shards of broken pottery scattered around.

Barton gave Zander a dirty look and mouthed, 'Is this your fault?' at him.

Then he put his hand on Kelly's shoulder and said, 'It's okay. Nothing can be that bad.'

She glanced up though moist eyes. 'I'm pregnant.'

30

Zander dropped the mug he had just picked up, smashing yet more crockery. Barton imitated a goldfish, while Strange scrunched her hair. Zander slipped his coat off a chair and sneaked toward the door.

Barton frowned. 'Wait outside, Zander, and don't let anyone in.'

Barton pulled his chair over and sat down next to Strange. 'Do you want to talk about it?' He expected her to say no.

'Maybe.'

'Okay, take a moment while I see if we have some intact crockery in a drawer.'

She smiled. 'Sorry.'

'That's all right, most of them were beyond filthy and no doubt responsible for half the departments' sick days. There's nothing like necessity to force a change.'

He took his time making them both a drink. He covertly watched her wipe her face and even reapply a bit of make-up before he plonked himself back down.

'They weren't tears of joy, then, and the broken cups aren't some sort of Greek celebration thing that I wasn't aware of?'

'No, quite the opposite. Sorry for dragging my problems into work, but I don't know what to do. I'm not far off thirty and I want children, but not just yet, and not under these circumstances.'

'Is the father not about?'

'Kind of, but he's not ready for kids. He'll run a mile.'

'You haven't told him?'

'I haven't been able to see him for three weeks.'

'Ah. I understand.'

'Exactly. To be fair, we only met up when our schedules permitted.'

'You have options. How far along are you?'

'Nine weeks, I think. I only found out a few days ago. My periods are erratic because I have polycystic ovaries. I don't tend to miss two in a row though. I've got a scan tomorrow.'

Police work had involved Barton in many situations like this. Each different in its own right. There were no correct answers, only correct decisions and only the woman could make the first one.

'In summary, Kelly, you are pregnant, but it's unlikely the father is going to be pleased, and therefore possibly not interested. You aren't ready for children yet as you are focused on your career and aren't in a loving relationship. You thought you wouldn't be able to have children easily, so, without even considering the moral implications, you are wondering whether this might be your only opportunity.'

She laughed. 'Brutally put, but yes.' She opened her mouth to say something else then stopped. After a big inhale, she told him anyway. 'I was just so attracted to him, and I've never been too worried about getting pregnant because of my condition. It was our fifth date, and I hoped it was going somewhere.' She rolled her eyes.

'Do you have anyone close you can talk to who can come to the appointment with you tomorrow?'

Her cheeks flushed red. 'Not really. My parents spend most

of their time abroad for their health. I haven't made any real friends here yet.'

Barton returned to his early thoughts about lonely lives. Many of them could be people you wouldn't expect.

'Would you like me to go with you?'

She didn't even pause. 'Yes, please.'

'Done.'

Barton's ringtone interrupted them. He checked it and frowned.

'Answer it, Guv. We'll know more tomorrow. Thanks for the chat. I'd appreciate it if you don't tell anyone.' She took the opportunity to escape from the room.

'Of course,' he said to no one. He pressed the green phone button on his mobile. 'DI Barton.'

'John, it's Celine Chapman here. Brick's gone missing.'

31

Barton told Celine to hold the line a moment while he returned the chair to his desk so he could make notes. 'Okay. When did you last see him?'

'Yesterday. We had lunch together.'

'What's the panic? It's not even twenty-four hours. He could be doing anything.'

'He didn't turn up for work today.'

'So what? He might be sick or busy or late. Why are you concerned? Loads of people haven't arrived this morning because of the weather.'

'He didn't ring in sick, and he's not answering his phone. There's no one at his house either. I've been around and checked. His car's still there.'

Barton considered the facts. 'It's too early for us to put resources into looking for him. People go off and do things without telling their partners all the time.'

'Brick wouldn't let me down. People don't do that to me, John.'

Barton thought for a few seconds and suspected that was true. Still, even if she had the hump, why involve the police? 'Why tell me? What are you thinking?'

This time the silence was on the other end of the phone. Finally, she answered. 'It feels wrong.'

'Because of what happened to Terry Sax?'

'Exactly.'

'You never got back to me with any further information, Celine.'

'I never found any. Look, I don't expect to see Brick's face on the evening news asking if anyone's seen him. I wanted to let you know he'd gone because it's out of character. We're both aware what happened the last time someone went missing in the snow.'

32

Barton told Celine he'd look into it and finished the call. It might be nothing, or it might be everything. He spent the rest of the afternoon completing paperwork and put the word out about Brick's unscripted holiday. After a quick word with Zander about keeping Kelly's news quiet, he was debating a trip to the vending machine when he received an email from Records.

They had retrieved the information regarding the murder all those years ago. There were PDF attachments, which he opened. As always with the microfiches, they resembled poor quality photocopies so it wasn't easy to make out. There was more than he'd thought there would be, so he made a brew, bought a Mars bar, and sat down to read.

After an hour, he revisited the notes he'd made. Geoffrey Stevens, aged forty-three, murdered outside his home. He suffered four puncture holes in his back from a sharp implement of some kind. The coroner suspected a pointed weapon or sharpened tool because the tissue was not damaged in the way a knife would cause. He described it as a frantic attack.

He read that those wounds would have caused death had a slit throat not beaten them to it. They found the body in the snow, slumped against his front door. No murder weapon was recovered. There seemed to be few leads and no witness statements. The man had criminal connections and went under the alias Goof. There were no arrests, and the murder remained unsolved.

Barton stood by the window and considered the similarities. This sounded more uncontrolled than the Terry Sax murder. There wasn't anything in the case files to connect the two and it seemed highly unlikely they were related to each other. That said, as he stared into the snow, the hairs stood up on the back of his neck.

33

The next day, Celine Chapman rang in the early afternoon to say Brick still hadn't shown up. Nearly forty-eight hours had passed since he'd last been seen. Barton told her to come in and file a missing person's report, but she refused to visit the station.

He was about to say she couldn't be too concerned, then, when he realised that he wanted to talk to her. A worried person would be less likely to cover any natural reactions if he slipped in a few devious questions. She said she'd be at the Herlington car park at 17:00, and he agreed to meet her there.

DCI Naeem discussed the fifty year old case with him and said she'd park the information for the moment. Barton reiterated what he knew about Brick and, although the sum of the new information meant little, both of them had a suspicion the case might crack soon. The mood in the office was gloomy, but that was just as likely to be because of the snow. Everyone loved it to start with, but it soon became annoying and inconvenient.

DS Strange's appointment for the scan at the maternity unit was at 16:00 and at 15:30, Barton drove her there in his car. Understandably, she'd been quiet all day. The temperature lifted to around zero but the wind had strengthened too. Traffic was light even though the gritters had done their job and cleared away the surface snow. Banks of it crowded the verges, giving the road the feel of a racetrack.

'Thanks for coming with me.'

'I'm pleased you want me there. Don't you have to wait until twelve weeks for an ultrasound?'

'Normally, yes, but because of my polycystic ovaries they wanted to see exactly how far gone I am and to make sure all is progressing as expected. It's possible there could already be problems or that I've miscarried. I didn't want to pay another fifteen pounds for a pregnancy test.'

Barton smiled at her. 'You can buy little strips for about ten pence and then pee in a pot and put them in. We did it for Baby Luke as it took six months for Holly to fall pregnant. We used loads of them.'

'Baby Luke? Isn't your son four now?'

Barton laughed. He could look back at that period fondly now; the excitement for the first few months as they waited for the blue line to appear. After half a year, the novelty wore off with a vengeance and Barton dreaded checking. The very next time, the test was positive. Funny how life happened that way. If you want something too much, it doesn't happen. He turned the radio on to distract them but the next song it played was the original Beatles version of 'Yesterday'. Barton daren't glance at his passenger.

They arrived and struggled to find a space to park. Even though Peterborough's new hospital was only a few years old, it was already groaning under the burgeoning city population. When they got out of the car, they shielded their eyes. Snow had turned to stinging, freezing rain and the temperature had dropped dramatically.

Barton knew about this rain from the accidents when he'd worked traffic. It fell through cold air and became super-cooled. When it hit the frozen road, it spread on contact and formed a perfectly smooth, transparent layer of ice so when the surface looked wet, the whole road could in fact be a sheet of ice. With this wind, it drove horizontally into them. They both hustled into the building and chuckled at each other's red faces in the queue at the maternity desk.

The place was busy and a perfect reflection of how multicultural Peterborough had become as it resembled a United Nations conference. There was only one seat spare, into which Barton guided Strange. She sat but shook her head at him. 'I hope you aren't going to carry me into the appointment.'

The clock clicked onto 16:30 by the time the waiting room thinned out, and they still hadn't been seen. Barton considered showing his warrant card but hated doing that sort of thing unless it was necessary. He knew if he did, the nurses would bump them up the queue as the emergency services tended to look after each other, knowing how busy they were, but Barton only had Celine Chapman to see, and she could wait.

A free seat came available next to Kelly, and he slid onto it. They'd both been people watching as soon as they arrived. It was hard not to. Here was life at its rawest. They'd seen tears of joy and despair, faces of hope, and ones of sorrow. But all these individuals, from whatever country they came, had waited patiently and courteously. It reminded Barton that the vast majority of the population were nice people, just trying to get by. He also noticed Kelly's hands gently resting on her stomach.

At 16:35, they heard Strange's name. The nurse guided them to a quiet, slightly darkened room with a bed and a monitor in it. Strange perched on the side of the bed while Barton tried to lighten the experience.

'If you don't want to lie down, do you mind if I do?'

'Congratulations, Mr Barton. You're having a Big Mac.'

'Let me guess, triplets?'

'I doubt they'd be able to tell – there'd be too many fries in the way.'

The sonographer grinned as she arrived and saw them laughing. She asked Strange to lie on the bed and undo her shirt. Barton sat on the seat next to her, unsure where to look.

'So, Ms Strange, how far along do you think you are?'

'About nine weeks.'

'Okay, let's see. The gel will be a little cool, so prepare yourself.' She pulled a pair of blue gloves on and squirted a large amount of a clear substance below Kelly's belly button. She tucked a tissue into the top of the trousers and slid a probe around Kelly's lower stomach while she gazed at the screen. Seconds drew out. Barton stopped breathing and Kelly's hand came over and hovered near his. He took it and tried to exude confidence as they both peered at the grainy image.

'Right, there's the baby. If you look closely, there's the heart beating.' She pressed a button on the keyboard and a rapid heartbeat echoed around. 'Very normal – 175 beats per minute. Measuring from head to bottom would make my guess eight weeks and five days. We'll wake it up a little. There, look, arms moving, and legs, which is great. Congratulations to you both. Let me get you some pictures.'

The woman and Barton turned to a weeping Strange. Tears pouring down her face. She wiped her eyes and took a deep breath. 'Can I ask a question?'

'Of course.'

'I have polycystic ovaries. Does that increase my risk of miscarriage?'

'There is evidence that PCOS is a risk factor, but we don't really know. There are always so many factors involved in a pregnancy. Did you ask your doctor about it when you planned to get pregnant?'

'It wasn't really planned. In fact, I didn't know if I was going to keep it until now.'

The sonographer rested her hand on Strange's shoulder. 'There's a lot of literature in the waiting room. Grab yourself some leaflets and have a read. You'll need to book in for a twelve week scan because we can't do the nuchal fold test until that point.' At Kelly's blank face, she checked her watch. 'Are you in a rush? Because I finish my last appointment in half an hour and can answer any questions you might have then.'

Barton couldn't help a glance at his own watch to see a time of 16:45. He didn't want to look up afterwards.

'Go, John. I'll be fine here. I want to read everything they've got and I'm sure I'll have loads of questions. It will be time well spent getting my head around it all. There'll be cabs outside.'

'It's okay. I can wait.'

They both still held hands. She gave his fingers a firm squeeze and let go.

'John, I'm pregnant, not dying. Get out of here.'

Barton thanked the sonographer and grinned at her.

'Make sure the taxi driver is careful. The roads will be bad.' He paused after standing and said, 'Good for you, Kelly.'

As he closed the door behind him, the sonographer whispered, 'Men!'

34

THE SNOW KILLER

I glance at the clock and see the time is approaching five. My body has calmed down, and I am strangely cool headed. The news had nothing of any importance on it, local or national, so I've decided to strike now if possible. Big Chapman often leaves the office around this time. I remember her father lording it from that office while his children ran riot outside, taking things from unlocked cars and terrorising the shoppers. It's no wonder Britney runs part of their business out in the open.

My clothes have dried and I slide my arms into the white coat. My jeans are stiff coming off the radiator, but only the wellingtons have any dampness. The drawer on the sideboard is stiff, and the pistol rattles inside when I manage to yank it open. I keep it loaded, just in case. It holds six rounds. I used one of them making sure it still worked, and to see how loud the bang was, but five bullets should be more than enough.

I'll need my head visible for this if it's going to work. Stepping outside the front door, I gasp at the weather. It's like being hit in the face with tiny ball bearings. I pull my hood up, lean forward into the wind, and with short, careful steps, walk up the path.

Baggswell Lane, the route to the shops, has many tall trees

and fences along it, and I'm protected from the worst of the conditions. I only meet one other person; a lunatic on a push-bike. A balaclava cocoons his head, and I can't make out any features. The lights are on at the shops, and I'm disappointed to see the units so clearly. The odd person scuttles from doorways with their heads down but they disappear as quickly as they emerge.

A few vehicles are stationary with their headlights on. I recognise the expensive behemoth that Big Chapman owns. The strong beam from its lights displays the blistering hail to good effect. She's parked it up in the far corner near the building that holds the dentist's. I shuffle forwards with the wind directly in front of me. It whips the air away so fast that I struggle to breathe. I hold onto both sides of my hood to keep it in place.

A car drives out of its space, causing me to stop. It glides past within touching distance, but I can't recognise any features through the windows, and it's unlikely they would see me either. It is now or never. I grab the handle of the pistol in my big side pocket and step forward as though I'm heading to the dentist entrance. A gust blows my hood off and whips my hair around.

I stagger a little, edging towards the driver's side door of the huge vehicle. A hand wipes the side of the frosted window and a brown face presses against it. She's seen me. I expect the car to roar away. Instead, the door clicks open and she pushes it wide.

Big Chapman stares at me like I'm insane. The inside light reflects off her leather coat. Her lopsided smile is amused. I detect kindness and genuine concern. A question flashes before my watering eyes. Do I kill again?

35

DI BARTON

Barton made his way to the exit uplifted, as he often was by his experience of the NHS, despite another late running appointment. Few of the staff didn't go the extra distance every day. It had been an emotional moment for him too, so it must have been a roller coaster for Kelly. He smiled at the recollection of her peaceful face when she said she planned to keep the baby. That was the right decision for her, and he was sure she wouldn't regret it. He laughed and got an odd look from a passing porter. For sure there would be tough times, but a baby might be all she needed in life. After all, plenty of parents raised them on their own.

Barton inserted his ticket into the machine and paid the fee after double-checking the outrageous price. He was wondering if it counted as a claimable work expense when the freezing rain reacquainted itself with his face. His only thought now was getting to the car with his eyesight intact. If anything, the rain came down harder now. Angry, grey clouds boiled above, and the gloom that threatened earlier had arrived with gusto.

He cursed at the line of traffic out of the hospital. He was minutes ahead of rush hour, but everyone wanted to get home early. He could rat-run on the back roads to beat the queues, but once you were on the parkways around Peterborough, it was usual to maintain a decent speed. He chose the latter and was wrong. Tonight's weather broke the rules. He found himself drifting along at twenty miles per hour. There were no blues and twos fitted to his car but maybe that was just as well, he thought. Abandoned vehicles littered the side of the road as though giants had thrown them there. People's lives changed in conditions like this.

The song on the radio finished. Barton's concentration on the traffic conditions meant he hadn't heard a word. The presenter took over.

'Take care on the roads tonight, all you commuters. We're getting reports of terrible conditions, and most of the routes around the city are barely moving. Keep your distance. The council tells me the gritters are struggling as the grit won't stick on the surface and is just getting washed away. Then more ice forms. It's a no win situation. In the US, this freezing rain is known as an ice storm.'

Everyone else must have been listening, too, as Barton's speed dropped to ten miles an hour. He cursed but then steadied his breathing. Celine Chapman would still be there if Brick hadn't turned up. She was clever enough to know the weather might delay him.

He joined the slip road to Orton Malborne and the shops, and got stuck in another queue. It wasn't usual to meet a known felon to discuss their worries about a different criminal matter, but he had the strange feeling that Celine wanted to help. A detective's job had never been straightforward. At some point in the future, he hoped they'd arrest the Chapmans. Someone close to them would get caught, and loyalty was easily discarded when heavy sentences became a real possibility.

At the roundabout, he swung onto Malborne Way. He'd be there in less than a minute. His gut tightened without warning.

36

There's no time for thought and reflection. That should have taken place fifty years ago. They've buried the fat lady. The choir has sung. After all, I saw it leaving the church. I'm too old and too cold for change.

'What the hell are you doing out in this weather at your age?' shouts Big Chapman.

I put a hand on the top of the car door to steady myself and reply.

'Cleaning the streets.'

An act of kindness by her doesn't negate the lives she's ruined with drugs. Stealing those people's futures means you must forsake the right to one of your own. My father accepted that. The men who killed him understood it. And as the smile drops from her face, this lady knows it too.

She still cries out in defiance, 'No!' but the wind screams louder. The bang of the Webley pistol isn't loud. What sound there is gets blown into the clouds. I blast her again in the side, reach over, and turn off the car ignition. She attempts to lean over to the passenger seat but her insides are already ruined, and she slumps back into her seat. Her eyes slant right at me in shock and shame.

I pull the screwdriver from my other pocket and show it to her face. Her gaze follows the point as it moves towards her neck. I rest it against the skin.

The car door is heavy as I slam it shut. I pull my hood up again and hold it in place. The wind rips at it as I leave the lee of the vehicle. I glance up to see a young lad staring over in the distance. It's too late to run or hide.

I need to walk near him to escape into Baggswell Lane. As I approach, he backs away and sprints across the road, past the chip shop and the bookmaker's, and through an underpass. I turn into the entrance to the lane and notice a familiar car, driving too fast for the conditions, screech and slide into the top of the street that leads to the car park. Fear stirs my legs. I find a semi-jog I'm pleased I still have the ability to achieve, and the policeman's vehicle slips from view. The gravel slides under my feet, but it isn't treacherous.

I slow when I arrive at our cul-de-sac and walk to the end. My vision blurs as I approach my home. My strength empties out as though a gasket has blown. The last few strides are almost impossible. I cry as my key drops from my fingers. The back door is unlocked, I recall, and, using the fence as support, I stagger inside.

The heating turning itself on stirs me some time later. I must have collapsed fully clothed on the sofa. Even my wellingtons are still on my feet. The room warms up fast. The bungalow has long radiators and small rooms. Sleep is coming and I won't resist. My final thought as my eyelids close and the world dims is that this could be it. But there's just one loose end to tie. Only one more lesson to give. One last wrong to make right.

37

DI BARTON

A desolate, urban landscape greeted Barton. Grey, watery light blurred the streetlamps and headlights. Frantic windscreen wipers revealed people huddled in shop doorways and making breaks to the bleak housing estates through layers of spitting rain and sleet. He hammered his brakes as a car pulling out of the car park swung too wide, then edged in.

The traffic had melted some of the snow during the day, and it'd become an icy slush. It crunched in places and slipped in others. Soon it would be a hip breaking glacier full of ridges and crevices. There was no mistaking the Chapmans' Porsche. He noticed the vehicle vibrate and smoke poured out of the exhaust as though the engine had just started. Checking his watch, he realised he was fifteen minutes late. Maybe she'd given up waiting.

Barton drove to the right to cut her off. He expected the big car to swing past the dentist's but it crept forward and picked up speed. There was something unnatural and jerky about the movement. The car struggled and then revved. It did head towards the dentist's, but instead of stopping, it accelerated. Barton slammed on the brakes, dashed from his car, but could do nothing to stop the Porsche smashing into the thick brick posts at the entrance.

The engine roared and stalled as he arrived at the driver's side. He yanked open the door, and a horrific scene greeted him: Celine Chapman slumped over the steering wheel with a screwdriver sticking out of the side of her neck. Her eyes opened a fraction.

Twenty years of training clicked into place, and he immediately grabbed his phone and dialled 999. There was no point ringing Control because they could take a minute to pick up and time wasn't on Celine's side. The wind curled over the roof of the car and blew the smell of cordite and fresh blood into Barton's nose. Harsh, biting snow blasted it away. He crouched to speak.

'DI Barton. Herlington shops car park. Outside the dentist. Ambulance needed. Heavy blood loss. Life in danger. Police needed. Notify command chain. Attempted murder.' He cut the line.

At that moment, Celine dropped back off the steering wheel and into her seat. Her hand came up to the tool in her neck. There wasn't actually an enormous amount of blood pouring from the wound so he hoped that meant the weapon might not have penetrated the main veins and arteries.

'Don't touch the screwdriver, Celine. Leave it in place. The medics are coming. Breathe slowly.'

Celine tried to speak but only a gargled sound came out. Her right hand dropped off the wheel, and she managed to pull her coat back. Barton peered down and couldn't prevent himself saying, 'God,' at the blood that oozed rapidly from her side.

'I'm going to get a towel from my car to stop the bleeding.'

For the second time within an hour, a hand hovered in front of him. He took it.

'N-n-n-n-n-o,' she said.

He let go of her hand, pulled his jacket off and then his jumper. He made the latter into a pad and pressed it hard against the two close-together bullet holes.

'You'll only need to hold on until the medics arrive.'

He felt a faint pressure on his hand, and she twisted her head slightly towards him. A small smile lifted her cheeks. She didn't believe that. Her body convulsed, and she gurgled. 'Ahh-h-h,' came out, and blood trickled from the side of her mouth. Her eyes stayed on his. She squinted. There was determination to talk.

'O-o-o-o-l-l-l-d,' she gasped.

'What do you mean? You want me to hold you? I can hear the sirens, Celine. They're almost here. Hang in there. Stay awake. Keep those eyes open.'

He realised he sounded like someone who had watched too many Vietnam war films when the helicopters came in to rescue the wounded. Her eyes bulged, but lost their focus. A large breath, more a release than anything, pushed more blood from her shredded lungs. The gasp tailed off and the mist it created, and Celine's life, disappeared.

The police and emergency vehicles poured into the car park. Zander prised Barton's fingers from Celine's grasp. Paramedics lifted Celine from the seat, placed her on a stretcher, and quickly shunted it into the well-lit interior of an ambulance. Barton watched through the back door as they inserted an airway. A female paramedic shook her head and closed the door.

One explanation occurred to Barton on this professional hit. It was a sign.

38

DI Barton woke the following morning at 8:00. He couldn't remember the last time he'd slept for ten hours. After nipping to the toilet, he slid himself back into the warm sheets. A lukewarm cup of tea sat next to the bed. He decided to let yesterday's events wash over him.

Once the body had been removed, the crime scene felt strange. A bitter day with a crumpled car and a bloody seat didn't seem dramatic enough. The vehicle was so well made that the brick post had come off worst. Zander had put Barton's coat back on him and guided him to a patrol car, where he shivered uncontrollably despite the heater blasting out warm air. Barton had seen people die before, most police had, but it was different when someone familiar died before their time. He had some affection and respect for Celine, even if she lived on the wrong side of the law.

Zander returned from the shops with a coffee and asked the constable driving the response car to drive them home. Barton protested half-heartedly, but he was emotionally drained. The driver tried to make small talk for a while. It wasn't often he had two men from CID with reputations like theirs in his car, but

Zander eventually told him it had been a long day, and he got the hint.

Holly and the kids were finishing dinner. She knew the look and drove the children into the lounge with promises of ice cream from the freezer. Zander remembered where they kept the whisky. He poured them both half a tumbler and sat opposite Barton at the table.

They talked for a while. Holly quietly came in and cooked a frozen pizza for them, which Barton didn't touch. Baby Luke said he could smell it and ran off with the biggest slice. Zander probed around the hospital visit with Kelly but remained tactful enough not to ask for details. He asked Barton for a run through of the events leading up to the murder as a message confirmed Celine's death on arrival at the hospital. He made notes in Barton's pad for him while events remained fresh. Zander then went into the hallway and Barton heard him talking to a person he assumed was the boss, DCI Naeem.

Zander informed him there was a meeting for everyone at 10:00 the next morning. CSI were all over the crime scene, and any PC or DC who answered their phone was being sent to the area to look for witnesses.

Zander received another call half an hour later. Apparently, Britney Chapman had arrived at the scene. The scene guard ended up tussling with her as Britney refused to take no for an answer. They don't teach you street fighting at training school. In true Britney style, she wasn't happy with just getting through. She had to go too far. Luckily, DC Ginger Rodgers arrived and threatened her with a dose of PAVA spray and a whack from his baton. Zander and Barton were amazed that Ginger had been wearing his holster. Luckily, there was still an ambulance present, which took the officer to hospital.

Ginger arrested and cautioned Britney, and drove her to the station in his car where all her fight drained away on the news she'd spent a lifetime dreading. In a way, Britney being arrested worked out nicely as at least she remained safe in custody and could be questioned in the morning. Barton noticed Zander hadn't drunk his whisky, so he had his glass, too.

When Zander left, Barton climbed the stairs, took off his clothes and dropped into bed. He dreamt of blood and snow.

Holly came up at 9:00 with another cup of tea while Barton drowsed. He stirred and caught her sneaking away.

'Hey, why didn't you wake me?'

'Zander said to let you sleep. You don't need to be in 'til ten.'

'Okay. I'll grab a shower. What's the weather like?'

'It's not as cold, but the snow's not melting. Forecast is for a thaw tomorrow and milder for the rest of the week before a really bitter spell, minus five or something, for a couple of days. Winter's last gasp. Then, apparently, spring will be sprung.'

Barton gave her a quizzical look.

'I'm only repeating what the forecaster said.'

'Did he forecast a quick fry-up?'

'It's already on. You have half an hour. Do you remember Zander saying he'd give you a lift in?'

Barton jumped out of bed and trotted down the stairs in his dressing gown eight minutes later. He found himself whistling. Strange's news excited him. There was nothing like seeing a new baby, although Barton got a perverse pleasure from watching the joyful expressions on new parents' faces, knowing they had no idea what lay ahead.

Barton let his thoughts return to the events of the previous evening. It was sad for the Chapmans, but they led that kind of life. A brutal murder out in the open like that must have been seen. There were bound to be more clues. He now dared to believe they would catch this cold killer.

'Help yourself: oven and microwave,' Holly shouted to him as she passed him in her suit. 'I take it you'll be late, so do what you've got to do. I'm doing spag bol for the kids when they're back. There'll be a plate for you when you get home.'

His wife had treated him if the smell was anything to go by. Barton's belly rumbled. He hadn't eaten since yesterday lunchtime, which was virtually unheard of for him. He pulled a tray with eight sausages and another containing four hash browns out of the oven. Then burnt his fingers removing a big bowl of nuclear beans out of the microwave. The frying pan had oil in it and a box of eggs at its side with a spatula resting on top.

Ten pleasurable minutes later, the eggs remained intact, but the rest had filled a giant hole. He released a small burp, marvelled at his good fortune, and went upstairs to change.

It felt as if it might finally be above zero when he stepped outside. He even had fifteen minutes to spare to nip and get a newspaper. For some reason, the kindness of the doctor from the appointment with Kelly at the hospital was at the forefront of his mind. When he returned from the shops, he stared down the cul-de-sac and thought of the old bloke who had been confused in the street. Deciding to take the initiative, he strode along the path.

The thick snow on the pavements remained treacherous, so Barton took his time. He didn't know which house the man lived in for sure but didn't care. Door knocking was second nature to a copper. He had a recollection of the guy coming out of a bungalow on the right. A house on that side had the brightest red door that Barton had ever seen. It stuck out a mile with the snow resting underneath it. Might as well start there, he thought.

Barton's wife had wanted their door replacing with a red one when it split last year. She said a red door in feng shui meant welcome. That was one of the few arguments he won when he explained they wanted to live there quietly, considering his profession. He said it would be like having a target on their house. She settled for a red tumble dryer, which he joked had murdered their electricity bill.

The door opened and, instead of the man, the old lady who'd taken him shopping that day peered at him. It was hard to age her as she wore plain clothes and just a touch of lipstick. She stared at him with a small grin and widened her eyes.

'Morning, Officer.'

'Are you all right?' he asked.

'Just a bit of blurred vision. It's probably the glare from the snow. Luckily, you're big enough to recognise. Enjoy your eyesight and hearing while you still can, young man. And don't get me started on knees!'

'Erm, okay. You don't live here, do you?'

'No. After that day he got lost, I occasionally pop over to ask if he wants anything from the shop. He usually says no, and I see him go by himself later. He's not in great form today. I had to let myself in. To be honest, he doesn't say much. He never has.'

'Can I talk to him? I don't know his name.'

'I call him Mr Smith.'

'That's very formal.'

'It's an old joke, and, as I said before, he's very reserved, secretive even. He told me to call him Jen last time I visited. I asked why and he said that's what his mates call him. The funny thing is, in all my visits here, I haven't seen any friends.'

'Okay, I'll give Jen a try.'

'Go into the lounge, but he might not remember you. If he gets cross, which is possible, just leave.'

Barton didn't like the sound of that but tentatively pushed open the door. He edged into a stifling hot room where the man dozed in a chair. Barton could see the top of his shirt was buttoned up incorrectly. A sheen of sweat glistened on his forehead. He decided he wouldn't wake him. The woman had entered as well.

'Toasty in here?' Barton commented.

'Yes, nice isn't it? I put it on full whack because he forgets.'

Barton wasn't sure if she was joking or not. 'You have a key?'

'Yes, he insisted one morning. I don't think he remembers some days, but I rarely use it. He usually leaves the back door open because he can't hear the front doorbell, just in case he has a fall. It's like many old-age illnesses. Sometimes you're okay, others not. Social services came around shortly after I started coming. They've been pretty good. I agreed to do a fridge clear-out once a week to stop him eating out-of-date food. They left CO alarms and fire alarms. But they said he's getting close to the end.'

'I thought you said he's fine most of the time?'

'Not *the* end, but the end of independent living. He's deteriorating, and he hasn't got any family. You can do a lot of damage with forgetfulness. We don't want him leaving the gas on and blowing up the street. Besides, I don't really know him, and I'm not in the arse-wiping business.'

Barton laughed as he stepped towards the door. 'I hear it's a dirty job.'

She smiled, but it was only half of one. 'When you're elderly, your biggest fear is being a burden and losing your dignity. This place is familiar to him and therefore comforting, whereas the outside world constantly changes, I suspect the curtains and carpets here are twenty years old. That TV is probably older than you are. Leaving this bungalow will kill him.'

Barton doubted they had flat screens forty years ago but still nodded. He left her doing the washing-up and walked up the middle of the road where the snow mushed underfoot. Zander's vehicle had pulled up outside his house and Barton let out a groan. The Colonel from opposite ploughed through the slush and parked his mobility scooter next to the car. His head virtually entered the driver's window.

Barton got in the car next to Zander and placed his newspaper in the glove box. He leaned forward so he could see their visitor.

'Morning, Colonel. You well?'

'I just asked this fella about the murders.'

'I don't reckon he did them,' Barton replied.

Zander stifled a snigger and put the car into gear.

'No, no, I expect not. I wondered, maybe it's the Snow Killer. Come back for more victims.'

Zander turned the engine off. 'Who's the Snow Killer?'

'Ages ago, we had three murders in the snow. Around here, they were. One of them was amongst the graves at the church. The rumour was that they received a note before they died, telling them to watch out.'

'How long ago did this happen? Is the culprit still in prison?'

'They never caught anyone for it, but I don't think the authorities searched very hard. The people killed had lengthy records. It probably saved the police time and money.'

'Twenty years ago, thirty years?'

'Fifty years, more maybe. They say on some nights when it snows, a ghost can be seen placing flowers at the graves.'

Barton exchanged a glance with Zander. 'Okay, thanks. We'll look into it.'

The Colonel's face seemed to drop at that news, and he turned and sped away. Barton tapped Zander on the arm. 'Every time I speak to him, I feel like drinking immediately afterwards.'

'Do you think the boss will move the meeting to the pub?'

That reminded Barton of a team building trip at a bar a few years back. Most of the youngsters drank soft drinks and made their excuses. Barton, Zander and Rodgers had turned it into a session and weren't at all productive the next day. Those changes were for the best, but he couldn't help missing the old days. Zander interrupted his thoughts.

'I wanted a quick chat. That's why I said I'd pick you up.'

'That sounds ominous.'

'I hope not. How have I appeared of late?'

Barton considered the question. 'Back to normal.'

'Right. I took all the family pictures down and cleared out my boy's room and his wardrobe. The constant reminders kept me depressed. This murder case gave me something else to focus on. Being with the team and seeing how everyone has ups and downs has given me perspective as well.'

'Sounds reasonable. What's the problem?'

'Diane came around last night to get the rest of her things. She called me "unfeeling" and some other nasty stuff. Said I was trying to erase my son's memories. I wondered what you thought.'

The terrible loss of his friend's son had made Barton consider how he would handle losing a child. He'd even discussed it with Holly. She'd called him morbid and told him it didn't bear thinking about. He'd seen others go through it before and knew the answer to Zander's question.

'You do what's best for you, mate. I wouldn't want to be reminded of it all the time either, but everyone's different. I couldn't talk about my dad after he died, but we do now. It's nostalgia in a way, and that's often tinged with sadness. You'll get the pictures out again when you're ready. As for Diane, she's only lashing out.'

'That's what I thought. It seems crazy how we are with each other now, especially after how close we were.'

'It's all over for you two, then?'

'Yeah. She blames me for distancing from her, but we grieved in different ways. I can't see a way back.'

They'd reached the station by then and Zander parked the car. When they got to the office, DC Rodgers took one look at their long faces and said, 'Looks like the entertainment's arrived.'

40

DI BARTON

DCI Naeem waited for them to settle down. Barton detected the energy in the room. An event like this would also cause drama in the criminal fraternity for sure. The Romanian crews that ran the north of the city were a ruthless bunch, and they wouldn't be able to believe their luck, if they weren't the culprits. Because it was so unexpected, it might take a while before the others moved in, but react they would.

'Quiet, please, thanks for your promptness this morning. I'll summarise, even though I'm sure you know the story. A few months ago, someone executed a man with loose connections to the Chapmans. There were no witnesses, and the evidence didn't lead us anywhere. In many ways, it was a flawless crime. The chance of solving that murder without further information is unlikely.'

'Where's the top brass today?' shouted DC Rodgers.

Naeem ignored him. They all knew that upper management wouldn't want to be visible in a failure, and that was what the Terry Sax case had been until this point.

'Since then, we've had nothing. Then, on Tuesday, Brick disappeared. Celine Chapman was unusually worried about her boyfriend. He still hasn't shown up. Is he dead? Or did he kill Celine in a lovers' tiff?'

Most of those present chuckled at that.

'I would suggest it's likely that Brick is deceased and I doubt he's responsible for Celine's death. If Terry Sax ran drugs for them, it's possible Brick did. With Celine gone, the hierarchy of their gang has been destroyed, and they'll be ripe for a takeover. What are your views on that, DI Barton?'

Barton stood up and walked to the front. 'Personally, I think Terry Sax and Brick were collateral damage. All of you should be aware that Celine is, was, a despot. To save Ginger asking, that means she held absolute power, tolerated no subversion, and governed oppressively. She ruled by fear but she also had respect, and those close to her reaped the rewards. Were there any witnesses from last night?'

'No, incredibly. No one's rung in so far.'

Barton shook his head. 'I know this is their hood, but thousands visit those shops every day. Someone must have seen something.'

'Think of the weather. People had their heads down in that freezing rain. The wind would have whipped the sound away.'

'Even gunshots?'

'The top ballistics guy is coming here this afternoon. He'll have a look at our body. I spoke to him yesterday, and he said that most people's experience of weapons is from war films where there's multiple firing, or movies about robberies inside buildings where the bangs are amplified. One or two shots in an open space with an average calibre pistol in adverse conditions would be easy to miss. Might sound like an engine backfiring. We have so few guns in this country that most people wouldn't have heard one firing without watching TV programmes.'

'What about the post-mortem? Forensics on that screwdriver?' asked Barton.

'Mortis said he'd have the post-mortem done by this afternoon. I spotted the CSI lady, Sirena I think her name was, and him on site. They gave me their initial observations last night. Combining them both, the conclusion is two blasts from close range with a moderately powerful gun. From the powder burns, most likely a pistol. The screwdriver was probably inserted into her throat after the shots. Mortis said it was unnecessary to kill the victim as one of the bullets passed straight through the lower abdomen and came out the other side, which would have caused extensive bleeding, and the other one hit higher and exited the chest cavity.'

DS Zander picked up on that immediately. 'Torture? Although why not take the screwdriver with you? Why commit a professional hit that you might get away with, but then leave a clue behind?'

DS Strange put her hand up. 'We had this kind of thing in London all the time. It's a message. They wanted it found. They know that adds extra shock to the killing. There won't be any fingerprints on the weapon. My guess is the type of implement used will match Terry Sax's back stabs. They wouldn't leave the gun like they do in American films because they are too hard to come by over here. They might want to use it again.'

The room remained silent while they digested that piece of information.

'Good call,' said Naeem, who had been writing the facts down on a whiteboard. 'Who's next? Will more people be targeted?'

A fairly new officer, DC Malik, shouted out the obvious. 'Britney's got to be next.' Someone threw a paper cup at him and received a rebuking scowl from Naeem.

'Correct, Malik, thank you. Rodgers, do that again and I'll throw something heavier at you. We state the obvious in this room because everything isn't always obvious. This looks simple. A gang are trying to take over. They eliminated a few soldiers, maybe others we don't know about, and now they've taken out the boss. Let's discuss what's going to happen.'

DS Strange spoke. 'There's a power vacuum. Will Britney

step into it? She doesn't seem the managerial type, more operational. How will this affect the building business they were running?' She stopped talking. A dawning expression came over her face, and she smiled at Naeem.

'Yes, Kelly, you've got it. Speak up.'

'We're thinking drugs. What if it's a building competitor? I would say it's unlikely to be a local firm, but it might be an east European gang.' She slumped back in her seat. 'It could be either of them, over anything.'

Naeem took over. 'Now we're getting somewhere. Put your opinions to one side. As the great Kuato said in *Total Recall*, "open your minds". We follow the obvious leads first but there will be surprises in this case. Find out what's happening to the business in Celine's absence. Is it still functioning? Britney has refused to talk to us since we arrested her. She might have had a breakdown and killed her sister. Is she scared? Does she think she's next? Locate Brick. Check the CCTV at the shops. Anyone got anything else to add?'

'There are going to be a lot of nervous people in the area,' Zander said. 'My belief is that Britney won't take on the construction business. She doesn't have the experience to manage a company like that, nor the drug trade. Without her sister, she'll crack up sooner or later. The runners will be filling their pants. Let's talk to them, apply some pressure.'

'I suspect that the supply chain will falter,' said Ginger. 'People with habits might lose their ability to score. Someone having a cluck is a sitting duck for strong questioning!' He grinned.

Naeem good-naturedly threatened to throw a pen at him but let him continue.

'Also, that was a close kill. With Brick missing, Celine wouldn't allow a masked killer to wander up and blow her away. I believe she recognised the shooter, or it was someone she wouldn't expect.'

Malik couldn't help himself. 'She wouldn't be expecting Kuato.'

They all chuckled, but Barton thought that was the best work DC Rodgers had done in years. He would look forward to seeing what HOLMES produced.

'That's brilliant stuff, Ginger,' he said. 'Think like that, everyone. It might have been a friend, or maybe a kid. We know some of these youngsters don't value their own lives, never mind others'. Fifty quid buys you a lot these days, perhaps even a minute's work with a loaded gun.'

They all paused to acknowledge that worrying fact.

Naeem clicked her fingers to regain their attention. 'Finally, do any of you have a mad idea? Something outlandish that seems stupid. Is a thought itching at you, and you're not sure why? Remember, sometimes we don't solve these cases for ten years. Technology moves on. People's motivations change. Confessions occur on death beds. As always, keep your notes detailed, store evidence correctly, get everything typed up. Suspect everyone. John, what's on your mind?'

'You recall I told you about the historic case? Well, we did have a bit of a lead earlier. It's unlikely, but my neighbour said someone called the Snow Killer rampaged around here over fifty years ago. They were never caught.'

'Why the Snow Killer?' asked Naeem.

'I'm not sure, but I assume because they killed in the snow. There were two more victims. We have the information on the first one, and that has a similar modus operandi to the Terry Sax murder. I'll get the files pulled on the other two murders. It's way out there but worth a look.'

Ginger burst into a laugh. 'So, if we see Victor Meldrew smoking a cigar and waving an Uzi around, it's case solved?'

It was too good not to laugh at, and they all joined in. Barton smiled as, even though the tension had eased, everyone remained focused.

Naeem nodded thoughtfully. 'This is showtime, people. DI

Barton, allocate roles, please. I'll talk to the media and upstairs. Things could get very messy on the streets in a few days as the fallout hits those remaining.' She sat down and gave Barton the whiteboard pen when he arrived at the front.

'Zander, are you staying to work? Okay, take a DC and check out the shop CCTV situation and visit the business premises. DC Malik, ask intel to chase up those historic murders and do a full background check on Celine Chapman. Give a few local building companies a ring as well and sniff about.'

Barton dished out the rest of the immediate tasks and left the most important one for him and Strange.

'We'll talk to Britney Chapman. She will want revenge.'

41

DI BARTON

DI John Barton and DS Kelly Strange sat opposite Britney Chapman in the interview room with the introductions and statements completed. Barton didn't expect Britney to crack but to some extent he was wrong.

'I'm sorry for your loss, Britney,' said Strange.

'I bet you are.'

'I respected her,' Barton added. 'And she respected me.'

Britney leaned forward in her chair. 'You can respect her and want her dead at the same time.' Defiance and strength shone from her. Barton recalled her age; she was only nineteen. Being born into such a criminal existence meant there was little chance of escaping that way of life. Her path had been set at birth. That would make her street smart though, and she wouldn't tell them a thing by being pressured.

'We want to find out who killed her. Any help you give us will speed up that process,' said Strange.

'I'm not saying shit to you. You never did anything for me.'

Barton leaned in to her. 'Remember, we've arrested you for assaulting a police officer.'

It would take more than that to faze Britney, so he changed tack.

'You don't seem very upset to me. You sure you don't need a solicitor?'

Britney's eyes narrowed at his implication, and then she laughed.

'Man, Celine said you were good. You are sneaky. I respect *that*. And because of that, I will tell you one thing, and then you will not hear a single word more from me, however many times you pick me up.'

'Go on.'

'I am a survivor. I do not show fear or weakness. Crying in front of you devils isn't part of who I am. I don't talk to the police. End of.'

'You'll get your own revenge, that it?' asked Strange.

'Girl, you are dumber than you look.'

Barton smiled and thought he understood. 'This empire, or whatever you want to call it, is Celine's thing, isn't it?' The girl leaned back in her seat but didn't speak. 'You aren't a business-woman and weren't involved in any of the big decisions. Your sister loved the power. She wanted control.'

This time a tear trickled down Britney's cheek. She stared from Strange to Barton. 'That's right. The construction thing means nothing to me. All I needed was to be with Celine. Yeah, I would have done whatever she asked, but she looked out for me. She always did. But I'm a kid. I enjoyed the drama of running with the other youngsters. We messed around and had some fun. It was just a game to me.'

'What are you going to do now?' he asked.

'I'm done with it all. Sure, I'd like to hurt whoever did this. But I get how it rolls. Celine didn't see this coming, so I haven't got a clue. In our neighbourhood, folk die. I've seen what happens to those who won't let go and live for retribution. They end up in the same box they wanted to send others to. I'm getting out now. I have the chance of a new life waiting for me. Maybe this is an opportunity to start from fresh with my own people.'

'What about the business? Will you allow it to fold?'

'Don't be daft. Celine was smart, you understand that. Speak to Hunt and Froome Solicitors. It's set up. There's a PA in our office. She can run the show until they sell it off. Even in death, she put me first. I'll get money, but I've never needed it. I wanted the life for us that I see others have, you know, holidays and things. But I'd have been happy in a caravan at Skegness. Retaliation won't bring my sister back, and she was all I cared about. The game's over for me. We lost.'

Barton and Strange exchanged a glance. He decided to warn her. 'We think they'll be after you next.'

'What for? I've got nothing. Word will be out soon enough that I'm done. Whoever wants this area has it now. That's your problem. Don't even dream about putting any surveillance on me. If I find anyone acting suspicious near me, I'll assume the worst.'

42

When Barton came out of the interview room and returned to his desk, DC David Whitlam, a solid but serious detective with three years' experience, hovered nearby. He was a big, rangy lad who spent much of his leisure time with DC Malik in the gym.

'We've had two calls from potential witnesses. A lady called to say she heard fireworks and might have seen something. A man said a sound reminded him of shooting and he observed a car being driven erratically.'

'Excellent. See both of them and take statements.'

'DS Zander also rang in. He wants you to attend the mini-mart and look at the CCTV. He thinks there's someone on it you'll recognise.'

Barton looked forlornly at the kettle and picked his coat up off the back of his seat. He tapped DS Strange on the shoulder and raised his eyebrows at her. 'We might have a lead.'

* * *

Barton and Strange got in the pool car and swapped a smile over yesterday's shared experience.

'How you feeling?' asked Barton.

'Don't start that crap. Until I'm waddling around like a duck and mainlining chocolate, I'm still the best you have.'

'I hear you.'

'Seriously, I made the right decision. I'm happy with it, but I don't want reminding of it at every touch and turn. There's no need for special treatment.'

'What baby? You know how forgetful I am.'

'That's better.'

They drove in silence, but Barton couldn't help himself. 'When are you telling the father?'

She scowled but, by her deep breath, he could tell she wanted to talk. 'That's not as easy as it sounds. I've been trying to contact him, but he's not picking up.' She picked up her phone, typed and then put it down. 'I didn't want to send a text with the news, but he deserves it.'

Barton laughed. Someone was about to have a life altering surprise. 'That should get his attention.'

'Yep, now back to business. Where are we heading?'

'To the Herlington centre. Zander's seen something on the CCTV.'

'Do you believe Britney's retiring and not looking for payback?'

'My gut tells me to believe her. I feel like I know her a bit because we've picked her up so many times. She rarely lies and says little. This is the first time she's given us a proper idea of her thoughts.'

'Has your belly ever been wrong?'

'Of course not. Don't ask my wife that question though.'

They pulled up next to the car park where there were barriers around the entrance from the night before. Lights blinked on a low-loader parked alongside Celine's car. Various CSI peppered the scene. Barton recognised the CSM from the first victim, Sirena. He waved, but she didn't notice. Strange grinned at him.

'It's called manners,' he said.

'It's called micro-flirting.'

Barton ignored her.

Zander was waiting for them outside the minimart. 'Afternoon,' he said. 'The manager has been showing me the CCTV.' He pointed up at a camera above the door. 'Unfortunately, it doesn't point in the right direction, just outwards from the shop towards the road.'

'Right, what did you see?'

'At the time we think it happened, there's a kid in the distance. It's bad quality with the weather, but it looks to me like he's watching something. He then turns and runs away, really, really fast.'

Barton leaned in closer. 'Okay, let's take a look.'

The sweaty manager, who would have been more suitable supervising the fish and chip shop over the road, knew his CCTV. 'We always make sure it's working, and it's backed up. You can imagine that in this area, we have a lot of thieving weasels. It's more a deterrent because, even if we catch the kids nicking stuff, nothing gets done.'

That wasn't a discussion Barton wanted to get into today, so he didn't take the bait. He watched the film and, as Zander said, it looked promising.

'Can you zoom this in at all?'

'No, I'll get you a copy, and you'll be able to do that.'

'What's it stored on?'

'Flash drives.'

'My colleague here, Sergeant Zander, will be taking this flash drive, thank you. It's evidence of an offence and will be an exhibit. You may have a copy, of course.'

The kid's image was too fuzzy for details, but he really did sprint. Sadly, he didn't veer towards the shop door when he ran by, but kept in the middle of the path. Barton wondered where he would be running to. He stood up and clicked his fingers.

'He'll have run past the bookies a bit further down. It's under cover, so there won't be the same problems with clarity. I bet they'll have CCTV on their door as well. Kelly, stay here and make sure this gets sent in. Then go and chat with the CSM and check if they've found anything of interest. Zander, let's see if you've picked a winner.'

He instructed the DC who was working with Zander to give Strange a lift home when she finished and assist her as she required.

No one spoke in the bookmaker's but it was noisy. An old guy seemed mesmerised by the virtual racing, and both fruit machines flashed and buzzed. Other than that, it was empty. The manager twiddled a pen and raised his eyebrows as they approached. He whisked them out the back and got the recording up from the previous day, where they could see a young lad race past at breakneck speed. With clearer quality and freeze-frame ability, they grinned at a decent image.

Zander smiled. 'Todd "Flying" Finn, no less.'

Barton had guessed it was him as well. He was another sad story from the surrounding area. Finn had been a promising runner but got caught up in a commercial burglary. Five kids were seen leaving business premises loaded up with stolen stationery. They refused to talk, and therefore all of them received records for it because the judge found everyone guilty. CCTV would be cruel to Finn again. He'd dropped out of his athletics club and then given the police the runaround. Finn became the king of smash and grab, nipping in and grabbing what he wanted, and fleeing as if he were running from a fire.

Later, after his seventeenth birthday, he got involved with the Chapmans and disappeared from the robbery scene. Why steal pens and pencils when other things paid better?

'We know it's Finn, but I've no idea where to find him. His mum washed her hands of him a long time ago,' Zander said.

The manager cleared his throat. 'Good news. That rude little tyke has been seeing a bird who lives two doors from me. He's in here every time my back's turned, playing the machines and trying to put a bet on, even though I know he's underage. The girls who work here are scared of him. I told him off for being rude to people, and he told me that if I spoke to him like that again, he'd cut me up.'

Zander took down the address of their next appointment and pointed across the road when they got outside. 'I like it when they live nearby.'

As they walked over, Barton wondered if Zander was tempting fate.

43

Barton sent Zander to the rear of the terraced house. There were few areas in the city worse than this one. Multiple cars on bricks competed with abandoned white goods and sofas for the parking spaces. Youngsters in tracksuits pedalled away as they arrived.

There was no doubt Finn would try to run when he saw who had popped around to see him. Barton knocked on the door, and a small woman of about eighteen, with a baby in one hand and a can of lager in the other, opened it. He could hear machine-gun fire and shouting in the background. Her glazed eyes scowled at him, but she stepped away as he showed his warrant card. Barton didn't need asking twice, and he followed her into a tiny hallway.

'I'd like a quick word with Finn. In there, I assume?' Barton pointed at a closed door on the right.

The girl nodded, handed him the lager, and walked away into the kitchen behind her. Barton pushed the other door open and blinked as the cigarette smoke stung his eyes.

'Yo, about time. Any longer and I'd have died of thirst.'

Barton rested the can of lager on Finn's shoulder; Finn didn't look back. He took the drink while maintaining his rate of fire on the screen in front of him. Barton spied a table full of cans and a *Men's Health* magazine with two lines of white powder on it. A ten pound note lay half unfurled next to the cocaine.

'Good game, Todd?'

Barton had his second surprise of the day. Without even looking around, Todd Finn jumped off the sofa and flipped over the table. He turned to Barton with blazing eyes and a rounders bat in his hand. Barton filled the only door out of the room. It took Finn's spinning mind about three seconds to recognise Barton and his predicament.

'Shit.'

'Shit, indeed. I need a word.'

'I got nothing to say to the likes of you.'

'It's just a few questions to do with yesterday.'

Todd's eyes shifted sideways. 'I can't talk, you know that.'

'You know who died?'

'Of course.'

'Then what are you scared of?'

'They both dead?'

'Britney's retiring from the business.'

'I'm still not saying anything. A retired Britney is more dangerous to me than you'll ever be.'

Barton gazed around the messy room. That poor baby would grow up around people like this. He knew he couldn't change that and nicking Finn for possession of some coke he'd argue was only for personal use wouldn't help his investigation.

'All I want to know is what you saw.'

'I saw nothing.'

'The cameras show you staring in the direction of yesterday's incident. You look shocked and you ran like you wished you owned a motorbike.'

Finn stared at the floor and shook his head.

'Just tell me what you saw.'

Finn looked up, set his chin, and still shook his head.

'Okay, fair enough. I have six officers outside. They will

come in here, search your house, and get the social involved with that baby. We can have the sniffer dogs here in an hour or so. Then I'll parade you all the way through your estate in cuffs. And we'll be smiling. It's a murder inquiry, so it's okay to keep you locked up for ages. What with you being the suspected killer.'

Todd's mouth shot open. His brain raced for an out that didn't exist.

'Okay. I'll talk, but I'm not giving no statement. Off the record, and you leave me alone.'

'It'll need to be good.'

'I clocked Celine's car and went over to see if she'd seen her sister, Britney. You know, I wanted to catch up.' Barton let out a long breath but said nothing. 'I was waiting to cross the road when I heard a crack. It was kind of muffled but I know what a gunshot sounds like. I hear them all day.' He gestured to the console on the floor. 'Celine's motor was in the corner. A person stood next to the open door. Then another bang, and her car lit up for a second. It had to be a shooting.'

'Who did it?'

'I don't have a clue. That's the truth. The sleet was coming in, and I couldn't see. I waited for a few seconds, and the person walked towards me. No way I'm hanging around.'

'What did they look like?'

'Just a person, with a hood pulled down at the front. I don't think he noticed me, so I ran.'

'What did he have on?'

'A big grey coat and wellies. That's all I remember before I chipped off.'

'Were they tall, or fat?'

'They weren't your size.' The cheeky imp had the nerve to grin. Barton stepped towards him. 'Small, I don't know, a bit smaller than me maybe.'

Todd weighed about ten stone and looked five and a half feet tall. 'What else?'

Todd shrugged then smirked. 'Yeah, they walked funny. Like they were drunk. You know, leaning over to one side.'

Barton smiled too until the baby cried. 'I'm going to need a written statement after all.'

'You said—'

'I didn't say anything of the sort. Here's the deal. I'll send a plain-clothed constable here tomorrow morning. You have a decent tidy up, like a good boy. Make it safe for that baby. I'll forget what I spotted on that magazine if you toe the line. Don't let me down. Britney would be less forgiving than I am.'

Todd nodded. He maintained eye contact, but it wasn't confrontational; sad almost. Barton guessed he wasted his breath but had a go, anyway.

'All this stuff you're doing rots your brain. If the powder doesn't do it, the games will. You've got a pretty girl out there, a warm place, a nice baby. Have you thought about doing the right thing? You could start running again?'

The lad considered it for a moment. The innocence dropped from his eyes as he replied. 'Who says that baby's mine?'

44

When Barton got back outside, Zander appeared to be chatting up an attractive neighbour hanging out her washing. He glanced up at the sky and admired the patches of blue. About time; he'd had enough of snow for one year.

'Are you ready, Zander? Sorry to leave you out in the cold. Must have been tough waiting for me.'

Zander waited to talk until they were in the car. 'Nice girl. Slovenian. Thought I was from the council and wanted to show me her plumbing.'

Barton shook his head but still smiled. 'Don't tell me any more. I don't suppose she had anything to say about Flying Finn.'

'No, usual story. She knows he's up to no good, but she has to live here. No one wants to talk to us, John. Maybe if I returned and fixed her pipes, she'd cooperate?'

Barton brought Zander up to speed on Finn's information. A grey coat wasn't much to go on, but at least it spoke of progress. Zander said he'd get control to pass on the word when they got to the station. Barton explained that they'd let Britney off with a caution for the assault. There wasn't any point in taking that further. Finding your sister had just died was quite a mitigating factor. The officer she hurt only had light injuries and wouldn't hold a grudge. That sort of thing came with the role. If you couldn't stand the odd bruise or personal insult, then you were in the wrong job.

They observed Britney leaving the police station from the front exit as they returned to the building. Barton considered driving her home, but a hot drink and some contemplative time appealed more. Besides, she could afford a taxi. He also had the solicitors to contact to see if he could find out anything about the Chapmans' business.

He had a note on his desk to ring DC Malik on his mobile phone.

'Malik speaking.'

'Barton here. Got your message. Where are you?'

'Having a fag. I'll be back in the office in a minute.'

Barton filled the kettle while he waited. The young officer returned panting, which Barton appreciated.

'Fire away.'

'There's surprisingly little to go through on Celine Chapman. She's been under surveillance numerous times but is seemingly clean and has been for years. I spoke to a guy I know in Records, and he said he'll have the information about the other two historic murders for us tomorrow. He checked out the causes of death for me and rang back a few minutes ago. One killed by what they thought was a small-bore rifle and the other a hammer. No screwdrivers or pistols involved.'

Barton tutted. That certainly made it less likely to be the workings of the Snow Killer. He would leave that angle for now. They had plenty of other stuff to be going on with.

'Thanks. I'll need you to see a Todd Finn tomorrow morning to get a statement. I'll email you the details.'

'Yes, sir. I also spoke to two local builders. They both said the same thing. The Chapmans are well-liked subcontractors. They don't take on huge contracts themselves. They have a team, a bit like temps. Apparently, the building trade is a nightmare for jobs running over. If that happens, the Chapmans are your first port of call. Even though they're pricey, their work is top notch, and deadlines are never missed. Neither of them had a bad word to say.'

'Did you ask about competition?'

'Of course. The idea of Romanian builders knocking out rivals amused them no end. If you have a costly build that needs finishing fast, you pay for the best, not get any old cowboy in. A few Portuguese crews are up to it, but not too many foreign firms would be. The simple truth is there's too much work out there as it is. Nobody needs to worry where their next job is coming from. One of them banged on for five minutes about stamp duty making it too expensive to move house, so the rich are extending and improving. I think we're in the wrong trade, sir.'

He thanked Malik and dismissed him. DS Strange came back in at that point and stood by his desk.

'Mortis was there at the scene. He's done the post-mortem of Celine and it's straightforward. Well, it was after he told me it in a language I could understand. No drink or drugs in the system. In fact, she had been noticeably healthy. Cause of death, gunshot wounds to the torso, leading to internal bleeding. The screwdriver injury was superficial in comparison.'

'Why did he go back to the scene?'

'He wanted another look at the vehicle. Again, the angle of entry of the bullet came in low like with the direction of the stab wound in the first murder. Assuming it's the same person, then he concluded that the person responsible is likely to have been on the short side.'

'You mean like a dwarf?'

Strange smiled. 'Long day, John? No, not a dwarf; he means closer to five feet than six.'

'Shame. That would have narrowed down the suspects. How certain of that is he?'

'Not very. They could have just been holding the gun low. He wanted to give you anything he could.'

Barton settled at the PC to update his notes. There were a lot of them. He was pondering whether paperwork would be called computer work in his lifetime when DC Whitlam returned from talking to the two eyewitnesses.

DCI Naeem had informed him she'd be out of the building at an award ceremony for a retiring officer and would miss the wash-up at 17:30, so he took Whitlam into her office for some quiet as Zander had been distracting him by humming 'Rhinestone Cowboy' for the last hour. He suspected the Slovenian girl had something to do with that.

The young officer ambled into the room. Barton remembered Holly saying to him that most people are nervous when they talk to managers above them. It's how you control it that counts. Whitlam took his notebook out of his pocket and spoke with confidence. Barton smiled to himself. Whitlam didn't seem unduly bothered by anything, in a good or bad way.

'I've had words with them both, sir.'

'Go on, but call me John.'

'The first lady, Katherine Symonds, couldn't find her glasses when she got home from the dentist's and went back. She was very old. Ninety. Told me six times, I think, just in case I missed it. She saw an unusual flash from a big car in the distance and someone in a white coat leaving the scene.'

'How could she tell if she couldn't see anything?'

'Said she can see shapes and colours.'

'Great. A defending barrister would have an orgasm hearing that. Wait, how come she left without her glasses? Surely she must have realised as soon as she got outside that she couldn't see.'

'That's what I said. She thought the weather had misted up her glasses until she tried to take them off and found they weren't there.'

Barton covered his face with his hands and spoke through his fingers. 'What about the other witness?'

'That was an elderly gentleman as well, one who walks his

dog every afternoon around that time. Said he heard a strange bang. It made him suspicious, so he kept an eye out for anything unusual. Told me he'd been to Korea. I wasn't sure what difference his holiday destination had to proceedings, but I took a note of it. He provided a superb description of a car being driven in an unsuitable way for the conditions.'

'Did he take a number plate?'

'Yes, we tracked the driver down.'

'And?'

'I'm talking to him now.'

'Blue Land Rover, eh?'

'That's the one.'

'Excellent. It's a fair cop. A few years at HMP Butlins might do me some good. I don't suppose our witness could be the culprit?'

'Unlikely, with him having no legs.'

'You said he was walking his dog!'

'He had an electric wheelchair, but the dog was walking.'

'Thank you, that will be all.' Barton rested his forehead on the keyboard. It was sticky and smelled funny.

'Final thought, sir. Do you think the airlines gave him a discount when he flew to Korea?'

Whitlam had gone when that penny finally dropped, which was just as well. He decided to gather his thoughts before returning to the incident room and chairing the meeting. There were always stragglers. He shook his head at Whitlam's legroom joke. It seemed even that sombre officer wanted to be a comedian.

45

DCI Naeem's desk phone rang a minute later. Barton picked it up to hear the voice of the woman herself. She had decided not to put surveillance on the younger Chapman. It was hard to know what Britney would do if she noticed. She'd been informed of the danger, so they were covered. Naeem had also asked the drug squad about Celine and come up with some interesting information. Barton raised his eyebrows at the news and put the phone down.

He strode to the meeting room where bodies struggled for space. Nothing like progress to rekindle interest.

'Quiet, please,' said Barton. 'I'll make this quick because I know you have plenty to work on. Other traders confirm the Chapmans' building business is well respected and very profitable. We still have feelers out, but that line of enquiry is colder after speaking to them.'

'Britney Chapman has been released...' he paused to let the half-hearted boos subside '... and tells us she is going straight.' This time he waited for the cheers to finish before continuing. 'It's possible she'll remain a target as, to me, this case seems personal. The Terry Sax hit could have been a warning to Celine. Maybe they wanted her to fear for her safety. Interestingly, the latest intel about Celine is that she was so far removed from the drug dealing that it's possible she wasn't involved any more and may not have been for a long while.'

Many mouths opened at that revelation. 'It could be that the Chapmans had gone clean after all; the elder one at least. DC Whitlam, tell us the figures that the builder estimated their business made a year?'

'Turnover of two or three million. Profit of half.'

'Now, we know you can make more selling drugs, but you have to shift considerable weights to earn that kind of money. Why bother if you could live a life of luxury without the risk of twenty years in prison? Perhaps it isn't the drug angle at all. Is it someone from their past who wants revenge?'

He let that wash over them before announcing the most credible information they had. 'Mortis reckons the killer is fairly short. Five feet and a few inches probably. The attacker was seen leaving the hit. They had a big white or grey coat on. It's likely they ran through Baggswell Lane to the nicer houses in the area.'

'Your area, sir?' Ginger smiled.

Barton gritted his teeth. 'Yes, towards my house. Some rich people live near me. Who's to say they couldn't be the murderer? That brings us nicely on to the Victor Meldrew angle. It's natural to think of a killer as a young person or an ex-soldier who knows how to use a gun. One of the witnesses described the person as running as if drunk. Perhaps they were, or they could have a health condition like a hip replacement. Trust me, everyone's capable of murder. A gun levels the field. Even Mike Tyson can't bite the ear off a gun.

'I'm looking for people to knock on doors in my village tonight. We've focused on the rougher estates. That might have been our mistake. Who's keen?' Six raised their hands, including DS Strange, which would be sufficient for the job. 'Kelly, if you could arrange that. I'll name the streets right after this meeting. Be careful, everyone. Avoid any risks. This person is clearly armed and dangerous. If anyone acts suspiciously, record it and leave. We can always go back with the Armed Response Vehicle.

'Guilty people don't answer their doors in general. But there could be something incriminating on their property. A careless gangster dropped a live round on his drive up north somewhere, and it was that which got him nicked. It's going to thaw a bit tonight too, and then completely tomorrow, which may reveal incriminating evidence. I'm wondering if one of those things might be Brick.'

The laughter died away as they realised what he meant.

'I'm visiting the solicitors who are managing Celine's estate later. They probably won't be able to tell me anything, but I've a hunch that Celine will have left detailed instructions.' Barton had decided his physical presence in the solicitor's office might yield better results.

'Any questions?'

'Do we know who Celine spent her time with?'

'Only Brick and her sister were regularly seen in her company. I'm beginning to wonder if a mistake was made in killing Terry Sax. Maybe they thought he was someone else. Mortis said he expects to confirm from analysing the screwdriver and metal traces in Terry's back that the weapon was used in both murders although it's still possible they were unrelated. Anyway, taking Celine out raises the game. Even though Britney said she's had enough, I suspect we wouldn't be the only ones to be surprised by that fact. Everyone will expect her to take over. All options remain. It could even be an old-fashioned serial killer killing people every time it snows.'

That got a few chuckles too, but Barton instantly thought of his mother. *Many a true word is spoken in jest* was one of her favourite quotes. Barton felt as if the net was closing in on the guilty party, but was it closing fast enough?

46

DI BARTON

Barton found the roads much more amenable without the ice, and arrived at the solicitors' in a matter of minutes after giving Strange her instructions for that night. It was 17:55 when he pulled up. There were numerous other vehicles in the car park, but when he tried the front door, it wouldn't open. He waited outside until a heavy-set man with thick glasses pushed the doors wide. Barton's eyes widened at a face from the past. One of his old rugby friends locked the doors behind him.

'Bill?'

'John?'

They froze next to each other for a couple of seconds before shaking hands warmly. Bill Hunt was obviously doing very well for himself. Barton gestured towards the sign on the door. 'All yours?'

'Half mine. I met the other partner, Sam Froome, at uni. It's good to see you, John. Must be twenty-eight years since we played together. You look great. Not a social call, is it?'

'Yeah, we need a prop for Sunday. How you set?'

'I prefer to watch these days.'

Barton couldn't tell if his joke had fallen flat or not. What he did realise was that, after twenty-eight years, he didn't know this guy at all. At least he had the same trouble with his waistline as Barton. At Bill's impatient face, he cut to the chase. 'I'm investigating the death of Celine Chapman. I'm sure you're aware of it. Her sister said your company will manage the estate.'

Bill considered his reply. 'My partner deals with that account. He'll be back in on Monday – he should be able to answer some questions then.'

Barton noticed Bill Hunt's eyes slip to the building and guessed that his partner remained inside. Why would he want to delay? 'How about I come by first thing? Nine o'clock.'

'It's Saturday tomorrow.'

'It's important.'

Bill nodded. 'I'll let him know. Someone will be here. There are limits to what we can tell you though, short of you having the necessary authority. Goodnight, John.'

Barton watched him leave. The man hadn't said anything unexpected, and he could just be stopping his colleague from being interrupted late at night, but something felt wrong.

He got in his car and drove the brief distance home. The best part of working in a place like Peterborough had to be the distances. Within fifteen minutes, you could drive to virtually anywhere in the city.

A strange sight greeted his eyes as he arrived at the village green outside his home: the Colonel and Britney Chapman deep in conversation outside the Colonel's house. Britney paced from side to side and gestured wildly. The Colonel pointed. Barton bumped up onto his driveway and when he'd parked and checked again, they were watching him. Britney walked away leaving a scowling Colonel staring after her. Barton strolled over the grass to him with interest.

'How's things? What was that about?'

'Bloody kids. Smoking weed near my front door.'

Barton decided to humour him. 'Shall I bring her in for questioning? Get the water board out? They confess in the end.'

An unusual expression crossed the Colonel's face. When he answered, he failed to look at Barton. 'No, don't bother. She's only a girl. We were all young once.'

Barton shrugged. It'd been one of those days.

Barton slipped his shoes off and wandered towards the noise in the kitchen, where he found Holly and the kids sitting around the table laughing at Luke.

'You're home early. Just in time for the incredible candle-making boy,' said Holly.

Barton sat opposite his youngest son and couldn't help chuckling at the long drip of snot that swung from his nose. Holly grabbed the kitchen roll and went to wipe it off.

'No, Daddy do it,' said Luke.

'It will be my pleasure.'

Luke gave him a hug after and climbed on his lap. His headache receded as he listened to his older children having a normal conversation around what happened in *Doctor Who* at the weekend. He leaned back in his seat and exhaled. He thought of Zander and Strange returning to empty houses. It was hard to recall living on his own.

'John, your mother sent a letter to us asking if we'd forgotten about her.'

'What? Why didn't she ring?'

'She said that phone you got her to replace the old one is too complicated, and the buttons are too small.'

'I wondered why she hadn't been replying to my texts.'

'We should visit her. It must be two months since we went.'

'It's not that long, is it?'

Holly checked the calendar and nodded at him. 'Kids,' she said, 'who wants to go and see Nanny on Sunday?'

'Yeah, I'll go,' said Lawrence.

'That's only because she always gives you a tenner,' said Layla.

'You not coming, then?'

'No way, I've got loads of things I need to buy.'

Holly chuckled. 'Very mercenary, guys. What about you, Luke?'

'No. Nanny doesn't have any fun toys.'

The kids left the room sharpish as talk of whose turn it was to do the washing-up began. In the end, Barton washed and his wife dried. Holly put the tea towel on the radiator when she'd finished and gave Barton a peck. 'You okay? You seem distracted.'

'These two murders have affected me more than usual, and I reckon more will die before we solve them. It feels like we're being played with.'

'How so?'

'Whoever killed Celine left a screwdriver hanging out of her neck. It let us know that the previous murder was linked, but doesn't really give us much more chance of solving it. The killer wants something, but I don't know what it is. If it's fame, we're in trouble as that means more of the same. It's a strange thing to say, but I feel a bit unstable. I've been noticing other people's lonely lives, and I haven't been to see my own mother in two months. That's bang out of order when she's on her own.'

'Come on, John. These things happen. She had three kids. She knows how time flashes past when they're young, and it's a struggle to focus on anything else. You go more often than your sisters.'

'Well, they do live miles away.'

'It's a 120 mile round trip for us, too. Don't beat yourself up. We'll go on Sunday. I love your mum's stories about what a disgusting child you were. Maybe she'll give me ten pounds as well.'

Barton shrugged. He walked to the fridge and took out a bottle of Budweiser. When he turned to Holly, she'd cocked her head to one side.

'That was a good line, surely worth a small grin.' She stepped over and pushed the sides of his mouth up. 'What's got into you lately? Humour is how we cope with life. That's the thing I love most about you. Even when it's all going pear shaped, there's always a glimpse of a smile in the back of your eyes.'

'Sorry, sweetie. I'll try harder.'

'Come on, let's have some fun.' She took his hand and dragged him to the lounge. 'We can do some kissing in front of the kids.'

Her laugh was an infectious one. He joined in and almost forgot the sense of foreboding that cloaked him.

48

DI BARTON

The next morning, Barton parked up outside the solicitor's and walked into the reception. Bill Hunt was waiting for him. He guided Barton into a small room just off the entrance and asked him to take a seat.

'Coffee?'

'No, thanks. I know you're busy, Bill. I appreciate you turning up at the weekend. Is your partner coming in?'

'We're flat out with a fraud case. He got stuck in Nottingham all week and won't be back until tomorrow. He's been meaning to look into Celine's case since her death but hasn't had time. I came in earlier and read through it instead.'

'I understand you can't give me any details. What I wanted to appreciate was more around how organised she was. Britney said her sister prepared for everything. I'm getting a feeling Celine wasn't who we thought she was.'

'I didn't know her well, but my partner, Sam, came to be quite taken with her. She'd had a rough start as a child. It wouldn't be overstating things to say she broke the law as a younger woman. The picture Sam painted this morning was of someone who turned her life around. She wanted to do everything above board. The business is placed in trust for her sister's benefit. She is almost the sole beneficiary of the will.'

'Almost?'

'Again, this is between you and me. There are numerous bequests to various charities. Decent sums of money too. I'm telling you this because it's a tragedy for her to be killed after overcoming so many obstacles in her short life. We want you to have the facts to help solve her murder. She would have wanted that, even though she didn't tell us that specifically.'

'I really appreciate this.'

'Don't thank me too swiftly. We received an envelope from her in the post yesterday, marked for Sam's attention, only to be opened by him. I remembered receiving it when you came last night.'

Barton realised he'd been wrong when he thought Bill's eyes had strayed to the building because his partner remained in the office. Bill continued after a rueful shake of his head.

'I'd put it on his desk for when he returned. There was an envelope in the letter, only to be opened in the event of her death. Reading it now, I should have looked at it as soon as I heard.'

'Why?'

'There was a note saying that if she died in suspicious circumstances, then this letter should be handed to DI Barton personally. It's open because she also wanted us to read it.'

Barton took the letter off him and slid an A4 piece of paper out.

John,

If you're reading this, I'm gone. We've not always been on the same side but I hope Sam Froome will tell you I really did go legit. I'd be lying if I said Britney was a saint, but she is my concern. She's my heart. About four months ago, I received this card through the post. Someone hand-delivered it to add to the weirdness. I almost mentioned it to you when Brick disappeared but hopefully he'll be fine still.

I don't know what it means if anything. But if I'm gone, then my sister is in danger. Please protect Britney and stop her getting hurt.

For a pig, you weren't so bad.

All the best,

Celine.

A small plain piece of paper nestled in the bottom of the envelope, about the same size and thickness as a business card. It was blank on one side. Barton turned it over.

Fear the north wind. Because no one will hear you scream.

Barton shivered, and the card slipped through his fingers.

'What does it mean, John?'

'I'm not sure, but what I do know is that Britney is in trouble.'

Barton shook hands with Bill at the door. 'Is there anything I can do to help?'

'No, not really. When will you discuss the will with Britney?'

'As soon as we contact her.'

Barton thought for a moment. 'If you get hold of her before I do, make certain she sees this note and rings me. I'll have someone go around to their house and warn her now. They'll tell her to ring your mobile.'

Barton sat in the car and, while he waited for the traffic to let him onto Thorpe Road, a nursery rhyme surfaced from his distant past. *The north wind doth blow and we shall have snow.* Blue filled the sky when he peered up. But he remembered his wife's words concerning winter's last gasp in a few days.

He was just about to pull into the stream of vehicles when his phone rang. He checked the screen. 'Yes, Zander.'

'It's Brick. We've found him.'

49

DI BARTON

Barton put the car back in gear and remembered that he'd been driving around with the petrol light on. Cursing, he decided to fill up before attending the scene. From what Zander had said, Brick wasn't going anywhere. He turned right instead of left and hit the traffic on the town bridge. The glorious twelfth century cathedral loomed in front of him. At forty-four metres, it was still by far the highest spot on the horizon for miles around. Few in England were aware of it. He had a feeling that Peterborough would be remembered for something completely different.

Typically, there was a long queue at the forecourt, and Barton found his temper fraying. After a frustrating twenty minutes, he parked his car at home. He could walk the same route to see Brick that he did to gaze upon Terry Sax. Brick had been discovered about 150 metres from the first body. When he arrived at the edge of the field, he wasn't startled to feel déjà vu as he stared at the scene. The tent and cordon were already in place. Barton took a deep breath and walked towards the throng of people.

It was the same constable, PC Zelensky, on duty at the cordon, and this time she just let him in with a grin and marked him on the clipboard. He noted the graze on the side of her face

– a souvenir from her fight with Britney. The tent was next to a copse of trees. Sirena, the CSM who had worked Terry and Celine, was there talking on the phone. She finished the call and gave him a big smile. 'Morning, John. We have to stop meeting like this.'

He grinned back. 'Another perfect crime?'

She looked up. 'To be honest, probably not far off. Mortis is in there with the body. I'll let him talk to you about the deceased, but the scene won't tell us much. The snow around the victim is quite solid, as is he. I'd estimate he's been dead for days at this point. It's reasonable to guess he was concealed after death, and further heavy snow buried him. Then each new snowfall would cover him further. If it hadn't thawed, we'd never have found him.

'Snow melts from top to bottom, so any melting would have had water running through the snow onto the body. At night, that would refreeze. You can see that the field is clear of snow, but there's still a bank next to the copse. The fact it hasn't gone indicates it's been days, not hours. I'll bet there's a fair amount of traffic around here, too: dog walkers, kids, animals. All the rubbish here won't help, either.'

Barton cut in. 'The homeless sometimes sleep in these woods.'

Sirena frowned. 'The conditions are similar to the Terry Sax case, and nothing concrete came from that scene. If you've had people living in here, then not much we find will be of use. We might uncover shell casings nearby. It depends on how professional the hitman was.'

'Someone shot him?'

'To begin with.'

At that point, Mortis exited the tent. Sirena nodded. 'I'll be in touch.' With a final wink, she walked over to others in protective clothing who filtered through the trees.

Mortis had a strange expression on his face.

'What's up with you?' asked Barton.

'Got an admirer, have you?'

Barton followed his gaze to the departing back of Sirena. 'Don't you look at me in the same way, Mortis?'

'I wish my wife beamed at me like that. Come on, put some boot covers on. I'll give you the sixpence tour.'

Zander stood next to the body. 'Morning, John. Where's the coffee?'

Barton gave a shrug. 'I thought you'd already have brought it.'

'Wait until I tell the boss. Right, the victim was found earlier this morning by a Polish chap on his way to work. He suspected someone had dropped an expensive coat. I assume he meant to have it for himself. He panicked when he noticed a man inside. I heard you talking to Sirena, who sickeningly seems to have a soft spot for you, about the poor chance of recovering evidence.

'The finder said he assumed the guy was alive for some reason and spent a while trying to free him. He stamped all over everything by the look of it and dislodged the hammer. By the time uniform arrived, another weirdo had leaned over it. We think he might have planned to rob the dead man, too. Ginger is searching him as we speak over in the car park for the BMX track.'

Barton stared at Brick's lifeless face. He observed the caved-in skull. Thankfully, the man's eyes were closed. An evidence bag contained a hammer. Another one had a wallet in it. He noted the leg closest to him had a small bleeding red circle.

'Gruesome.'

'Indeed,' said Mortis. 'I haven't been here much longer than you, and the CSI have only just finished their part. We're about to examine the body from head to toe, but there are four distinct, obvious injuries. He's partly frozen, making algor and rigor mortis fairly useless. The snow would have had an insulating effect and also kept the body in the same place. We will be able to tell from liver mortis the position at death. Zander told me he's been missing for three days. That seems reasonable to assume as a time of death at this moment. His stomach may help with a time if it has cornflakes or a kebab inside.

'To add to that, judging by the size of him, he would have been killed right here. No one could lug this man about.'

Gesturing to the head and blood-stained clothing, Barton queried the cause of death. 'Which came first, chicken or egg?'

'He has three gunshot wounds. The holes look fairly small, so it wasn't a large calibre weapon. The two in the leg would be very painful and incapacitating but not fatal. Shot three looks like it went through a lung. If it hit a major blood vessel, he wouldn't have lasted long. The damage to the top of the head with that hammer would kill instantly if he was still alive.'

'You'd need to be pretty strong to do that kind of harm.'

'Surprisingly not. The skull isn't designed to withstand a blow from a hammer. Remember your physics lessons? Force equals mass times acceleration.' Mortis rolled his eyes at their blank faces. 'Smallish heavy end, swung with reasonable effort. Maybe the first impact cracked the skull, and the second entered it. It's a grisly death however you look at it.'

'Post-mortem today?' asked Barton.

'No, first thing tomorrow. But I doubt you'll get much from it that I haven't told you already.'

Barton turned to Zander. 'I don't suppose the guy you found with the body was seventy-five years old?'

He shook his head. 'More like twenty-five. You still considering the old person angle?'

'Maybe. We're missing something. Hopefully I'll have the information about those other murders when I check my email.'

'Kelly said it was an unusual experience speaking to people in your area, and that there were loads of militant retired folk capable of dodgy deeds.'

Barton rubbed his eyes. 'This is crazy. We've got three deaths on our hands now. They're all obviously linked in some way. Yet, we don't really have much. What if it is this Snow Killer from fifty years ago? That's serial-killer territory. All we need is a reporter getting hold of that, and we'll have Chiefs and Commissioners breathing down our necks and bringing in outside help.'

'How did it go at the solicitors'?'

'He helped, to be fair.' Barton updated him with everything new he'd learnt and mentioned the note.

'Fear the north wind?' said Zander. 'That sounds like something a snow killer would say. We need to find Britney.'

'I'll leave that to you. Release a Be-On-The-Lookout for her. Can you drive straight to her address and have a chat? Get a uniform to camp outside if she isn't around. We can't make her come in but, surely, she'll see the danger. I'll have a word with this weird bloke and go back to the station with Ginger.'

'What if we can't find Britney?'

Barton struggled to believe what he was about to say but said it anyway. 'I don't think she's in trouble until it snows again.'

Barton caught up with Ginger as he let a tall man out of his car.

'Confession?' he asked.

'No. Mr Dwayne Tyne is about to leave. I've taken a statement from him, but he didn't see anything. I believe him when he says he just noticed the body and stopped.'

The man peered through Barton with a slack jawed expression of indifference. 'Can I go now?'

Barton glanced at Ginger, who nodded. 'Sure, Dwayne. Are you going to be all right? Can we give you a lift home?'

'No, it's okay. I enjoy walking. It's good for you. I don't like the snow because it's slippery, but I love wind and rain. It makes you feel happy.' He grinned at them both before abruptly turning and marching away.

Ginger and Barton tried not to smile.

'I take it he wasn't our criminal genius?'

'Nope, Homer Simpson would thrash Dwayne at Snap. I searched him. All he had on him was a bank card and an old mobile phone. He unlocked that for me because he couldn't remember his number, so I had a quick scoot through his texts and calls. I read a lot of puerile stuff about wrestling and *The Lord of the Rings*, all sent to the same friend.'

'Okay. Where does he live?'

'In that block of flats with the communal kitchens near you, where the council puts people they struggle to house.'

'Criminal record?'

'Nothing, which surprised me, although he seemed oblivious to the other murders around here. He didn't seem to be interested. Dwayne loved being in the police car though, it being his first time. Said it was very exciting.'

'Shame he didn't confess, eh? Wait a few days and call on him at home to make sure he isn't having flashbacks or something from seeing a dead body. He might have remembered something else.'

'Okay. The Polish guy is in the ambulance. He started hyperventilating. It definitely wasn't him either.'

'Great. Can you give me a lift back?'

'Sure.'

Barton had received a reply from DCI Naeem confirming she was in her office. He got in the car and made sure Ginger had the recent intel. He had always found that talking to the officers involved on a one-to-one basis brought results. They enjoyed throwing ideas at him knowing they wouldn't be ridiculed. Sometimes the team had the answers between them, but nobody had put them together.

'You've been doing this job a long time, Ginger. What do you think of the ancient Snow Killer angle?'

'Nothing astounds me any more. It's unlikely because they are meaty crimes, but pensioners nowadays are different from how our grandparents acted. My neighbour's parents backpacked through India last year and they're both nearly seventy. An eighty year old near me still works at the supermarket and jogs to work. Look at the Hatton Garden Heist. Three of them were pensioners.'

'The MO on two of the other hits is similar to Brick and Celine's. They have to be connected. Maybe it's a revenge attack of some kind.'

'But why? None of the people killed were born when they occurred. We weren't alive either. Although annoyingly, I knew there were unsolved murders from way back in Peterborough. I should have mentioned it.'

'I suppose I did too. In fact, I only read last week that a quarter of all homicides in the UK are unsolved. Who knows? Perhaps our guy did loads of them.'

51

DI BARTON

Barton found an empty seat back at the station and logged onto his email. The report on the historical killings had landed. DCI Naeem arrived as he pored through the information.

'Give us an hour, Boss. It looks like this is it.'

'You sure?' she asked.

'The similarities are chilling.'

Barton made notes as he read, with his mind processing the material. He couldn't see any mention anywhere of the words *Snow Killer*. He was momentarily distracted by childish giggling over near the photocopier. Ginger and an open mouthed Malik leaned into one another. Ginger did an over-exaggerated hand gesture from his chin to his navel, clearly pretending to be heavily pregnant. He whispered something to Malik, and they both chuckled.

Barton's frustrations over the last few months solidified. With Frankenstein style grace, he walked over with stiff limbs and a mad expression. The two men didn't see him until too late. He grabbed both of them by the knot of their ties and shook them. His voice came out as a growl.

'What are you doing?'

Ginger's face reddened, and Malik's eyes closed. Barton

wondered if he'd passed out and took a deep breath. He eased his grip. 'You insulted a sergeant whom I like much more than you two scrotes.' Malik's eyes opened, but neither man returned his blazing stare. He pushed Malik to one side and bent down so they faced each other. 'Get out of here. If I catch you gossiping again today, I will impregnate you.'

He glanced around after Malik had fled and was relieved to find an empty room. He stepped back from Ginger and folded his arms. 'Talk.'

'It was just a joke.'

'How did you know?'

'She's been throwing up in the morning.'

Barton stared at the ceiling. 'Everyone knows?'

Ginger nodded.

'Let it be known that I will be furious if I see or hear anything else similar. What is wrong with you? You're in your forties and gossiping like an old woman. You've got so much talent, but half the time you're a drain on the department. Is that how you want to be remembered?'

He expected Ginger to shrug it off, but instead he felt a connection. The man's eyes welled up. 'It won't happen again.' He sniffed.

Barton would put money on Ginger feeling his age in the same way he was. But as opposed to having a family like Barton, Ginger was twice divorced and childless.

'You understand these kids look up to you. Why don't you be someone they really respect? Or one they remember many years from now when they reflect on who helped inspire them at the start of their careers?'

Barton returned to his seat and continued to analyse the information. After he'd read it all twice, he found the Google icon and, with a few clicks, brought up the weather forecast.

As Barton made his way to DCI Naeem's office, DS Kelly Strange arrived at work after starting late due to last night's door knocking exercise.

'Kelly, come with me. I'm updating the boss, so you may as well hear it at the same time.'

'Sure, I can report last night's findings to you both.' She widened her eyes and blinked theatrically to let him know she had something interesting to tell them.

When they got to the DCI's closed door, Barton stopped. 'How's everything else?'

'All good, actually. The man responsible, as we shall call him, rang me, and he's coming over tomorrow night. Said he'll bring a takeaway. Assuming it's not to take away the baby, it sounds positive.'

'Excellent. Still happy with your decision?'

'Very much so.' She nudged him on the arm with her fist. 'I can't wait for maternity leave.'

Barton wondered how she'd feel changing ten nappies a day. He knocked on the office door, which Naeem opened.

'Come in, you two. I hate working Saturdays, so let's get on with it. I'm up to speed with Brick's demise. Are we any closer to solving this? There's a lot of people interested now, and an arrest or even a suspect would be helpful. If there wasn't such a blood-bath in London at the moment, this place would be crawling with shiny buttons.'

She sat behind her desk. Barton paused to allow Strange to take the first seat in front of her. Barton peered over Naeem's shoulder at a picture of her family on the wall. There were two boys: a handsome roguish one wearing a skin-tight shirt, and a studious one with pink glasses. He coughed to stop himself laughing. Even so, he had a grin on his face when he started talking.

'I'd like to hear an update from DS Strange on last night, but I do have a few theories.' Barton cleared his throat and managed to look serious. 'The first is a straightforward revenge attack or maybe vigilante killings. The second is a serial killer from the past come back to life for reasons unknown.'

Naeem drummed her fingers on the desk and gave him a suspicious glance. 'I know which one I'd rather be reporting back. Okay, Kelly, fire away.'

'Right. I split the six DCs into pairs due to the fact we could be disturbing a murderer. We covered the six streets you requested. I flitted between the teams as back up. It was the usual mixture of annoyed or bored householders. There were plenty of unusual people. Your street in particular had some weirdos, John. One guy informed me Margaret Thatcher would sort the criminals out. When I explained she died years ago, he told me not to be so stupid and slammed his weird, bright red door in my face. Another answered her door in her underwear, which gave the two DCs a shock as she had plenty of curves.

'An older woman explained she had Parkinson's and didn't go out much, and a guy who lived near the green told me three times he was eighty years old. He then stated that he hopes the Snow Killer has returned because the police are useless. However, a man down Baggswell Lane said he had seen someone in a white coat on the night of the murder. He'd been cycling home from work. He was heading to your end, John. The time fits. He couldn't give a description due to the conditions apart from they were not particularly tall.'

Barton perked up. 'That matches with what Flying Finn told us he saw. It's still not much, although apparently we all shrink as we age.'

'Let's hear these theories, then, John.'

Barton opened his notepad. 'The most likely initial explanation is a drug related crime to take over the Chapmans' area. The picture I've built up now on Celine is that she's legit and has been for years. Little Chapman is still dealing, by my reckoning. She uses street kids to move her product but, judging by the lifestyles of all of them involved, Britney included, I don't believe it's on a huge scale.

'However, if we assumed Celine was involved then it's fair to say that somebody else could have thought the same thing. They may also have guessed that Brick and even Terry Sax were involved. If it wasn't money related then maybe it was for revenge. If we look into any drug related deaths or overdoses in the recent past, we might find someone with a dead friend, child or relative, who now holds a grudge.

'They might have decided the police weren't up to the job and taken it upon themselves to put matters right.'

'Sounds possible,' said Strange. 'I can check out the recently deceased angle tomorrow. Oh, that's Sunday. Will we get paid double time?'

Naeem laughed. 'That's the only thing I know that won't be happening over the next few days.'

Barton was on a roll and continued without listening. 'That leads us to the vigilante theory. Maybe there isn't anything as drastic as an overdose in the background. The Colonel who lives near me says he wishes the Snow Killer would take out all the junkies. He could mean drug addicts or drug dealers.'

'Definitely not him though?'

'No, he's knackered; bad hips, back, the lot, and it wouldn't be very cunning to mention the Snow Killer if he was him. He will be the eighty year old you spoke to. It might be someone like him, though, who is either younger, or fitter. As Ginger reminded me earlier, some elderly people pump iron, do yoga, and all sorts nowadays. The Colonel is a peculiar bloke, but a murderer, no. So, I'm guessing a fit, short, older, angry person is responsible.'

'Was he a colonel?' asked Strange.

'Good question. That would indicate a military background and familiarity with guns,' said Naeem.

'No,' said Barton. 'I asked him that when I first met him. It was a moniker from a team he used to manage years ago, and it stuck.'

'What next?' asked Naeem.

'I've seen the files for the three historic kills. The first happened at a house in Woodston, which is about a mile away. Someone stabbed and killed a criminal nicknamed Goof in a similar manner to Terry Sax. It was more brutal, but perhaps the culprit was younger. The second murder, if you can believe it, occurred with a small-bore rifle in the churchyard just up the road from me. He was known to the police too. The third victim, another felon, got beaten to death with a hammer in a field near The Boy's Head pub.'

Naeem leaned back in her seat. 'Bullseye.'

'I know.'

'Where's The Boy's Head?' asked Strange.

Naeem answered. 'Oundle Road, about a mile from the latest murders. It's a Tesco Express now. Go on, John.'

'The Boy's Head was only around the corner from where they found the first body. All three men were known to associate with each other. The notes on the first murder are much more detailed. I'll check with Records if there's more, but the information on the second two is sparse, almost like the record is far from complete.'

'They could easily have lost or misplaced items from back then.'

'Yes, that's what's annoying. I can tell they discovered the victims in the snow from the crime scene descriptions. But there's no mention of a *Snow Killer*. However, most of the detail is in regard to the first murder, so there wouldn't have been a link at that point.'

'No suspects?' asked Strange.

'Nothing. They interviewed people from the pub and surrounds, other villains by the looks of things, but no one said anything. If they were taken out by another crew, or belonged to a bigger operation, it's not surprising that nobody talked. It could have been a hired gun from out of town. He turned up, took them out, got called the Snow Killer by the media for the last one, but his job was done by then, so he disappeared. The case went cold.'

'But now we have three more deaths with remarkably similar MOs. Could it be someone who killed them all back then and quit, but now they've started up again?' said Naeem.

'That's perfectly possible. We may never know for the earlier deaths, but the person responsible could still be living here. Maybe they've killed again, and it's not been linked. Or it might be a bloke who lived at the same time and now copies the murders. It's reasonable to assume that we might have a serial killer on our hands.'

Naeem stood and paced the room, clearly thinking fast. 'We should warn people to stay in. I'll talk to Headquarters. This will be national news tomorrow. They'll be calling it serial killings, whether we like it or not.'

Barton noticed Strange was deep in thought. He continued. 'Let's look at the facts we do know. These aren't random kills. All the victims have been criminals or at least been involved in crime. Joe Public is probably safe if they keep out of the way. I'm guessing it's someone from back then. Our suspect is going to be over seventy, male, shortish, and own a white coat. They will live in the area, possibly even go to the church.'

Strange got to her feet. 'The hammer was left at the scene. So was the screwdriver. This person wants us to know they did it.'

'Maybe they're taunting us?' added Barton.

'What would be more worrying,' cut in Naeem, 'is if they have a message. They may be coming to the end of their lives and need their story heard. They want the world to recognise they are the Snow Killer.'

Strange agreed. 'Yes. That would be bad. Like a zealot, they'd have no anxiety over getting caught or killed. Anyone who gets in their way would be in extreme danger.'

Naeem had been making notes as she spoke. 'There's no point in having a big meeting as we don't have enough staff on. These are the tasks we need to look at. We ought to get an Armed Response Vehicle driving around the area asap, two if possible. We need more information on overdoses in the city for the revenge angle. Someone should also talk to the vicar at the church. I want officers watching Baggswell Lane, the field where Brick was taken out, and maybe the BMX track where Terry died.'

She tutted. 'My old Chief Super attended the awards thing last night. I didn't think to ask him, but he worked this area years ago. I'd guess he was a DCI like me then. I'll get hold of him and see if he remembers the case. Does it say who the Senior Investigating Officer was, John?'

'An Inspector Griffin.'

'Right, let's find out if he's still alive and able to shed any light on the subject. God, I need more bodies for this. Are you both free tomorrow?'

Barton sighed. 'I'm seeing my mother in the morning and she's cooking for us. I haven't seen her for a long time, and I want to check she's okay.'

Naeem sighed. 'All day?'

'I can be back mid-afternoon. I'll pop into the church on the way. There's bound to be a service around ten in the morning.'

'That will have to do. It's crazy to think there's a homicidal nutcase out there, and we still have little concrete idea of who they could be.'

Barton's phone rang. He answered it and stared at Naeem as she listened. 'It's a message from Zander. Britney is nowhere to be seen. He posted a uniform on her door but I reckon we should upgrade that to some armed personnel. She has to be the favourite for the next target. Zander is out hunting down her underlings for her mobile number or whereabouts. He's also put out a BOLO (be on the lookout) for her. Let's hope we get to her before the killer does.'

'Agreed,' said Naeem. 'I've never known anything like this. It could be a tough day tomorrow.'

Barton was the final person to stand. 'We do have a bit of time. The murders occurred when it snowed, and I checked the weather forecast. We aren't due any on Sunday.'

'When are we next likely to get some, John?' asked Naeem.

'Monday.'

53

Barton woke at 5:00. He lay there with his pulse racing. They say many people have a sense of impending doom before something terrible happens. And that was how he felt. Next to him, Holly made the weird gentle clicking snore thing she often did when she was exhausted. He flushed hot. He couldn't recall the last time he took the kids out to give her a break. Was it over a month since he'd cooked her a decent meal? He didn't even know where they kept the ironing board. Barton pushed those depressing facts aside and focused on the case. He took a deep breath. The finale approached.

'Get up if you can't sleep, John.'

Smiling, he slipped from the covers and discovered he was fully dressed. He couldn't remember going to bed. He moistened his dry mouth while recollecting draining the vestiges of a bottle of wine. He relieved himself and stopped to look at Luke and Layla sleeping. Life goes on.

When he got downstairs, he found defrosted bacon on the cooker. With the oven fired up, he took five plates from the cupboard and flicked on the kettle. Was it the last supper or the final meal of the condemned? While he poured juice for everyone, Barton tried to push the melancholy from his mind. He'd always been pragmatic. Perhaps he should talk to a professional.

Having to wake the kids was usually unnecessary when the smell of bacon wafted through the house. He plated the sandwiches up and they arrived in thirty second intervals, Layla last of all.

'Where's the brown sauce?' she said.

'Next to the houmous in the fridge. I thought you wanted to be a vegan?'

She gave him an if-looks-could-kill scowl and then smiled. 'Love you, Daddy.'

Recently, he'd endured a big spiel from her about how a typical pig factory generates the same amount of raw waste as a city of twelve thousand people, but it wasn't a day for cheap point scoring. He stared forlornly at the single remaining slice of bacon, and ate it out of the pan.

The family managed to take turns in the bathroom without killing each other and then clambered into Barton's Land Rover. He looked forward to seeing his mother, though he knew it would still be bittersweet when he remembered his father. The kids loved being with his mum, too. Even Lawrence didn't moan. He found her honesty highly amusing. Barton thought Lawrence enjoyed the fact that, with Nanny, he would always be a child and could enjoy being spoilt without thinking it reflected on him badly in some way that only a teenager would understand.

Barton stood next to the car and shivered. He pulled chilled air into his lungs. He didn't need to see a forecast to know what to expect. His phone rang as he climbed into the driver's seat. It was DCI Naeem.

'Boss, any news?'

'Kind of. I finally managed to reach the retired DCI. He remembers the events in Peterborough vividly.'

'Excellent. What did he say?'

'To some degree, what we already have. The victims were

three drinking buddies who ran for a drug kingpin. Known crooks, but nobody could get anything to stick. He said they were pretty surprised they got taken out because they were just minions. At the time, they thought it was the start of a gangland war, but it all stopped after they were killed.'

'Does he still know this Griffin character who worked the cases?'

'That's one of the important pieces of information. He hated this bloke. He said Griffin oversaw the first murder but didn't seem bothered after that. Loads of paperwork got misplaced, leads weren't followed up, and the investigation lost focus. He suspected Griffin was dodgy because normally he behaved like a terrier with cases. Nothing stuck obviously, and he went on to have quite a distinguished career.'

'Is Griffin still alive?'

'Yes, very much so, and he lives down your street.'

'What? You're kidding.'

'No, small world, eh? He's at number nineteen. Perhaps you'd like to have a word with him when you return from your mum's.'

'No problem. We're just setting off. I'll call in on the way back. Have they found Britney yet?'

'No, there's no sign of her at all. Zander has her mobile number now after threatening that Todd Finn, but it goes straight to voicemail. I've been able to get an armed unit parked on her street. They'll be there for a few days. It's going to freeze tomorrow. Snow's forecast too. In fact, it's likely to be blizzard conditions. They offered the helicopter today and tomorrow, but it won't go up in bad weather.'

'Jesus. Perfect conditions for our killer. Did he mention anything about that?'

'He confirmed you were right. The papers started using the Snow Killer line after the third murder, but because there weren't any more, it went quiet. When I mentioned the snow angle, he remembered something else.'

'Why do I have a feeling I'm not going to like this?'

'He said that about two years beforehand, more people lost their lives in the snow.'

'More criminals? Didn't they link them?'

'I asked that. They tried to connect them, but they had a very different MO. An entire family were shot in the countryside. They believed that to be a professional job as the father was a known hitman.'

'They have to be connected.'

'That's what I said, but the father came from London. It had all the hallmarks of a mob killing. About a year later, they nicked a bagman down south, and he told them that everyone knew the guy killed had stolen money from the bosses.'

'Shit. And those murders occurred in London?'

'No, in Lincolnshire. Isn't that where you're going today?'

'Yep. Was he confident the incidents were unrelated?'

'He said Griffin did the investigative work because he'd had some involvement in both cases, but he didn't find any connection. He couldn't remember the details exactly. I've got Records pulling everything today. Whatever they have, I'll get by this afternoon.'

'The family were only shot? No screwdrivers, knives or hammers involved?'

'He doesn't think so. It was a long time ago, and he wasn't as interested in that case. The weird thing is that he can recall the headlines for the family murders in the news the next day. They called them the snow killings.'

54

Barton pulled off the drive with a grimace.

'Everything okay?' Holly asked.

'Not really. I've a feeling the case has taken a turn for the worse. I just need to nip down the bottom and check out a house.'

He drove down the cul-de-sac. Before he got there, he guessed the answer. Sure enough, number nineteen was the bungalow with the big red door. He did a three point turn and accelerated away.

'I also need to pop into the church.'

Holly nodded and jerked her thumb to the back of the vehicle. Surprisingly, the kids were behaving. Layla was playing games on her tablet, Lawrence was listening to music on his phone, and Luke only had to look at a car and he'd fall asleep.

Barton pulled out of Black Ermine Street and drove three hundred metres along the road to the church. It was amazing that he hadn't heard about the grisly murder there. A few cars lined the verge. He noted from a board outside that a service started in thirty minutes. The big wooden entrance door had been opened in readiness.

Barton could see the vicar inside, bent double, placing hymn books on the pews, and walked up to him. The man's hands shook as he worked. When Barton cleared his throat, he peered up at him through rheumy eyes.

'Ah, come for the service? Excellent, we need fresh blood, especially youngsters like yourself.'

Barton felt bad disappointing him, but he'd never been the God-fearing type. Besides, the last time he'd donated blood, the nurse had said something similar.

'Maybe next week. I just have a few questions around something that happened fifty years ago in the churchyard.'

'I'll try to help. Sixty years, I've been here. It was in my time. Not much happens here that I don't know about. We used to get hundreds at communion in those days. We only had twenty turn up last Sunday.'

'I'm Detective Inspector Barton, and we've been investigating the murders that I'm sure you've read about in the news.'

The vicar nodded, yet Barton sensed a noticeable shift in concentration in the man's eyes. He didn't comment though, so Barton continued.

'In the 1960s, a man got shot here amongst the graves. Can you tell me about it?'

The vicar turned around and proceeded to distribute the hymn books. After a few seconds, he stopped. 'Nasty business that, but a long time ago. I can't remember the details.'

Barton squinted. 'I thought little escaped your attention here?'

The vicar returned to stand in front of Barton. He stood taller.

'Someone shot a man. He died. They never caught anyone for it. That's all I'm aware of.'

Barton didn't believe that to be accurate, although he wasn't quite sure how to probe further without calling him a liar. He decided to leave it for the moment. It was over an hour's drive to Lincoln, and he would use the time to mull things over. At the door, he remembered something the Colonel said.

'A neighbour told me that the churchyard's haunted. That a ghost can sometimes be seen, late at night or really early in the morning, putting flowers on the graves. Is it true?'

The side of the vicar's face twitched. 'This place is full of ghosts, Officer. I find it safer to let them be.'

55

The children kept silent for the whole journey. Holly slept as well. She stirred as Barton turned the engine off outside his mother's house.

'Have the kids been okay?'

'Perfect. We'll have to wake Luke.'

They all clambered out and waited while Barton rang the bell. His mother opened the door with a cheerful look. 'Morning.'

Luke stepped forward and hugged her legs. 'Nanny, are you going to give us some money?'

'Luke!' admonished Holly.

'That's all right. Yes, I am.' She stuck her hand in her pocket and gave each of the kids a crisp ten pound note.

'Cool, thanks, Nanny,' said Lawrence. 'Does that mean we can go home now?'

'Lawrence!' shouted Barton.

'I was joking.'

His mother just laughed. 'John never beat around the bush when he was young either. Come in, then. I've made a lasagne. John, you help me set the table while I put the kettle on.'

The others moved into the lounge while Barton went to the

dining room. He stared at the set table. His mother chuckled behind him.

'Cheer up, my boy. Let's have a sherry.'

He sat on a chair. His mother had never been a 'hugger', as she called them, but she loved him. Actions spoke louder than words, and she'd always been supportive. She paid the deposit on his first home and often told him she was always a phone call away, although that would be more comforting if she actually answered the damn thing.

She plonked a sherry in front of him. Barton was pleased no one else could see the tiny glass in his paw.

'It's good to see you. Sorry about the phone business, but I think it's okay now. My boyfriend showed me how it works.' Sherry came out of Barton's nose. 'Just kidding. A woman at my bridge club has the same model. I didn't even know it had a camera.'

'That was quite a shock. I had some frightening images in my mind.'

'Don't be silly. Besides, why stick to one man when I can play the field?'

Barton was pleased his mouth was empty. He didn't have the energy for a sparring contest. 'I'm glad you've mastered the phone. We started to get worried about you.'

'Who? Me? I'm fine. Better than fine actually. I've been going Nordic walking with Tilly from number six. I'm as strong as a bull. Where do you think you got your strength from? Your dad was just fat.'

Another strange vision entered his head of her and Tilly skiing down the motorway. 'You don't feel old, then?'

'Of course not. Us women are more resilient than you men. Is everything okay with you? You look exhausted. I thought you'd applied for a desk job.'

'I did, but I didn't get it. Generally, I'm okay, although it all seems to be a struggle at the moment. I know it sounds ridiculous, but I feel down all the time.'

His mother put her empty glass on the table. 'Well, maybe not too ridiculous. Your father struggled with depression.'

'Really? I never knew that.'

'People didn't talk about it back then. Your dad rarely said anything to me. Young'uns nowadays can't wait to bleat their problems to all and sundry. Poor me, I'm so sad. A kick up the arse would sort them out, or a week in a coalmine.'

'I'm beginning to understand why he failed to mention it.'

'You pull yourself together. Don't do what he did and drink yourself into an early grave. Another sherry? After that I must get the lasagne out of the oven.'

Barton stared at her retreating back with his mouth open.

'Are you working on all those murders?' she asked on returning from the kitchen.

'Yes. That's not helping my frame of mind either.'

'There are some sick people out there.'

'You don't say. You need to be a complete psycho to kill like that.'

'Well, they reckon the really dangerous monsters are those who don't realise they are one. They think they're just doing a job. They should be strung up when they're caught.'

'We don't do much of that nowadays. Here, do you recall a family being killed around here about fifty years ago? The only information I have is that it was here in Lincolnshire.'

'Gosh, if it's the one I think, it was a long time ago. Do you know what? I do remember because they shot the kids as well. Although if I'm right, one of the children survived.'

56

Through the dining room window, Barton watched the others chowing down on their dinners while he tried DCI Naeem's phone again. He gave up and rang DS Strange.

'Kelly, how's things? Are you at the station?'

'Yes.'

'I'm trying to get hold of the boss. Any idea where she is?'

'She's gone into a meeting. I was just talking to her.'

'Okay. Can you pass a message on when she comes out?'

'Sure.'

'There were more killings in the snow over in Lincolnshire a few years before the ones in Peterborough.'

'Yeah, she told me. Although she said that it's unlikely to be connected.'

'That's right. However, they didn't kill the whole family. My mum reckons one of the children survived.'

'No way. Did she know names or ages?'

'She can't remember. She seemed to think it wasn't a young child but couldn't be sure.'

'That's interesting. If they're still alive, it would really help to talk to them and get some background.'

'Correct. Have we got any information from Records yet?'

'We've had bad news regarding that.'

'Great, there's a delay?'

'No, there aren't any files.'

'You're kidding me. Nothing at all?'

'No, the woman there said it's rare but not completely unheard of. Especially if the case wasn't solved. The box could have been hanging around the station and been thrown out.'

'Or someone threw it out.'

'What makes you say that?'

'I get the feeling that somebody didn't want to solve these cases. I'm talking to the retired detective who failed to solve the Peterborough murders when I get home. We'll see what he says when I pin that on him. There must be some info somewhere.'

'Apparently the newspapers keep records of all their issues. It'll be on microfiche. A slaughter like that would have made front-page news. She checked online and said it won't be a problem, but she was only working 'til noon on overtime and had finished for the day. She promised to sort it first thing tomorrow morning.'

'Okay. It could well be the same person. A ruthless paid assassin takes out the family for one contract then is hired for three more hits a couple of years later. If the survivor is still alive, they may even have a description.'

There was silence from the other end before Strange quietly added, 'Didn't you mention that the three men were criminals? Maybe they slaughtered the family in Lincolnshire?'

'You're right. Perhaps one of the father's connections found out and had them killed in retaliation.'

'What if the child who lived was a teenager? They waited two years and took revenge for the murder of their parents and sibling.'

Barton almost said it wasn't likely that a teenager could commit such horrific murders against three full-grown men in their thirties when he recalled the viciousness. Those three men suffered. They didn't die quickly. It was personal. 'That's good thinking, Kelly. A bit of a leap perhaps, but the child would only be about sixty-five now, which is young enough for more mayhem.'

'True. I agree it's unlikely, but the cases do seem to be connected. You wait, the details will come back and the one who survived will have been two years old.'

Barton laughed for the first time that day. 'An actual baby-faced assassin. There is definitely something unusual going on though. I spoke to the vicar at the church this morning. He said he's been resident sixty years, and even he was peculiar.'

'The whole world is behaving oddly at the moment. Before I forget, DCI Naeem wants everyone in at 6:00 tomorrow. I'm cream-crackered, the heating's playing up and it's absolutely freezing in here, so I'm going to go home to have a bath.'

'Good, don't overdo it in—'

'Don't say it!'

Barton smiled again. 'I'll be in then as well. That's assuming I fail to extract any pertinent information out of Inspector Griffin. He's got Alzheimer's, so I doubt it.'

Barton terminated the call, entered the house and stared at his lasagne.

'Is it snowing yet, Daddy?' asked Luke.

'No, it is freezing though. It's probably too cold for snow.'

'How can it be too cold to snow?' asked Layla.

'It's a phrase. I think it's something to do with the water vapour in the air.'

'But I want snow,' said Luke.

'Wait a minute,' said Lawrence. 'I'll look it up.'

He took his phone out of his pocket and ran his fingers over the screen for ten seconds. 'Wikipedia knows all,' said Lawrence. 'Basically, if the temperature gets to minus 8 °C, 17.6 °F, you are unlikely to get heavy snow.'

'What temperatures are we expecting this evening and tomorrow?' asked Holly.

Lawrence fiddled with his phone. Barton's stomach gurgled. 'Tonight will be minus 7, and tomorrow's going to be minus 3.'

'Is that good or bad, Daddy?' Luke stared at him with the utmost interest.

Barton stared out of the window. 'Definitely bad.'

I've stopped taking my medication these last few days. I'd been sleeping poorly and, even when I did get some rest, crazed visions filled my dreams. When I was awake, people shimmered at the periphery of my vision, and dark thoughts dragged me into a gloom. It's possible that my actions poisoned my brain. But this morning, after two days pill free, I feel like a different person after a good night's sleep.

A car pulls up outside. It must be the doctor. I missed my appointment yesterday and, with him being a caring man, he rang to find out why. I suppose I have known him twenty-five years, but acts of kindness are rare nowadays. Perhaps it's his compassion that's making me wobble at the finish line. The body buried in the snow has made the national headlines. Peterborough is on the map. They say he was just a simple bricklayer, but if he hung around with the Chapmans, he knew. The detectives will be searching for Britney. I wonder if they've found her.

I open the door to let Dr Patel in and spot the police helicopter in the distance. That will be the third time today that it's been overhead. I also chanced a walk this morning and noticed an officer down the lane and another one at the shops. Maybe Inspector Barton does have some idea what he's doing. I bet they are looking for someone in a white coat. They must have linked the case to my previous acts. Their minds will struggle with the concept of an elderly serial killer. I was young and silly once, too, but they'll understand in the end.

Dr Patel smiles at me as I let him inside. He squeezes my arm in greeting. He's often done that since the diagnosis. Maybe he knows I'm on my own, and I appreciate any human contact. It lets me know I'm here, and that others notice me. The whole country will know who I am shortly. My family will be remembered.

'You've stopped the medication, then?' he asks.

'Yes, I was slowly going mad with such poor sleep quality,' I reply.

'That's a frequent complaint with that drug. Exercise will help considerably. We could try sleeping pills in the short term to see if your body settles down, but I hate prescribing them.'

'That sounds daft. If one tablet causes insomnia, surely it's a better idea to stop taking it rather than continuing and popping another pill to knock me out.'

'I know, but you're running out of options because this is the second drug we've used. What's left doesn't tend to be as helpful. Have you had any other side effects?'

'Like what?'

'Hallucinations or delusions?'

'What's the difference?'

'Well, the first is seeing things that aren't there, whereas delusions are unusual thoughts that aren't based on reality.'

'Let me make you a quick cup of tea, and I'll think about it.'

I've boiled the kettle already. I consider Sandy Janes; also known as Brick. Was he innocent, and I imagined he was bad? I read today that Celine Chapman had turned her life around. Could Terry Sax have actually been a quiet man? Am I wrong about them all?

I stop and stare in the mirror before bringing in his drink. I look old but with sleep my eyes are still young. When did my hair get so grey? I had such white teeth, too. Now I'm conscious of smiling at people.

When I return to the lounge, the doctor fidgets near the window with his back to me. I realise we are a similar age. He stoops nowadays. I hope he isn't lonely.

'Sometimes I see shadows.'

He spins around. What was he thinking? He nods at me. 'How about impulsive or compulsive behaviour?'

'I don't know the difference between them either.'

'Impulsive behaviour is when an individual can't resist the temptation to carry out certain activities. People might do something like going shopping and give no thought to the future or to long-term consequences of the money they spent, just the immediate reward. Compulsive behaviour is when a person has an overwhelming drive to behave in a certain way. Excessive gambling is an example. They may continue to act in that manner even if they no longer get any fun or benefit from it. That behaviour might be out of character.'

I give him a small grin. 'I have been a little ruthless with people of late.'

He returns the smile. 'That's probably an age thing. I don't possess the patience I used to either. Please, stick with the pills and try the sleeping tablets to see if they work.'

I feel the frown forming before I display it. 'Nothing will really help, will it? I studied up on the endgame, and it's bleak. Being so independent, it's a horror I can barely comprehend.'

He takes a sip of his tea and smiles. 'Good cuppa. I admit what you have is progressive and, with no support, you'll end up in a care home. Live for the moment. Treat yourself to things you might not usually have done.'

'Be more impulsive?'

He laughs. 'Exactly. Take your pleasures while you still can.'

His smile drops. 'I have noticed a change in your mood that I haven't seen before. I'm not sure what it is, perhaps anger at the diagnosis. Don't waste the rest of your days sitting around with dark thoughts. Do something purposeful.'

He always was a perceptive man. Earlier, something else occurred to me when I checked the medical websites. Who better to ask than a doctor?

'Do you know anything about Traumatic Brain Injuries?'

'I've seen many in my career. Why, who's had one?'

'Me, actually, many years ago. I discovered that the effects might be long lasting.'

'Very much so. Most people recover, but some experience depression, memory loss, balance issues, even problems with judgement and aggression. An interesting piece of research I read said that, when screened, just under half of prisoners reported that at some point in their life they had experienced a serious blow to the head that rendered them very dazed or confused. Obviously, that's an indicator of a TBI. If you had one yourself, that may have been a factor in you developing your condition. Imagine that. An impact to the skull years ago could cause odd behaviour all this time later. Your untimely degenerative damage to the brain might be a result of that blow.'

He stays for fifteen minutes. I wonder if that's how long he usually spends with patients or if he enjoys my company. Not that I listen much after his comments. When I was shot, they really did take my future. That makes me vengeful. Any doubts about my path are removed. I pop a pill in front of him. I don't suppose it matters if I don't get any sleep tonight.

The clock strikes one the moment he leaves. I grab a Milky Way from the fridge and turn the TV on. Grinning, I return to the kitchen and take another bar from the packet. Very naughty. The news is a brief round-up. Peterborough has already lost its spot in the sun as London has just had its thirtieth murder so far this year. Not bad going considering the time of year. Today's forecaster is a middle-aged woman in a smart suit with a towering pair of heels. She looks lovely.

'Britons can expect a shock to the system tonight as temperatures drop sharply after a spell of unseasonably warm weather. Most of northern Scotland is in for sleet and flurries of snow tonight, while further south the mercury is unlikely to rise above zero all day tomorrow.

'Some areas in the south of England enjoyed temperatures as high as 15 °C, 59 °F over the weekend, but even those parts will feel the cold by tomorrow.

'It will turn a lot chillier this evening as the wind strengthens and turns more northerly – we might see sleet and wet snow in northern areas. But the east of the country will take the brunt of the bad weather, and we could hit minus 5 °C, 23 °F.

'Snow is forecast this afternoon and overnight. It will probably only be a few centimetres, but tomorrow morning is the danger period. Freezing temperatures and more downfalls in the morning will also combine with a strong wind. This could cause drifts and the possibility of whiteout conditions, especially on roads.'

It's time. I fall back in my chair and let out a huge breath. The Snow Killer's story ends tomorrow. I think of the police presence nearby and guess they are close to solving it. They will be at my door soon, and if they catch me, I'll have to die in prison. Most disagreeable. Going out in style as planned is much more tempting.

I ring A2B Taxis and book one to take me to the Marriott Hotel. I've been there once before. There's a lovely jacuzzi and steam room. It's pricey but they can cook my last meal. I can't stay here. They should have the snow link by now. This area will be crawling with uniforms tomorrow. The detectives may be solving it this second. Perhaps I should have gone earlier because the news warned of the imminent storm.

I fetch my suitcase from the spare room. I look at my white coat and place it in the bottom. My warmest clothes go in as well. There's only the need to take one outfit. I'm looking forward to the eat-as-much-as-you-like breakfast. I pick up the envelope addressed to the newspaper with my life history in it. My story will be told. The hotel can post that for me.

That just leaves the pistol, which I fetch from its usual location. I slide it in the case between my clothes and click the lock shut. It makes a clunk when I put the case down. I'm glad it's not loaded. There's only one round remaining, but that's enough. I still have the Stanley knife.

58

Barton arrived home and helped usher the children inside. The heating had been left on due to the risk of frozen pipes, and he gasped with the warmth. He didn't fancy going out again, but at least he only had to call in about eight houses away.

He regretted not putting a hat and scarf on as he plodded down the already icy path. The street was empty. He cursed when no one answered. He turned to leave when he remembered the woman telling him Griffin couldn't always hear the doorbell. When he reached the back, he stared at another red door. He knocked twice and a shadow appeared through the glass.

The old guy peered around the door. He stared blankly at Barton.

'Mr Griffin, it's me, Inspector John Barton, from the end of the road.'

'Aye, what do you want?'

'I'd like to talk to you about a case you worked on years ago. I believe you'd reached Detective Inspector at that point.'

His shoulders straightened. 'Come in for a bit.'

Barton stepped inside and closed the door behind him. 'I won't take up too much of your time.'

'I'll try to help. I struggle with the present, but oddly I can still remember my first ice-cream sundae. To be honest, I feel lost all the time, as though I'm supposed to be somewhere, but I don't know where that place is. I fall asleep in my chair and wake to an unfamiliar room. Then unknown worries stop me sleeping at night.'

'I'm sorry to hear that.' Barton was too tired for more platitudes. 'Now, the murders I'm interested in took place fifty years ago. They were more like three executions. Very brutal.'

'I recall a case a long while ago. I don't believe they were ever solved.'

Barton detected a change in the tone of the man's voice. Griffin had selected his words with caution. Barton knew he would remember the serious crimes he'd investigated until the day he died. 'There can't be too many murders you didn't solve.'

'What is it you want to know, Inspector Barton?'

Barton considered his words carefully. The meek old fellow from moments ago had vanished. He now spat Barton's name out. Barton imagined a younger man with real strength of character.

'Why couldn't you find the killer?'

'They were the perfect murders. No fingerprints or evidence except some common footprints. We had nothing and waited for another victim, but the third one was the last.'

'Did you think of connecting them to the murder of the family over in Lincolnshire a few years beforehand?'

Griffin's eyes narrowed. 'I can't remember much about that. I understood it was a London thing. We dismissed it. Why are you bringing all this back up?'

'As you know, we've had three grisly deaths here in the last six months. An avenue of inquiry links the murders then to the ones now. We're expecting more information tomorrow morning.'

'Don't be preposterous. That's so long ago that everyone must be dead.'

'You're still alive.'

'Only just.'

Barton expected anger, yet instead he detected concern. He pressed on. 'One of the children survived. Could they have been about revenge?'

'What's that got to do with the present-day murders? How are they related to the past?'

'We haven't found a link apart from the method of killing. I don't suppose you have any theories?'

'No, maybe all my memory is bad now. Sorry, I can't be of any help. Goodnight to you.'

Griffin walked around him and opened the door. Sharp eyes challenged Barton to leave. Barton stopped on the threshold, turned, and noticed the trembling in the hand that held the door. What did he know? He thought about the lack of evidence in the later murders and the missing files in the family's slaying. Could Griffin have been linked to organised crime in the past? Was he paid to leave those cases unsolved? Another anomaly crossed Barton's mind. 'Why were you called Jen? Didn't you say your name was Mr Smith earlier, when it's Griffin?'

'No, I didn't.' The frail man placed his hand on Barton's chest and shoved him off the doorstep.

'I'm retired. Don't come back.'

The door closed quietly, which was more disconcerting than a slam. Barton plodded to his house deep in thought as the first few flakes floated through the air.

59

DI BARTON

Barton emerged the next morning with bleary eyes and scowled at the freezing conditions. It had snowed steadily through the earlier part of the night and his boots crunched through the crystals. Bad snow for snowmen, he thought, as it wouldn't stick together. The wind was getting up as well, which made his eyes water as he removed the sheet from his car. Gusts of snow blew off the neighbour's roof and covered his clear windscreen.

The Land Rover's temperature gauge indicated minus 6 °C. He had hauled himself from his bed twenty minutes early to allow time for the big engine to warm up. Comfortable now, he drove down the street with his lights on even though they weren't needed to see in the strange twilight conditions. Would the Snow Killer be out in this? Would he kill tonight? Often after Barton went to bed, he woke up with solutions. It was almost as if his brain had arranged the jigsaw pieces during the night. Instead, this morning he had woken to doubt and mistrust of his own judgement.

When he got to the station and placed his coat on the back of a chair, DC Whitlam asked him to nip to the front desk to sign a card for a woman in Forensics who had resigned. While he was there, a sharply dressed Asian lad in his twenties arrived. Barton listened in as he recognised one of DCI Naeem's sons.

'Hi, my girlfriend left this behind earlier. I only noticed after she drove off. She said she had a really busy day ahead. Can you pass it on to her?' He handed over a mobile phone.

'Who's it for?' asked the man on the desk.

'Detective Sergeant Strange,' he replied with obvious pride. 'Thanks. I didn't think she would want to be without it.'

The lad turned around and almost bumped into DCI Naeem.

'Oh, hi, Mum.'

'Aryan. What are you doing here?'

'It's a long story. I'll be in touch.' He kissed his mother on the cheek and left.

Barton raised an eyebrow at his boss, who said, 'That was rather cryptic.'

Barton watched her leave as his brain dragged up the memory of Naeem telling him that Aryan played the field. He decided it might be best to keep out of it. Hopefully it would all work out for Kelly. Although, imagine having DCI Naeem as the mother-in-law.

The incident room heaved with staff when he arrived. Zander caught his eye over the top of them and held up a coffee cup. Barton sidled through them and smiled. 'Nice one. How are things?'

'Up and down.'

Barton shrugged. 'I'm sorry, mate. I keep meaning to ask you out for a beer, but I never seem to have any free time.'

'No, I'm okay. I've been seeing that Slovenian girl and been going up and down.'

Barton laughed. 'Good for you.' He still checked his friend's face.

'I'm cool, John.'

Barton gave him a look, but DCI Naeem clapped her hands

together at the front of the room and the comment was forgotten.

'Morning, everyone. Thanks for coming in early. The intelligence we have for the current spate of murders may seem a little tenuous. However, if we follow every lead it isn't going to jeopardise the investigation in any way. Personally, I'm in agreement with the historic angle. The matching weapons used are too similar for there not to be at least some kind of copycat connection.

'It's 6:15 now, and, as I'm sure you can tell, the conditions are deteriorating fast. If it is someone who kills in the snow, this may be our last chance to catch them as the weather should break on Wednesday. Then we're into March and we probably won't get any more until the end of the year. DI Barton thinks that our killer has a message to send, so he or she may have something else to prove. Prime time has to be dusk onwards. It's going to be dark not long after 16:00. We will have at least one Armed Response Vehicle in the area at all times, today and tomorrow. They are outside Britney's house at present. Still no contact, DS Zander?'

'No, her phone's been turned off, although it rang last night. Whoever answered didn't talk, and then cut me off when I did. There's no message-leaving facility.'

'Keep trying, please.'

'Can't we use her mobile to locate her?' asked DC Ginger Rodgers.

'Good idea, I'll try to get permission for that, but, seeing as she is not a suspect, it's not guaranteed. We can argue her life is at risk, although I suspect she will be on the move anyway. That's what I'd do. Okay, so eyes peeled for Britney and anyone else looking suspicious in the vicinity. Usually we focus on young males but, in light of what we know, it could be anyone of any age. There's talk of whiteout conditions later, especially if more snow arrives to match the stronger wind. It will be tempting to keep in the warm, but we must stay observant.'

'Stay frosty, ma'am?' said Ginger with a smile.

'Exactly. It's a big area. DS Strange, I want your team to cover south of the shops where Todd Finn lives. It dawned on me that he could be a target as well. DI Barton, chase the newspaper articles via Records as soon as they start work, or go direct to the website if necessary. That angle is yours.'

'DS Zander, your group take Baggswell Lane and the shops. Uniform are patrolling the field and estate behind. DC Rodgers, check in on that guy who was found staring at Brick's body.'

'I look forward to seeing Dwayne again. Any development on the footprints?' he asked.

'Thanks for reminding me. DC Whitlam, did CSI make any progress with that?'

Whitlam rose to his feet. 'There were loads of different types as the crime scenes were contaminated. However, there is one that occurred at all the incidents. They've been matched to a standard brand of wellington boot sold by Shoe Zone. I've spoken to their head office. They have five hundred stores in the UK alone, and after the inclement weather started, they have been selling anything up to thirty thousand pairs a week. They estimate they've sold hundreds of thousands of that particular style since they began stocking them.'

A ripple of laughter spread through the room at Naeem's exasperated face. She took a deep breath and was about to speak when the loud beep-beep of an incoming text message cut her off. Ginger chuckled louder at that, but Naeem stunned him with a fierce glance and pointed finger. Zander reached into his inside suit pocket and pulled his mobile phone out. His fingers danced over the screen.

'It's from Britney's mobile number: "*Stop calling me. I get that you think I'm next but if you don't know where I am then the killer won't know either.*"'

Naeem's jaw bunched. 'I do not share her confidence. This killer has been one step ahead of us all the way.'

60

I stir from a deep slumber. I ate so much at breakfast that I fell asleep on the bed afterwards. The pills have numbed my thought processes again and, despite the nap, I'm groggy. I've missed the eight o'clock taxi, having slept past that time, and rebook it for nine, which is only fifteen minutes away. No matter, there's little to do. The shower blasts some of the fug from my mind, and I pull on my winter clothes. This white coat has been my suit of armour. I check the final round is in the pistol and place that and the Stanley knife into my pockets. Uncle Ronnie's keepsake from his father can come too, for when the moment arrives.

The taxi driver doesn't acknowledge me, just drives away from the hotel when I get in the back seat. I wonder if it was him who had a wasted journey earlier. He's going in the right direction, anyway. He drives past the business park with the flash new offices. It seems this place changes by the hour. I've enjoyed seeing the city develop over the years. Some find the expansion and multiplying population unsettling whereas I've loved the anonymity it provides.

I don't feel nerves. I rarely have. Was that another part stolen from me on that wintry night? It's possible that Britney isn't at the girlfriend's place, but that's where I'd go if I were her. When the you-know-what hits the fan, people like Britney find they have few friends.

Still, I may be wrong. What will I do if she isn't there? Maybe I should just put the last bullet in my own head. No, I have a plan for myself. That's back up in case they try to save me. I know where I want to die.

I tell the man to stop on the small stone bridge that gives Stonebridge its name and give him fifty pounds and ask him to wait. If I haven't returned in a few minutes, he can keep the change. There's a path through to the property. It's much colder than I expected. The wind swirls the snow into mini-tornados, and I watch my step. It wouldn't do to fall at this late stage.

A few days ago, I hung around outside Britney's girlfriend's building. A leaving cleaner told me about the sheltered housing. There are eight flats with their own bathrooms and two communal kitchens. People don't tend to stay long.

The owner of one of the neighbouring properties' was keen to have a moan to me about the occupants. Loud, late music being the main point of irritation. She knew most of the culprits by sight and pointed to the flat that had been the worst recently.

I'm guessing the cause is Britney, who's been hiding at her girlfriend's place. Typical that she didn't think to keep a low profile. She always did like her music. She likes women, too. It's funny reading the papers nowadays. They seem to think lesbians, gays and transgender rarely existed before now. They were about. Perhaps people were just nicer to each other in those days.

I suspected the inhabitants would be late risers, hence my plan to get here early. I may have missed them by oversleeping. A man smokes outside. I might as well ask for confirmation.

'Hi, I'm looking for the flat with the young lady and the baby.'

I can tell straight away that the guy isn't the full ticket. He's one of those whose mouth opens as their brain tries to engage.

I'm reminded of Special. She did that sometimes. Then she'd laugh as she had forgotten what she was thinking about. I try a different angle.

'Hi, it's nice to meet you. My name's Ronnie. I want to visit the young family.'

His simple smile splits his face. 'Dwayne, I'm Dwayne. There's a baby in number one. I hear it when the music isn't too loud.'

It is the flat that the neighbour pointed out. 'That's very good. Which one are you in?'

'I'm opposite in number three.'

'I suggest you get back in there. It's getting worse out here. I'd hate for you to catch your death.'

I follow him inside. He points at the first flat on the right and giggles. He puts his finger to his mouth and goes, 'Shhh.' There you are. Ignore different people at your cost. They can often understand what's going on. When his door shuts, I push my hood back, grip the pistol, and knock on the door. A young girl opens it up enough to peek through. I smile. She recognises me but can't place from where. Our paths have crossed at the shops and in the street. She wouldn't see danger. She pushes the door wide.

'Is Britney there?'

'She's asleep in bed.'

I point the gun at her chest. 'She'll get up for me.'

61

DI BARTON

Barton spoke to the woman in Records who'd kept to her word by arriving early and finding the information online. She rang the company, and they'd agreed to email her a PDF of *The Times* newspaper the day after the family had died, and the copies from the following week. The chilling headlines on that first morning were simply: Snow Killings. Barton had just received the email that she forwarded to him. Only the initial facts appeared on the front page. He was flicking through the later pages when DC Rodgers waddled past looking as if he'd been inflated with a pump.

'I'm off to see that slow fella in the hostel who we caught peering at the body. He's in flat three.'

'Cool. Ask him if he knows the Chapmans. You sure you don't need a few more layers?'

'It's protection from snow and bullets. I think if I fell over, I would bounce back up again.'

'Ginger. I wanted to say I was out of order when I grabbed you the other morning. I shouldn't have done it.'

'Hey, forget about it. We're old school and I should know better. I'll make it up to her.'

Barton found himself alone in the office when Rodgers left.

He read the newspaper of the day after the murders again. It contained very little detail. He rubbed his hands and decided a drink would warm him up. Someone had foolishly left some Cup-a-Soups on the side. A chicken one would be just the job. He sat down and resumed his search.

The incident dropped from the front pages quickly, as if the press struggled to get hold of any facts. Barton wondered if the police withheld information from them for the purposes of the investigation, or for reasons unknown. He finally found the names of the deceased. Alan and Vicky Smith, and their disabled six year old daughter, Michelle. A fifteen year old child had survived but remained under police protection in hospital with serious injuries. Their details were being hidden for the time being.

Barton rubbed the sides of his forehead and grimaced. It was the name Smith, again. Think, you idiot. A common surname, but still. The age of the victim worked. They'd be less than seventy now and around eighteen when the later murders were committed. He cursed at the lack of information, then another email pinged through from the woman in Records.

John, I read the newspapers I sent you but couldn't find the details of the child who survived. I flicked through the next few weeks' front pages. They have thumbnails on their website. I came across this. I've blown up the image, and it's a little blurred, but the information you want is there. If you bear with me, I'll ring the company again to get the whole paper. I thought you'd want to know straight away.

Barton clicked on the photograph she'd sent. The picture of the survivor stared out at him. He frowned. The kid reminded him a bit of Oliver Twist. The headline declared: Snow Killings Survivor Vanishes from Hospital. Then he read the child's name. Barton's stomach turned over. How could he have been so stupid?

Britney charges from the bedroom as the girl backs away. She freezes at the sight of the gun, which follows her progress.

'You two, on the sofa.'

Britney's fingers tighten on the knife at her side. I point my pistol back at her girlfriend. 'Last chance.' They sit down.

It's a gloomy, damp room. I step to the cot and look in. The baby is fast asleep and appears clean, warm and well fed. I peer into the bedroom, which looks empty.

'Who are you?' demands Britney.

'I'm the Snow Killer.'

'You're crazy.'

'I killed Terry Sax, your sister, her boyfriend, and now I'm here for you.'

Britney's face whitens. She bares her teeth. The other girl sobs into her hands. Britney jumps out of her seat. My gun stays pointed at the crying form.

'You going to shoot us all, that it?'

'No, Britney. I've come for you alone. Unless you make it difficult for me.'

'Why, what did I do?'

We chuckle together; I admire her spunk. I know she was

born into a life she couldn't escape from and got on with it. But now it's caught up with her.

'You sell drugs and ruin lives.'

'You're mad. My sister was a businesswoman. Brick a builder, hence the name, dummy. And Terry just a junkie, and not even much of one. He only scored off me every month or so.'

I can't help my right eye flickering. Have I been wrong? My hand shakes uncontrollably, and I have to put the pistol in the other hand. Then her comment sinks in. 'You admit to being a drug dealer?'

She realises her error. Her face droops as she accepts that this might be it. I expect a desperate lunge, but instead she sits down.

'The others won't get hurt?'

'No. I promise.'

'What's wrong with your hand?'

'I have Parkinson's disease.'

'Are you dying? Is that why you're doing this?'

Clever girl. 'My family were killed years ago. It was drug related. I murdered the men responsible, but nothing changed. I watched you and your sister break the law for years. You, in particular. Do you remember breaking my bottle of sherry?'

'Shit. Do you know when I left that night, I had a weird feeling I'd done something that would come back to bite me. So, you're taking out the trash before you check out, that it? Am I the last? Someone new will only take over from me.'

'You're the last. Well, it will finish with me.'

The girlfriend's snuffles strengthen considerably. Britney sighs. 'Can I tell her to go in the bedroom with the baby?'

'Yes, fine.'

The girl doesn't need further permission. She scoops her child up, leaves, and slams the door shut before either Britney or I move. Britney leans back in her seat.

'Are you ready, Britney?'

'Not just yet. If I have nothing to lose then I've got something to say. Perhaps you'll have another target. I've heard your story. Now hear mine.'

I assume she's playing for time. There's no rush, and I give her a nod.

'My father beat us kids rotten. He was a cocaine-snorting psychopath at the weekends. He had no idea what he was doing. By Tuesday, he would be back to work and running his business. He'd apologise for his actions even if he couldn't remember them. Then it'd all start again on Friday night. Celine said she didn't kill my dad. She did though. I know it because of what he did to me.

'We knew all the guys who he scored his drugs off. Everyone did. I went to the police and gave them their names. I was a minor and my conditions for cooperation were that they kept Celine and me out of it. A father and son ran the scene back then. They got eighteen years. Someone stabbed the father to death in prison.

'They learned their trade from their grandfather. He was a ruthless man who'd run a big empire before handing it down to his offspring. He's still alive, and hates me because he suspects I gave the police enough information to trap them. I ruined his life. He fumed when Celine and I took over. What could he do? He was an old man with a dodgy back. He was yesterday's news. You should wipe out the Colonel before you go. It would be a favour to me.'

The Colonel. What were Hardy's words all that time ago, just before I beat him to death with the hammer? He said that the Colonel ordered him to do it.

'Tell me about this Colonel.'

She talks, I question. It must be him. Five minutes later, I am incredulous of life's little peculiarities. The Colonel is the short-tempered old fart who lives next to the green. For over fifty years, I've been walking by the house of the man who ordered my family killed. He's been living near a policeman for about ten. Unbelievable.

I stand to leave. 'Come with me. We'll pay him a visit.'

'No way. You're the Snow Killer. You'll shoot me outside.'

My reputation precedes me. She stands and stares me down, which is unsettling. I can't place my thoughts in the right order. I have to finish this, but I need to get to the Colonel. Another thought occurs to me.

'Where do you get your drugs? The Colonel?'

'No, he's retired. I buy them in bulk from a Bulgarian guy. It's well cheap. Do you want to know where to find him?'

I shake my head. The whole world is at it. I'm too tired for much more.

'Do not talk to the police. I'm going to see him now.'

'I'm not saying anything about this. You understand? I don't want you caught because he has to pay.'

I consider my options. She looks so young in just an over-sized T-shirt. I realise she must be freezing.

'Do you deserve to live?' I ask.

'I want a chance,' she says.

My finger flexes on the trigger. Her eyes close. The enclosed space magnifies the bang. It's deafening. Britney's mouth opens and closes. She stares down at the wound and collapses onto the sofa. I open the door and hear Dwayne's door open. An enormous round man with ginger hair comes out of his room. I raise my arm and point the gun at his head.

'Back inside. Anyone steps outside in the next five minutes, I start shooting.'

The ginger man remains calm, as if he's been in this position before. Police. I don't have much time.

63

DI BARTON

DI Barton's phone rings. Ginger's name is on the screen.

'Barton.'

'It's me, I'm with Britney. She was staying with her girlfriend at the same hostel as bloody Dwayne Tyne. The Snow Killer's just shot her. I've rung for an ambulance and everything else. You aren't going to believe this.'

'I might, if you're about to tell me it's a woman.'

There's a pause on the line. 'How did you know?'

'The child who survived was a fifteen year old girl called Veronica Smith. She disappeared from the hospital after leaving for some fresh air with her uncle. I presume your shooter is in her late-sixties.'

'Yes, that's right.'

'It has to be her. We've managed to determine her date of birth, but there's no Veronica Smith listed in this area. There isn't a Veronica Smith on the local electoral roll either, never mind trying to match the age. Is Britney going to make it?'

'Yeah, she got shot in the leg, but she's not talking. She also warned her girlfriend not to say anything. I'm not sure why. I'll get the guys out looking if you want, but the Snow Killer is armed and dangerous. PAVA spray won't be enough.'

'The Armed Response Vehicle should be on its way. Do you know which direction she went?'

'No, I thought she was going to shoot me. Her finger twitched on the trigger while she pointed it at my head. It was a horrible feeling. I had total clarity that I didn't want to die. Crazy eh? I never believed for a moment the killer would be an old woman. There must be quite a few living around here.'

Barton suddenly remembered. 'Oh my God. I know who it is.'

64

DI BARTON

The snow fell. More a fine mist as opposed to big flakes. It swirled and fluttered as the passing cars blew it around, which meant he couldn't see much further than the end of his bonnet. Luckily, he didn't have far to go. When he pulled into the village and the traffic eased, he put his foot down and controlled the skids. He'd told Ginger to wait at the property for him and to arrange for the armed unit to cover the building. DC Malik clenched his fists next to him. Barton still hadn't been able to get hold of DCI Naeem.

He arrived at the property as a woman in a green uniform helped Britney into the back of an ambulance. Barton stopped them from closing the rear door.

'Half a minute?'

'And no more,' said the paramedic.

'Tell me what you know, Britney.'

Britney stroked the thick bandage on her leg. She smiled at him.

'I think it was Meryl Streep.'

The paramedic laughed and slammed the door shut.

DS Strange, ashen faced, appeared at his shoulder. Barton almost asked after her health but settled for a breezy, 'Okay?'

'Fine,' she replied.

Sirena, the CSM, had been in the police station when he'd left and said she'd follow. She drove into the area in front of them and gave Barton a wave that reminded him of one he'd received in an assembly at school from a girl who then proceeded to stalk him.

Strange tutted next to him. 'She's an oxymoron.'

'What's one of them?'

'In her case, she's an intelligent fool. Bright lady, but she must be mad to find your lumbering ass attractive.'

Barton smiled. His relationship with Strange was changing. Two uniforms were leading the baby and mother towards a patrol car with flashing lights. Barton found Ginger inside the shared kitchen. He had contained the crime scene. Two very normal men with rifles stood next to him as well as DS Zander and DC Whitlam. Barton nodded at the younger rifleman.

'Listen up, guys,' said Barton. 'That retired Inspector Griffin who lives down my street had a neighbour in his bungalow when I visited a while back. At the time, I didn't know Griffin's name. When I asked her, she said that she calls him Mr Smith. He was asleep. When I mentioned that to him later, he didn't know anything about it; said his name had always been Griffin.'

Barton stared at their blank faces. 'Her name is Smith, not his. She was messing with me.'

'Wow, that is icy behaviour,' said Whitlam.

Barton glowered at him. 'Do you admire her? Scary is a better description, there is no wow.' Barton thought for a moment. 'She was short, yes?'

Ginger nodded.

'This little old lady lives down your street?' asked Strange.

'I'm an idiot. I've also seen her in a white coat. I just never thought it would be a woman. She's been living as Ronnie Smith, not Veronica. Let's go there now and at least block the cul-de-sac off. How about you boys kick the door down?'

The younger of the two armed men laughed. 'I'm not kicking

anything with a loaded gun behind it if I can help it. Your man here brought me up to speed on the whole thing. You think she'll have returned to her house after being rumbled?'

Barton frowned. 'Probably not. She'll know we're looking for her now that Ginger's seen her close up. Unless she's gone back for an OK Corral type ending.'

'Exactly. We don't have the equipment for that sort of situation. I'll ring for the Tactical Firearms Unit. They'll send a van. They've got smoke grenades, sniper rifles and the rest if necessary.'

'How long will that take?' asked Strange.

'They should be here within the hour,' the older rifleman answered. 'I'm on that team too, so I understand the procedures. We all have other jobs because we have few shootouts.'

Barton knew that. He had never been at a scene where they'd called the TFU.

'Call them up, then. What's your name?'

'I'm Jules Cureton. Call me Jules. Everyone knows Alistair.'

'Yes, I trained Alistair when he first started.'

Alistair, a short barrel-chested man with a Scottish accent, laughed. 'Aye, and it took me a long time to unlearn it afterwards.'

'Okay, Jules, Al, what's the process with approaching the house?' asked Barton.

They got Barton to explain the layout of the street. He filled them in on what he suspected and the history of the snow killings.

Jules replied. 'We'll cordon off the road halfway down. She's armed with a pistol at least, so she might be a threat to the public. However, this sounds like scores being settled. If she's there and in the bungalow and there aren't any hostages, at least she's contained.'

Al took over. 'This isn't TV. That's her house, and she knows the layout. Going in there blind would be extremely dangerous and unnecessary if lives aren't at risk. We'll cover the exits and she'll come out when she's ready. If she leaves shooting, we take her down, but they rarely do. Most times they give up or turn the gun on themselves.'

'Will we go down the street with sirens blaring?'

'I was coming to that,' said Jules. 'It's a residential road. We need to get everyone inside or preferably elsewhere if they've got somewhere they can go. That'll be easier if people aren't panicking. We'll park up like we're visiting a friend. I doubt she will have gone back anyway. In this weather, even if she has, she may not even see us. Once the area is controlled, the negotiator will communicate by loudspeaker or we'll ring them if we can get the number. Failing that, we throw a mobile phone through the window.'

Barton's phone rang. He spoke quickly and quietly and finished the call.

'That's DCI Naeem. She's on her way. Go ahead with the containment but don't try to initiate contact until she arrives. She'll sort the negotiator.'

Zander cleared his throat. 'I'm poised and ready.'

Barton wondered about the man's state of mind for the job, but of all the people present, only Zander had trained for it. Barton briefed those attending with the order in which the vehicles would arrive and sent DC Whitlam to the hospital to see if he could prise any more information out of Britney.

Had he missed anything? There didn't seem to be anyone else as a target he could think of now she'd got to both of the sisters. Was her work done? He couldn't say why, but he didn't think so.

65

Barton cast a worried look at his house as they coasted down the street. He needed to stop this killer. In his mind, he expected an empty, barren wilderness devoid of life and a view littered with frozen cars. Instead, he gazed at two little kids in bright yellow jackets sliding in the snow at the end of the cul-de-sac. A shiny blue car drove past them, which must have just come out of a garage to be so clean. Barton stopped fifty metres from the bottom of the street where Jules said they would form an outer cordon to keep people and traffic out.

The response vehicle carried on and parked opposite the house but on the other side of the road. The man who lived next door to Veronica Smith shovelled snow from his path. He slowly rose as the men with guns took positions to cover the house. The shovel dropped from his hands.

Jules beckoned Barton's team to start. They'd agreed that the detective team would clear people off the street while the firearm pair covered the property. Jules and Al wanted to get the road empty as fast as possible and thought that it was safer to do it straight away rather than wait for a shooter to come out blazing.

Barton's people spread out. Shovel guy's mouth dropped

open and he moved towards his kids. Barton directed Strange and Rodgers to collect the kids. He instructed Zander and Malik to go to each house and inform the residents.

Barton approached the now worried man.

'I'm Detective Inspector Barton. We have a situation here and need everyone in their houses. Are they your children?'

'Yes.' He put his arm around their shoulders after they were shepherded over. 'What's happening?'

'We'll go inside to discuss this.' It wasn't a choice.

Barton asked Strange and Rodgers to help the door knockers, especially as Smith's bungalow looked so innocuous. There were no lights on, and the lounge curtains were wide open.

Once inside the neighbour's house, the man took his kids' coats and boots off, gave them a bag of crisps each, and plonked them in front of the TV. He ushered Barton into the kitchen.

'I don't understand,' he said.

'I can't explain too much, but there could be a dangerous person next door.'

'In Ronnie's bungalow?'

'Yes. How well do you know her?'

The man considered his answer. 'Not particularly, to be honest. She's quiet. We see her walking around, and she says hello. She sometimes buys the kids sweets from the shop, but she gives them to me, not them. Just so I'm happy and can stop them eating them all at once. I usually clear her path of snow.'

Barton couldn't remember the condition of the path. 'How long have you been out in the street today?'

'A good while. At least three quarters of an hour. We came straight out after my wife went to work, so 9:00.'

Barton wracked his brain. Britney was shot after that, so if the Snow Killer had returned, this man would have seen her coming.

'Did you see Ronnie return to her house this morning, around 9:15?'

'No, that's what I'm trying to say. I saw her yesterday morning when she was getting in a taxi. I asked her if she wanted her path cleared and she said no because she'd be away for a few weeks.'

'You haven't seen her since?'

'No, she had a suitcase with her. I assumed she was off to the airport or something.'

'Okay. Hopefully we'll get this resolved fast. Do you have somewhere else you can stay today? A relative?'

'My sister lives just around the corner in Baggswell Lane. I could go there.'

Barton shook his head. 'That's too close. No, stay here for the moment. Do not set foot outside and keep away from the windows at the rear and side. Pull down the blinds if you have any. I'll be back soon.'

Barton had a final thought. 'Can you recall the name of the taxi company?'

'A2B. I remember because it's the same firm I use.'

When he returned outside, DCI Naeem approached on foot. They got in Barton's car.

'The neighbours have been informed. Anything else to update me with?'

'I've just spoken to the immediate neighbour. She left yesterday with a suitcase, telling him that she was going away for a while. Took an A2B taxi. The house looks empty. He's been shovelling snow and playing with his kids out here since nine. He didn't see her come back. I don't think she's there.'

'Right. I'll check the situation with the ARV guys.'

'I reckon I should go and knock. We're wasting time here.'

'Don't be daft, John. I know you want to solve this, but we don't do anything stupid. There's no risk to anyone if she's in there. We don't want her to start shooting. The TFU will be here soon. Control the neighbours for me.'

'I'd like to be the negotiator.'

'No problem. Shall I see if they have a course running this morning for you?'

Barton sighed. The course had been on his development plan for seven years.

'The more time we spend here, the better chance she has of getting away.'

'We don't put lives in danger, you know that. The duty Super is Braithwaite. He's initiating the major incident plan and will be Gold Commander. He'll make the calls with Firearms and the Tactical Advisor. They've summoned a negotiator. I'm Bronze Commander dealing here until the unit arrives.'

'Shall I just get a few coffees from my house?'

'That's the spirit, John.'

'I was joking.'

'We'll only try to initiate contact when everyone's here, and further decisions will be made from that point onwards. We could be here for days.'

Barton stomped back to his home. And still it snowed.

66

DI BARTON

Barton left his house twenty minutes later with three flasks and some plastic cups. Holly had agreed to take their family to a friend's house until the situation was resolved. DCI Naeem was still in his car. 'Anything?'

'No. The property looks very empty.'

'I'll ring A2B taxis. I should have done it straight away, sorry.'

'That's okay. I didn't think of that immediately either. Zander rang them. They were a little evasive, so he's gone down to talk to them personally.'

The Firearms Unit parked up, and Barton spotted heavily armed men slip down the sides of the neighbouring houses. Naeem remained permanently on the phone. The remaining neighbours had been warned to keep away from the windows. Barton could see another cordon further up. He noticed the odd vehicle stopped there and turned around. Just the BMW of the Armed Response team and the newly arrived truck were behind it.

Malik knocked on a window and told them that everyone they'd spoken to in the other properties had left. Barton asked after the retired Inspector, but Zander had said no one answered the door. At that point, Naeem finished her call and let out a deep breath.

'What's the plan, Boss?' said Barton.

'We watch the property. It looks dead but Gold Command doesn't want any risks taken. He wants her alive.' Naeem rolled her eyes at him. 'The negotiator's ETA is five minutes. He'll deal from my car. If we have no contact by midday then they'll deliver a mobile phone.'

The negotiator turned up thirty minutes later. Barton recognised him. He was a florid man who smelled as if he'd run behind schedule because he'd been to Burger King. Barton liked the smell and the man. He knew his job. Two hours later, after repeated failed attempts with the loudhailer, two armoured men edged towards the front door. One held the ballistics shield while the other posted an envelope containing a mobile through the letter box. They both retreated. The snow had stopped, so Barton could see the front window. Nothing moved.

Three hours later, Barton watched as an armed team of four battered the door down with a ram. Five minutes later, one of them came out. She indicated an empty house to Naeem.

Naeem and Barton made their way inside. With a shattered entrance, it felt like walking into a freezing crypt. On the kitchen table they found a note to them.

Dear Police. Thanks for popping in. If you have the chance, water the plants.

Two hours later, the armed officers had departed apart from Jules and Al, who secreted themselves under a neighbour's carport. They would be relieved by another unit at 22:00. The road was reopened, and the team left. They'd leave the situation like that for the moment in case she returned but that didn't seem likely. A neighbouring county needed the Firearms Unit for a drugs raid. CSI would arrive in the morning.

There had been no sightings or further intel on Veronica

Smith. A taxi card was found in the house, but Zander had already tracked her to the Marriott Hotel where she'd left her clothes and wash bag. A despondent team returned to the incident room. DCI Naeem entered the office. Her shoulders drooped like many others.

'Thanks for today,' she said. 'It's been a strange one. The girl who survived the shootings in the sixties was a Veronica Smith. She vanished, never to be seen again. We've confirmed the identity of the shooter as Ronnie Smith. It looks like the same woman, but their dates of birth don't match. A year younger and a different day and month.'

Zander put his hand up. 'She could have changed it when she took the name Ronnie Smith.'

'Yes, that's most likely. Britney Chapman will be fine. The bullet penetrated the fleshy part of her thigh. Why wasn't she killed like the others? Ginger said that he didn't disturb the shooter. She was already finished so where is she now? Her house has been left as though she won't be returning, and her toothbrush, amongst other things, remains in the hotel room.'

'She could be leaving the country,' said Strange.

'There's no passport for Ronnie Smith. Her cupboards are full of medication, which we've linked to Parkinson's disease. We can't get to her medical records, but that makes me think she might be ending it soon. Any thoughts? Yes, John.'

'I don't understand letting Britney live at all. Look how ruthless she's been with the other kills. We must have missed something. I know we're checking other hotels, although I assume she would pay in cash. Her family are all dead, so that limits our options. She literally could be anywhere in the country.'

Ginger spoke up. 'Not with Parkinson's. I don't believe she intends to live very long. She'd need to keep in touch with her doctor for repeat prescriptions, or she would've taken the pills with her. Perhaps she's going to do something dramatic. She might already have taken her own life.'

'I've got a theory.' Strange jumped to her feet. 'Shit, why

didn't I think of this before? We thought Celine was the big cheese, but she'd been straight for years when she died; a model citizen, in fact. Britney still dealt, but she's hardly the type to be running a crime syndicate. Where is she getting her product from? There's got to be someone fairly local further up the chain.'

Naeem wrote Britney's name on the board. 'Brilliant, Kelly.' She pointed an arrow upwards from Britney. 'Who is it here? Britney doesn't want to tell us anything as it incriminates her. Did Smith spare her because she revealed this person's name? I bet that's where she's gone. The head of the snake is all that remains. We need to find out who Mr or Mrs Big is around here. If the Snow Killer is still alive, they're going to be next.'

It's just past nine at night, and the Colonel and I are struggling. After shooting Britney, I strode to the Colonel's property as fast as I could. Unsure what to do and not wanting to hang around in the cold opposite the detective's house, I rang his doorbell. He opened it and clung to the doorframe. It was difficult to believe the things that Britney told me. But time has no friends. We all wither under its assault. I know that as surely as anyone.

He attempted to shut the door on me but stopping him was no effort at all. I shoved him into the house and he wobbled backwards, glancing at the floor with fear. When I got him back to the lounge, he collapsed into an armchair, gasping. I hunted through his drawers to find something to restrain him. I might have known he'd have duct tape. Well, it was actually packing tape, but that was fine for a weak old man. I wound it around the big recliner, under his armpits, and around his chest. It made me laugh – the ridiculousness of it – until I remembered what he'd done.

This wasn't planned. I intended to go to the church up the road. This morning should have been the end. I could have lain down next to my family in the far corner of the frozen church-yard and joined them.

The Colonel remembered seeing me over the years but he just knew me as someone who lived near his house. Nothing more. So, I talked him through a story about an innocent young girl and her family from long ago. Three assassins were ordered to kill them all, but one of the children survived. With ice in her heart, she avenged those deaths by taking the murderers' lives. She became the Snow Killer. The final man to die, in his desperate attempt to stay alive, gave up a name. His commands, he implored, came from the Colonel.

Even back then I understood that everybody lies, and I'd had enough. The men who killed my family were dead themselves. It was the moment to move on, but not, as it turned out, move house. Fate has a sick sense of humour. I spent the next fifty years waving and passing the time of day with the man who instructed those men to wipe out all who were dear to me.

I wanted the truth but the Colonel refused to provide it. Threatening him with the gun didn't work. Death rarely strikes terror into the old. It holds no fears for me. I placed my pistol on the floor and drew out the Stanley knife. Tape over his mouth silenced the screams. It's a gruesome task, cutting someone for answers. We played that game for an hour.

I realised he'd die happy if it meant his secrets departed with him. He was as ready for the end as I was. This world frightened and confused him in the same way as it did me. I found a first-aid kit in the bathroom. I removed some of the tape and patched him up, but most of the blood had dried anyway. He fell asleep, and I allowed him to dream. Shadows lengthened and I, too, dropped off. He was staring at me when I woke. Before I was fully roused, he spoke.

'Do you believe in God? I refused to have faith. But now, I wonder. I'd like there to be something more. I'd love to see my son and daughter again.'

I rubbed my eyes. 'I think you'd struggle when it came to the final judgement.'

'Is it too late to say sorry?'

'Do you regret your choices? Tell me the truth.'

'I suppose you deserve answers. I might as well give you them. Judging by the way you walk and those tremors, your race is nearly run.'

I rose from my seat and made a pot of tea. I wasn't sure I wanted to hear the facts now they were forthcoming. I placed his cup next to the recliner and cut the ties that restrained his hands.

He spoke slowly and with thought. 'I never knew your family. I ran the Peterborough drug business for a mate in London who brought the stuff into the country. I worked hard but fair. There were punishments, for sure, but no one died. He dealt with bigger volumes and his penalties were on a grander scale. Your father worked for him in a variety of roles. Delivery-man, dealer, but mostly as a hitman. London is a different place. He had become a hopeless, reckless addict. My friend wasn't his boss, heroin was. And that was his downfall.

'He ripped my pal off twice, once for drugs and finally for money. Most people don't get a second chance, no one a third. Your father didn't deserve one. I got ordered to kill him. They said to spare nobody. You'd be surprised at how many children seek revenge when they grow up.' He coughed or laughed. It was hard to tell. 'Look at you. This is what he tried to prevent. Luckily for him, he's long gone.'

I didn't feel anger. These were facts, not feelings. I would respond in kind.

'My sister had severe disabilities. I'm not sure what you call it nowadays. Additional needs or something. She wasn't capable of seeking retribution.'

'I didn't know that. How could I? After the hit was done, we forgot about it. We read you'd survived, but you were a child with brain damage. Years later, when the others began to die, we were involved in a turf war. I never suspected an eighteen year old girl would come back from the dead and take them out in that way. Anyway, my crew won the battle. The fighting stopped, and life continued. I had a wife, children, and finally grandchildren. If I'm honest, I didn't think about your family again, or the other people I hurt over the years. When my wife died of cancer and my daughter died of an overdose, I started to wonder if Him upstairs had it in for me. Vengeance is mine, sayeth the Lord.

'I had a stroke a decade ago. He must have been watching. My son ran the business with my grandson until the police finally caught them. We'd had a good run, and they were only arrested when someone grassed us up. I guessed it was the bloody Chapmans. The judge jailed the whole crew apart from me. They had superficial evidence on my involvement from years back, but I struggled to walk more than fifty metres. I couldn't cause much trouble in a wheelchair.

'Someone stabbed my son to death in prison, and I'll be gone by the time they release my grandson. Criminal friends aren't real friends, and now I'm alone. Justice was served though because you killed Celine and her boyfriend. Do you know I'm Britney's godfather? We were close once. She used to come and stay when she was young. The last words she said to me were, "I'll piss on your grave." I suspect you threatened her, and she dropped me in it. The circle is nearly complete.'

We drank our tea and listened to the weather against the windows and ominous ticks from painted radiators. I wondered where mercy had gone. I had none. Besides, I doubted his sincerity. 'You don't seem sorry to me.'

He smiled.

I'd turned the lights off when I entered. We'd spoken in the gloom with the only light reflecting from the swirling snowflakes. I left my seat and cleared a hole in the misty window. Hours ticked by as I considered my existence. I began at the night when Special died. Thoughts of Uncle Ronnie crowded my mind for a while, and then my memory jumped to my later actions. I relived the recent killings and how I got to be standing where I am now. Was there anything in between the deaths? Nothing of substance, it seems. Where did fifty years go?

Mine is a life highlighted by death. So much water under the bridge; so much blood in the snow.

* * *

I duck down from the window as headlights from a large car cruising into the cul-de-sac opposite dazzle me. It's the detective. Standing next to the curtain, I watch him climb from the vehicle. He looks my way. Has he seen me? What do I do now? He disappears into his house but comes out shortly afterwards carrying something. Through the spiralling snowflakes, he fades down the path towards my end of the street.

I decide the original plan still works. A final question remains. It's the last piece of the puzzle. Slowly, I turn to the Colonel.

'We're going for a walk. Don't worry, it's not far. Just along the road to the church. You can apologise to my parents in person.'

'I can't walk that distance.'

'I know you have wheels. Is there a finer place to ask for forgiveness?'

'What if I don't want to go? What's the worst you can do?'

He heaves himself to the edge of his seat and, with a rolling technique, gets to his feet. Despite that, he stands there proud. He's enjoyed an existence that he denied my sister. My heart freezes, and I see a way.

'Or should I kill you here? Better still, I'll maim you in such a manner that you live the rest of your life in a nappy. Blind and castrated.'

As I suspected, he doesn't want that being his legacy. We put our coats on at the door in silence, as though we are leaving a fine restaurant after a bad meal. Crime does pay, and his electric scooter glints brilliantly when I turn on the light. I support him into it and whisper in his ear.

'I have one last thing for you to tell me on the way.'

His eyes narrow. The doorway has been modified, and it's

easy getting out of the front door, but the wind screams. An unearthly squall speeds the scooter along the icy ramp and onto the drive. It slips and slides down the paving, through the twirling mist that fills the air, and out of sight.

I leave the door swinging and tread through the grass for a better grip. I find the Colonel at the edge of the road. His hat has gone and manic eyes stare at me. He laughs, pushes the lever forward and trundles across the street onto the far pavement. I can't see anyone else around, but that isn't surprising. I can hardly see anything. The wind pauses, and I shuffle after him, nearly losing my balance on the ice.

Even in my boots, progress is slow, and I realise he's trying to escape. His urge to survive surprises me but at least he's heading in the right direction. A thumping gust shoves me, and I bounce off a wall. My shoulder throbs, but the structure stopped me from being blown away. Dim yellow street lights fail to pierce the white air around me.

I'm blinded by a blast of icy particles and bump into his chair. He's stuck in a thick bank of snow. I tug him free and hold onto the handles at the back. It pulls us to a deadly conclusion. His ride must be state-of-the-art because it copes with my weight and the snow covered gravel of the path to the church-yard with ease. The front gate is unlocked. Someone must be inside the church as the lights are on. Floodlights beam up the side of the stone walls. The soft glow of those and the fog make the church look as if it's floating on a cloud.

I pull the lead out of the battery at the rear of the chair.

'Not quite ready to die, then, Colonel? Now, answer my final question.'

68

DI BARTON

DCI Naeem sent them all home at 21:00 after the paperwork was done and the last few leads chased. There were no further developments. Barton cruised into the village and parked on his drive. The weather had taken a severe turn for the worse. The wind bucked and screamed as though in pain. It whipped the dry snow around, making him feel as if he were struggling on the peak of a mountain. It wasn't even snowing, but the visibility had switched from fifty metres to ten in seconds. The thought of hot soup was calling him. He had an early start again in the morning.

The Colonel's house was uncharacteristically as dark and empty as Ronnie Smith's residence had been. Barton considered checking on him but couldn't really be arsed. He thought he saw someone move near the window. The man would no doubt moan about all the disruption during the day when he collared him next.

He remembered Al and Jules parked up at the bottom of the cul-de-sac. They'd had a long day, too. With that in mind, he nipped into his house and took a pack of ready-to-eat small sausage rolls out of the fridge. After a minute in the microwave, they were soggy, but the lads wouldn't care. Four each should be enough. Holly came into the kitchen as he popped the spare two in his mouth. She shook her head and he tried to talk, burning his tongue in the process.

He grumbled to himself along the path. She constantly told him to eat healthily, so why put things like that in the fridge? If he was a heroin addict, she wouldn't leave syringes full of the good stuff in the salad box and tell him to use his willpower.

Halfway down the street, the wind picked up again. The snow swirled in all directions. Visibility dropped to near zero, and he assumed that this was what they meant by a whiteout. The surrounding houses disappeared, and if he hadn't known the street like the back of his hand, he might have got lost. The police X5 remained in the carport next to retired Inspector Griffin's property. He could make out two fuzzy round lights. As he approached, the only thing that stood out was Griffin's red door.

He had a thought. Zander probably didn't know to knock on the back door earlier because Griffin wouldn't hear the front doorbell. They'd asked the other neighbours if they had any idea where Ronnie Smith might have gone, but no one knew anything about her. Barton did know that she'd spent some time with Griffin. Maybe he could point them in the right direction.

He walked around the rear of the property and hammered on the door. Griffin answered it in a shirt and badly tied tie combined with a pair of pyjama trousers. The fronts of the former were stained, and the latter had a worrying wet patch at his groin.

'Morning. Burton, isn't it, from down the road? How can I help you?'

Barton was unsure whether it would just unsettle the man to correct him. 'How are things? Are you okay?'

'Fine. Watching the news. I'm going to have a cup of coffee, I think.'

By all accounts, this individual had wielded considerable power by the end of his career in the force. He'd never been a friendly man: in fact, this was the nicest conversation Barton could remember having with him. But this seemed a poor end to a life. He wouldn't wish this lonely confusion on anyone.

'I'll make it. You go and sit down.'

Barton ushered him into the lounge. His breath froze in the air. He inspected the gas fire and deduced it had been blocked off. The TV show seemed to be a documentary about the sex trade in Thailand. He wasn't sure if Mr Griffin would enjoy that or not. Instead, he put it on BBC1 and settled Griffin in his chair. Barton flicked the kettle on and located the boiler while he waited. He found it on continuous. The thermostat in the lounge, though, had been turned as low as possible. At three degrees, it clicked. Twenty-two should be fine, he thought.

The cupboards were surprisingly well stocked. Within a few minutes, Barton had discovered a large jumper on the back of the sofa, placed it over the man's head, made him a strong cup of coffee, and set a plate with five chocolate digestives and an immense piece of Victoria sponge in front of him.

'Has Mrs Smith from over the road been around?'

'Who?'

'The lady who lives opposite and helps out?'

'Ah, her. She pops over on Sundays, so maybe today?' His eyebrows raised, so Barton agreed with him, despite it being Monday.

'Yes. Do you know her very well?'

Griffin's face dropped. 'Sorry, lad, but I can't remember. I can't seem to recall much about her. I don't think she likes me, but I guess she must do if she comes over.'

'I don't suppose you're aware of any places she visits, or people she meets?'

'What did you say her name was again? She's lived opposite me for a long time. I remember her telling me to get a red door when I told her I needed a new one. I can't recall if that was recently or years ago. She said it would look nice in the snow. Pleasant lady. I tell you where I do see her. She goes to the church up the road. I've often seen her putting flowers on the graves.'

'Do you know which ones?'

Griffin rubbed his forehead. 'That's silly. I don't know that either. I suppose it must be where her family are buried.'

69

The information that the Colonel has given me is in some ways more dramatic than finding out who he was. It's been a day of surprises. The Colonel looks pleased to have shocked me. I point the gun at his privates. 'Out.' He struggles from the chair.

A heavy door clangs behind us. The vicar in full robes fills the doorway, bathed in golden light. His bent back sways as his gaze takes in the scene. I'm too far away to see the colour of his eyes, but I remember they are piercing blue. His look falls upon the Colonel and hardens. I can tell he knows, perhaps, everything. Whose confessions does he hear? No one says anything to the police, but everyone likes to ease their guilt. How many secrets will he take with him when he leaves?

His stare passes to me and softens. His face shows recognition and understanding. He's heard what I did and who I am. He will have seen me amongst the tombstones. I wonder why he didn't tell? Was he scared of me, or maybe he accepted my balancing of the scales? I suspect he protects his own weaknesses. Those of fresh hare and stolen TV sets.

The Colonel cries out, 'Help!'

After making the sign of the cross, the vicar retreats into the radiance behind him. The door bangs shut with finality. Uncle

Ronnie said he'd saved his life once. Maybe he's returning the favour.

I poke the Colonel in the back with the end of the pistol and direct him towards my family's plot. The wind buffets us as we stare at the three headstones. There's a space next to the smaller one for another.

A flurry sprays our bodies with ice from the surrounding bushes. The Colonel drops to his knees. His face is white and he looks as if he could be dead already. He isn't, because his head turns in the direction of the sirens at the same time as mine.

Barton left Griffin's house and stood in the beam of the police vehicle next door. Jules popped his head out.

'Jesus, I spotted a dark figure and thought it was her. You're lucky. We discussed filling you with lead and asking questions later, but neither of us wanted to open the window.'

'Very amusing. Let me in, it's freezing out here.'

Barton climbed into the warmth of the BMW X5. It felt like stepping out of an air-conditioned aircraft into the heat when you arrive in a tropical country. He handed them the sausage rolls. Al held the bag up.

'Couldn't you have pinged them in the microwave?' he asked.

Barton didn't bother to explain. 'I take it she hasn't shown?'

'We have no idea,' said Al, stuffing a roll in his mouth. 'Ah, nice. Warm too.'

While Al munched with a smile, Jules explained. 'We can't really see anything from here. It clears every now and again when the wind dips and it stops snowing, but she could easily have sneaked home without us noticing. The commanders told us to keep an eye out but not engage. They don't expect her to return, and they don't think Joe Public is at risk. What are you doing here, anyway?'

'The plan was to bring you those healthy snacks. Then I had an idea to ask the guy who lives opposite if he had any idea as to where she might have gone. Maybe he knew about other friends, that sort of thing.'

'What did he say?' asked Jules.

'He didn't know the day of the week, so we have to take his info with a pinch of salt, but he said she goes to the local church-yard. A line of thinking is that now she's got to Britney, she'll commit suicide. If her family are buried there, she might have visited for one final goodbye, or even to die next to their graves.'

'It's possible. Are you going there now? Stay out in this too long and it would be suicide. We'll come with you. We aren't doing any good sitting here. It'll only take a few minutes, and if she's there, you'll have back up.'

'Okay, do you want to let Control know?'

'Yeah, sure. The radio isn't working, but my mobile's fine.'

Al pulled out of the carport and crawled down the street. At points, the car slid around as though they were driving on a frozen river. Jules rang Control and said he'd call in fifteen minutes with an update. Barton remembered DS Strange and DC Rodgers were on call tonight. He sent them both a text to say he was en route to Orton Longueville church after an idea and that he'd keep them posted.

The guys in the front didn't seem worried about the almost featureless landscape. Barton noticed a light on at the Colonel's and the door swinging in the breeze, but heavy snow had begun to fall once more. Al distracted him by putting the sirens on.

'Best to let her know we're coming this time,' he said. 'If she's caught exposed, she might shoot first.'

Barton directed them to a place to park at the front of the church. The men marched to the boot of their vehicle to get their weapons while Barton walked to the gate and peered over it. The stone tower shimmered in and out of view a hundred metres away. The walls appeared to be a mass of twirling steam with the lights shining on them, as if they were smoking. He scanned the graveyard for signs of life. Suddenly, a figure came out of nowhere pointing a gun. He stepped back from the gate, but she was already leaning against it and targeted his chest.

'Freeze, Inspector Barton. If you'll pardon the pun.'

71

Barton's eyes fixed on the pistol. Dark liquid dripped from the handle. He glanced up into the pale face of a well-kept pensioner. She even wore a touch of bright red lipstick. She'd been wearing that the time he had nearly run her over. He recalled she was wearing a white coat. Celine had tried to talk as she died. He'd thought she was saying hold, but did she mean old?

Calm eyes returned his look. He didn't know what to do. This woman had seen her family killed. Who could predict her mental state? She was the Snow Killer. One mistake and he'd die on this frozen ground.

He heard the sounds of rifles being loaded behind him. He put his hands up and shouted over to the two men. 'Don't shoot. We're talking.' He turned back and watched her finger move onto the trigger.

'I'm talking,' she said. 'You're listening. I'm sure you have the background story of the Snow Killer by now. The press will receive a letter upon my death. There were things I didn't know though. I only discovered some information today. When I avenged my family all those years ago, the final victim mentioned that his boss had ordered the hit. A man they called the Colonel.'

Barton shuddered, and it wasn't through the cold. A thin voice echoed through the graves. 'Help me. I'm here.'

She scowled. 'There will be no saving him.'

'Come on, Veronica. There's been too much killing.'

Her eyes narrowed. 'From what I've learned today, perhaps there hasn't been enough. This chapter needs closing. Captains, Majors, Colonels, wall-to-wall corruption, you police couldn't catch a cold, even in this weather.'

Barton realised he risked provoking her but decided to try to talk her down nonetheless.

'Some of those people you killed were innocent.'

A tear trickled from her right eye. She wiped it away with the back of her hand and sighed. A sad smile flickered on her face.

'Perhaps. I'm trying to close the circle, but maybe I'm just making a new one.'

'Why did you kill Brick and Terry?'

'Are you trying to tell me Terry was innocent? He had a record like a screenplay.'

'Okay, perhaps. Brick, though, was only a labourer. He led a simple life. There was no malice in him at all, and certainly no criminal record.'

'He dated a known drug dealer.' Veronica's voice crackled.

'We thought so, too. Celine had been involved in crime when she was younger but went straight years ago. We were wrong about her as well. We've been picking her up and trying to charge her for stuff she knew nothing about. She'd turned her life around. Brick met her after that. She was just an attractive, successful businesswoman to him.'

Her head dropped and he pressed his advantage, urging her. 'Let him go. No one else needs to die, least of all you. We can get you the help you need. I know you're also a victim in this.'

He thought for a moment she would hand him the gun. An icy blast whipped her words away.

'What did you say?'

'I said, nice try. Everything comes back to my parents' deaths. People who kill don't get leniency. The Colonel will die tonight; so will I. Unless you'd prefer me to escape? Then you could use my name to scare children. This time it would be a bogey-woman. Has there ever been a purer wind than the one blowing through this city? And no, I won't surrender. Why would I? I'd spend the rest of my days rotting in a cell, surrounded by the types I want to rid the world of. Perhaps this was what I was born to do. I spent fifty years treading water. Only now, when I'm dying, do I feel alive.'

'Have mercy, Veronica.'

'The time for forgiveness has passed.'

Barton realised that the young girl, the victim, from all that time ago had gone. This woman needed locking away before she decided someone else deserved her form of justice. He focused on the pistol, only noticing then that it was pointing towards his chin. Seconds drew out as flint eyes bored into his. A laughing Baby Luke was who he thought of as she pulled the trigger and the hammer hit home.

72

THE SNOW KILLER

I can feel the snipers aim on my forehead like a laser beam. I drop behind the gate and scuttle away bent double. My back itches as I wait for a bullet to tear through it. I contemplate returning to the Colonel, but I'm out of ammunition. Those men will kill me, given the chance. They know I'm dangerous but won't consider me a difficult target. What's an old woman with an empty pistol and a Stanley knife going to do against armed policemen with rifles?

They underestimate me. These are my streets. I've been laying flowers in this churchyard for half a century. Every blade of grass, divot, headstone and hiding place is etched into my being. I recall the hole out the back to escape through. I could run now, but the Colonel doesn't deserve to dodge his sentence.

A strange fizz echoes through the gloom and the floodlights die. Then the lights in the church are gone. The wind howls in defiance, too. The tomb that I want is right at the rear. I dodge between the graves and with horror realise that the stone panel has slipped off and is resting on the floor. I ram my hand into the black space and thank the God who deserted me for this last piece of luck. The rifle slides out. I check the magazine: three bullets. There's no margin for error.

73

Al and Jules surround the kneeling Barton.

'Are you all right, John?' asked Jules.

'I'm fine.'

'I thought she shot you,' said Al.

'She did. It wasn't loaded.'

'Could it have been a dud bullet? Was the gun old?'

'It looked ancient, but she knew. She smiled and said, "You get a second chance." I can't believe I pissed myself.'

Despite the seeping chill, Barton's face flushed red. Another begging cry for help carried to them on the wind.

'Don't worry about that. You won't be the last. Only a madman would have done differently,' said Al.

Barton was too shocked to feel relief. Al's comment registered, though. They'd been one step behind in this entire investigation. Not a single person had seriously considered a woman might be responsible, and an old one at that. He imagined his mother with a gun and shook his head. She'd probably be worse.

'John, you still with us? We need to go in. There's someone alive in there. Ring Control and update them. Bring everyone here.'

'The man in there will be the Colonel. But he's already dead.'

A faint cry sounded to contradict his words, but they both knew what he meant.

'John, we're trained marksmen. She won't get away,' said Al.

Barton stood and pulled his phone from his trousers. They'd underestimated Veronica Smith from the beginning. She'd killed at least six people in a variety of different ways. He stared at the backs of Al and Jules as they moved into the churchyard with their weapons raised. Al put out a flat palm gesture to stop Jules. Al cupped his ear. Barton couldn't hear anything as another blast of dry snow stung his head. Using two fingers, Al directed Jules to the left and weaved to the right himself.

Barton watched their tactics, but he finally understood that they were the hunted. She'd stabbed men in the back in the exact place to incapacitate them, shot Brick from a distance only to wound, and blasted Celine in the side so she died slowly with no hope of survival. She was black hearted for sure, but someone had taught her to kill.

He screamed, 'Be careful. She's more dangerous than you think.'

Too late. The men had faded into the mist.

THE SNOW KILLER

The snow has stopped, and I can make out two dark figures in bulletproof vests as they separate. My white coat gives me an advantage. As I hide behind a horse chestnut tree, I realise that I'm no better than those I kill. Hopefully, all this evil will die with me. First, the police need teaching a lesson. No one can save the Colonel.

A line of dense, stunted trees sits along the edge of the graveyard. They have a gap behind them where a small person such as me can creep out of sight. They'll head to the Colonel, so I will need my eyes on him. It's quiet as I crawl through the dead leaves. I have the rifle in the cradle of my arms, just as Uncle Ronnie taught me. There's a hole in the foliage up ahead, and it's perfect. I settle into position.

The Colonel is as still and white as the surrounding statues. The first man comes into view on my left about forty metres away. He stops and takes cover at a large stone with a cherub draped over the top. Mrs Brown's daughter, Daisy, if I recall. Died, aged three, of diphtheria in 1969. He pauses then assumes the position and crawling style that I did. He pulls himself towards the Colonel.

The other guy rises next to a plinth with a weeping, winged

angel leaning over the dead. Mrs Crane's only son, Tommy, still-born in 1974. I remember Mr Crane coming once a week for thirty years, always alone. This second, younger man is more eager, less cautious, and, with a last look around, he sprints towards the prone Colonel. As he puts his hand on the Colonel's neck, I squeeze the trigger and shoot the policeman in the hip just under his vest.

He cries out then immediately silences himself. I hoped the wind would hide my direction, but the branches above me splinter with the impact of bullets. Semi-automatic fire sprays my position. The Virgin Mary, leaning over the grave of Stella Draper who went to sleep in 1985, shatters, blasting stone powder into the atmosphere. I frantically shuffle away as quickly as I can. The initial adrenalin that had kept me going is depleted. My right leg is numb, and the arm on that side trembles. Another volley of shots hits the wall where I hid seconds ago, although it's too random to have been from someone who knows where I am.

I sneak out of my cover, edge around the side of the war memorial, and arc back so I'll be directly behind the more alert shooter. I lean against the headstone of Corporal Craddock, who gave his life for our future, aged eighteen, at Dunkirk, and stare through the sights. My target gestures to his injured partner. He crawls forward on all fours. I pause my breathing and pull the trigger. The bullet enters his right buttock, rewarding me with a howl. He turns and I aim again. Everyone seems very young to me. I watch his life flash before him and raise my head from the sight.

I don't need to offer twice. He drags himself along on his non-injured side towards his colleague. With a brief desperate glance at my position, he pulls the other man and himself out of view. That leaves the Colonel, who lies on his back with his head resting on a granite kerb. He stares at me. Sirens blare nearby.

I waste the remaining round in the Colonel's throat because he doesn't move. The snow killed him and that is right. Moving as fast as I'm able, I skirt away from where I imagine the policemen to be and limp towards the gap in the fence at the back that my dog found all those years ago. It's still there, but the bramble almost beats me. I discard the useless rifle and head for my final task.

Barton listened to the approaching sirens. The last five minutes had dragged out like torture. He'd flinched at each gunshot. There were clearly two types of weapon being fired. A lighter gun and the heavier sound of the AR15, which he recognised from firing one himself at a range. He'd also caught cries of pain from deep voices. It was quiet now. He held his head in his hands. The final report came from the quieter weapon.

The wind had dropped dramatically, almost as if events were over. Tiny flakes of snow fell again as a staggering Jules dragged Al's body out towards the main path. Barton couldn't stop himself. He ran forward, crouched, and, with a silent roar, picked Al up like a sleeping child. He staggered from the churchyard and returned for Jules. Jules hobbled out with support, gasping with pain.

When Barton helped him to the ground, he grabbed Barton's collar.

'She's armed, small calibre rifle. She's fucking deadly, man. Don't go in there. Do not go in there.'

'Calm down, you're okay.'

'I lost it, John. It was complete panic. I sprayed bullets everywhere like a novice.'

'What about the Colonel?'

'He's gone.' Jules shuddered. He attempted to control his breathing. 'She could easily have killed us all.'

Barton examined the wounds. They looked painful but not life threatening. The bullets were still in Al's hip and Jules' arse. Barton's trousers remained wet.

The other Armed Response Vehicle arrived first, then DS Strange and DC Rodgers. Further approaching sirens filled the night. The Tactical Firearms Unit was on its way back and no one was allowed anywhere near the churchyard.

Barton hunched over and held his head.

'Let's take you home,' said Ginger.

He didn't want to go, but he had nothing left. They stopped outside his house.

'Thanks, guys,' he managed as he attempted to push the car door open.

Ginger got out and opened it for him.

'How did you know she'd be at the church?'

Barton gave him a weary smile. 'I asked Griffin down the road where she might be. He said she often went there and left flowers on the graves, so we guessed her family were there and that was where she might be heading.'

'Clever. Shall we pop down and see if he has any other ideas?'

'I suppose it can't hurt. Veronica's probably still holed up in the graveyard. His house is number nineteen. If she turns up, do not engage her. Just drive away and come here.' Before he slammed the door, he added, 'Make sure you go around the back as he won't answer the doorbell.'

I lurch through the woods at the back of the church. A gentle flurry blinds me with ice-white particles as I step into the open and head towards the green near to the BMX track. A dog with a flashing lead bounces around at the copse where the bricklayer died. It's hard to comprehend what I've just done. When did I decide that shooting the police was okay? I've changed. It's almost time to lie in the snow and retire.

Instead, I fill my lungs and force myself onwards. A small lane links up to the road that Black Ermine Street is on, and I stagger along it. I stare at the Colonel's house with the swinging front door. The streets are empty, as you'd expect on such a bitter night. The clouds above have almost disappeared and a full moon gazes down on me. I need to return to my house to get Mr Griffin's back-door key. My damaged front door makes me smile.

I take a piece of paper and write a farewell note, just in case they don't link everything up. Griffin's part in all of this will not die with him. Who knows which stones may upturn? I pad across the road and go around the back.

He's in the kitchen when my key lets me in, peering into his garden. Yet again, there's no surprise at a levelled pistol.

'Do you know who I am?' I ask.

He regards me with an open face. 'No, get out.'

'I am the child who survived the snow killings fifty years ago. I was responsible for the three men murdered in the snow near here, and it was me who killed today.'

There's still no response, so I continue. 'I've just had a chat with the Colonel down the road. He told me some interesting things. I wondered why they arrested nobody for the murder of my family. It turns out you pulled the strings. When Goofy, or Goof as you called him, was killed, you were the investigating officer. You didn't want those cases solved as it might have led back to you.'

It's weird how someone with Alzheimer's can't remember the present, yet the past can play like a soap opera they're unable to stop. All the evidence leads to this worn-out man in a too big green jumper and battered slippers.

'How dare you? I'm a decorated officer with a distinguished career.'

The lack of conviction is damning, even if I didn't know the truth. I shake my head. 'Try again.'

His face drops, but again I am far from convinced. 'They made me do it. They threatened my family.'

'It's strange you say that. The Colonel mentioned that you and he were friends at school. He struggled to believe you joined the force as you were the worst of all of them. He didn't know my father. The people my father stole the money from came from London. The Colonel said it was you who contacted him and requested the hit. It was you who ordered them to slaughter everyone.'

'Are you here to kill me?'

'Yes, I am.'

I circle behind him. My right leg almost gives way. I put my hand with the gun on the work surface to stop me dropping it.

I beckon with my other hand. 'Outside, in the garden. Don't worry. You won't need your coat where you're going.'

He walks past me meekly, out the door, and treads into the middle of the lawn. There's a small bench next to his pond. I tell him to sit on it. He doesn't bother to move the snow, just drops himself down. His breathing struggles with the numbing air.

'Any last words?'

'I don't really understand. I'm not really sure where I am. Why am I on my own?'

'I assume that's because you are a heartless cretin. You have Alzheimer's, which is why you're so confused. Don't fret, you aren't missing much.'

A loud knock sounds on the back door. The snow softens my steps as I tiptoe towards it. A young woman and an older man stand there. I watch them for a few seconds. It looks as if the police have finally solved the case. Maybe there's hope for the future. I clear my throat and wave the pistol in their direction.

'Evening, Officers. Please come into the garden. I'd hate to start shooting.'

They freeze at first. That's understandable. I back away and they follow. The woman's face pinches as she sees the man on the bench. 'Mr Griffin, are you all right?'

'I'll be asking the questions,' I say. I don't think he heard her anyway as his head lolls forward. 'Why are you two here?'

'We came to ask him if he had an idea where you might be,' says the ginger man who wears an enormous thick coat.

'My God, you still haven't got a clue. Can't you see all roads lead to this man? I'm sure someone will put two and two together before his funeral.'

I throw the gun at their feet. They glance at each other, open their hands, but don't move. Understandably so. Eventually, the woman steps forward and picks it up. I expect her to point the weapon at me. Instead, she surprises me and checks if it's loaded. It isn't. The last bullet is in Britney's leg. She throws the gun in the bushes anyway.

'You're under arrest,' she says without conviction.

'Save your breath. We're leaving. Now you're here, you can join us.'

I take Uncle Ronnie's hand grenade out of my pocket. His father agonised over whether to pull the pin out as the enemy approached but I have no such dilemma. No one moves. They wouldn't have been expecting this. I hold it up slowly and remove the pin. There's a moment of worry as the seconds tick by. Is the grenade still live? A final breeze blows snow off the fence tops and, for a second, the world is swallowed in white. Everyone vanishes. As it clears, I see the ginger officer yank the woman back and step in front of her.

77

DI BARTON

His house was still when Barton opened the front door and entered. His family should all have been in bed and the silence confirmed that. It felt so warm and safe. He walked into the lounge and smiled at the mess. His shoulders shook as he fought back a sob. Barton sat on the edge of the sofa. Then he stood up, recalling what he'd done to his trousers. He picked up his little man's T-Rex figure and kissed it on the head.

Would they have caught Veronica by now? The more he thought about it, the more he struggled to understand why she had stayed to shoot the policemen. She could have just finished off the Colonel and left. What next? Would she kill more people? Was there something else she needed to do?

She blamed the police for everything. That was rich considering what she'd done. But she spat out the word 'corruption'. What had she said: wall-to-wall corruption, and then Major and Colonel? He couldn't imagine anyone he worked with being corrupt, or being involved with dealing drugs. Not nowadays. This wasn't about the present, though. He understood that now. He'd guessed himself that the cases back then weren't conducted properly. Who better to hide evidence than the person investigating it?

Inspector Griffin's name was all over the documents. Could he have been involved? If he was, he might get a midnight visit from the Snow Killer, never mind Strange and Rodgers. Suddenly, it dawned on him. Captains, Majors and Colonels. They were ranks in the British army. What came next? General. What had Veronica said about Griffin – that he told her his mates called him Jen? Could that be short for General?

Barton put his coat back on and stepped out of the door. Veronica had shown that even the police were fair game if they got in her way. Barton had told Ginger and Strange to steer clear of any trouble. But if the Colonel had informed the Snow Killer about a General, then she would be heading there next.

With a dry mouth, he hurried down the street. And that was when an almighty boom filled the air.

I try to open my eyes, but only one of them cooperates. All I see are grey clouds above, and I can't hear anything at all. Strange to experience total silence. I'm not in pain, but my mouth is incredibly dry. It takes a few seconds for me to realise I'm on a sheet of ice. My head drops to the side, and I see I'm in the frozen pond. The General waits in his seat except now he doesn't have a face.

My aches are also absent, only this terrible thirst remains. I can touch slippery ice under my left hand. My right hand feels strange. When I raise my arm, I realise that it's gone.

My chest constricts, and I try to pull air into my lungs but manage only a shallow breath. There isn't any chance of me getting up. In fact, I barely have the energy to keep my remaining eye open. It's as though someone is gently pulling it shut.

Detective Barton materialises in my view with frantic eyes. He looks behind him and puts a hand to his mouth. His chin thrusts forward as he stares down at me.

'Why?' he mouths.

As my eye finally closes, I attempt a smile. 'He knows why.'

79

Barton sat on the bed and stared at Kelly Strange's sleeping face. He had no tears left. He'd arrived to find three bodies lying on the snow and a bloody corpse on a small bench. The air seethed with the taste of metal and the sickening smell of burning flesh. Strange and Ginger Rodgers were still breathing. Veronica Smith died as he stared down upon her.

Ginger's body rested slightly on top of Kelly's and it was obvious, looking at his blackened back, that he'd taken the brunt of the explosion. Barton rang for an ambulance. Strange sobbed. Ginger's layers had protected everywhere apart from his head. Barton used his hand to staunch the bleeding while he screamed at Ginger to open his eyes.

The paramedics were already at the church, so the ambulance arrived two minutes later and blue-lighted the pair of them away. DCI Naeem ran to him and grabbed his shoulders. He didn't remember much else.

Kelly's injuries were superficial apart from a piece of shrapnel entering her lower back. He didn't know exactly what damage that had caused, but she'd miscarried the baby. They kept her sedated, but she had been told. The tears that leaked down the side of her face at times broke his heart a little more.

The door opened behind him, and Zander walked in. They hugged without embarrassment. Zander had gone to check on Ginger, who'd been scheduled an emergency operation on his brain.

'How's Ginger?'

'The worst news, I'm afraid. There's nothing they could do. They're contacting his next of kin before they turn the machine off.'

Barton reflected on what Ginger had said. He did make it up to Kelly, just as he said he would, in the most noble way possible. Barton nodded at Zander's matter-of-fact words. That was what this job did to you. Where did all the hurt go? When was it all too much?

'Naeem's retired with immediate effect. I've spoken to DCI Cox, as we'll now be calling her, at the station. We're not expected back in for a week. The workload's light, anyway. I guess the whole city is stunned.'

'It's my fault. I let them head down there. I should've known.'

'You can't think like that, John. She was a sick woman. It's her fault, not anyone else's.'

Barton thought back to the quiet old lady. She hadn't seemed crazy to him. Dark and vengeful, of course, but she knew what she was doing. He wondered what he'd do if someone slaughtered his family. He decided not to think about it too honestly. Mortis had done the post-mortem and found the sliced skin on the Colonel's chest. He shuddered as he imagined that happening.

Barton had also read Veronica's parting note and the final picture had been revealed. A cold-case team in London dug deep into the new details. Careers would end; reputations were in tatters. Old people, he mused; disregard them at your peril.

Britney hadn't cracked despite another attempt from Zander. Barton had gone to visit her private room this morning, but she'd disappeared during the night. He wished her well.

Barton visited the vicar, too. He left thinking that the man knew more than he was letting on. Especially when he said cryptically, 'Be sure your sins will find you out.'

The door opened again; this time, DCI Naeem and her son, Aryan, entered. Judging by their red eyes, they also had a tough path ahead. Thoughts of what might have been would darken the rest of their days.

Naeem embraced Barton as well. 'Thank you, for everything.'

Zander squeezed Barton's shoulder. 'Come on, John. Let's go into town and get hammered. We've got days to sleep it off.'

Barton let himself be led out of the building and slumped in the passenger seat of Zander's car. He'd never wanted to be drunk so much in his whole life. He knew without a shadow of a doubt that he wouldn't be the same again. None of them would forget the Snow Killer, but what he needed right now was oblivion.

ACKNOWLEDGEMENT

Many of those who helped with my previous books have again given freely of their time, and their assistance and support remain greatly appreciated. However, the stand-out supporting act for this novel is Julian. He retired recently after twenty-five years in the police and kindly offered to answer any questions I might have, not realising that it was going to be about a million.

I couldn't have done it without you.

MORE FROM ROSS GREENWOOD

We hope you enjoyed reading *The Snow Killer*. If you did, please leave a review.

If you'd like to gift a copy, this book is also available as a ebook, digital audio download and audiobook CD.

Sign up to Ross Greenwood's mailing list for news, competitions and updates on future books.

http://bit.ly/RossGreenwoodNewsletter

ABOUT THE AUTHOR

Ross Greenwood is the author of six crime thrillers. Before becoming a full-time writer he was most recently a prison officer and so worked everyday with murderers, rapists and thieves for four years. He lives in Peterborough and *The Snow Killer* is the first instalment in the DI Barton series.

Follow Ross on social media:

 twitter.com/greenwoodross

 facebook.com/RossGreenwoodAuthor

ABOUT BOLDWOOD BOOKS

Boldwood Books is a fiction publishing company seeking out the best stories from around the world.

Find out more at www.boldwoodbooks.com

Sign up to the Book and Tonic newsletter for news, offers and competitions from Boldwood Books!

http://www.bit.ly/bookandtonic

We'd love to hear from you, follow us on social media:

facebook.com/BookandTonic

twitter.com/BoldwoodBooks

instagram.com/BookandTonic

CPSIA information can be obtained
at www.ICGtesting.com
Printed in the USA
LVHW051613120221
679183LV00009B/955

9 781838 894474

'This is classic Richard Stark, the grandmaster of American crime fiction, who brought Parker back to life by popular demand after a 20-year break. Parker, of course, is probably the genre's most captivating anti-hero ... In *Ask the Parrot*, he's showing little sign of ageing, and neither is Stark's prose – it's as lean, hungry and tightly plotted as ever. Superior entertainment.' *Daily Mirror*

'Richard Stark is an old-style pro ... entertaining.' *Observer*

'Stark's spare, downbeat style brilliantly evokes the amoral antihero as he shrewdly manipulates the reader ... Stark keeps the reader in suspense right to the satisfyingly ambiguous end.' *Scotland on Sunday*

'Richard Stark is the doyen of the modern hard-boiled crime novel. I have every one of his novels. Read *Ask the Parrot*, and find out why Stark is the kind of writer who, whatever else you're reading, you stop dead and read his latest.' *Independent on Sunday*

'Do you like your crime fiction pared to the bone, with never a wasted word? Are you addicted to narratives that move with bullet-speed velocity, in which every action is fraught with reined-in-menace? Then Richard Stark ... is undoubtedly your man ... The Parker books are treasures – and this latest is vintage Stark ... A recipe for jet-black humour along with the usual bruising exposition – and the ranks of Richard Stark fans will be swelled by a book as trenchant as anything we've had from this author.' *Daily Express*

'The nonpareil, the hard-boiledest of the hard-boiled, one of the darkest and best-loved names in all of noir: Richard Stark ... The brilliance of the books lies in their blurring of the distinction between madness and sanity, justice and mercy ... Parker is truly frightening ... The plot is classic Westlake deadpan rhapsody, a vision of endless roads and featureless towns, landscapes and people unravelling.' *Guardian*

'New readers tempted to seek an introduction to Westlake alias Stark through this novel will not be disappointed ... It is wonderfully laconic with a plot structure that condenses 48 hours of Parker mayhem and tightens like a noose ... A memorable and enduring character.' *Sunday Herald*

'Lean, clean, page-turning prose ... The crisp prose is straight from the cooler.' *Metro*

'The writing is tough and hard-boiled with short sharp bursts of violent action.' *Birmingham Post*

'Starts at a clip and just keeps on going ... High class, hugely enjoyable.' Tangled Web

RICHARD STARK (a.k.a. Donald E. Westlake) has won three Edgar Awards and was deservedly named a Mystery Writers of America Grand Master. Famously played by Lee Marvin in *Point Blank* and Mel Gibson in *Payback*, Parker is Stark's most enduring creation. Richard Stark lives in New York State with his wife.

ASK THE PARROT

Richard Stark

Quercus

First published in Great Britain in 2007 by Quercus
This paperback edition published in 2007 by

Quercus
21 Bloomsbury Square
London
WC1A 2NS

A CIP catalogue reference for this book is available
from the British Library

ISBN-10 1 84724 098 4
ISBN-13 978 1 84724 098 9

10 9 8 7 6 5 4 3

Printed and bound in Great Britain by Clays Ltd, St Ives plc.

PART ONE

PART ONE

ONE

When the helicopter swept northward and lifted out of sight over the top of the hill, Parker stepped away from the tree he'd waited beside and continued his climb. Whatever was on the other side of this hill had to be better than the dogs baying down there at the foot of the slope behind him, running around, straining at their leashes, finding his scent, starting up. He couldn't see the bottom of the hill any more, the police cars congregated around his former Dodge rental in the diner parking lot, but he didn't need to. The excited yelp of the dogs was enough.

How tall was this hill? Parker wasn't dressed for uphill hiking, out in the midday October air; his street shoes skidded on leaves, his jacket bunched when he pulled himself up from tree trunk to tree trunk. But he still had to keep ahead of the dogs and hope to find something or somewhere useful when he finally started down the other side.

How much farther to the top? He paused, holding the rough bark of a tree, and looked up, and fifteen feet above him through the scattered thin trunks of this second-growth woods there stood a man. The afternoon sun was to Parker's left, the sky beyond the man a pale October ash, the man himself only a silhouette. With a rifle.

Not a cop. Not with a group. A man standing, looking down toward Parker, hearing the same hounds Parker heard, holding the rifle easy at a slant across his front, pointed up and to the side. Parker looked down again, chose the next tree trunk, pulled himself up.

It was another three or four minutes before he drew level with the man, who stepped back a pace and said, "That's good. Right there's good."

"I have to keep moving," Parker said, but he stopped, wishing these shoes gave better traction on dead leaves.

The man said, "You one of those robbers I've been hearing about on the TV? Took all a bank's money, over in Massachusetts?"

Parker said nothing. If the rifle moved, he would have to meet it.

The man watched him, and for a few seconds they only considered one another. The man was about fifty, in a red leather hunting jacket with many pockets, faded blue jeans, and black boots. His eyes were shielded by a billed red and black flannel cap. Beside him on the ground was a gray canvas sack, partly full, with brown leather handles.

Seen up close, there was a tension in the man that seemed to be a part of him, not something caused by running into a fugitive in the woods. His hands were clenched on the rifle, and his eyes were bitter, as though something had harmed him at some point and he was determined not to let it happen again.

Then he shook his head and made a downturned mouth, impatient with the silence. "The reason I ask," he said, "when I saw you coming up, and heard the dogs, I thought if you *are* one of the robbers, I want to talk to you." He shrugged, a pessimist to his boots, and said, "If you're not, you can stay here and pat the dogs."

"I don't have it on me," Parker said.

Surprised, the man said, "Well, no, you couldn't. It was about a truckload of cash, wasn't it?"

"Something like that."

The man looked downhill. The dogs couldn't be seen yet, but they could be heard, increasingly frantic and increasingly excited, held back by their handlers' lesser agility on the hill. "This could be your lucky day," he said, "and mine, too." Another sour face. "I could use one." Stooping to pick up his canvas sack, he said, "I'm hunting for the pot, that's what *I'm* doing. I have a car back here."

Parker followed him the short climb to the crest, where the trees were thinner but within a cluster of them a black Ford SUV was parked on a barely visible dirt road. "Old logging road," the man said, and opened the back cargo door of the SUV to put the rifle and sack inside. "I'd like it if you'd sit up front."

"Sure."

Parker got into the front passenger seat as the man came around the other side to get behind the wheel. The key was already in the ignition. He started the car and drove them at an angle down the wooded north slope, the road usually visible only because it was free of trees.

Driving, eyes on the dirt lane meandering downslope ahead of them, the man said, "I'm Tom Lindahl. You should give me something to call you."

"Ed," Parker decided.

"Do you have any weapons on you, Ed?"

"No."

"There's police roadblocks all around here."

"I know that."

"What I mean is, if you think you can jump me and steal my car, you wouldn't last more than ten minutes."

Parker said, "Can you get around the roadblocks?"

"It's only a few miles to my place," Lindahl said. "We won't run into anybody. I know these roads."

"Good."

Parker looked past Lindahl's sour face, downslope to the left, and through the trees now he could just see a road, two-lane blacktop, below them and running parallel to them. A red pickup truck went by down there, the opposite way, uphill. Parker said, "Can they see us from the road, up in here?"

"Doesn't matter."

"They'll get to the top in a few minutes, with the dogs," Parker said. "They'll see this road, they'll figure I'm in a car."

"Soon we'll be home," Lindahl said, and unexpectedly laughed, a rusty sound as though he didn't do much laughing. "You're the reason I came out," he said.

"Oh, yeah?"

"The TV's full of the robbery, all that money gone, I couldn't stand it any more. *Those* guys don't get slapped around, I thought. *Those* guys aren't afraid of their own shadow, they go out and do what has to be done. I got so mad at myself – I'll tell you right now, I'm a coward – I just had to come out with the gun awhile. Those two rabbits back there, I can use them, God knows, but I didn't really need them just yet. It was you brought me out."

Parker watched his profile. Now that he was talking, Lindahl seemed just a little less bitter. Whatever was bothering him, it must make it worse to hold it in.

Lindahl gave him a quick glance, his expression now almost merry. "And here you are," he said. "And up close, I got to tell you, you don't look like that much of a world-beater."

He steered left, down a steep slope, and the logging road met the blacktop.

12

TWO

The name on the town sign was Pooley, and it wasn't much of a place. One minor intersection was controlled by a light blinking amber in two directions, red in the other two. A gas station stood on the corner there, along with a shut-down bank branch, a shut-down bar, and a shut-down sporting goods store. Twenty houses or so were strung along the two narrow roads of the town, three or four of them boarded up, most of the rest dilapidated. An old man slept in a rocker on a porch, and an old woman a few doors down knelt at her front-lawn garden.

Lindahl drove straight through the intersection, then three houses later turned to the right into a gravel driveway next to one of the boarded-up houses. Behind the house, at the rear of the property, a three-car brown clapboard garage had been converted to housing, and that was where Lindahl stopped.

"You go on in," he said. "It isn't locked. I'll take care of my rabbits."

Parker got out of the Ford and walked over to what had originally been the middle garage door, now crudely converted to a front door next to a double-hung window covered on the inside by a venetian blind.

He pushed open this door and stepped into a dim interior, where the smell, not strong, was cavelike, old dirt combined with some kind of animal scent. Then he saw the parrot, in a large cage on top of the television set. The parrot saw him, too, turning his green head to the side to do it, but didn't speak, only made a small gurgling sound and briefly marched in place on its bar. The newspaper in the bottom of its cage was not new.

The rest of the living room was normal but seedy, with old furniture not cared for. The television set was on, sound off, showing an antacid commercial.

Lindahl's anger was money-based. He wasn't supposed to be needy, living like this, shooting rabbits to feed himself. Hearing about a big-scale robbery had made him angrier and depressed and self-hating; which meant there was something he should have done about the money he felt was rightfully his, but he hadn't done it. And now he thought that talking with a bank robber would help.

Parker spent the next five minutes lightly tossing the place: living room, bedroom, bath, kitchen, utility room with oil furnace. Three more rifles were locked to a wall rack in the bedroom, but there were no pistols. Lindahl lived here alone and didn't seem to have much correspondence with anybody. He had a checking account with $273 in it, and wrote checks only for standard items like phone and electricity, plus ATM withdrawals for cash. A $1,756 deposit every month was labeled "dis"; disability?

Lindahl would tell him why he'd rather talk to a bank robber than turn him in. Whatever the reason, right now Parker needed it. The only identification he carried was no good any more, now that the police had the car he'd rented with it. For the next couple of days, in this part of the world, it would be impossible to travel anywhere, even by foot, without having to show ID every once in a while.

When Lindahl walked in, carrying his rifle and two white plastic bags, Parker was in the living room, seated on the chair that didn't face the television set, leafing through yesterday's local blat. From the headlines, it seemed to be all small towns around here, no cities.

Parker looked up at the door opening, and Lindahl said, "I'll just take care of this and wash my hands," and went on through to the kitchen. Parker heard the water run, and then Lindahl came back, now carrying only the rifle, loose in one hand. "One more thing," he said, and went into the bedroom, and Parker heard the click as the rifle was locked into its place on the wall.

Now at last Lindahl came out to the living room and sat down on the left side of the sofa. "I've been trying to think how to tell you," he said. "I'm not used to talking to people any more."

He stopped and looked over at Parker, as though waiting for a response, but Parker said nothing. So Lindahl made his sour chuckle and said, "I guess you're the same."

"You have something to tell me."

"I'm a whistle-blower," Lindahl said, as though he'd been planning some much longer way to say it. "My wife told me not to do it, she said I'd lose everything including her, and she was right. But I'm bullheaded."

"Where did you blow this whistle?"

"I worked for twenty-two years at a racetrack down toward Syracuse," Lindahl said, "named Gro-More. It was named after a farm feed company went bankrupt forty years ago. They never changed the name."

"You blew a whistle."

"I was a manager, I was in charge of infrastructure, the upkeep of the buildings, the stands, the track. Hired people, contracted out. I was nothing to do with money."

"So whatever this is," Parker said, "you shouldn't have known about it."

"I didn't *have* to know about it." Lindahl shook his head, explaining himself. "What we had was a clean track," he said. "The people working there, we were all happy to be at a clean track. There's a thousand ways for a track to be dirty, but only one way to be clean, so when I found out what they were doing with the money, it just hurt me. It was like doing something dirty to a member of my own family."

The strain of getting his point across was deepening the lines in his face. He broke off, made erasing gestures, and said, "I need a beer. I can't tell this without a beer." Rising, he said, "You want one?"

"No, but you go ahead."

Lindahl did, and when he was seated again, he said, "What they were doing, they were hiding illegal campaign contributions to state politicians, running them through the track. Laundering them, you might say."

Parker said, "How would that work?"

"A fella goes to the track, he bets a thousand dollars on a long shot on every race, he drops eight thousand that day. Just that day. That money stays in the system, because he did it with credit cards, but a lot of little penny ante bets from other people disappear. Bets made with cash. So the guy didn't give the politician the eight thousand, he just lost it at the track, but a little later it shows up in a politician's pocket."

"The horses gave it to him."

"That's about it," Lindahl agreed. "When I found out about it, I was just stunned. We never had dope at the track, we never had fixed races, we never had ringers, we never had the mob, and now this. I talked to one of the execs, he didn't see the problem. They're just helping out some friends, nobody from the track is making any money off it. This is just trying to get around some of those stupid pain-in-the-ass regulations from Washington."

"Makes it sound good," Parker said.

"But it isn't good." Lindahl swigged beer. "This is just corruption everywhere you look, the politicians, the track, the whole idea of sports. I talked it over with my wife, we talked about it for months, she told me it was none of my business, I'd lose my job, I'd lose everything. We never had a lot of money, she said if I threw our life away she wouldn't stick around. But I couldn't help it, I finally went to the state police."

"You wear a wire?"

"Yes, I did." Lindahl looked agonized. "That's the part I really regret," he said. "If I just said look, this is going on, then I'm just the guy who saw it is all. But the prosecutors leaned on me, they got me to help them make their case. And then, at the end, the politics was just too strong for them, it all got swept under the carpet, and nothing happened to anybody but me."

"You knew that was going to happen."

"I suppose I did," Lindahl said, and drank some more of his beer. "They talked me into it, but I suppose I talked myself into it, too. Thinking it was best for the track, can you believe that? Not best for me, best for some goddam racetrack named after cow feed, I should have my head examined."

"Too late," Parker said.

Lindahl sighed. "Yes, it is," he said. "Everybody told me don't worry, there's whistle-blower laws, they can't touch you." He gestured with the beer bottle, indicating the room. "You see where I am. My wife was true to her word, she went off with her widowed sister. I haven't had a job for four years. I get a little disability from when a horse rolled over me, years ago, I don't even limp any more, but I'm the wrong age and the wrong background and in the wrong part of the country to find anybody to hire me to do anything. Even flipping burgers, they don't want somebody my age."

"No, they don't," Parker said. "So you've been kicking yourself that you didn't get even. Because you think you could get even. How?"

"I ran those buildings for years," Lindahl said. "I've still got up-to-date keys for every door out there. I still go out every once in a while, when there isn't any meet going on, when it's shut down like a museum, and I just walk around it. Every once in a while, if I find a door with a new key, I borrow a spare from the rack and make a copy for myself."

"You can get in and out."

"I can not only get in and out," Lindahl said, "I know *where* to get in and out. I know where the money goes, and where the money waits, and where the money's loaded up for the bank, and where the money's stored till the armored car gets there. I know where everything is and how to get to everything. During a meet, the place is guarded 24/7, but I know how to slide a truck in there, three in the morning, no one the wiser. I know how to get in, and then I know how to carry a heavy weight out."

Lindahl had already carried a heavy weight out of that place, but that wasn't what he meant. Parker said, "So once they cost you your wife and your job, you decided to rip them off, get a new stake, go away and retire in comfort."

"That's right," Lindahl said. "I've been thinking about nothing else for four years."

"Why didn't you do it?"

"Because I'm a useless spineless coward," Lindahl said, and finished his beer.

THREE

"Or it could be," Parker said, "you're just not that dumb."

Lindahl frowned at him. "In what way?"

"You go in there some night," Parker said, "three in the morning with your truck and your keys and your inside knowledge, and you load the truck up with their cash, and when they find the cash gone next morning, nothing broken into, what's the first thing they say? They say, 'Do we have a disgruntled ex-employee around here?'"

"Oh, I know that," Lindahl said, and laughed at himself, shaking his head. "That was a part of the whole idea. It wasn't just the money I wanted, was it? It was revenge. I want them to *know* I got back at them, and not a goddam thing they can do about it."

"You're just gonna disappear."

"It's happened."

"Less than it used to," Parker told him. "Right now I'm sitting here listening to you instead of getting to some other part of the country because I don't have any safe ID."

21

"Well, you stirred them up," Lindahl said. "You robbed their bank."

"Robbing their track will stir them up, too."

"Let me tell you the idea," Lindahl said. "The way the track operates, the losers pay the winners, so the track never has to start off with cash. They take in enough from the first race to pay the winners, plus some more, and go from there. The track take is about twenty percent, that's the piece I'm after. At the end of the day, the cash and the credit card slips are all put in boxes and on carts, and the carts ride down to the basement in the freight elevator. They're wheeled down the corridor to what they call the safe room, because it's all concrete block, no windows, and only the one door that's metal and kept locked. Just past that is the door to the ramp that comes up to ground level at the end of the clubhouse. That door is kept locked, and the gate at the top of the ramp is kept locked. Monday through Friday, the armored car comes an hour after the track closes, backs down the ramp, loads on the day's take. Saturday and Sunday they don't come at all, and they don't show up until eight Monday morning, when they pick up the whole weekend's take."

"So your idea," Parker said, "is go in there Sunday night."

Lindahl shook his head. "Saturday night," he said.

"Those boxes are heavy. Once the pallet is put down there on Saturday, it isn't touched again till Monday morning. I go in there Saturday night with boxes look just like their boxes, because I know their boxes. I take the full ones, I leave the empty ones. Now I've got thirty-six hours before anybody knows anything. How far could I get in thirty-six hours, spending only cash, leaving no trail?"

Everybody leaves a trail, but there was no point explaining things to Lindahl, since it was all a fantasy, anyway. Parker might be able to make use of Lindahl's access if things were quieter around here and if he could collect a string of two or three sure guys, but there was no way for Lindahl himself to reach into that particular fire and not get burned.

It wasn't Parker's job to tell an amateur he was an amateur, to remind him of things like a driver's license, license plates, fingerprints, or the suspicions created by spending cash in a credit card economy. So he said, "You gonna take the parrot with you?"

Lindahl was surprised at the abrupt change of subject, and then surprised again when he saw it wasn't a change of subject, after all. "I never thought about that," he said, and laughed at himself again. "Be on the lookout for a man and a parrot." Turning to look at the parrot as though he'd never noticed it before, he said, "That's who

I am these last few years, isn't it? Who else is gonna get a parrot that doesn't talk?"

"Not at all?"

"Not a word."

Lindahl studied the parrot an instant longer, while the bird cocked his head to study Lindahl right back, then gave that up to start rooting under its feathers with its beak, eyes wide and blank as the buttons on a First Communion coat.

Turning back to Parker, Lindahl said, "That's how little I'm interested in talk, the last few years. I better not take him, but that's no hardship. I'll do fine on my own. I won't start any conversations. Is that one of yours?"

Lindahl had nodded at the television set. Parker leaned forward to look to his right at the screen, and filling it was some old mug shot of Nick Dalesia, who had been one of his partners until just now. *Nicholas Leonard Dalesia* it said across the bottom of the screen.

So they had Nick. That changed everything.

"You want the sound on?"

"We know what they're saying," Parker said.

Lindahl nodded. "I guess we do."

A perp walk showed. Dalesia, wrists cuffed, head bowed, looking roughed up, moved in jerky quick steps from a state trooper car across a broad concrete sidewalk to the side entrance of a brick building in some county seat where this was the courthouse up front and the jail around on the side. New York State Police, so Nick, too, hadn't gotten very far. As many uniformed state troopers as could do it squeezed into the picture to hustle Nick along from the car to the building.

Parker leaned back, not looking at the set. Three of them had pulled the job and stowed the cash away rather than try to get it through the roadblocks. It was a given that if one of them got nabbed, that one would turn up the cash as a way to make his legal troubles a little easier. You might give up your partners, too, if you knew enough about them. Give the law anything you could if you were the first grabbed. Otherwise, don't get grabbed at all, because there was nothing left to trade.

So the money was gone. It had been a rich haul, but now it was gone, except for the four thousand in Parker's pocket, and he still had to work his way out of this minefield. He said, "You say the meet's going on now, at this track of yours?"

"Two more weeks," Lindahl said, "then shut down until late April."

"So there's three Saturdays left, today and two more."

"We couldn't do it tonight," Lindahl said, looking startled.

"We can go there tonight," Parker told him. "A dry run, see if it's possible."

Lindahl looked both eager and alarmed. "You mean, you'd work with me on this?"

"We'll look at it," Parker said.

FOUR

Parker stood and crossed to the door, then raised the blind covering the window next to it. The boarded-up house standing between here and the road was a two-and-a-half-story wood-framed structure, probably one hundred years old, its original color long since time-bleached down to gray. Every door and window, except one small round window in the attic, was covered by large sheets of plywood, themselves also gray with age. Parker said, "Tell me about that place."

Lindahl got up to come over and stand beside him, saying, "A woman named Grothe lived there, forever. She was retired from somewhere in state government, lived there by herself, she was in her nineties when she finally died."

"Why's it boarded up?"

"Some cousins inherited the place, had nothing to do with this part of the world, gave it to a real estate agent to sell, years ago. But nobody's buying anything around here, so after a while the town took it over for taxes, boarded it up to keep the bums out."

27

"Ever been inside it?"

"Can't. It's sealed up. And who'd want to? Nothing in there but dust and dry rot."

"Who do you rent this place from?"

"The town. It's goddam cheap, and it oughta be. Who's this?"

A black Taurus had turned in from the road, was driving past the boarded-up house, headed this way. Lindahl gave Parker a quick look: "Are you here?"

When there's no place to hide, stand where you are. Parker said, "I'm Ed Smith, I used to work with you years ago at the track, I moved to Chicago, I'm back for a visit."

"Smith?"

"There are people named Smith," Parker said as a heavyset man in a maroon windbreaker got out of the car. "Who's he?"

"Oh, yeah," Lindahl said as the man shut the car door, glanced at Lindahl's Ford parked beside him, and started forward. "What the hell is his name? Fred, Fred something."

Fred saw them both in the window and waved. Under a red billed cap, his face was broad and thick, dominated by a ridge of bone horizontally above his eyes.

"Rod and Gun Club," Lindahl said, and opened the door. "Fred! Jesus, it's been years."

"You're still on the rolls," Fred said, and gave a quick nod and grin at Parker.

"Come in, come in," Lindahl said, stepping back from the doorway. "This is Ed Smith, he's visiting. You aren't after me for dues, are you?"

Fred gave that a dutiful laugh and stuck his hand out to Parker, saying, "Fred Thiemann. You a hunter, Ed?"

"Sometimes."

"I can offer you a beer," Lindahl said, sounding doubtful.

"No, no, no drinking," Fred said, "not at a time like this. You know about those bank robbers come over from Massachusetts."

Parker could sense the strain in Lindahl's neck muscles as he didn't turn to look at Parker, but instead said, "They caught one of them, didn't they?"

"Not that far from here. The state police figure the other two are holed up in this area someplace, so they sent out a request, American Legion and VFW posts, outfits like ours, just take a walk around any woods or empty spaces we've got, see do we turn up anything. It's the weekend, so we're getting a big turnout." He shrugged, grinning with both delight and embarrassment. "Like a bunch of kids, playing cops and robbers."

"Like a posse," Lindahl said.

"Exactly," Fred said. "Except, no horses. Anyway, a

bunch of us are meeting at St. Stanislas, we'll look around the Hickory Hill area. Nobody expects to find anything, but we might help keep those guys on the run."

Parker said, "How'd they catch the first one?"

"He tried spending the bank's money," Fred said. "Turns out most of that was new cash, they had the serial numbers."

The four thousand dollars in Parker's pocket was new money. He said, "That guy was careless."

"Let's hope the other two are just as careless," Fred said. "We didn't have a phone number for you, Tom, so I said I'd come over on the way, see do you want to come along. You, too, Ed."

Lindahl looked at Parker. "Would you want to do that?"

"Sure," Parker said. "The safest place around is gonna be with the posse."

FIVE

"Tom," Parker said, "you'll have to loan me a rifle. I didn't bring one."

Lindahl gave him a startled look, but then said, "Sure. Come on in and pick one."

Fred Thiemann said, "Want me to wait for you boys?"

"No, you go on ahead," Lindahl told him. "It'll take me a couple minutes to get ready. I'll see you at St. Stanislas."

"Fine. Good to meet you, Ed."

"You, too."

Thiemann left, pulling the door shut behind himself, as Lindahl turned toward the bedroom. Parker followed, and when he stepped through the doorway, Lindahl was glaring at him, face suddenly blotched purple.

"You get out of here!" It was a hoarse whisper, almost a choked scream. "As soon as Fred drives off, you clear *out*!"

"No," Parker said.

"What?" Lindahl couldn't believe it. "You can't stay here, you're a *fugitive*!"

"We've got our agreement," Parker told him. "We'll stick to it."

"We will *not*! Not for another second."

Parker looked from the bedroom doorway out through the front window. "Fred just drove off," he said. "What are you going to do, holler? At that empty house up there? Are you going to try to take down one rifle and not two?"

"When you said – when you said, give me a rifle – Jesus, I came to my senses, right then and there. You could kill people I *know*."

"If I'm the only man there without a rifle," Parker said, "how does that look? What am I there *for*?"

Lindahl dropped backward to sit on the bed, hands limp between his knees. "I was out of my mind," he said, talking at the floor. "Brooding about that goddam track for so many years, then thinking about *you*, and by God if you don't show up, and I was just running a fantasy. A fantasy." Glaring at Parker, trying to look stern, he said, "I'm not giving any fantasy a *rifle*. You just take off. I got you this far, you're on your own. I won't say a word about you."

"Doesn't work," Parker told him. "You're accessory after the fact. You took me off that hill, you drove me home, you introduced me as somebody visiting with you. You show up at this saint place without me, what do you say to Fred? And what if I *am* caught, and Fred sees my picture on the television? What do you tell the cops?"

"I was crazy," Lindahl whispered, as though to himself. "I don't know what I was thinking."

"Revenge. I'm not going to shoot your friends, now that you've suddenly got all of them. I'll carry a rifle because that's what everybody's doing."

Lindahl looked at him. "What if we find the other guy? What if you're trying to help him get away?"

"I wouldn't try to help him get away," Parker said.

Lindahl frowned at him, trying to understand what he meant, and then his entire body slumped. "You mean, you'd kill him."

Parker would, to protect himself, but he didn't want Lindahl thinking about that. "I'll keep away from him," he said. "And he'll keep away from me. He's probably long gone from here, anyway."

Lindahl seemed unable to move forward. He continued to sit on the bed, staring at nothing at all, slowly shaking his head, as Parker went to study the four rifles in their locked racks on the wall.

The top two were nearly identical, Remington Model 1100, single-barrel shotguns, the top one a

20-gauge, the other the slightly longer and heavier 16-gauge. The other two were both lever-action rifles, one a Marlin 336Y, firing a .30-30 Winchester cartridge, the other a Ruger 96, firing the .44 Magnum. All four weapons were old but well cared for, and might have been bought used.

Parker turned back to Lindahl, still slumped unmoving on the bed. "Lindahl," he said.

Lindahl looked up. There was very little emotion in his eyes, so he was scheming down inside himself somewhere.

Parker said, "You and me, we'll go with this posse crowd. We'll take the two lever actions, no round in the chamber, that way neither of us can get off a snap shot. We'll stay with those people as long as they're out there, then we'll eat something and come back here."

"I don't want you here," Lindahl said, dull but stolid.

"Listen to me. We're talking a few hours out there. What you wanted – what you thought you wanted – was revenge. You'll have those hours to think about it. When we get back here, you tell me, either you still want to take down that track or you don't. If you do, we'll go look at it. If you don't, I'll leave in the morning."

"I don't want you here."

"You've got me. You brought me here, and you've got me. If it wasn't for your friend Fred, I could lock

34

you in your utility room and not worry about you. But if we don't show up at this saint place, Fred's going to start wondering this and that. So we've got to do it. Let's go."

Lindahl shook his head in a slow dumbfounded way. "How did this happen?" he wanted to know.

"You made your choice when you saw me come up the hill," Parker told him. "Back then, you could have shot me, or held me there for the dogs, figuring there's got to be a reward. But you looked at me and said, 'This guy can help me.' Maybe I can. Or maybe you'll change your mind. We'll know when we get back. Do you have a spare coat? Something right for the woods?"

Lindahl blinked at him, confused. "A coat? I have a couple coats."

"And boots, if you've got them. These shoes aren't much use outdoors. Do you have extra boots?"

Lindahl didn't want to be dragged away into this other conversation. "I have boots, I have boots," he muttered, shaking his head. "But no. Take my car. Just drive away."

"Right into their arms," Parker said. "Look at me, Tom."

Reluctantly Lindahl looked up.

Parker said, "Do you want me to think you're trouble, Tom?"

Lindahl frowned, looking at him, then his eyes shifted away and he shook his head. "No."

"So you'll loan me a coat and a pair of boots. And you want the Ruger or the Marlin?"

SIX

The red and black wool coat was loose, but the lace-up boots fit well. Parker carried the Marlin, a thirty-four-inch-long single-shot rifle weighing six and a half pounds, with a five-shot tubular magazine. They put both rifles on the floor behind the front seat and drove away from Pooley, not the way they'd come in. They'd gone about six miles when they reached the first roadblock, two state police cars narrowing the road to one lane, cars and troopers sharply sketched in the late afternoon October sunlight against the dark surrounding woods.

As they slowed, Parker said, "You'll talk."

"I know."

The trooper who bent to Lindahl's open window was an older man, heavyset, taken off desk duty for this emergency and not happy about it. Lindahl told him his name and his membership in Hickory Rod and Gun, and that they were on their way to St. Stanislas to join the search.

The trooper stepped back to look in the rear side window at the rifles on the floor and said, "Whole county's filling up with untrained men with guns. Not how I'd do it, but nobody asked me. You got your membership card?"

"In the Rod and Gun Club? Sure." Reaching for his wallet, Lindahl sounded sheepish as he said, "It's a little out of date."

"Doesn't matter," the trooper said. "Doesn't have a photo, anyway." He nodded at the card Lindahl showed him, without taking it, and said, "Leave it on the dashboard so if you're stopped again they'll know who you are."

"Good idea." Lindahl put his membership card on top of the dashboard where it could be seen through the windshield.

The trooper, sour but resigned, stepped back and said, "Okay, go ahead."

"Thank you, sir."

They drove on, through hilly country, still mostly forested, many of the trees now changing to their fall colors, crimson and russet and gold. There were apple orchards, darkly red, and scruffy fields where dairy cows had once grazed, now mostly vacant, though here and there were groups of horses or sheep or even llamas. The houses were few and old and close to the ground.

They climbed awhile, the road switching back and forth through the partly tamed forest, then came to a town with a sign reading *St. Stanislas* and a steep main street. What they were headed for was not a church, but an old Grange Hall, its clapboard sides painted a medium brown too many years ago, with the metal signs of half a dozen fraternal organizations on stakes along the roadside out front.

A dozen cars were already in the parking lot beside the building, and Lindahl put the Ford in with them. They got their rifles, then walked over to where a group of men milled around the closed front door. They were mostly over fifty, hefty and soft, and they moved with checked-in excitement.

Lindahl knew all of these people, though it was clear he hadn't seen any of them for some time. They were pleased to see him, if not excited, and pleased to meet Parker as well, introduced as an old friend of Lindahl's here on a visit.

Parker shook hands with the smiling men who were hunting him, and then a state police car arrived and two uniformed men got out, the younger one an ordinary trooper, the older one with extra braid and insignia on his uniform and hat.

This is the one who went up on the steps leading to the Grange Hall and turned around to say, "I want to thank you gentlemen for coming out today. We have two very dangerous men somewhere in our part of the world, and it's an act of good citizenship to help find them and put them under control. You've all heard on the television the crime they committed. They didn't kill anybody, but they caused a great deal of property damage and put three armored-car employees in the hospital. The weapons they used are banned in the United States. We don't know if they're still carrying those weapons, or if they might have others as well. We do know they *were* armed and *are* extremely dangerous. We ask that no one go off by himself, but always have at least one other person from your group in sight. If you come across one or both of these fugitives, do *not* try to apprehend them yourselves. These are professional criminals, desperate men facing long prison sentences, and they have no reason not to shoot you down if you get in their way. If you believe you've found them, get that information to us or to some other authority at the earliest possible moment. Try to keep them in sight, and do not under any circumstances exchange gunfire with them. Trooper Oskott has artist's drawings of the two men that we'll pass among you, and then your club president, Ben Weiser, will describe to you the area we'd like you to patrol. Ben?"

Ben Weiser was a man in his sixties, as overweight as most of the rest of them, with absolutely no hair on the top of his head but very long gray hair down the sides and back, covering his ears and his collar, so that he looked like a retired cavalry scout. As Trooper Oskott moved among the group, handing out sheets of copy paper, Weiser said, "It's nice to see just about everybody here, and even an extra volunteer, Ed Smith over there, brought to us by Tom Lindahl, so I guess that makes up for all the times *Tom* didn't show up. Glad you're here, Tom. Welcome to Hickory Rod and Gun Club, Ed."

Parker took the two sheets the trooper handed him and looked at them while Weiser went on being folksy and another man went into the Grange Hall and came back out with an easel that he set up on the top step. The drawing of himself he'd seen before, on the television set in the diner before the law had arrived, attracted by his rental car. Nobody in the diner had looked from the screen to this customer among them and said, "There he is!" and nobody here in front of the Grange Hall turned to say, "Ed? Isn't this you?"

The other drawing, he knew, was supposed to be McWhitney, his partner back then, and if you knew McWhitney and had been told this was supposed to be him, you could see the similarities, but McWhitney himself could walk past this group right now and not one of them would give a second look.

Artist's drawings didn't bother Parker. What bothered him was the four thousand dollars in traceable cash in his pocket and the lack of a usable ID. Until he replaced

41

both of those, the best place for him was right here with the search party.

"Tough-looking guys," somebody said. "I'm not sure I *want* to find them."

That got a laugh, and then somebody else said, "Oh, I think Cory and me could take 'em, couldn't we, Cory?"

"I'll hold your coat," the one next to him said, and while that got its own laugh, Parker looked at the two of them, Cory and the one whose coat he'd hold.

They were a little younger than most in the group, a little rougher-looking, both dressed in jeans and boots and dark heavy work shirts. They might have been brothers, with the same thick dark blond hair hanging straggly around their ears, the same easy slope of the shoulders. The one who thought he and Cory could take the fugitives had a black patch over his left eye, which inevitably gave him a piratical look, as though he were the tougher brother. With that eye, now, he peered around at the group, slightly challenging, watching out for somebody else he could take. His good eye brushed past Parker, and Parker looked away, not needing to be noticed too much.

Meanwhile, up in front of them, Ben Weiser said, "Here's a government survey map," which somebody had put on the easel, but then had to hold there because otherwise the breeze would blow it off. Weiser then went on to describe what area they were expected to search in, saying things like, "You know the old Heisler place," which they all did.

Parker paid little attention to the details, because this wasn't a part of the country he knew, but it was interesting to see the approach they had taken. They were guessing that the men they wanted would have left the main roads, and possibly the secondary roads as well, though why they should think bank robbers were woodsmen wasn't clear. But the approach was to cover back roads and dirt roads and dead-end roads that weren't used any more, and particularly to cover abandoned buildings, old farmhouses and barns, and even a railroad station up where a town no longer existed because its iron mine had given out more than a century ago.

Which was where Parker would be searching, along with Tom Lindahl and Fred Thiemann. The decision had been made that the search parties should consist of groups of three, and Weiser explained the reason. If they *did* come across one or both of the fugitives, one of their group could go off to raise the alarm without leaving one man alone to keep the quarry in sight.

The men, who had arrived here separately or in pairs, now sorted themselves into threes and headed for the cars. Lindahl's SUV was roomier than

Thiemann's Taurus, so they'd use that, with Lindahl driving, Parker beside him as before, and Thiemann in back with the rifles.

They joined the exodus from the Grange Hall parking lot, followed a couple of other cars for the first mile or so, and Lindahl explained, "This place we're going to, called Wolf Peak, was a mining town way back when."

"Before the Civil War," Thiemann put in from the backseat. "The whole Northeast was iron mines, but the Civil War used it all up."

"Wolf Peak went on till the end of the century," Lindahl said, "with the tailings, and some lumbering, but the younger generations kept moving away, and when the railroad stopped going up there, around 1900, that was the end."

Thiemann said, "The houses were all wood, so they burned or rotted, but the railroad station was good local stone. The roof's gone, but the walls are solid. I hunkered down in there myself once, out hunting and here comes a thunderstorm."

"There might be a couple other hidey-holes up around there," Lindahl said, "but mostly it's the railroad station."

Spreading himself comfortably across the backseat, Thiemann said, "What I'm guessing about these robbers, I'm guessing they're city people, and they aren't gonna know what it means to try to hide out in a place like this."

Parker said, "How's that?"

"People like Tom and me," Thiemann said, "we been here generations, it's like we got our grandparents' memories mixed in with our own. We *know* this chunk of the planet Earth. No city person's gonna know a city like we know these hills. A stranger tries to move through here, tries to hide out in here, somebody's gonna see him and say, 'That fella doesn't belong.' You can't hide around here."

"I see what you mean," Parker said.

Leaning forward a little, Thiemann said, "Where you living these days, Ed?"

"Chicago," Parker told him. "I don't know it very well."

Thiemann grinned. "You know what I mean, then," he said, and sat back.

Their road trended mainly uphill, and a few miles later crossed a larger road, where a police presence had been set up. The trooper this time, a younger one than the first, walked over, saw Lindahl's membership card on the dash, and waved them through. Grinning, he called, "Happy hunting!"

A few miles later Lindahl made a left onto a road, a two-lane blacktop in crumbling condition, that angled steeply up. "There's a couple houses just up ahead," he said, "that they keep the blacktop for. After that, it's dirt."

"Shake the teeth right out of your head," Thiemann commented.

He was close to right. After the second small occupied house, the woods settled in closer on both sides, the hill grew even steeper, and the surface they drove over was more corrugation than road. Lindahl drove slowly, trying to steer around the deepest holes.

Parker said, "Was the railroad line near the road? I don't see any sign of it."

"They pulled up the tracks for scrap during World War Two," Lindahl told him. "It's only a couple more miles now."

First there were stubs of wall, stone or brick, in among the tree trunks on both sides of the road, then a couple of collapsed wooden buildings, crumpled down to a third of their original height, and then, ahead on the right, the railroad station, squat and long, roofless, with narrow tall window sockets and remnants of a concrete skirt around its base. Maple and cherry trees had grown up inside the station, some taller than the roofline. The woods on this slope were so thick that only narrow angles of sunlight reached the ground, like spotlights that had lost the performer they were supposed to follow.

Whatever level parking area had once existed around the station was long overgrown. Lindahl simply stopped on the rutted road in front of the building, and all three got out. Thiemann carried his rifle, a bolt-action Winchester 70 in .30-06, while Lindahl opened the left rear door and took out both of the other rifles. Parker walked around the front of the Ford, held his hand out, and after a second, Lindahl, with a strong and mistrustful frown, gave him the Marlin.

Vines covered part of the building, including hanging down over the doorless front entrance. "You want to be careful with that," Thiemann said, pointing toward the doorway. "That's poison ivy."

"There's probably wider doors around back," Lindahl said, "for freight."

They walked around the building, and there was really nothing at all any more to say what it had originally been, no platforms, no railbed, no rotting luggage carts. The place might have started, long before, as a temple in the jungle.

One of the doorways on this side was broad, and clear of vines. They stepped through, and Thiemann pointed to the left, saying, "That's where I hunkered down that time, waiting for the storm to go away." Then he peered more closely at that corner and said, "What's that?"

They moved into the building, toward the left corner,

and a little stack of old cloth had been piled there, ragged old blankets and towels. It looked like a mouse nest, but it had been put together by a man.

"You're not the only one got out of the storm here," Lindahl said. Looking up, he said, "It's the best protected spot, I guess, with those tree branches."

Bracing himself with his rifle butt against the root and dirt floor, Thiemann squatted down and felt the pile of cloth with his left palm. Solemn, wide eyed, he looked up and mouthed, just barely loud enough to be heard, "Warm."

Lindahl stared at Parker. His hands were clenched tight on his rifle, the way they'd been the first time Parker had seen him, on the hill ahead of the dogs.

Parker said, "Heard the car coming."

Thiemann stood. "He's nearby, then." He was excited, almost giddy, but trying hard to hide it, to seem mature and professional.

Lindahl, speaking mostly to Parker, said, "Do you guess he's armed?"

"Not if he was trying to get through roadblocks."

"If he's holed up in here," Thiemann said, "he isn't getting through any roadblocks."

Parker knew this wouldn't be McWhitney they'd found, but had no reason to say so. "Could be somebody else," he said.

Thiemann scoffed at that. "Way the hell up in here?"

"Could be you, once."

Thiemann shook his head, getting irritated at having his fantasy poked at. Pointing at the pile of cloth, he said, "I didn't make myself a bunk, and" – finger pointing skyward – "there's no thunderstorm. So let's take a look at what we got up here."

They left the station, Thiemann going first at a half-crouch, rifle ready in both hands in front of himself. Outside, he stopped and looked across the space where the tracks would have been, and into the woods. He had become very still, all eyes and ears, studying that wild land over there, sloped steeply down to the right, clogged with low shrubs in among the narrow trunks of the second-growth forest.

Parker and Lindahl waited, a pace behind Thiemann, and after a long minute Thiemann took a backward step toward them, without looking away from the woods. "You see where I'm looking."

Ahead, and just to the right. Parker and Lindahl looked there, too. Parker didn't know if Lindahl saw anything, but he didn't; just more shrubs and more trees.

"Little branches broken on that multiflora there," Thiemann murmured. "That stuff's miserable to get through. See how he forced his way?"

"You know, I do," Lindahl said. "Very good, Fred."

"Not that different from hunting a deer." Thiemann nodded at the woods. "You two flank me left and right, I'll go through where he went through."

They set off slowly, Lindahl giving Parker one quick worried look behind Thiemann' s back, but then concentrating on the terrain ahead.

The land was broken, tilted, full of rocks; very slow going. There was no way to be quiet about it, their feet crunching on old leaves and fallen branches, their bodies shoving branches out of the way. They moved about ten yards forward, and when Parker looked back, the lower part of the station building was already obscured by the undergrowth, only the uneven roofline still visible. It wouldn't take long to get lost in here.

"Freeze!"

That was Thiemann, a dim uncertain shape through the woods to Parker's left.

A sudden loud rustle and clatter ahead of them was someone running, running desperately through the unforgiving forest.

"Fred, hold it!" That was Lindahl, invisible beyond Thiemann, sounding panicky.

"Halt, goddammit!" Thiemann again.

The sound of the shot was a dead flat crack in the open air, like two blocks of wood slapped together, without echo.

"Fred, don't!"

Too late; there was one hoarse scream, and then a great turbulence on the forest floor. Parker moved forward toward that thrashing. To his left, Thiemann moved more cautiously, bent low.

Whatever had been hit was now lunging around out there, agitating the shrubbery, making a racket. Parker got to him in time to see the blood still bubble from the hole in the man's back, the color of wine, the thickness of motor oil. The man, facedown on the leaves and branches, jerked his arms and legs as though swimming through the woods.

And then he stopped. The blood from the hole in his back bubbled less, and pulsed to an end as Thiemann arrived, panting as though he'd run a mile. He stared at the man on the ground as intently as if he'd just given him birth. His voice hoarse, he said, "Which one is he?"

"Neither," Parker said.

Lindahl came to join them, from farther to the left. "How is he?"

"Dead," Parker said.

Thiemann was trying to get the artist's drawings out of his pocket without letting go of his rifle. "Damn," he said. "Damn! Tom, hold this a sec."

Lindahl took Thiemann's rifle, and Thiemann got out the two papers, unfolded them, and went down on one knee beside the dead man. He was clearly reluctant to touch the body, but had to turn the head in order to see the face.

"He's not one of them," Parker said.

Thiemann wasn't ready for that, not yet. This man on the ground in front of them was small, scrawny, old, with thin gray filthy hair and a thick gray untended beard. He wore tattered gray work pants and a moth-eaten old blue sweater, stained everywhere. Lace-up black shoes too big for him were on his feet, without socks, the ankles dirty and scabbed from old cuts.

The face, when Thiemann used both hands to turn the dead man's head, was bone thin, deeply lined, with scabs around the mouth and under the eyes. The eyes stared in horror at something a long way off.

Thiemann squirmed backward, rubbing his fingers on grass and leaves. "He's some old bum," he said. His voice sounded the way the dead man's staring eyes looked.

Lindahl said, "Fred? You didn't get a good look at him?"

"He was . . . running. What the hell was he running for?"

Parker said, "Men with guns chased him."

"Shit." Thiemann was trying to find some rope to grasp, something, some way to get his balance back. "Doesn't he know? The whole countryside knows.

Everybody's out looking for the bank robbers. Nobody wants *him,* what the hell's he running for?" He stood leaning, looking at nothing, arms at his sides.

Lindahl said gently, "Fred, that guy wasn't up on the news. He's up in here, he's some old wino, he goes down sometimes and cadges or steals, but he doesn't keep up with current *events,* Fred."

Thiemann said, "I'm feeling, I can't, I gotta . . ."

Parker and Lindahl grabbed him, one on each side, and eased him down until he was seated on the ground, the dead man just to his left. Not looking in that direction, he pushed himself around in a quarter circle until he was faced away from the body. "Do you think," he said, much more humbly than before, "do you think we should bring – it – him, bring him out? Or should we just tell the troopers where he is?"

"No," Parker said.

Thiemann looked up. "What?"

"We don't tell the troopers," Parker said. "We don't tell anybody."

Lindahl was holding his own rifle in his right hand, Thiemann's in his left. Looking warily toward Parker, moving as though he wished that left hand were free, he said, "What do you mean, Ed?"

"They told us," Parker said, "don't exchange gunfire. Even if this was one of them, we weren't supposed to shoot. He isn't one of them, he isn't armed, he was shot in the back." Parker looked at Thiemann. "If you go to the troopers with this, you'll do time."

"But—" Thiemann stared left and right, looking for exits. "That isn't right. We're like deputies."

"Search," Parker said. "Observe. Don't engage. If you go to the law, Fred, it's bad for you, and it's bad for us."

That snagged Thiemann's attention. "Bad for *you*? Jesus, how is this bad for you?"

Parker could not have the law interested in this trio of hunters. He wouldn't survive five minutes of being looked at by the law in a serious way. But what Thiemann needed was a different reason. "You shot an unarmed man in the back," he said, to twist that knife a little. "A man who isn't one of the ones we're looking for. Tom and I were right here with you, and we didn't stop you. That means we're part of it." Looking at Lindahl, Parker said, without moving his rifle, "You know what I'm saying, Tom. It's just as important for us. This thing didn't happen."

Lindahl, face paler than before, understood both what Parker was telling him and what Parker was telling Thiemann. He said, "My God, Ed, you mean, just leave him here? You can't do that to a human being."

"Tom," Parker said, "what that guy was doing to himself was just as bad, only slower. He didn't have

54

much of a life, and there wasn't a lot of it left. What difference does it make if he dies back there in that ruin from exposure or starvation or DTs or liver poisoning, or if he dies out here from Fred's bullet? He's dead, and the animals around here'll take care of the body."

"Jesus," Fred said, and put his shaking left hand up to cover his eyes.

"I can't even think that way," Lindahl said.

"I'm thinking for you," Parker told him. "This is a bind we're in, and the only way out of it is that it didn't happen."

Lindahl looked helplessly at the dead man, at the huddled shape of Thiemann, at Parker. "Should we at least . . . bury him?"

Parker scuffed his toe on the stony ground. "In this? How? Even if we had three shovels, and we don't, it would take hours to make a hole in this ground. And what for? Fred, what animals you got up around here, besides deer?"

Thiemann seemed surprised to be spoken to. Slowly he took his hand away from his eyes and squinted upward, toward Parker, but not quite meeting his eye. "Animals?"

"Predators. Scavengers."

Thiemann sighed, long and shuddering, but when he spoke, his voice was calm. "Well," he said, "we got coyote, not a whole lot, but some."

"Bobcat," Lindahl said.

"That's right," Thiemann agreed, and gestured skyward. "And a whole lot of turkey buzzards."

"They'll get here," Lindahl said, "right after we leave."

Thiemann shook his head. "Well, no," he said, "not that fast. A few hours later, it's gotta get—" He stopped, squeezed his eyes shut, shook his head. "God *damn*!"

"You thought it was the right guy," Parker told him. Now that Thiemann wouldn't be any more trouble, it was best that he not get excited. "It could have happened to any of us."

"That's right, Fred," Lindahl said.

Thiemann spread his hands. "I was just so— I thought, Wow, I've *got* him! Me! I've got him!" He shook his head again, disgusted with himself. "When I said we were acting like kids, I didn't really mean it, I thought it was a joke. It wasn't a joke." Looking now toward Lindahl, he said, asking forgiveness, "I never killed a man before. A human being. I never killed anybody. Deer, you've got venison, you've got . . . ."

"A reason," Lindahl suggested.

"I'm not sure I can even do that any more." Thiemann looked around, but not toward the body. "Would you guys help me up?"

They did, and he said, "I can't do this any more, I

gotta go home, I gotta, I don't know, get by myself somewhere. I can't do this today."

Parker said, "You got a wife at home, Fred?"

"Sure," Thiemann said, "and one daughter still in college."

"Can you tell your wife things? Can you trust her?"

That drew Thiemann's startled attention. "Sure I can trust her. But tell her about" – with a hand gesture behind himself, toward the corpse – "about that?"

"You've got to tell somebody," Parker said. "You can't put it where you can't ever talk about it, because it'll eat you up. You won't last. And you can't talk about it with anybody else, not even Tom here. Tell your wife, talk it out with her."

"He's right, Fred," Lindahl said. "Jane will help you."

Thiemann made an awkward shrug, uncomfortable with himself. "Get me back to my car, will you?"

They started back through the thick shrubbery toward the ruined railroad station. Thiemann hadn't asked for his rifle back, seemed not to want to know it was his, so Lindahl carried them both under his right arm, leaving his left arm free to push through the branches along the way.

Parker lagged behind the other two a pace, watched their backs, and decided what to do about them. The continued roadblocks in this part of the world, his lack of usable ID, even his lack of usable cash, meant he had to stick with Lindahl if possible, at least for now.

But how reliable was Thiemann? If he did talk with his wife, and if she was sensible, if she understood what was best to keep him out of trouble, it should be all right. But if Thiemann started to talk to anybody else, anybody at all, it would unravel in a minute. And Parker wouldn't know there was a problem until Lindahl's house was surrounded.

The other choice was to shoot them both, take Lindahl's Ford, get away from here. Until he left this county, Lindahl's membership card in Hickory Rod and Gun Club, displayed on the dashboard, would get him through the police blocks, particularly if he left the rifle prominently on the backseat. Not the Marlin, Lindahl's Ruger, the only weapon here that would not have been fired.

But the trouble wasn't just this county. The trouble extended for a hundred miles in every direction. To have a place to hole up was the most valuable asset he could hope for right now. If either Lindahl or Thiemann looked enough like him to make it possible to use their identification, it would be a different thing.

Lindahl suddenly turned his head, frowning at Parker with a question in his eyes, but Parker was simply pushing through the brush like the other two, the Marlin held loose in the crook of his right arm, hand nowhere near the lever or the trigger. Parker nodded at him, expressionless, and Lindahl faced the station, just ahead of them now, and pushed on.

SEVEN

They sat in the Ford the same as before, Lindahl driving, Parker beside him, Thiemann in the back with the three guns. The first few minutes, driving down the washboard road, no one spoke, but then Thiemann, as though he'd been brooding on this a long time, said, "I'm really in your hands now, aren't I? You guys."

Lindahl shot a quick glance at the rearview mirror but then had to watch the road. "In our hands? What do you mean, in our hands?"

"Well, you know this . . . thing about me. You know I killed a man."

Parker half turned so he could look at Thiemann, and rested his forearm atop the seat back. "We all have to trust each other, Fred. Tom and me, we're not reporting it, so that puts us in the same boat as you."

"Not exactly," Thiemann said, sounding bitter. "Not quite, Ed *Smith*. Not exactly."

With another quick look at the mirror, Lindahl said,

"What's the matter, Fred? You know me. We've known each other a long time."

"Not *for* a long time, Tom," Thiemann told him. "Not for years. You don't come to meetings, you don't go anywhere. I haven't seen your face in three years. You're like a hermit."

"I'm not *that* bad," Lindahl said, but as though admitting that yes, maybe he was that bad.

"Everybody knows," Thiemann told him, "you turned sour when you lost your job."

Lindahl didn't like that. "Oh, do they? Everybody knows? Everybody talks about it a lot, do they, Fred?"

"Nobody has to talk about it," Thiemann said. "Everybody already knows. You lost that job, you turned sour, your wife walked out, you don't act like you're *anybody's* friend. I don't know you any more. I don't know you much more than I know this fella here, except I know he talks smooth and he talks fast."

"Fred," Parker said, "you just tell your wife, Jane, what happened today and see if *she* wants you to turn yourself in. If she does, it doesn't matter what I say."

"Oh, I know what she'll say," Thiemann said, as though the knowledge made him angry. "Keep out of trouble, don't make things worse, you can't bring that man back, it's over and done with."

"Absolutely right," Lindahl said.

Leaning forward, his face closer to Parker so he could talk to Lindahl's profile, Thiemann said, "The one thing she won't tell me is forget it. I'm never gonna forget it."

Lindahl said, "None of us are, Fred. That was a bad moment for all of us."

Parker could see that Thiemann thought he was supposed to be punished now, but he was smart enough to understand he couldn't punish himself without punishing other people, too. First his wife, and the daughter still in college. But Tom Lindahl after that.

So what Thiemann was doing back there now was trying to separate himself from the other people who'd get hurt. Tom Lindahl was a stranger to him, a hermit who had turned sour. His wife wouldn't give him understanding, she'd just give him boilerplate stock responses. He couldn't think about these unworthy people, he could only think about himself.

The daughter would be harder to dismiss. That might hold him in place. In any case, the dangerous time was between now and when Thiemann reached his home. If his wife was there.

Parker said, "Fred, is your wife home now?"

"Yeah," Thiemann said without much interest. "She works at a hospital, but not on Saturdays."

"That's good," Parker said.

They drove in silence again until they were back down

on the county road and along it to the intersection with the roadblock, where the smiling trooper recognized them and waved them through. Lindahl and Parker waved back, but Thiemann sat crouched into himself, staring at the back of the seat in front of him. Then, just after that, Thiemann roused himself and said, not to either of them in particular, "I don't know if I can drive."

Parker looked at him, and Thiemann's face was very pale now. He'd been in shock since it had happened, but the shock was just beginning to bite in, taking blood from the parts of him where it was needed, like his brain.

Lindahl said, "You want me to drive you home, Fred?"

"But then there's the car," Thiemann said, "way the hell in St. Stanislas."

Parker said, "I could drive you in your car, Fred, and Tom could follow and pick me up at your place."

Lindahl tossed a sharp look at Parker. "You mean, I follow right behind you."

Parker said, "That's the only way I'm gonna get back to your house, Tom. Fred, you want me to do that?"

Thiemann frowned at Parker, then at the back of Lindahl's head, then at Parker again. "I think so," he said. "I think I got to do that. Thanks."

EIGHT

Several cars were in the Grange Hall parking lot, left by people doubling into another team member's car, as Thiemann had done. It looked as though no one else had come back yet. Among the vehicles parked here was a state police car. Seeing it, Parker said to Lindahl, "You talk to the trooper. I'll go with Fred to his car. Fred took sick after we checked out the railroad station. Nobody there."

"Okay."

The trooper was getting out of his car. It was the older one with the braid, who'd addressed the group before. Lindahl steered around to park next to Thiemann's Taurus, then they all got out onto the blacktop.

As Lindahl went off to talk with the trooper, Thiemann fumbled in his pocket for his keys, finally got them out, then couldn't get his fingers to work well enough to push the button that would unlock the doors. "Damn. I can't—"

"Give it to me."

Thiemann looked at Parker and didn't want to hand

over his keys, but then he did. Parker buzzed the doors open and looked past the SUV hood to where Lindahl and the trooper were talking. Lindahl seemed to be doing the job right, with no problem from the trooper.

Thiemann opened the driver's door, then stood looking confused. "I should be on the other side," he said.

"I'll get your rifle," Parker said.

"No!"

It was a sharp response, loud enough to make both Lindahl and the trooper look this way. Calm, quiet, Parker said, "You want to leave it with Tom?"

Thiemann blinked, and nodded. "For now," he said. "Yeah, just for now. I'll pick it up . . . . sometime."

"I'll tell him. You get in on the other side, I'll be right back."

"Yes, okay."

Carrying Thiemann's car keys, Parker walked over to Lindahl and the trooper, who were both still looking this way. "Afternoon," he said to the trooper.

"Afternoon. Everything all right there?"

"No, Fred's all loused up."

Lindahl said, "You ask me, he's got Lyme disease."

"Well, we've got a lot of that around here," the trooper said.

"Headache," Parker said, "and a lot of confusion. I'm gonna drive him home."

"Good idea."

"Tom, he says you should hold on to his rifle, he'll pick it up later." Parker shrugged, and offered the trooper a faint grin. "That was the 'no' he shouted," he said. "I think he's afraid he might accidentally shoot himself."

"Stumble with a rifle in your hands," the trooper said. "It's happened."

"Tom, you ready to follow me?"

"I think so. Okay, Captain?"

"Fine," the trooper said. "Thank you for your help."

"Anytime," Lindahl told him.

They started away, and the trooper called, "Tell your friend to get tested. You don't fool with Lyme disease."

"I'll tell him," Lindahl promised.

They walked on, and Parker said quietly, "I guess that's some sort of local disease around here."

"You get it from a tick in the woods," Lindahl told him. "It's a very mean disease. But you know, I bet Fred would rather have that right now than what he's got."

NINE

Parker got behind the wheel of the Taurus, adjusted the seat for his longer legs, started the engine, and then looked at Thiemann, who sat slumped beside him, staring at nothing, deep in his own thoughts. Parker waited, then said, "Which way?"

"What? Oh. Christ, I don't know what's the matter with me."

"You got shook up," Parker told him. "It's natural. Which way?"

"Uh, left out of the parking lot."

Parker drove that way, seeing Lindahl's SUV steady in his rearview mirror. "If I'm gonna make a turn," he said, "tell me before I get to it."

"Yeah, I'm okay now. I'll be okay."

"Good."

They drove two miles, and Parker became aware that Thiemann's attention had gradually shifted from his own interior landscape to Parker's profile. Thiemann frowned at him, quizzical, seeming to try to understand

67

something. Parker said nothing, and then Thiemann faced front and said, "There's a stop sign coming up. You'll turn right."

"Good."

They made the turn, and ahead was another road-block. Parker lowered his window, eased over to the shoulder, and waved Lindahl to overtake him. When Lindahl did, his own passenger window open, Parker called to him, "We're with you, you've got our guns."

Lindahl nodded and drove ahead, Parker now following him. He said, "Tom know the way to your house?"

"Sure."

"Good. He can lead the way, you don't have to worry about telling me."

"Probably good."

Ahead, Lindahl slowed for the barricade. The cop there, local, not state, saw Lindahl's membership card on the dash and waved him through, but Lindahl stopped, long enough to give the message. The cop looked toward the rifles on the floor in back, then nodded, waved Lindahl through again, and did the same to Parker; not grinning like the other one, but not stopping him, either.

They drove on awhile in silence, trailing Lindahl now, and then Thiemann said, "You didn't like that road-block."

"It's easier if they'll wave you through it. And we wanted Tom out front to lead me."

"Yeah, but you didn't like the roadblock."

"I don't like any roadblock," Parker said. "They make me nervous. People get tensed up, sometimes accidents happen."

"Nothing makes you nervous," Thiemann said.

Parker looked at him, then back at Lindahl up ahead. "What's that supposed to mean?"

"I got the wind knocked out of me, up there, when I shot that guy."

"Sure you did."

"Tom felt it, too. But you didn't."

"Maybe I just don't show things that much."

"Maybe. But you were pretty cool. You knew what we should do and why we should do it. Tom and me, we wouldn't have thought to leave that poor guy up there for the scavengers to eat. The first thing you said to me, what scavenger animals do we have around here?"

"Because you were in trouble, Fred," Parker told him. "You know you were. And Tom knows it, too."

"The second you saw that roadblock," Thiemann said, "you were opening the window, getting off the road. You knew exactly what to say to Tom."

"It was easier to get waved through on Tom's ticket than have to stop and go through all that."

"Just show ID," Thiemann said.

"It was easier not to."

Thiemann looked out the windshield, not saying anything more, but thinking it over. He was suspicious of something, but he didn't know what. He had sensed the otherness in Parker, but he didn't know what it meant.

An older Cadillac convertible, bright red, top down, big as a speedboat, came the other way, suddenly honking madly. The three guys in it, middle-aged, in their bright orange or red hunting caps, waved hands with beer cans in them at Lindahl, who honked and waved back but didn't stop. Neither did the Cadillac, which went on by, the three guys all grinning and shouting things, now at Parker and Thiemann. They were very happy. Parker nodded but didn't honk.

"That's part of our group," Thiemann said.

"I know."

"They shouldn't be drinking. That's the worst thing you can do." Then Thiemann turned away with a grimace. "Almost the worst thing."

Ahead, Lindahl signaled for a left, and Parker did, too. "How much farther?"

"A couple miles." Thiemann turned toward him again. "You don't think much of us, do you?"

"How do you mean?"

"Not just those guys with the beer," Thiemann said.

"All of us, running around, being man hunters. You could see in those troopers' eyes, they thought we were all just a joke. Useless, and a joke. And I could see it in your eyes, too. You think the same thing."

Parker followed Lindahl around the turn. Thiemann's sense of Parker's otherness, which had led him toward suspicion, had now led him to embarrassment instead; Parker wasn't an alien from outside them, unknown and untrusted, he was a judge from above them, finding them wanting. Good; that moved Thiemann away from a direction that might have caused trouble.

"Isn't that right, Ed? You think the same thing?"

"Not a joke," Parker said. "You just don't have the training. I suppose, if you'd been trained, up there in the woods, you wouldn't have moved quite so fast."

"Not quite so fast." Thiemann barked a laugh with no amusement in it. "You'd think, with the training, the trained guy'd be faster."

"The trained guy knows *when* to be fast," Parker said.

"You trained, Ed?"

"Some."

"I thought so. It's here."

This area was more suburban than country, with curving roads flanked by neat small houses on large green lots. Lindahl, signaling for a right, didn't turn but came to a stop just beyond a driveway. At the other end of the driveway was a tan stucco ranch with attached two-car garage.

Parker, turning in at the driveway, said, "Which garage?"

"Doesn't matter, they're both full of junk."

Parker stopped, switched off the engine, and opened his door. But Thiemann went on just sitting there. Parker said, "The sooner you talk to her, the better."

"What the hell am I gonna *say*?"

"Honey, I made a mistake today."

Thiemann's expression was haggard. "That's a hell of a way to put it."

"It's what happened."

"A mistake."

"Let's get out of the car."

They got out of the Taurus and looked at each other across its top. "I keep thinking," Thiemann said, "it's a good thing for me you didn't get impatient. I don't know why I keep thinking that."

"I got nothing but patience," Parker told him. "I'm on vacation. Go talk to your wife."

"I will. Maybe I'll see you around, before you leave."

"Maybe," Parker said.

TEN

Parker got into the Ford, and Lindahl immediately shifted into drive. Then, looking at the empty suburban street as it curved away in front of them, he said, "How is he?"

"You know him better than I do."

"Not in something like *this*." Lindahl gave Parker a quick uneasy look, as though not sure how to explain himself, then faced the road. "This isn't something that just happened," he said. "He shot a man. I can't even imagine that."

"You tried to stop him."

"He was just too—" Lindahl paused while he turned out of the suburb onto a country road. "Fred likes to be in charge," he said. "He likes to think he's the guy can take care of it, whatever it is."

"Can he take care of what he's got now?"

Another quick glance. "What do you mean?"

"He's in shock," Parker said. "So right now he doesn't know what he's thinking. Also, down inside, he

73

has the idea he ought to be punished. That could lead him to the law, which would be bad for everybody."

"Especially you."

"No, especially Fred. He may like to pretend he's in charge, but he's in foreign territory now. His grandfather's memories aren't gonna help him."

Lindahl snorted. "I bet he's sorry he said that."

"Maybe, later."

"I'll tell you something could help him," Lindahl said, "that he wouldn't ever talk about. His oldest son is in jail."

"How did that happen?"

"He was in the army, they sent him to the Middle East, teach those people all about democracy. He met a couple young local guys taught him a few things of their own. These are fellas walk into your house, walk out with stuff they didn't have before."

"Uh-huh."

"Not like you. Small-time. Impressed George, though. He came back, he told everybody about them. They even had a special slang for them. *Hawasim,* it means looter." Lindahl shrugged. "I guess it's not as easy to be a looter in a war zone."

"Probably not."

"Young George thought he was *hawasim* himself, now he's doing three to five in Attica. The last thing Fred wants is to be in the next cell."

"Good."

They drove on, silent a while. Parker thought the shock of a son in prison must have been almost as strong for Thiemann as the second shock that had hit him today. Would the double hit make him likelier to withdraw into himself, stay quiet, not make trouble? Or would it make him spin out of control?

"I want to do it," Lindahl said.

There had been close to ten minutes of silence in the car, and now Lindahl spoke abruptly, as though not wanting to forget what he had to say. Or as though not wanting the chance to change his mind. The words had been forceful but flat, Lindahl's expression intense.

Parker said, "The track?"

"I hadn't seen any of those people for years," Lindahl said. "What'd Fred say? Three years? He's right, I don't know them any more, and they don't know me. They don't give a shit about me."

"They haven't seen you."

"They have an opinion about me," Lindahl said, "and that's all they need. You heard what Fred said. I lost my job, lost my wife, turned sour, end of story."

"You didn't give them any other story."

"Because it's true." Lindahl nodded at the road in front of them, agreeing with himself. "As long as I stay around here," he said, "I'm just what they think I am.

75

A hermit, Fred said. Didn't destroy my life just the once, destroy it all over again every day." Another emphatic nod, this time with an emphatic glare in Parker's direction. "As long as I'm here," he said, "that's who I am, there's no hope I'll ever get out of this. I have to go down and take that money from the track because otherwise I'm dead here, I'm just walking around dead, all by myself." He laughed, a bitter sound. "With a parrot that doesn't talk."

"We'll drive down there," Parker said. "After dark."

Lindahl took a long shuddering inhale and slowly let it out. "I'm a new guy," he said. "I don't look it yet, but that's what I am."

ELEVEN

With the sound off, the television set seemed to be saying that nothing much had happened. Parker gave Lindahl back his outer coat and boots, and then Lindahl went off to find some take-out food. "You don't want any of that rabbit I got," he said. "And neither do I, any more."

"Fine," Parker said.

Lindahl shrugged into his coat. "There's nothing real close around here," he said. "I'll probably be an hour."

Parker said, "If you run into anything I should know, call here."

"You're not going to answer the phone." Lindahl looked startled.

"No, I'm not. But I'll hear what you tell the answering machine."

"Oh. Fine. Good."

Lindahl left, and Parker went back to the kitchen where, first time through, he'd seen a drawer of tools. First taking the wad of four thousand in new cash from his pocket, he stuffed it deep into the bad-smelling garbage bag under the sink, washed his hands, and turned to the tool drawer. From it he selected a hammer, a Phillips-head screwdriver, a flathead screwdriver, a hacksaw, and a flashlight. He also took, from the bedroom, a right-handed black leather glove. Then he left the converted garage, carrying everything, and walked over to the rear of the boarded-up house.

It was now almost seven in the evening, twilight, just enough illumination left in the sky to see what you were doing. The few houses he could see with lights in their windows looked darker than the rest of the world. No traffic moved out on the road, no sounds could be heard but the small movements of little animals.

Parker stopped at the rear door of the house to study what was here. The door was up two concrete steps from ground level, with filigree iron railings on both sides. A piece of half-inch plywood had been cut to fit between the railings, then screwed to the door frame on both sides and across the top. There were a total of fourteen Phillips-head screws, which would have been put in with a power drill, a tool Lindahl didn't have.

The big question was what length screws they'd used. For half an inch of plywood, a one-inch screw would be plenty, but a guy with a power drill wouldn't mind putting in longer screws, if they were handy.

Parker put on the glove, picked up the Phillips-head

screwdriver from the concrete step where he'd laid all the tools, and went to work. The first screw didn't want to budge, having been put in position here a long time ago. Two-handed, he gave it quick hard twists, and at last it unstuck and then turned as smoothly as if it had been oiled.

One-inch; good. Parker pocketed it and went on to the next.

Some of the screws were a little easier, some a little harder, but it all came out to the same; a quarter hour to remove all the screws. Then he pulled the plywood back, to show beyond it an ordinary kitchen door with four windowpanes in its upper half. The doorknob had been removed, because it would have stuck out in the way of the plywood.

The next step was to alter the screws to his own purpose. Turning the sheet of plywood sideways, he leaned it against the front of the railings and put all the screws back in place except for one low on the left side. He turned the screws in only partway, leaving less than a quarter inch of the head still jutting out. He then used the hacksaw to slice off all the screw points back flush to the wood before seating the screws completely into place as before. Now, when the plywood was in position, it would look the same as before, but a simple tug at the top would pull it free.

The screw he hadn't put back he fixed into the upper middle of the plywood on the house side, turning it in only partway, so that it wouldn't show on the outside. From inside the house, that would now be the handle to pull the plywood back into place.

Next was the door. He removed the glove, held it against the pane of glass nearest the missing knob, and hit it with the hammer. The muffled jingle of the breaking glass echoed mostly into the house. Knocking the last couple of shards out of the way, he reached in, found the knob still in place on the inside, turned it, and the door had not been locked; no reason to.

He pushed the door open and stepped in, feet crackling on the broken glass. Turning back, he picked up the plywood and moved it into position, guided by the iron railings that flanked the door. When he pulled the plywood upright against the wall by the screw he'd just added, it fit snugly into place, the shortened screws sliding into the previous holes just enough to hold.

Now the house. The plywood over all the doors and windows made the interior completely black. Switching on the flashlight, Parker saw the house had not been stripped. When the town fathers had sealed it up, they'd still hoped to find a buyer someday, so the plumbing was still here, and the electric fixtures, even the sink and a thirty-year-old refrigerator with its door propped open by a plastic milk box. The electricity and water had been switched off, but that was to be expected.

Parker moved through the dusty empty rooms and found nothing he didn't expect to find. A coating of gray on the floorboards, walls faded to a dull noncolor, long cobwebs in the corners and around the blinded windows. No one had been in here since the plywood had been put up.

Back in the kitchen, he put the flashlight on the counter near the back door; if he had to come back, there wouldn't be time to find some other light source.

There was nothing else here he needed to do or know. He left the house, pulled the door not quite shut, set the sheet of plywood in place, and went back to the converted garage to wait for dinner.

TWELVE

"We've got a problem tonight," Parker said, "getting to this track of yours."

Lindahl put his beer can down. "What's that?"

They were seated in the living room, eating acceptable pizza, Lindahl drinking beer, Parker water. Outside, full dark had arrived. The silent television set showed sitcoms, so nothing else had happened. In its cage, the parrot seemed mostly asleep, though every once in a while it swiveled its head and made a small gurgling sound and marched a bit in place.

Parker said, "They're looking for two men. They don't know if the two men are still together or if they separated. Once we get where your gun club card doesn't count for anything, when we come to a roadblock and they see two men in the car, they'll want ID from both."

"And you can't show any."

"Nothing useful."

Lindahl thought about that, chewing pizza. "The

funny thing is," he said, "once we get to the track, I can help you with ID, but not before."

Parker frowned at him. "Help? How?"

"Every employee carries an encoded ID card," Lindahl told him. "You wear it in a plastic sleeve hangs around your neck. I'm the one bought the machine, I chose it, I know how to use it. I could take your driver's license, photograph it, change the information in the machine, print it out on one of our own laminated blanks. It won't be perfect, but it'll look a lot like the real thing."

"But not till we get there," Parker said.

"If my vehicle had a trunk—"

"No."

"Well, it doesn't, anyway. But the point is, if we can get you there, we can solve your ID problem."

Parker thought about that. He saw what to do, but he didn't like it. Lindahl was so unsure of himself, Parker needed to keep him on a tight leash, but now he couldn't. If Lindahl had time off by himself, would he decide the hell with it, let's call in the cops?

Whatever the odds, Parker would have to risk them. He said, "No, you don't need me there. This machine of yours, it takes mug shots to go on the ID cards, right?"

"Sure."

"There's already a picture on my license. You're going to keep everything the same on it except the name and the home address. You don't need me there to make the change, you only need the license."

Lindahl frowned. "You mean, go there by myself. That way, I'd have to go all the way there twice tonight."

"The second time, I'll drive," Parker said. "It's the only way we can do this, Tom. I can't leave here without identification."

"It's over an hour, each way."

"It's up to you," Parker told him. "We do it this way, or we don't do it. Which do you want?"

Lindahl eyed his beer can. "I'd better switch to coffee," he decided, and got up to go to the kitchen.

THIRTEEN

Lindahl drove off a little before nine. Ten minutes later a knock sounded at the door. Parker was seated in the living room, beside the silent television set, not looking at it, waiting a little longer before going out to explore, but now somebody was here.

Parker waited, not moving. The front door, and the window next to it, were fitted into the original garage door space so sloppily that sound came through from outside, one or two people talking low, somebody scuffing his feet. Then there was a louder, harder knock and a voice called, "Ed! Ed, you in there?" Very aggressive, pushing hard.

Ed? Not looking for Lindahl. No; somebody who had watched and waited for Lindahl to leave, then came over to knock on the door, because it was Ed he wanted to see.

The voice was slightly familiar, recently heard somewhere. Not Thiemann, somebody else.

"Goddammit, Ed, be sociable! Open up this door!" And whoever it was rattled the doorknob, but since the door wasn't locked, he unexpectedly lurched into the living room, holding the knob to save himself, barking a laugh of surprise and embarrassment.

It was the one-eyed guy with the black patch from the meeting this afternoon at St. Stanislas, and coming in behind him, more cautious and wary, his coat holder, Cory. They both looked at Parker, who stayed in his chair.

The one-eyed man said, "What's the matter, Ed? How come you don't open your door?"

"It's not my door," Parker told him.

"You can answer," the guy insisted. "When somebody comes along, polite, and knocks in a very polite way, and calls out your name, you can answer, can't you?"

"I'm not in a mood for visitors," Parker told him.

The one-eyed man was both surprised and offended. "Not in a *mood*! You hear that, Cory?"

"Cal," Cory said, a small warning.

But Cal wasn't a man to take warnings. Glaring around the room, he stepped over and dropped backward onto the sofa, facing Parker, saying, "Well, I feel like a visit." Then he blinked with sudden delight and pointed past Parker, crying, "Cory, looka *that*!"

"It's a parrot," Cory said.

"Goddam, it *is* a parrot! That's what *I* oughta have." Leaning toward Parker, gesturing at the patch that covered his left eye, he said, "You can see how that would go with me, can't you?"

"It belongs to Tom," Parker said.

Taking a step forward, Cory said, "Cal doesn't mean he wants it. It just tickled him, that's all. You know, because of the patch."

"I don't want a goddam *bird*," Cal said, and now he was discontented again. Leaning forward ever closer to Parker, he said, "I bet you don't know we're twins."

"I knew you were brothers," Parker said.

"Yeah, but not twins. It's because of this goddam—" He made an angry swiping gesture toward the patch. "If I could get," he started, then erased that in the air, and sat back, showing himself calm and logical. "The situation is," he said, "if I could get the plastic surgery and the glass eye, I could look just exactly like this handsome fella here."

"The insurance wouldn't pay," Cory explained.

"I wasn't that drunk!" Cal yelled, angry again. "And it was that other sonofabitch's fault, anyway." Leaning forward toward Parker again, now confidential, he said, "All I need's a little money, Ed, you can see that. Where'm I gonna get that kinda money, Ed? I'm a *carpenter* at the modular home plant over in LeForestville, me and Cory both, where we gonna get fifteen, twenty thousand dollars?"

"I don't know," Parker said.

"I bet you got some money, Ed," Cal said, smiling like he was friendly, showing crooked teeth. "I bet you could help out a fella, if you wanted."

"Quid pro quo," Cory said, to explain things.

So the artist's renderings had done their work, after all, at least with these two. Parker said to Cory, "What's the quo?"

"We don't need to go into all that," Cal said, impatient, sitting back, waving that idea away. "We're just friendly, that's all, a couple friendly guys, helping each other out. Just Cal and Cory Dennison and good old Ed – what was it? Smith?"

"That's right," Parker said.

"Funny kind of name, that, Smith," Cal said, twisting the name to make it sound strange as he winked his good eye at his brother and said, "You don't hear it much. Not around here, you don't."

Parker said, "Get to the point."

"The point?" Cal seemed surprised, as though he'd thought they'd already reached the point. "It's just to be pals, that's all," he said. "Be of, you know, *use* to each other. Like if we could do something for you. Or like, it should happen, you might have a stash of money around somewhere, you'd probably want to help a friend with this bad fucking eye here."

Parker said, "That's Tom Lindahl's sofa you're sitting on."

Cal grinned and shrugged. "So?"

"Get up from it."

"Oh, I don't think so." Cal spread his arms and legs out, settling into the sofa. "Everybody's gotta be somewhere, you know. Even those—"

"No, they don't," Parker said.

Thrown off, not getting to make his clever remark about how even the missing bank robbers have to be *somewhere,* wink, wink, Cal blinked his one eye at Parker and said, "What?"

"Some people," Parker said, "don't have to be anywhere." He got to his feet, aware of them both tensing up as they watched him. To Cory, he said, "You're the one with brains. What do you do now?"

"Hey, listen," Cal said.

But Cory patted a hand downward in his brother's direction, looking at Parker as he said, "Maybe we'll talk tomorrow. Maybe with Tom here."

"Ask him," Parker said.

Cory nodded. "We'll do that. Come on, Cal."

Cal looked up at his brother and decided not to argue. He moved to get up, but the sofa, rump-sprung and saggy, was hard to get out of. As he tried to get to his feet while making it look easy, Parker made a small fast gesture with his hands, nothing in particular, but Cal lost his balance and sprawled back onto the sofa.

"You want to be careful," Parker told him.

"Come *on,* Cal," Cory said, and stuck a hand out, which Cal angrily took, to be hauled up out of the sofa. They moved toward the still-open door, Parker following, seeing their battered red Dodge Ram out there, with the fitted steel toolbox bolted to the bed. They stepped through, and Parker stood in the doorway behind them. "Always be careful," he told Cal. "You wouldn't want anything to happen to that other eye."

As Cory pulled him toward the pickup with a hand on his elbow, Cal glared back, face distorted, crying, "Never mind the good one! What about *this* one? What about *this* one?"

Parker shrugged. "Ask the parrot."

FOURTEEN

Cory drove, so there was no squealing of tires, burning of rubber. Parker watched the Ram go, then stood in the open doorway another five minutes, listening to an absolutely silent night, before he stepped outside, shut the door, and walked down the driveway.

There were two tall streetlights at diagonal corners of the intersection down to his left, but otherwise the road was dark, with here and there the dull gleam of lights inside houses. Parker walked first to his right, past a dark house, then a house where an older couple played some sort of board game in a brightly lit living room, then another dark house, a boarded-up house, and then the last on this side, where a woman muffled up in robes and blankets as though she were on a sleigh in Siberia sat alone to watch TV.

This first walk through the town was simply to get a sense of it, and the sense was of leftovers, of people still in the stadium after the game is done. There were no children watching television, no toys on porches, never more than two people visible in any house. These were the respectable poor, living in retirement in the only place they'd ever known. They wouldn't have much that would be of use to Parker, though there might be one thing. Older not-rich people in an isolated community: Some of them might have handguns.

Down the other side of the road, Parker passed the gas station, closed for the night, with light from a soda machine in front of the office illuminating the pumps and a small night-light gleaming on the wall above the desk inside.

Up till now, there had been no traffic at all through this town at this hour, the blinking signal lights at the intersection controlling nothing. But as he walked just beyond the gas station, Parker did see a car coming this way from the blackness outside the town. He continued to walk, continued to look at the houses, and the car rapidly approached, its high beams becoming troublesome just before the driver dimmed them; which meant he'd seen Parker and was doing the polite thing.

The car slowed, coming into the town, then went on by Parker, who kept walking at a steady pace. A few seconds later he heard the tire-squeal as the car made a U-turn, and here it came again, the opposite way, slowing beside him.

Not a cop. A beat-up older Toyota four-door, some dark color. The passenger window slid down as the car came to a stop beside Parker, and the driver alone in there, a woman, leaned toward him to say, "Can I help you?"

He could keep walking, but she'd just pace him, so he stopped and turned to her. "To do what?" he said.

She didn't seem to know what to do with that answer. She looked younger than the people of this town, probably in her thirties, dashboard-lit in such a way as to give her face harsh angles and extremes of light and shadow. She said, "Are you looking for an address or something?"

"No."

"I just thought— People don't usually walk around here."

"I do."

"But you don't live here."

"I visit here."

"Oh." Now at last on familiar ground, she pasted what was supposed to be a friendly smile on her face and said, "Who are you visiting?"

It would cause less trouble and suspicion just to answer her. "Tom Lindahl."

"Tom! I'm surprised. I thought he was—" Then it occurred to her she might be about to say something insulting about Lindahl, and this might be a friend or relative, so she laughed, an uncomfortable sound, and said, "You know what I mean."

"You thought he was a hermit."

"Yes, I suppose. Yes."

"He is a hermit," Parker said. "But I visit him."

"Well, why not?" she said, moving her hands on the steering wheel as though sorry she'd stopped. "I'm glad he has . . . I'm glad he has visitors."

"And now," Parker said, "I'm doing my after-dinner walk."

"Of course. Well . . ."

She didn't know how to end the encounter, but he did. He nodded and walked on, not looking back. After a long moment of silence back there, the car abruptly burst into life, with another U-turn squeal of tires, and receded quickly into silence.

A few minutes later, nearing the end of his walk-through, he came to the house where the old man had been asleep earlier today on the front porch. Now the only illumination from that house was the fitful blue-gray glitter from a television set, and when Parker looked in the living room window, the same man, in the same clothing, sat asleep straight up on the sofa, the television light playing across him like reflections from a waterfall.

So this was as good a place as any to start. When Parker looked back, the Toyota with the inquisitive woman was gone. He walked around to the back of the house, which from this angle was similar to the boarded-up house he'd entered earlier, including even the concrete steps up to the back door flanked by filigree iron railings.

Taking from his pocket a credit card that had no function any more except what he was going to use it for now, because it had the same burned name on it as the driver's license Lindahl had taken away with him, he slid it down the jamb between frame and door, worked the bolt back from its recess, and pushed the door open. It squeaked, very slightly, but above that he could hear the screams of police sirens and raucous music from the television set at the other end of the house.

This was a smaller structure than the boarded-up house, only one story high, not much larger than Lindahl's converted garage. The messy kitchen was unlit, and so was the small dining room in front of it, crowded with furniture as though the owner had at one point moved here from somewhere larger. A bedroom off the dining room was clearly a seldom-used guest room, so he backtracked to the kitchen, opened a side door there, and found the bedroom.

There were two places people usually kept a handgun inside a house, both in the bedroom: either in a locked box atop a dresser or in a locked drawer in a bedside table. There was no box on top of the dresser in here, only coins, socks, magazines, and a very thin wallet, but the lower of two drawers in the bedside table was locked.

Parker opened the drawer above that one, felt in the near-darkness through a jumble of medicines, flashlight, eyeglasses, and a deck of playing cards, and found the key. He closed that drawer, unlocked the other, and took out a Smith & Wesson Ranger in .22 caliber, a stubby blue-black revolver with a two-inch barrel, moderately accurate across an average room, not much good beyond that. But it would do.

Parker pocketed the revolver, felt some more in the drawer, and found a small heavy cardboard box. When he took it out and opened it, it contained more cartridges. The box was almost full. Had the revolver never been fired? Possibly.

He pocketed both the gun and the box of ammunition, relocked the drawer, and put the key back in the drawer above. To the sounds of forensic explanation from the living room, he silently let himself back out of the house.

As he walked down the side driveway toward the road, the television sound abruptly shut off and lights came on in the living room, spilling out of the windows. Skirting that glow, Parker continued on out to the road, saw the old man just exiting the living room toward the rear of the house, and walked on back to Lindahl's place.

Would any of the people in these houses here have anything else of use to him? No. What he needed was a good amount of cash and clean transportation. He'd start to assemble those once he got the altered driver's license. If he got it.

Back at Lindahl's house, he saw that the answering machine had collected no messages, so possibly Lindahl was simply doing the job. Parker sat down to wait.

Lindahl had said the trip would take a little over an hour each way, and he'd left just before nine, so when the silent television set started the eleven o'clock news, Parker stood, watched the set until he saw there was no fresh news about the bank robbers, then left the house, still with all its lights on, and went over to let himself into the boarded-up house, pulling the plywood panel shut behind him. Using Lindahl's flashlight, he went upstairs, found the pull-down staircase to the attic, and climbed up.

The round window that was the only opening in the house that hadn't been covered with plywood was a pale blur to his right. Switching off the flashlight, he crossed to it and looked out. The window, at the rear of the house, was at head height, about a foot wide. Through it he could see Lindahl's place and a bit of the driveway, but nothing more. Revolver in one pocket and flashlight in the other, he leaned against the wall, looked out the window, and settled down to see what would arrive.

FIFTEEN

At twenty-five after eleven, a glow brightened the front of Lindahl's house, and then his black SUV appeared, moving slowly. It stopped in the usual place, and Lindahl got out, stretched, yawned hugely, and walked over to enter his house.

Parker watched. Nothing else happened over there. Then, after two minutes, the front door opened again and Lindahl stepped out, peering to left and right. He barely glanced at the boarded-up house. He might have called a name, but if he did, Parker couldn't hear it. In any event, after one more look around and a baffled headshake, he went back inside.

Now Parker turned away from the window. The attic was absolutely black, with a rectangular hole somewhere in its floor for the staircase. He took the flashlight from his pocket, closed his fingers over the glass, switched it on, and slowly separated his fingers until he could make out the area ahead of him and the beginning of the staircase.

Going down, he didn't bother to lift the attic stairs into their upper position. Reaching the back door, he switched off the flashlight and put it on the counter, then let himself out, put the plywood in place, and crossed to enter the house.

Lindahl was in the bedroom, but he came out when he heard the front door. The look of bafflement was still on his face. "Where'd you go?"

"Looking around the neighborhood. You did the license?"

Bewilderment was replaced by a proud smile as Lindahl took a laminated card from his shirt pocket and extended it. "Take a look at that."

It looked very good. It was the same New York State driver's license as before, colored in pale pastels, with the same photo of Parker on it, but now his name was William G. Dodd and he lived at 216 N. Sycamore Court, Troy. The card itself seemed to be just slightly thicker than those used by the state of New York, but not enough to attract attention.

"It's good," Parker said, and put the license away in his wallet. "Where'd you get the name and address, make them up?"

"No. Bill Dodd used to work there years ago, before he retired, and that address came off another guy's next of kin on his employment sheet." Shrugging, but pleased with himself, Lindahl said, "I figured we wouldn't want you living too close to the track."

Parker didn't see what difference it made, but let it go, saying, "You want me to drive?"

"God, yes," Lindahl said. "I got stopped three times going down, by the way, and twice coming back. I'm ready to not drive for a while. But just give me five minutes."

"Fine."

Lindahl turned toward the bedroom, then turned back, with a sudden sunny smile on his face. "I'm really going to do it," he said. "Even when I left here, I still wasn't sure, but the minute I saw the place I knew. It's been a weight on me, and now I'm getting rid of it."

"That's good."

"Yes. And it was a good thing we met," Lindahl said. "Good for both of us. Give me five minutes."

PART TWO

PART TWO

ONE

A billboard ahead on the right read

GRO-MORE RACING
Next Right

"That's the main gate," Lindahl said. "We don't want that. You keep going, about another quarter mile, there's a dirt road on this side."

The dashboard clock read 12:42. In the last hour, William G. Dodd's new driver's license had been inspected by two state troopers at roadblocks and found acceptable; which of course was more likely at night than by day.

On the drive down, Lindahl had alternated between a kind of buzzing vibrancy, keyed up, giving Parker little spatter-shots of his autobiography, and a deep stillness, as he studied his newly changed interior landscape, as mute as his parrot.

The main gate, when they drove past it, was a broad entry with parking lots to right and left, a line of entry booths, and the wide hulk of the clubhouse beyond. Large curved iron gates built around stylized outlined shapes of bulls were closed over the entrance. A few dim lights showed here and there in the clubhouse.

Parker said, "Who's in there now?"

"Two guards. That's the security office, that light way over to the right. There used to be just one guard at night, but then they found out the guy would usually fall asleep, so now it's two."

"Do they patrol? Make rounds?"

"No, they've got monitors in the security room, cameras and smoke detectors here and there in the clubhouse and the paddocks, burglar alarms on the ground-floor doors and windows."

"Are the guards armed?"

"Oh, sure. Handguns in holsters. They're in uniform, they work for a security company, that part is all contracted out. Here's where we turn."

The turn was a narrow dirt road unmarked except for a Dead End sign. Parker drove slowly, trying to see into the darkness to his right where the track would be. "Is that a wall?"

"Wooden wall, eight foot high, runs the whole perimeter. This road is used to bring horses in and out, supplies, ambulance when they need one. Up ahead here, turn right to the gate."

"Can they see these headlights?"

"No, there's nobody around in there except the guards in the security office. Those other lights are just for the fire code."

This gate was plain chain-link, eight feet high like the wall stretching away to left and right. Parker stopped just before it, the headlights shining through the chain-link fence onto the white clapboard end wall of the clubhouse. Tall white wooden fences angled out from the corners of the clubhouse at front and back, curved to meet the perimeter wall at some distance to both sides, making a large enclosed area, part blacktop, part dirt. A number of trucks and pickups and horse vans were parked along the wall to the left, with an ambulance and a fire engine along the wall to the right.

Opening his door, Lindahl said, "I'll turn off the alarm, then I can unlock the gate."

"Isn't there a security camera along here?"

"No," Lindahl said. "They only watch the inside and the paddocks. They're not worried so much about break-ins as fire. Or somebody wanting to hurt the horses. I'll be a minute."

Parker waited as Lindahl opened a metal box beside the gate, punched numbers onto the pad in there, then took a full ring of keys from his pocket, selected one, and opened the padlock securing the gate. He opened it wide, then gestured for Parker to follow him. He walked confidently in the headlight glare toward the clubhouse, then turned to wave to Parker to stop in front of more chain-link fence, this making a kind of three-sided cage extending out from the middle of the clubhouse wall.

Coming around to the driver's door, Lindahl said, "Leave the engine and lights on a minute, I want you to see this."

Parker got out of the Ford and went with Lindahl to the fence. The outer side of it was another gate, and inside, a concrete ramp sloped down to a basement level, then went straight under the building, stopping at a featureless metal garage door tucked back about eight feet.

"Inside there," Lindahl said, "is the corridor, with the safe room on the left. The armored car backs down, they open the door, and they load on the boxes. Food deliveries go down there, too, and all kinds of supplies. But we have to get in a different way now, so you can turn the car off and we'll go in that door over there."

The door was near the front corner of the clubhouse, solid wood with *No Admittance* stenciled on it. By the time Parker had left the Ford and walked over, Lindahl had this door, too, unlocked. "There's no cameras until we come to the main corridor," he said.

Parker said, "I'd expect more security."

"Well, it's a small track out in the country," Lindahl said as he led the way down the dim-lit narrow corridor past closed doors. "It has two twenty-four-day meets, spring and fall, and it's shut down the rest of the time. They've been wanting to sign on to a tote-board system so they could be open for betting at other tracks the rest of the year, but so far it hasn't worked out. I think the population around here is too small. So the track never makes a whole lot of money, and there's never once been a break-in in all these years. A couple times crazies tried to get at the horses, but nothing else. We go through here, it bypasses the main corridor."

Lindahl opened a door on the left, and they entered a broad low-ceilinged room with eight desks neatly spaced on a black linoleum floor. A fluorescent halo around a large wall clock gave illumination. Most of the desks were covered with papers and other items, including a leftover bacon and omelet breakfast on a green plastic plate.

"This is where the accounts are kept," Lindahl said, and pointed. "My office used to be— Damn!"

He had bumped into the wrong desk, causing the breakfast to flip over and hit the floor facedown. Lindahl stooped to pick up the plate, but the omelet stuck to the black linoleum, which was now a black ocean, and that omelet the sandy desert island, with the solitary strip of bacon sticking up from it, slightly slumped but brave, the perfect representation of the stranded sailor, alone and waiting for his cartoon caption. On the floor, it looked like what the Greeks call *acheiropoietoi*, a pictorial image not made by a human hand.

"I ought to clean that up," Lindahl said, frowning down doubtfully at the new island.

"A mouse did it," Parker told him. "Drop the plate on it and let's go."

"Fine."

Lindahl led the way across the room and out another door to another corridor that looked identical to the first. They went leftward, Lindahl still leading the way, Parker making sure to remember the route.

Lindahl stopped where the corridor made a right turn into a wider hallway. Pausing, he leaned to glance around the corner, then said, "Take a look. See the camera?"

Parker leaned forward. Some distance down the hall, on the opposite side, was a closed door with a small pebble-glass window and a pushbar. Mounted on the wall above the door was a light, aimed downward, flooding the immediate area and giving some illumination down as far as the end here. Above the light, just under the dropped ceiling, a camera was mounted on a small metal arm. The camera was at this moment pointed toward the other end of the hall but was moving, turning leftward toward the wall. As Parker watched, it stopped, hesitated, and began to turn back in the other direction.

Parker leaned back. "Tell me about it."

"It does a one-minute sweep, back and forth. Once it comes back in this direction and starts the other way, it looks down here for just a few seconds. After that, we have forty seconds to walk down the hall and through the door. That's the stairwell; no cameras. We go down in the basement. Here it comes."

Lindahl waited, seeming to count seconds in his head, then looked around the corner and said, "Good."

They strode down the hall, the camera continuing to turn away from them. Lindahl pushed open the door, and Parker followed him through, to a stairwell of concrete flights of steps leading up and down. A small light mounted on the wall above the door illuminated this section of stairs.

They went downstairs one flight to the bottom of the stairwell, where an identical door had an identical light over it. Lindahl said, "This is a little tricky, because if I open the door when the camera's faced straight across the hall, the guards might see the light change on their screen, so hold on."

He bent down to the small window, cheek against the glass and head angled back as he squinted up and out. "I can just see it when— Oh, good. Right now."

He opened the door and immediately walked briskly to the right. Parker followed. The end of the hall down here was very close, closer than upstairs, with a metal fire door in it. As he walked, Lindahl chose another key from his ring, quickly unlocked the end door, and stepped through. Following him, Parker looked back and saw the camera still turning away.

Once this door was closed, the space they were in was completely without light. "I don't want to turn the light on in here," Lindahl said, "because the camera might see it, around the door edges, I don't know for sure. Hold on."

Parker waited, leaning against the closed door. He heard Lindahl shuffle away, then sounds of a key in a lock and a door opening, and then lights went on, ceiling fluorescents, in a room on the right.

Lightspill showed him the space he was in. Empty, and longer than wide, it had a concrete floor, concrete-block walls, and a windowless metal garage door at the far end, certainly the same one he'd seen from outside.

A forklift truck stood in the near right corner. When Parker moved to the room Lindahl had illuminated, the doorway was a little taller and wider than average, to accommodate the forklift. Lindahl was now fastening the gray metal fireproof door to a hook in the concrete floor, to keep it open.

This would be the safe room, a windowless square low-ceilinged space in concrete block painted a flat gray. To the left, half a dozen smallish oblong metal boxes stood on a mover's pallet. Each box was marked with the logo *Gro-More Racing* in white letters on its long sides. Metal shelves on the right contained more of the boxes plus the kind of sectioned tray inserted into cash register drawers, and a toolkit and some miscellaneous supplies.

Lindahl said, "You see the setup."

"Yes."

"The track owns the boxes, so the empties always come back here. Every once in a while, one gets dented or the hinges warp, and they throw it out. They're careful, they put them inside black plastic bags in the Dumpster."

"But you know how it works," Parker said. "So you've been taking them home."

"I have seven." Lindahl's pride in his accomplishment immediately gave way to self-disgust. "I was brilliant," he said. "I worked it all out, every damn thing but coming down here and actually doing the deed."

Parker said, "You figured to move that stuff in your Ford?"

"No, that wouldn't work, I know that much." Lindahl shrugged. "For that, I need a little truck, like a delivery truck."

"Do you have one of those?"

"No, I'd rent it." Then Lindahl grinned at Parker, almost defiantly, and said, "Yeah, I know, just one more thing to tell the police I'm the one did it. But I don't *care* if they know, I'm long gone. I'd even leave the truck and the empty boxes at my place, because I won't be coming back."

That was true. Parker said, "Anything else to show me?"

"No, this is it, only we've got to go back out the way we came in. If you open that door to the ramp from outside, it flashes a light in security. You have to switch off the alarm on this side, and then open it. And then, if you close it and don't re-alarm it, the light in security goes on, anyway. So when we do it, next Saturday, *if* we do it – well, when we do it, we have to go in and out the same way, drive the truck out, come back in, lock up, switch the alarm on, walk around and up the stairs and out. Anything else you want to see?"

Parker pointed at the metal boxes on the pallet. "They locked?"

"No need."

"Open one."

"Sure."

The lids were two long flat metal pieces, accordion-hinged to the long sides of the boxes. Lindahl went to one knee in front of the pallet and lifted open the two parts of the lid, which was apparently pretty heavy. Inside, cashier drawer inserts like the ones on the shelves were stacked, it looked like three deep, but these were full of cash; paper money sorted into compartments from the left, coins to the right.

"These things really weigh," Lindahl said as he closed the lid and got to his feet.

"They look it."

"Anything else?"

"How much is in there, usually, on a Saturday night?"

"Probably more than a hundred thousand, less than one-fifty."

Parker nodded. Enough to keep him moving.

Lindahl, proud and anxious, said, "So what do you think?"

"It looks good."

With a huge relieved smile, Lindahl said, "I knew you'd see it. You ready to go?"

"Yes."

On their way out, up the stairs from the basement, Lindahl said, "You know, I know why you wanted *me* to open that box. You didn't want your fingerprints on it."

"That's right," Parker said.

TWO

Parker didn't speak until they were well away from the track, headed north, and then he said, "If we're going to do this, you'll have to do what I say."

"You're the pro, you mean."

"I care whether I get arrested or not."

"Oh, I *care*," Lindahl said. "Don't get me wrong, I don't have some kind of death wish over here. If those bastards catch me and put me in jail, they've beat me *again*. I don't want that. I'm not going to jail, trust me, that's not going to happen."

"You'd rather die first."

Lindahl grimaced, trying to work out an answer to that, and finally said, "Would *you* give up?"

"I don't want them on my tail," Parker said. "That's the point."

"They *were* on your tail. When I first saw you, they were right down the hill behind you."

"It's fresh in my memory," Parker assured him.

"That's why, if we go ahead and do it, we do it my way, and you don't argue."

"But I can say no, I guess," Lindahl said. "I can say no, I don't want to do that, and then we don't do it. Like if you say, 'Now we go kill the two guys in security,' I can say no, and we don't do it."

"I'm not out to kill anybody," Parker said. "It only makes the heat worse."

"Well, whatever it might be," Lindahl said. "If I don't like it, I can say no, and we don't do it."

"You're right," Parker told him. "You can always say no."

"Good. We understand each other." Lindahl nodded at the windshield. "Lights out there."

They had met only the occasional other moving car, this time of night, but up the road ahead of them now were the unmistakable lights of another roadblock. Those roadblocks would be in position all night tonight, and maybe tomorrow night, too.

The law was looking for two men, possibly separate but possibly together, so any car out late at night with two men in it attracted their interest. Also, with so little traffic out here on the rural roads in the middle of the night, the guys on duty were getting bored. For the first time, Parker and Lindahl were asked to step out of the Ford while the troopers did a quick flashlight scan of the interior. They

118

weren't patted down, though, and once again Parker's new license was accepted without question.

They were the only car at the roadblock, and when they left it, driving north into darkness, that cluster of lights in the rearview mirror was still the only illumination to be seen. Lindahl kept twisting around to look back at those lights, and it wasn't until they disappeared that he spoke again. "I guess you have an idea of what to do. About the track, I mean."

"Yes."

"I think it must be different from mine."

"Parts of it."

"Which parts?"

"In the first place," Parker said, "we don't take those metal boxes with us. There's no reason to lug all that weight around."

"The money's gotta be in *some*thing."

"Is there a mall around where you are? Someplace open on Sunday?"

"About forty miles away," Lindahl said, "over toward Albany."

"Tomorrow," Parker told him, "you drive over there. Get two duffel bags. You know what I mean, big canvas bags."

"Like the army uses."

"That's right."

Lindahl shook his head. "I don't know," he said. "You saw how much money was there."

"All we want is the big bills," Parker told him. "Nothing under a ten. And no change."

"Oh." Nodding slowly, Lindahl said, "I guess that makes sense."

"And also get two pairs of plastic kitchen gloves."

"For fingerprints; fine. Anything else?"

"No, that's all we'll need. And fill the gas tank, it's getting low."

"Sure." Lindahl was quiet for a minute, but then he frowned and said, "Why do I have to do all this tomorrow? There's closer places I can go to on Monday."

"Because we're taking the money tomorrow night," Parker said.

THREE

"No!" Lindahl was deeply shocked. "That's no good! We won't have any time at *all* to get away!"

"In the first place," Parker said, "let's get rid of that thirty-six-hour fantasy of yours. You can't go on the run, because you can't hide. Where do you figure to be, thirty-six hours later? Oregon? Where do you sleep? Do you go to a motel and pay with cash? A credit card places you, and the law by then is watching your accounts. So do you pay cash? The motel wants your license plate number. Oh, from New York State?"

"Jesus."

"Anywhere you go in this country, everybody's on the same computer. It doesn't matter if you're across the street or across the country, as soon as you make any move at all, they know where you are. You gonna try to leave the country? You got a passport?"

"No," Lindahl said. He sounded subdued. "I've never traveled much."

"Not a good time to start," Parker told him. "You

can't run away, you don't know those ropes. So instead of being the guy that did it and you're thumbing your nose and they'll never get you, you're the guy that *didn't* do it, and you're staying right there where you always were, and sure, let them go ahead and search, and you were home in bed last night same as any other night, and you don't spend any of that cash for a year. You want to pull the job and not do time for it? That's how."

"That's all . . ." Lindahl shook his head, gestured vaguely in the air in front of himself, like someone trying to describe an elephant to a person who'd never seen one. "That's different from what I had in mind. That isn't the same thing."

"You want two things," Parker reminded him. "Or so you said. You want revenge. And you want the money."

"Well," Lindahl said, and now he seemed a little embarrassed, a little sheepish, "I kind of wanted them to *know*."

"Because you were gonna disappear."

"But you say I can't do that."

Parker said, "You aren't used to the life on the other side of the law. There's too many things you don't know, too many mistakes you can make. You can have your money, and you can have your revenge, and maybe even a couple of your old bosses think you maybe did it, but they can't prove it, and you and your parrot just go on living the way you did before."

"That's not what I had in mind," Lindahl said again. "What I had in mind was, I *don't* live like this any more. I don't shoot rabbits for my dinner. I don't curl up in that crappy little house and never see anybody and everybody knows I'm that crazy hermit and nobody gives a shit about me."

"You did it for four years," Parker reminded him. "You can do it one year more. A little less. Next July, you tell a few people you're going on vacation, you're driving somewhere. Then you take the money and you go wherever you want to go—"

"Someplace warm."

"That's up to you. When you get there, you start a checking account, you put a couple grand of your cash in it every few weeks, you rent a place to live, you drive back up here, pack your stuff, tell whoever you're paying your rent to that you decided to retire someplace warm, and there you are."

Lindahl was quiet for a long while as Parker drove, the headlights pushing that fan of pale white out ahead of them, moving through hilly countryside, sleeping towns, here and there a night-light but mostly as dark as when the continent was empty.

Finally, with a long sigh, Lindahl said, "I think I could do that."

"I think so, too."

"It's like hunting, I see that. In some ways, it's like hunting. The main thing you have to be is patient. If you're patient, you'll get what you want."

"That's right."

"I'd have to— If that's what we do, I'd have to hide the money. I mean, really well, where they wouldn't find it. Where nobody would find it."

"I'll show you where," Parker said.

Surprised, Lindahl said, "You already know a place?"

"But the other thing you've got to do," Parker told him, "is get rid of those metal bank boxes. You don't need them, and you don't want any lawman to come across them, because you don't have any answers to those questions."

"You're right," Lindahl said. "I didn't think about them. They're just in the furnace room, stacked in the corner."

"Wipe your fingerprints off."

"They're still in the black plastic bags, from when they were thrown away in the Dumpster. I just left them that way."

"That's good. Take them with you tomorrow, find another Dumpster, maybe at this mall you're going to, get rid of them in a way that they won't come back."

"All right, I can do that." Curious, half turning in his

seat, Lindahl said, "You really know where to hide the money?"

"In the boarded-up house in front of you."

"Oh, I don't know," Lindahl said. "I don't think it'd be easy to get in there. Not without making a mess."

"I've already been inside," Parker told him. "It's all set up. I'll show you tomorrow."

"You've been *in* there? My God."

"In case it would turn out to be a bad idea to be in your house," Parker said.

"I'll have to see this."

Parker said nothing to that, and they drove in silence another while. It was well after four in the morning by now, and it would be after five before they got where they were going. And then Lindahl had a lot to do tomorrow.

"You know," Lindahl said about fifteen minutes later, "now it *is* real. When I first went back to the track, and looked at it, and realized I was still goddam mad about what happened and still wanted to get back at them, I thought then it was finally real, but it wasn't. It was still my fantasy, riding off into the west like somebody in the movies. Like Fred Thiemann saying we were a posse, only without the horses. That was *his* fantasy, and it sure bit him on the ass, didn't it?"

"Yes," Parker said.

"And my fantasy would have done the same thing. So now, for the first time, it really is real."

Lindahl looked out at the darkness and smiled. Parker didn't tell him anything.

FOUR

When they drove past the boarded-up house, coming into Pooley at last, Lindahl frowned at it and said, "You really got in there."

"We'll look at it tomorrow," Parker said. "We both need sleep."

It was nearly five-thirty in the morning, false dawn smudging the sky up to their right, suggesting the silhouettes of hills. The only lights showing in the town were down at the intersection, the streetlight and blinker signal and night-lights of the gas station.

Lindahl parked in his usual place and got out of the car, yawning. Parker, getting out on the other side, paused to listen. Not a sound anywhere. He followed Lindahl inside, where at first the television set was the only light source, but then Lindahl switched on a floor lamp beside the sofa, switched off the television, and said, "That sofa isn't bad. I'll get you a pillowcase and a blanket."

"You got an alarm clock?"

"Sure. What time should I set it?"

"Ten."

Surprised, Lindahl said, "That doesn't give us much sleep."

"You'll sleep when we're finished," Parker promised him.

FIVE

Lindahl kept yawning as they walked over to the boarded-up house. It was ten-thirty in the morning, and they'd been up half an hour, finishing a silent breakfast before coming out here to cold damp air, the sky a grayish white as though starting to mildew. Parker led the way to the rear door of the house, where he reached up to the top of the plywood and pulled it back.

"Uh!" Lindahl broke off in midyawn, staring in astonishment. "Was that always like that?"

"I fixed it yesterday."

Lindahl came closer to study the plywood, touching a finger to the stubby end of a sawed-off screw. "You cut them back."

"Right."

"And what's that one in the middle for?"

"To pull it closed when you're inside. Come on."

Parker pushed open the door and motioned for Lindahl to precede him. As he then stepped in and maneuvered the plywood back into place, Lindahl said, "Is that my flashlight?"

"Yes. We'll need it. In fact, turn it on now."

Lindahl did, and Parker closed them in, then said, "Give me the light, I've been through here before."

"Fine."

They went up through the black house to the attic, and Lindahl went over to look out the unblocked window. "This is where you were when I got back last night," he said. "In case I brought the police or something."

"That's right." Parker pointed the flashlight to the area behind the stairwell, where the roof angled down closest to the floor, leaving only a three-foot height of wall. Discarded there were a bent old cardboard suitcase and some rolls of curtains and curtain rods. "You put your duffel bag in with that stuff, and you leave it there until you go to your some-place warm. And once it's there, you put a couple full-length screws in the plywood, just in case anybody ever comes around to be sure everything's sealed solid."

"And I'll rub a little dirt on them."

"Good."

They went back downstairs and out, and while Parker put the plywood in place, he said, "I'll come along with you to this mall, see if there's anything I need. Let's go put those money boxes into your van."

"All right."

130

Parker put the pistol in his jacket pocket before they left. He had to drive again, because Lindahl was feeling the effects of four hours' sleep. The seven metal boxes in their sheaths of black plastic filled the rear seat so high Parker could only use the outside mirrors.

The first police blockade they came to was manned by the same sour older trooper as yesterday. "I saw you two before," he said as Parker handed over his new license.

"Untrained men with guns," Parker reminded him. "Hickory Rod and Gun. No guns today, though."

"At least nobody got killed yesterday," the trooper said, giving him back the license.

"Any more word on those two guys?"

"Not a peep." His total disaffection dragged the trooper's face down like a double dose of gravity. "You ask me," he said, "those two are on the beach in Florida this very minute. But nobody asked me."

"See if your boss will send you down there to look for them," Parker suggested.

"You can move along now," the trooper said.

They drove on, and Lindahl said, "You don't get nervous, do you?"

"Nothing to get nervous about. Keep an eye out for someplace to get rid of these boxes."

That was twenty miles farther on, a demolition site where an old bowling alley was being torn down, the two Dumpsters already half full of a great miscellany of stuff, the site empty and unguarded on a Sunday morning. They transferred the seven money boxes, dividing them into both Dumpsters to make them a little less of a presence, then drove on to the mall, a smaller older place with only one of its two anchor stores still up and running. The shops down the line between the living major retailer and the dead one made an anthology of national brand names. The parking area was a quarter full, so they could leave the car very close to the entrance, just beyond the empty handicapped spaces.

They went inside, and Parker said, "You go ahead. You want two duffel bags and two pairs of plastic gloves. I'm gonna look around, and I'll meet you on the way out."

"Okay."

Lindahl took a shopping cart and pushed it away into the sparsely populated store. Parker watched him go, then turned and walked back outside and headed down the row of secondary shops. On the way in, he'd picked the one he thought he probably wanted, a youth clothing store featuring baggy jeans and baseball caps and sweatshirts with penitentiary names on them.

Yes. Reaching that store, looking in the plate-glass window past the display of elaborate sneakers designed like space stations, he saw no customers, only the clerk, a skinny high school kid wearing the store's product as he moved slowly around, halfheartedly neatening the stock.

Parker went into the store, and the kid looked up, first hopeful and then blank when he realized this was unlikely to be a customer. "Yes, sir? What can I do for you?"

"Well," Parker said, and showed him the pistol, "you can open that cash register over there and then you can lie facedown on the floor behind the counter."

The kid gaped at the pistol and then at Parker, as though he'd lost the ability to understand English. Parker lifted the gun so it pointed at the kid's nose from a foot away. "Or," he said, "I can shoot you in the face and open the cash register myself."

"No, I'll do it!"

The kid abruptly moved, all jangly limbs, bumping into things as he hurried around the end of the counter and opened the cash register. He stepped back from it and stared at Parker. "You won't shoot me?"

"Not if you're facedown on the floor."

The kid dropped as though in fact he had been shot, and when he was on the floor, he put his hands over the back of his head, trembling fingers entwined.

Parker reached over the counter into the cash register drawer and removed the twenties and tens, touching only the money. Then he looked down at the kid and said, "Look at your watch."

The enlaced hands sprang apart, and the kid arched his back to look at the large round watch on his left wrist.

"I'll be outside for five minutes. If I look through the window and see you up, I'll shoot. Five minutes. Got that?"

"Yes, sir." The kid kept staring at the watch, body arched.

Parker turned away, left the shop, and walked back to the large store, where he went inside and found Lindahl on line at a checkout counter, only one other shopper in front of him. In his shopping cart were two dark brown duffel bags folded into clear plastic bags and two pairs of yellow kitchen gloves mounted on cardboard in shrink-wrap. He nodded to Parker: "Found it. You get anything?"

"No, I just looked around."

Lindahl's turn came, and he paid and got his purchases in a large plastic bag with the store's name over a smiley face. They walked out of the store, Lindahl carrying the bag and saying, "Should I drive back?"

"Sure."

Parker gave him the keys. In the car, they started out to the road, but then had to wait while a police car rushed by, lights flashing and siren ablare. Lindahl watched them go by, startled. "What do you think that is?"

"Nothing to do with us," Parker said.

SIX

They stopped at a run-down traditional diner for lunch on the way back. They chose a table beside the large window with its view out to very little Sunday traffic on this secondary road, and after they'd given the waitress their orders, Parker said, "Tell me about the Dennisons."

"The who? Oh, Cory and Cal? What do you want to know about *them* for?"

"They came to see me last night. Right after you left."

"They came— They were at *my* place?"

"They think I might be one of the missing robbers."

"Jesus!" Lindahl looked as though he just might jump straight up and out of the diner and run a hundred miles down the road. "What are they gonna do?"

"If I *am* one of the robbers," Parker said, "they think I must have a bunch of money on me."

"But you don't."

"But if I was and I did, I could give Cal money to get plastic surgery and an artificial eye."

"Oh, for—" No longer in a panic, Lindahl now looked as though he'd never heard anything so dumb. "They said that to you? You're the robber, and give us some of the money?"

"The robber part wasn't said."

"But that's what it was all about. And if you give them the money, they won't report you? Is that the idea?"

"I suppose so."

"That's a Cal idea, all right," Lindahl said. "He's jumped off barn roofs since he was a little kid."

"Cory's the smart one," Parker agreed, "but he follows the other one's lead. They say they're gonna come back today and talk to you."

Lindahl was astonished all over again. "Talk to *me*? About what?"

"Am I really your old friend Ed Smith."

Lindahl leaned back in the booth and spread his hands. "Well, you really *are* my old friend Ed Smith. I oughta know who you are."

"That's right," Parker said. As the waitress brought their plates, he said, "Over lunch, we'll work out the details of that. In case somebody talks to you and then talks to me."

"Good. We'll do that."

"We've only got to worry about today," Parker said, "and then we're done with it."

With a surprised laugh, Lindahl said, "That's right! Just today and tonight. The whole thing, it's almost over."

SEVEN

They got back to Lindahl's house a little before two. The vehicle parked in front of it was not the Dennisons' Dodge Ram, but a black Taurus that Parker recognized as Fred Thiemann's. Then its driver's door opened, and a woman in her fifties climbed out, dressed in jeans and a windbreaker. She must have been waiting for them to get back.

Parker said, "The wife?"

"Jane," Lindahl said, and looked worried. "What's gone wrong?"

"She'll tell us."

Lindahl parked next to the Taurus as Jane Thiemann went over to stand by the door to the house, waiting for them, frowning. Looking at her through the windshield, Parker saw a woman who was weighed down by something. Not angry, not frightened, but distracted enough not to care what kind of appearance she made. She was simply out in the world, braced for whatever the bad news would turn out to be.

Parker and Lindahl got out of the SUV, and Lindahl said, "Jane. How's Fred?"

"Coming apart at the seams." She turned bleak eyes toward Parker. "You're Ed Smith, I guess."

"That's right."

"Fred's afraid of you," she said. "I'm not sure why."

Parker shrugged. "Neither am I."

Lindahl said, "You want to come in?"

"Fred sent me for his rifle."

"Oh, sure. I have it locked in the rack in the bedroom. Come on in."

They stepped into the living room, and the parrot bent its head at Jane Thiemann in deep interest. She looked at the television set. "You keep that on all the time?"

"It's something moving. I'll be right back."

Lindahl went into the bedroom, and Parker said, "What was the urgency? Fred doesn't figure to use it, does he?"

She gave him a sharp look. "On himself, you mean?"

"On anything. He isn't hunting deer today."

Coming back from the bedroom, carrying Thiemann's rifle, Lindahl said, "Deer season doesn't start till next month."

She looked at her husband's rifle as Lindahl offered it to her at port arms, and said, "I'd like to sit down a minute."

"Well, sure," he said, surprised and embarrassed. As she dropped onto the sofa, not sitting, but dropping as though her strings had been cut, he stepped back and leaned the rifle against the wall. "I'm sorry, Jane, I forget how to be civilized. You want something to drink? Water? I think I got Coke."

Parker said, "You want the television off?"

"Yes, please," she said, and to Lindahl said, "I'd like some water, if I could."

Lindahl left the room, and Parker switched off the set, then sat in the chair beside it, facing the sofa. He said, "Fred's in shock."

"We're both in shock," she said. "But he's in more than shock. He's angry, and he's scared, and he feels like he's got to do something, but he doesn't know what. Thanks, Tom."

Lindahl, having returned to give her a glass of water with ice cubes in it, now stood awkwardly for a second, uncomfortable about taking the seat on the sofa next to her. He dragged over a wooden kitchen chair from the corner and sat on that, midway between Parker and Jane Thiemann.

Parker said, "What does he say, mostly?"

"All kinds of things. A lot about you."

"Me?"

"He doesn't understand you, and he feels that he has

141

to, somehow. The only thing he knows for sure, if it wasn't for you, this would all be different now."

"That fella would still be dead."

"Oh, I know *that,* we both know that, he isn't blaming you, he's blaming what he calls 'my own stupid self.' But if it had been just him and Tom up there, they would have gone to the troopers, and who knows what would have happened?"

"Nothing good," Parker said.

"Well, maybe." She drank some of the water, then sat holding the glass in both hands in her lap. "Or maybe they would have seen it was an accident," she said, "and that man was . . . he was only . . . wouldn't have relatives or—"

"Garbage," Parker said. "A man, but garbage."

"It's harsh when you say it that way," she said, "but yes. The troopers might have looked at it, might have seen what Fred was and what that other man was, and just said, 'Well, it was an accident, we won't make a big deal out of it.' Of course, *now* he can't do that."

"He never could," Parker said. "That fella has an identity. They'll find it, from fingerprints or DNA or dental records or something else. He'll have relatives, they'll want to be satisfied. Knowing their cousin is drinking himself to death is one thing; knowing he's been shot in the back is something else."

"Oh!"

"Fred wouldn't be hit with a whole lot," Parker told her, "but he would do some time inside."

"That's what scared him," she said, and now she did look as though she might cry, but shook her head and kept talking. "One of the things that scared him. The idea of . . . prison . . . we can't . . . we have our own—"

"Tom told me," Parker said. "Afterward, he told me. He had to."

"I haven't blabbed around to anyone else, Jane," Lindahl said. "Honest to God."

"Oh, I believe you." With that bleak look at Parker again, she said, "That whole thing hit Fred worse even than it did George. He's had to take pills to sleep, or he just lies there all night, thinking about that cell, imagining that cell. He's in the cell more than George is."

Parker said, "How long is George in for?"

"Oh, a year more, at the most," she said, dismissing it. "At the most. It was post-stress syndrome, everybody knows that's what it was. His army record couldn't have been better, everybody says so. Did Tom tell you he was wounded?"

"No."

"I wasn't telling stories, Jane," Lindahl said.

"I understand that." To Parker she said, "He was wounded, too. A roadside bomb." She slid her palm down over her left hip. "It burned a lot of skin off there and smashed a joint. He's got a plastic joint in there."

"So they'll let him out," Parker said, "as soon as they can."

"No more than a year."

Parker nodded. "Have you mentioned to Fred, George will want to see him when he gets out?"

She blinked at him. "Well, he knows— What do you mean?"

Nodding at the rifle against the wall, Parker said, "He's in pain right now. He might decide that thing's better than a sleeping pill."

Her eyes widened, and a trembling hand moved up toward her face, but she didn't speak. She'd known the same truth but had been trying not to think it.

Parker said, "When you take the rifle back to him, remind him, George will be very disappointed, all he's been through, if his father isn't there to say hello when he gets out."

"I will," she said. "That might . . ." She looked around the room. "I don't need any more water."

Lindahl jumped up to take the glass from her. "We're sorry, Jane," he said. "None of us wanted this to happen."

"It isn't you two, it's him. That's the worst of it, he knows it's him." She got to her feet, slightly unsteady. "I shouldn't be away from there too long."

Parker stood and told her, "With you on hand, he'll come through this."

"I hope you're right."

Lindahl handed her the rifle. "The safety's on."

"Good." She staggered slightly under the unaccustomed weight, which meant her husband hadn't introduced her to hunting. "I'll tell Fred what you said," she told Parker. "About George wanting him there, when he comes back."

"Good."

"I'll walk you out," Lindahl said, and did so. Parker waited, and then Lindahl came back in to say, "You were very sympathetic." He sounded surprised. "I didn't think you'd have that kind of sympathetic manner."

"I had to," Parker said. "You know Thiemann's thinking about killing himself. If he does, the cops'll talk to the wife three minutes before they find out what happened, and ten minutes after that, they're right at this door." Parker shook his head. "I'll be as sympathetic as I have to. Neither of us wants a gun battle with the law."

EIGHT

Three minutes after Jane Thiemann left, the door opened and Cal Dennison sauntered in, saying, "That lady had a gun."

"She's looking for the bank robbers," Parker said.

As Cory entered, shutting the door behind himself as he nodded a cautious greeting toward Lindahl, Cal laughed and said, "Well, I bet she come to the right place."

"No, the wrong place," Parker said.

Lindahl said, "Cal, you're jumping off half-assed again."

"Oh, I don't think so," Cal said, and pulled a much-crumpled sheet of paper from his pocket. Smoothing it as best he could on his dark gray shirtfront, he held it out toward Lindahl and said, "You tell me, Tom. You just go right ahead."

Lindahl, not touching it, reluctantly looked at the now familiar artist's rendering and grudgingly said, "Well, they look a little alike, I can see how they're a little alike."

"A *little* alike?" Cal swung to hold the paper out with both hands at its side edges, arms straight out as he aimed the picture at Parker and said, "Whadaya say, *Ed*? If you saw this fella comin down the road toward you, would you say, 'Looks like I got a long-lost twin brother,' or what?"

"He could be a thousand guys," Parker said.

"Not a thousand."

Lindahl said, "Cal, if this picture looks so much like Ed here, and everybody up at the meeting at St. Stanislas had a copy of the picture, and Ed was standing right there with us, how come nobody *else* saw it? How come everybody in the goddam parking lot didn't turn around and make a citizen's arrest?"

"It was that story in school," Cal said, and frowned deeply as he turned to hand the sketch to Cory. "That writer we had to read, all that spooky stuff. Poe. The something letter. All about how everybody's looking for this letter, and nobody can find it, and that's because it's right out there in plain sight, the one place you wouldn't think it would be. So here's a fella, and a whole bunch of guys get together to find him, and where's the best place he oughta hide? Right with the bunch looking for him, the one place nobody in the county's gonna think to look."

Voice arched with sarcasm, Lindahl said, "And you, Cal, you're the only one there figured it out."

"Could happen," Cal said, comfortable with himself. "Could happen."

"Not this time," Parker said, and Cory said, "Look at that."

They all turned to the television set, and there was the artist's rendering again, this time with superimposed red letters: FUGITIVE BANDIT STRIKES AGAIN.

"Jesus!" Cal said. "Where's the goddam sound on that thing?"

Lindahl stepped quickly over to the remote on top of the set and brought the sound on, an off-camera female voice saying, "—possibly still working together." The picture on the screen switched from the artist's rendering to a wide shot of the shopping mall where Parker and Lindahl had been this morning. "It was a slow morning at The Rad in Willoughby Hills Center until the bandit – or bandits – put in their appearance."

As the television picture cut to the exterior of the clothing store Parker had robbed, showing uniformed police going in and out of the place, Parker was aware of Lindahl vibrating beside him, shock and anger working their way through him but so far not erupting into speech. Parker's hand went into his right trouser pocket, lightly touching the pistol there. It would have to be all three of them, if it started now.

"Clerk Edwin Kislamski was alone in the shop at

eleven-forty-five this morning when a man entered, threatened Mr. Kislamski with a handgun, and robbed the cash register of over three thousand dollars."

The clerk himself now appeared, seated on a wooden bench against a green wall in what looked like the front room of a state police barracks. For some reason, he was wrapped in a thick cream blanket, as though he were a near-drowning victim. He clutched the blanket to himself with both hands. Above it, a kind of terrified half-smile flickered across his face like distant searchlights as he spoke: "I recognized him right away." An apparent cut, and then, "Oh, yeah, I got a real good look at him. I got a better look at him than I wanted."

"Hah!" Cal crowed. "I bet *that's* true! Change your pants, sonny!"

"Shut up, Cal," Cory said.

Now, on the television screen, outside The Rad, a woman reporter was seen interviewing some sort of senior police officer, with a lot of braid on his cap bill, but the sound was still the voice-over: "Captain Andrew Oldrum of State CID says there's reason to believe the other fugitive from the recent Massachusetts bank robbery was the driver of the getaway car."

Lindahl stared at Parker, who didn't look back, but shook his head. He needed Lindahl to remember not to act up in front of the Dennisons.

Now the interview was heard, or at least part of what Captain Oldrum had to say: "Given where they'd been spotted in the past, it looks as though they may be backtracking now, which would be a smart move on their part, if they can get into an area we've already cleared."

"Captain Oldrum, why would they risk so much to commit what, in comparison, is a very small robbery, after the multi-hundred-thousand-dollar robbery in Massachusetts?"

"Well, Eve, we have reason to believe, from the one bandit we've apprehended so far, that they no longer have that money on them. Also, even if they still have some of it, the other two know from that first arrest their stolen money's too dangerous to spend, because we've got the serial numbers. So what they need is cash they can use without drawing attention to themselves. Still, this robbery seems like a pretty desperate move, so it looks like we're a lot closer to them than we thought earlier in the day."

Now the cut was to the television studio, where the same woman reporter smiled at the camera and said, "Police are asking anyone who might have been shopping at Willoughby Hills Center at the time of the robbery, and might have seen the fugitives, or their vehicle, or anything at all that seemed suspicious, to phone the special number on your screen—"

"Let's call it," Cal said. "We got him right here." Laughing at Lindahl, he said, "And you got to be the driver!"

"Shut up, Cal," Parker said. "Tom, switch off that set."

Cal, suddenly bristling, said, "My brother tells me to shut up. You don't tell me to shut up."

As Lindahl killed the sound on the television set, Parker took a step forward and slapped Cal hard, open-handed, across the cheek, under the patch. Cal jolted back, astonished and outraged. Parker stood watching him, hands at his sides, and Cal, fidgeting, wide eyed, tried to figure out something to do.

"Okay," Cory said, stepping forward, not quite between them, but just to the side, like a referee. "Okay, that's enough. If it goes any further, you got me, too."

Parker half turned to him. "They say it was definitely one of the guys they're looking for, and they say he was at this mall, and I'm not. But let's say your brother's right. They just said on the TV the bandits don't have the money any more, or if they do, they can't pass it because the law's got the serial numbers. So if I am the bandit, I either don't have the money or I have money nobody can use. And if I am the bandit, why weren't you two dead last night?"

Cory had nodded through all of that, thoughtful, and now he said, "I don't know."

"What *do* you know?"

"Something doesn't smell right." Cory nodded toward his brother but kept looking at Parker. "Cal and me, we both noticed it, and we talked about it."

Cal had apparently decided the slap on the face was now far enough in the past that he didn't have to react to it at all, so, his aggressive style back, he said, "What are you *doin'* here, that's the point. Whether you're him or you're not him, and I still know goddam well you're him, but even so, how come you're here? What are you doin here?"

"Visiting my old friend Tom."

"Bullshit," Cal said. "Maybe those old farts at the gun club bought it, but we don't. We never did. I took one look at you up at St. Stanislas and I said, 'What's goin' on with that fella?' That was even before I looked at the picture."

Lindahl now stepped forward. He was paler than usual, and Parker could see he still hadn't completely adapted himself to what he'd just learned from the television set, but his expression was determined. "Cal," he said, "you never called me a liar before."

Cal turned to glower at him. "*You* gonna punch me now? I don't think so, Tom."

"Then don't call me a liar."

"Cal," Cory said, crowding in on top of whatever Cal had meant to say, "we're done in here."

Cal now had reason to glower at everybody. "*Done* in here? Whadaya mean, done in here? Now the guy's knocking off shopping malls!"

"That's nothing to do with us," Cory told him. "Come on, Cal. Tom, I'm sorry we busted in on you."

"Anytime," Lindahl said, though he sounded angry. "Just knock first."

"We will. Come on, Cal. Sorry if we upset you, Ed."

"You didn't," Parker said.

"Well . . ." Cory herded Cal to the door and out, Cal wanting to yap on about something or other, Cory pushing him out with nods and hand gestures, the two finally outside, Cory closing the door without looking back.

Parker continued to stand and frown at the closed door. After a minute, Lindahl gave him a puzzled look. "What is it?"

Parker nodded at the door. "Cory's scheming," he said.

NINE

Six hours. Six hours from now, Parker and Lindahl could leave Pooley and head south to the racetrack, which would be shut and dark and ready for them when they got there. That wasn't the problem; the problem was in the six hours.

Cory Dennison was out there somewhere, scheming, that was the first thing. He'd decided that, whoever Parker was, he was up to something the Dennison brothers would find interesting and should therefore be in on. So what would they do? Hang around the neighborhood? Watch Lindahl's house and SUV, follow them if they left? All the way to the racetrack?

All right; somewhere along the line he'd have to neutralize the brothers. But in a way, they were less trouble than Fred Thiemann, because they were at least sane and more or less sensible and knew what they wanted. Thiemann was none of those. He was a loose cannon, not at all under his own control, only partly under his wife's control. There was nothing Parker could do about him that wouldn't make it worse. If Thiemann were to die, at Parker's hands or his own or anybody else's, Parker would just have to forget the racetrack and hope to clear out of this part of the world before the law arrived.

Because once the law was interested in Thiemann, they would also be interested in Thiemann's partners in the manhunt. The wife would lead them to Lindahl, and that was the end.

What were the choices? He could tie up Lindahl right now, or shoot him if the man wanted to make trouble, and leave here in the SUV. He'd have the car's registration and the new driver's license belonging to William G. Dodd, and if stopped he'd say his friend Tom Lindahl had loaned him the car.

But if he did do that, and it turned out at the same time that Thiemann was eating his rifle, Parker would be on the road in a hot car and not know it. Or he could wait the six hours, ignoring the Dennison brothers and trusting Jane Thiemann to keep her husband in line, and the disaster would find him sitting here in Lindahl's living room with his feet up.

Another car. He needed a car he could safely drive, a car he could show up in at the roadblocks. A car with paperwork that wouldn't arouse suspicion, no matter what was happening back here in this neighborhood.

After the Dennisons left, Parker said, "I'll drive down to the corner, put some gas in the car."

Sounding bitter, Lindahl said, "Using some of the money you stole from that boy?"

Parker looked at him. "You got that wrong, Tom," he said. "I didn't take anything from that boy. I took some cash from a company has nine hundred stores. I needed the cash. You know that."

"You had that gun all along?"

"I'll be right back," Parker said, and turned to the door.

"No, wait."

Parker looked back and could see that Lindahl was trying to adjust his thinking. He waited, and Lindahl nodded and said, "All right. I know who you are, I already knew who you were. I shouldn't act as though it's any of my business."

"That's right."

"It's hard," Lindahl said. "It's hard to be around . . ."

The sentence trailed off, but Parker understood. It's hard to be around a carnivore. "It won't be for long," he said.

"No, I know. And I wanted to tell you," Lindahl hurried on, obviously in a rush to change the subject, "you don't want to go to that gas station on the corner. Go out to the right, eight miles, there's a Getty station. A straight run there and back."

"But this guy's right here. He's open on Sunday, I saw the sign."

"You don't want to go there," Lindahl insisted. "He charges ten, fifteen cents more per gallon than anybody else."

"How does he get away with that?"

"He doesn't," Lindahl said. "The only people that stop there are tourists or lost."

"Then how does he make a living?"

"Social Security," Lindahl said. "And he sells lottery tickets there, that's mostly what people go to him for. A lot of people around here are nuts for the lottery. And he also does some repair work on cars."

"I saw some cars there, I didn't know if that meant he fixed them or sold them."

"He fixes them, he's a mechanic," Lindahl said. "That's what he mostly used to do, somewhere down in Pennsylvania. He worked for some big auto dealer down there. When he retired, he came up here and bought that station, because his wife's family came from around here somewhere."

"But why charge so much for gas?"

"Just crankiness," Lindahl said. "He's a loner, he likes working on engines and things, listening to the radio in his station."

"Is he a good mechanic?"

"Oh, yeah." Lindahl nodded, emphatic with it. "He'll do a good job on your car, and he won't cheat you, he's fair about that. That part he takes pride in. I've taken my own car to him, and he's been fine. What it is, he'll fix your car, but he doesn't want to talk to you. I think he likes cars more than people."

"What's his name?"

"Brian Hopwood. But you don't want to go there."

"No, I'll stay away from him," Parker said. "I don't need somebody cranky, that overcharges. The Getty station, you say, eight miles that way."

"That's what you want," Lindahl agreed.

TEN

The Dennisons' red Ram pickup was nowhere in sight as
Parker drove a mile out of town, U-turned back past
Lindahl's place tucked back in behind the boarded-up
house, and stopped at the gas station, which was
brightly lit in the daytime like most such places, but still
had an air of emptiness about it.

There was one set of pumps, with service on both
sides. Behind them was a broad low white clapboard
building that was mostly overhead garage doors except
for a small office at the right end with fuel additive
posters obscuring the plate-glass window and the
smaller panes of glass in the door. To the right of the
building, along the rear line of the blacktop, were
parked half a dozen older cars, all with license plates
attached, so they were here for service, not for sale.

Parker got out of the Ford and read the hand-
printed notice taped to each pump: PAY INSIDE FIRST.
Taking out two of The Rad's twenties, he walked over
to the office, where another hand-printed sign beside

the door gave the hours of operation, including SUN 10–4.

He opened the door and heard the jangle of a warning bell, which was followed by classical music, something loud with a lot of strings that the bell had obscured for just an instant. Parker had expected a different kind of music, given Lindahl's description of Brian Hopwood, but that was the reason he'd come here, to understand the man and the operation.

The office was small and dark and crowded, as though brushed with a thin coating of oil. The desk was dark metal, covered with specs and repair books and appointment schedules and an old black telephone. A dark wood swivel chair behind it was very low, with the seat and back draped in a variety of cloth: old blankets, quilts, a couple of tan chamois cloths. On the back wall, a wooden shelf held an old cash register, next to a key rack with several sets of keys on it, each of them with a cardboard tag attached.

On the left wall of the office was an open doorway to the service area, through which a man now came, frowning as though he hadn't expected to be interrupted. He was short and scrawny and any age above Social Security eligibility. He wore what looked like army-issue eyeglasses with the thin metal wings bent into dips and rises, and grease-covered work clothes.

Wiping his hands on a small towel looped through his belt, he said, "Afternoon."

"Afternoon." Extending the twenties, Parker said, "I'm not sure it'll take that much. If not, I'll come back for change."

It was clear that Hopwood wasn't happy about that; two exchanges with a customer over one transaction. Still, he took the twenties, put them on the shelf in front of the cash register, and said, "Which pump you at?"

Parker peered through the poster-blocked window: "Three."

Hopwood bent behind the desk to set that pump and said, "I'll ring it up when you're done."

"Fine."

Hopwood was already on his way back to his work in the service area before Parker left the office. The man was without curiosity and would not be watching what Parker did, so he went first to the cars parked along the rear of the station blacktop. All were locked, their keys certainly on that rack in the office. A couple of them had personal items showing inside: a thermos, a blanket.

The law wanted people to keep their automobile registrations in their wallet or purse, but, in fact, most people leave it in the glove compartment with the insurance card, so at least some of these would be ready to go. If he needed one.

Parker went back to the Ford and pumped thirty-eight dollars and fifty cents' worth of gas. The car would have taken more than that, particularly with the high price Hopwood charged, but he wanted that second encounter.

Back in the office, Hopwood came from his work in response to the bell, and Parker said, "Sorry, that's all it took."

"Not a problem." Hopwood bent to see what the charge had come to.

"I'm staying with Tom Lindahl," Parker said.

"Thirty-eight-fifty. I recognized the car."

"On a little vacation."

"That right?" Hopwood made the transaction in the cash register and handed Parker a dollar bill and two quarters.

Parker said, "It says you close today at four."

"That's right." Squinting at the round white wall clock next to the service area entrance, Hopwood said, "You had plenty of time. An hour."

"When you close," Parker said, "is that it, you're closed, nobody here in case somebody shows up a little late? Or do you stay and work on the cars a little more?"

"Not me," Hopwood said, sounding almost outraged, as though somebody had asked him to lie under oath. "Four o'clock, I shut *down,* go home, say hello to the missus, have my shower, read the Sunday funnies until suppertime. I don't know what Tom Lindahl told you, but I'm not a nut."

"Tom said you were a good mechanic."

"Well, thank him for me." Nodding toward the Ford out by the pumps, he said, "I've managed to keep that thing going. Rides okay, doesn't it?"

"It does," Parker agreed. He pocketed his change, said, "Enjoy the funnies," and turned to leave.

ELEVEN

"Just a minute," Hopwood said, and when Parker turned back, his hand not quite touching the doorknob, Hopwood had opened a drawer in his messy desk and now there was a tiny automatic pistol in his hand, its eye looking at Parker. Flat in the still-open drawer was a smudged copy of the artist's rendering.

"Maybe you'll put your hands on your head," Hopwood said.

Parker didn't. Instead, he gestured toward the picture in the drawer. "You don't think that's me, do you? This isn't even a joke any more."

"I'm not foolin', mister," Hopwood said. The automatic that almost disappeared inside his fist was small but serious, the Seecamp LWS32, with a magazine of six .32-caliber cartridges. With its one-inch barrel, it couldn't have much effect across a highway, but inside this room it would do the job.

Now Hopwood moved the gun-holding hand in a

small arc, downward and to the right, to aim at Parker's left leg. "If I have to wing you, I will."

"I told you," Parker said, "I'm staying with Tom Lindahl. Call him if you want. That's his car right—"

"Last chance. Hands on top of your head."

With no choice, Parker started to lift his arms when the door directly behind him opened and somebody walked in. Hopwood lost his concentration as Parker took a quick step to his left, turning to see that the newcomer was the nosy woman who'd driven past him last night and stopped to ask him if she could help.

She was confused by the scene she'd walked into, reacting to the tension in the air but not yet noticing the small automatic closed in Hopwood's fist. "I'm sorry, did I—"

With both hands, Parker took her by the left elbow, spun, and threw her hard across the room and into Hopwood, who tried too late to backtrack out of the way, hitting the corner of his desk instead, knocking himself off balance. Then the woman crashed into him, and they fell diagonally in a jumble from the desk onto the floor. By the time they were separated and turned around and staring upward, Parker's pistol was in his hand.

"Stay right there," he said, and showed Hopwood the Ranger. "I don't wing."

"What is – what's—" She was still more bewildered than anything else, but then she saw the Ranger in Parker's hand and her eyes widened and she cried, "You! *You're* the one stole Jack's gun!"

PART THREE

PART THREE

Of the three men who'd pulled the bank job in Massachusetts, Nelson McWhitney was the only one who'd left the place carrying his own legitimate identification and driving his own properly registered pickup truck. The cops at the various roadblocks where he'd been stopped and the pickup searched had warned him against driving south toward the Mass Pike, because the heavy police activity had backed up traffic in all directions, so, even though his goal was Long Island, McWhitney drove steadily westward for hours, into the same areas where Parker found himself bogged down and Nick Dalesia found himself arrested.

He heard the news of the arrest on the truck radio and gave the radio an ironic nod and salute in response, saying, "Well, so long, Nick." A couple of miles farther on, having thought about it some more, he nodded and told the radio, "And so long money, too." That would be Nick's only bargaining chip, wouldn't it?

After Syracuse, McWhitney turned south, keeping to

smaller roads because they were less backed up, but still making slow progress. He finally gave up and found a motel outside Binghamton, then early Sunday morning got up into a still-police-infested world and made his way southeast toward Long Island, where his home was and where the small bar he owned was and where he had an appointment coming up with a woman named Sharon.

On even a normal day, he would have known better than to drive through New York City to get to Long Island, and this was far from a normal day. It was amazing how much fuss three guys with a simple bank plan could create. And, of course, having grabbed Nick Dalesia, the law was now hungrier than ever to gobble up the other two.

Driving down across New York State, he found himself wondering, was he himself maybe a bargaining chip for Nick? He thought back, and he didn't believe he and Nick had shared that much private detail, not enough so that Nick could pinpoint McWhitney on Long Island. He hoped not.

What he'd do, when he finally got to the neighborhood, was case it first. If Nick did know enough about him to turn him up, the surveillance on his home and bar would be far too large for him not to notice. Just go there and see.

He stopped for lunch at a diner in Westchester, then

headed south to the Throgs Neck Bridge to take him across to Long Island. The roadblock inspection at the bridge was the most thorough and intense yet, but then, once he got on the Island, life suddenly became much calmer. There were only a limited number of routes on and off the Island, so clearly the authorities believed they hadn't so far let any of the bank robbers through.

His neighborhood was quiet, like any Sunday afternoon. His bar, where he'd left a guy he knew in charge while he took his little "vacation," was also very quiet, almost empty-looking, which was also standard for a Sunday afternoon.

McWhitney parked the truck in the alley behind his building, went into his empty and stuffy-smelling apartment, opened a few windows, opened a beer, and switched on CNN. No further news on the bank-robbing front.

He wondered how Parker was doing among the straights.

TWO

Brian Hopwood, asprawl on his back on his dirty office floor, grinding pain in his left side where his rib cage had smacked into the sharp corner of his desk, useless little toy automatic still clutched in his fist, stared up past Suzanne Gilbert's thick mass of wavy auburn hair at the hardcase he'd been stupid enough to try to get the drop on, and he thought, Well, I'm not dead, so that's good.

Yes, it was good. If this hardcase here, this bank robber, had just wanted to clear these two pests out of his path, he'd have shot them without a word, without a warning like, "I don't wing." So in fact, he didn't want to shoot them, not unless they made it necessary.

Brian Hopwood had lived this long a time partly by never making it necessary for anybody to shoot him, and he was prepared to go on that way the rest of his life. Which meant shutting up Suzanne here. Heavier than she looked, now draped across him like a deer carcass lashed to a fender, half-twisted around with her elbow propping her torso up by bearing down into

Hopwood's stomach, she glared in discovery and outrage at the hardcase who had their lives in his hands, yelling at him, "You! *You're* the one stole Jack's gun!" As though this were Twenty Questions or something.

Jack Riley? It would have to be Jack Riley, but what the hell would Jack Riley want with a gun? Fighting that off, fighting his mind's habit of digression – that's what made him the first-rate loner mechanic he was, in a job that let his mind wander wherever it would while his hands and some other parts of his brain dealt with the particular problems of this particular automobile of the moment – Brian yelled, or tried to yell in a raspy hoarse croak that was all he seemed to have right now, "Suzanne, shut up and get off me! Mister, I'm putting the gun down, see? On the floor here, I can give it a push if you— Suzanne, get *off* me!"

She managed it, finally, rolling rightward off him, rolling over completely in a flurry of legs and tossing hair. She was dressed in black slacks and a gray wool sweater, so she didn't flash any parts of herself, but Brian's digression-ready brain did notice there was something very nicely womanly about that body in motion.

The hardcase hadn't moved, but now he pointed a finger of his left hand at Suzanne while holding the revolver still trained on Brian, and said to Suzanne, "Right there's good."

Suzanne had wound up in a splay-legged seated position, and did move some more, folding her legs in close into something like a loose lotus position while she glared up at him, but at least she didn't say anything else.

Then, as though Suzanne had been by that order effectively locked into a cage and put out of play, the hardcase looked at Brian again and said, "Tell me about her."

Tell me about her? She's right here; why doesn't he ask her himself?

He's the man with the gun, Brian, he gets to do it any way he wants. Brian said, "Her name's Suzanne Gilbert. She works nights at Holy Mary Hospital in emergency room admittance. Her grandfather lives just down that way."

"Jack?"

"Jack Riley, yeah, that's her grandfather."

And now Suzanne spoke up again; doesn't she understand the situation here? Apparently not, because, sounding aggrieved, she said, "Why *did* you take Jack's gun?"

He looked at her, and though his face didn't change into anything you could call a smile, Brian still had the feeling the question had given him some kind of amusement. "Just in case Brian here," he told her, "would draw down on me. You didn't stop to see your grandfather last night."

Last night? Brian looked from the hardcase to Suzanne, who didn't even look worried, much less scared, and he thought, What about last night? Now there was some other story here, and he wasn't in on it.

She said, "No, I just drive by, on my way home. Sometimes he can't sleep, and, if that happens, he'll sit out on his porch with the light on and I stop and we talk awhile. He knows I'll be there and it makes it easier for him, so these days he's sleeping more than he used to. Last night when I went by he was asleep in front of the television set, so that was fine, so I just went on home. I suppose that's when you broke in and stole his gun."

For Christ's sake, Suzanne, Brian thought, leave it alone. But the hardcase didn't mind. He just shrugged and said, "He didn't seem to use it much." Then he switched those cold eyes to Brian, considered him a minute as though he might decide after all he was the kind of pest you might as well shoot, and said, "When did you decide?"

"To be a hero?" Brian, beyond embarrassment, shrugged and looked away. "When I did it."

The truth was, it had grown in him. The customer had come in the door, had given him two twenties and said he was at pump number three, and went out again. Brian

175

had gone back to the brake drum repair he meant to finish before four o'clock closing time, and as he'd worked, his wandering mind gradually put together that customer's face with one of the two Wanted posters he'd put in his desk drawer because he hadn't wanted to throw away something given to him by the troopers but on the other hand didn't want to put those two faces on the wall to be an irritation and a distraction all the time. In very short order, the two faces had blended into one and he'd known the customer out there pumping gas was one of the bank robbers everybody was looking for. Driving Tom Lindahl's car, so God knows what had happened to Tom.

What to do about the bank robber? He'd decided it was a toss of the dice. If the guy pumped his forty bucks' worth and drove away, then the next time Brian stepped into the office he'd call the state troopers and tell them he believed he'd just seen one of the bank robbers in Tom Lindahl's car, and leave it up to them to catch the fellow. But if he came back in for change, that would be a message to Brian from On High that it was up to him to do the citizen's arrest thing himself. He had his little automatic in the drawer, and the sequence seemed simple: pull out the gun, hold the robber, call the troopers, wait.

Well, that sure worked out well, didn't it?

The hardcase must have been thinking the same thing, because he next said, "You'd have done better to wait till I was gone, then call the law."

"Oh, I know that," Brian said. "If you'd used up the forty and didn't come back in, that's what I was gonna do."

"Well, then, Brian," the hardcase said, "that should use up your stupidity for today, shouldn't it?"

"I sure hope so."

"So if I tell you to call your wife and say you're gonna be late, don't hold supper, might be nine or ten o'clock, you aren't going to be cute, are you?"

"Well, I never do that," Brian said. As long as he was relatively safe, he wanted to go on being relatively safe. "If I say that to her," he explained, "she'll know something's wrong, I won't have to try anything cute."

The hardcase waved that away, shaking his head and the pistol, focusing Brian's attention. "You got an important customer," he said, "or a close friend, somebody's got an emergency, got to drive to a wedding somewhere tomorrow, you've really got to get his car done."

Surprisingly, Suzanne spoke up at that. "Dr. Hertzberg," she said.

The hardcase looked at her. "Who's that?"

She said, "He treats a lot of the people around here. My grandfather." She looked at Brian. "And you."

"I suppose," Brian said. And he realized she was right, it was plausible.

The hardcase studied him, thinking about it. "If your wife doesn't buy it," he said, "I can't leave you two here."

"I know that," Brian told him. "Suzanne's right, Dr. Hertzberg's the one man I'd stay here for, work late. All right, I'll call her."

"Good. Suzanne, you stay where you are. Brian, get up and sit at the desk, and make every move slow and out in the open."

"Oh, I will," Brian promised, and did. His ribs gave him a few nasty jolts as he struggled upward, using the same corner of the desk for support that had earlier punched him, and when he was at last on his feet, he was breathing hard, as though he'd been running. The hard breaths were also painful, so he turned slowly and eased himself down into his desk chair, and then the pain receded and the breathing got easier.

"Give me a minute to catch my breath," he said, "think out what I want to say."

"Go ahead."

Brian looked over at Suzanne, and she was frowning at him with some sort of question in her eyes, but he couldn't figure out what. He'd known her for years, a pleasant if somewhat bossy woman, a granddaughter of

178

a neighbor, but he didn't actually know her very well. He wasn't the sort to chat up a divorced woman, living on her own the last few years, so when she frowned at him like that, her eyes full of some sort of puzzlement, he had no idea what she might be thinking, what it was she wanted to know.

"Do it now."

"Oh," Brian said, and looked at the phone. "Right."

Picking up the receiver, he noticed for the first time that some of the phone's buttons were much dirtier than the others. His hands were always dirty when he was working here, so, of course, those buttons must be dirtier because the number he most often called was his own home, to speak to Edna.

Yes; he tapped out the sequence on the dirtier buttons, and on the second ring Edna answered: "Three seven five two."

"Edna, it's me. I gotta stay and work late tonight."

"Wha'd, you find a tootsie?"

"Sure. We're going to Miami Beach together."

"Without your supper? That'll be the day."

"Well, that's the thing. Dr. Hertzberg, you know, he's gotta go to a wedding tomorrow down in Pennsylvania, he's got some real coolant problems here in that clunker he drives, I promised I'd have it for him first thing in the morning."

"I'm doing chicken curry."

"It'll reheat."

"Men. How late are you gonna be?"

"Maybe nine, ten."

"Why not just trade him a new car?"

"Listen, I'm not gonna argue with Dr. Hertzberg. He wants to go to that wedding."

She sighed, long and sincere. "And the man's a saint, I know, I know. I'm not gonna reheat it with you, I'm gonna eat it when it's ready and tastes like something."

He knew she wouldn't, she'd wait for him, and he found himself hoping very hard she wasn't going to have to wait forever. Just keep going along with the guy, just be grateful the guy was professional enough he didn't start blasting away the first time he saw an amateur with a gun, and a little later on tonight that chicken curry, reheated or not reheated, would be the most tasty thing he ever ate in his entire life.

"Well," he said, "I'll get there just as soon as I can."

"Say hello to the good doctor for me."

"Oh, yeah, I will."

It wasn't till he hung up that his hands started to tremble, but then they did a real dance. He was inside this sudden airless bowl here, and he'd made contact with the normal world outside the bowl, and it had shaken him much more than he'd guessed.

The hardcase, standing over by the door, said, "That's good, you did that fine."

"Thanks."

"Now I want the laces out of those boots."

"Sure," Brian said, knowing what that meant. It meant, unless something brand-new went wrong, he was going to live through this.

What he wore at the garage, because he was surrounded there by large, heavy, dirty things in motion, some of them also sharp, was steel-cap-reinforced boots, laced up past the ankle. He bent now to strip the laces out of the boots, and the hardcase said, "You got a Closed sign?"

"Over there, tucked in behind that file cabinet."

He went on stripping out the laces, and then the hardcase said, "You use this sign?"

"Every night."

"It says 'Closed' on one side, 'Open' on the other. How come you don't use the Open side?"

"People know if I'm here." The truth was, and Brian knew it, he didn't use the Open side because he thought it sounded like an invitation for a whole lot of people to come in and chat and fill up his day; who needed it?

The hardcase said, "Where do you put it? Window or door?"

"It goes in the bottom right corner of the window. It

slips in a space between the glass and the wood there. Here's the laces."

"Put them on the desk. Suzanne, get up. Slow! Come over here, pick up one of those laces. Brian, put your hands behind your back. Suzanne, tie his wrists together and then tie them to the metal crossbar on the chair. Go ahead."

"I don't know why you're doing—"

"Now."

Brian felt the rough movements of the shoelace wrapping around his crossed wrists as the hardcase said, "Not so tight the blood stops, but not loose. I'll check it when you're done."

"I was a Girl Scout," she said. "I know knots."

It felt to him she was doing it pretty tight. Had he read in a book somewhere where people could defeat being tied up by tensing certain muscles here and there? Well, maybe somebody could.

"All right, Suzanne, stand straight, wrists crossed behind you."

"I don't want somebody to tie me up."

"I tie you up, or I kill you. Kill you might be easier for both of us, you won't be tense any more. I only do it this way because it gives the cops less motivation."

The silence seemed to Brian to go on too long. If the guy shot Suzanne, wouldn't he have to shoot Brian, too? The cops would already be motivated, anyway.

Suzanne, wake up! Don't you know what we've got here?

But then the silence changed in quality, and it seemed to Brian he could hear the little sounds of the laces moving against flesh. No more discussion followed, no more argument; all to the good.

"All right, Suzanne, you're gonna sit against the wall here, I'll help you down. Fine. Legs out straight."

Brian's chair was on small casters that didn't work very well, but he could push himself back from the desk and turn just enough to see Suzanne seated on the floor, back straight, against the side wall, and the hardcase now down on one knee in front of her, tying her ankles with a brand-new set of jumper cables. Finishing, he looked over at Brian and said, "That chair rolls. I don't like that."

"I'm sorry," Brian said.

The hardcase got to his feet and went into the shop, where they heard him rummaging around. When he came back, he had some tools in his hands and a long roll of black electric tape. Putting it all on the desk, not saying anything else now, he moved Brian, chair and all, into the front right corner of the room, next to the door, with Suzanne on the floor to his other side. From here, of course, nobody out by the pumps looking in here would be able to see either of them.

The hardcase checked Brian's wrists and must have been satisfied, because then he used the electric tape to tie Brian's white-socked ankles to the chair legs, and used screwdrivers as chocks to keep the casters from moving. Finally he fastened the screwdrivers to the floor and the casters with more electric tape.

He was done with talking, apparently, and barely looked at them any more as he went about his work. Finished, he stepped back to look at what he'd done, while they both mutely watched. Then he went over to the key rack on the back wall, considered the keys and the identifying cards, and chose one. From where he sat, Brian thought he'd picked Jeff Eggleston's Infiniti, the best car he had here right now.

That was all. The hardcase came over to open the door, figure out the push-button lock arrangement, and, without giving them a glance, he left. From his position, Brian couldn't tell if he drove off in the Infiniti or Tom Lindahl's SUV.

"The arrogance of that man!" Suzanne cried. "To do a thing like this to perfect strangers, no excuse, no reason, no— I've never *seen* such a horrible, horrible . . ." She couldn't seem to figure out how to end the sentence.

"Suzanne," Brian said, trying to be kindly, to calm her down, "who he is, the situation he's in, he's gonna do pretty much what he wants."

Now Suzanne turned her outrage on Brian, as though it were all *his* fault (which it almost was). Voice dripping with scorn, caustically she demanded, "Oh, yes? Why? Is he supposed to be somebody *famous*?"

Brian stared at her. He thought, It's gonna be a long night.

THREE

Cal glowered out his side of the windshield as Cory drove the pickup truck. "If he was the guy, we'd be dead now," he quoted, twisting the words as though he wanted to spit. "That guy talks pretty big, Cory. We should of called his bluff right there."

"That doesn't do us any good."

"Does *me* some good." Cal looked around, and they were out in the country, Pooley well behind them. "Where we goin'?"

"To Judy's."

Their sister, younger than them, living on her own since the guy she thought she was going to marry went into the navy instead. "What for?"

"To borrow her car."

Cal scoffed. "Judy won't give us her car."

Watching the road, Cory said, "She won't give it to you. She'll loan it to me."

"Why? What do we want with her little dinky car?"

"We have to have a different vehicle," Cory told him,

"because Tom and that other guy know this truck. They'll see it in their rearview mirror, they'll know just what we're up to."

"Oh. Yeah, sure, naturally," Cal said, trying to pretend he'd thought of it himself, or at least might have. Then, needing to prove he could think of the details, too, he said, "But how you gonna get her to give it to you? You show up in this, you already got wheels, then you say, 'Gimme your car,' what are you gonna say? Because we're gonna take down a bank robber?"

"I got a job interview," Cory said.

Cal gave him a skeptical look. "What job interview?"

"I *say* I got a job interview. At that community college, in the computer arts department."

"They already turned you down over there."

"I know they did, and so does Judy." Cory nodded at the road ahead, agreeing with himself. "So what I tell Judy, I got another interview over there, this time I'm not gonna dress like a farmer and I'm not gonna show up in some pickup truck. I'm gonna dress like a guy teaches computer arts, and I'm gonna show up in Judy's nice Volkswagen Jetta. I'll tell her, and it's true, I'll even run it through the car wash first."

"Judy's down on me, you know," Cal pointed out. "If she sees me, she's gonna say, 'What are you taking *that* bozo to college for?'"

Cory laughed. "You're right," he said. "I can't have you in the truck when I get there. It's got to be just Judy and me."

"So whadaya gonna do with me while you're off bull-shitting Judy?"

"There's that diner about a mile before her place," Cory reminded him.

"Randall's."

"That's the one. I'll let you off, you have a cup of coffee—"

"Or a beer."

"Make it a cup of coffee. We gotta be sharp tonight, Cal."

"Okay, okay, I'll make it coffee. And you go off to Judy by yourself."

"And come back with the Jetta."

"And that so-called tough guy won't have an idea in the world we're sitting right on his ass."

"Right."

Cal frowned at the windshield, struck by a sudden thought. "What if they're already gone when we get back?"

"Whatever they're gonna do," Cory assured him, "they won't start in on it until after dark."

And that also made sense. Cal nodded at the road awhile, thinking, then said, "What do you suppose they're up to?"

"We'll find out when we see them do it," Cory said, and that was the end of that conversation until they reached the diner, a sprawling place that had originally been a little railroad car type of greasy spoon, but then kept adding on dining rooms and kitchens and bigger neon signs out front until now it looked more like an Indian casino than a place to eat. It was at the intersection of the smallish state road they were on and a bigger U.S. highway, and was always pretty full, though the food wouldn't bring anyone back.

Cory stopped near the entrance and said, "I'll be maybe half an hour."

"I'll sit by the window," Cal told him as he opened his door.

"Just have coffee, Cal, okay?"

"Sure, sure. Don't worry about me."

Cal got out, Cory drove away, and Cal went into the diner, where he had a cheeseburger, onion rings, and a beer.

FOUR

Usually Fred spent Sunday afternoons in fall and winter watching football games by himself in the living room while Jane read in the enclosed back porch that was a greenhouse in summer and the best view of the outside world in winter. Today, though, when she got home from Tom Lindahl's place with the rifle, though Fred was in the living room as usual, the television set was off and he was just sitting there, in his regular chair, slumped, not even looking toward the set but downward, past his knees at the carpet on the floor, brooding. He barely lifted his head when she walked in, trying to be chipper, saying, "I never knew this thing was so heavy."

"Oh, you got it," he said, though without much animation. "Good."

"Should I put it in the closet?"

"Sure. Okay."

She started out of the room, but couldn't help herself, had to turn back and say, "No football?"

"Ah, it's just same-old, same-old," he said, and shrugged, and didn't exactly meet her eye.

She herself had always thought football games were very much same-old, same-old, the same movements seen every Sunday, like ritual Japanese theater, only the costumes changing, but she didn't like to hear that sentiment come from Fred. She only nodded, though, and went to the bedroom and put the rifle in its place at the back of the closet, upright, leaning against the left rear corner. Then she went back to the living room, where Fred had not moved, and said, "I saw that man."

He roused a bit. "Uh? Oh, him."

"He's very strange, Fred."

"He knows what he wants," Fred said, which seemed to her a strange kind of remark.

"He did say something," she went on, "that I thought was odd, but maybe it was a good thing to say."

No response. She waited for him to ask what the strange man had said, but he didn't even look at her, so she had to go ahead without prompting. "He said George will want to see you when he gets home."

"George?" Not as though he didn't remember their own son, but as though he couldn't imagine why they'd been discussing him.

"Tom told him," she explained. "And he said George would want to see you when he gets home."

"Of course he's going to see me," Fred said, starting to get irritated. "What do you mean?"

"Well – just that we'll be together again."

He frowned, trying to understand, then suddenly looked angry and said, "Because I wanted my rifle back? It's *my* rifle."

"I know that, Fred."

"It's in the closet. You asked me, and I said put it in the closet. What do you people *think* of me?"

"I told you, it was just this odd thing he said, that's all."

"He'd like that, wouldn't he?" Fred said, looking sullen now. "Solve all of his problems for him, wouldn't it?"

"What problems, Fred? Now I don't know what *you're* talking about."

"Nothing," he said, turning farther away, brushing the air with his hands. "It isn't anything. Thank you for bringing it back."

Which was clearly a dismissal, so she went away again, paused at the kitchen to make herself a cup of instant coffee, and then went onto the porch, where the book she was currently reading waited for her on the seat of her chair.

Jane loved to read. Reading invariably took her out of the world she lived in, out of this glassed-in porch with its changing views of the seasons, and off to some other world with other views, other people, other seasons. Invariably; but not today.

Jane tended to buy best sellers, but only after they came out in paperback, so the excited buzz that had greeted the book's initial appearance had cooled and she could see the story for itself, with its insights and its failings. She was a forgiving reader, even when she was offered sequences that didn't entirely make sense; after all, now and again the sequence of actual life didn't make sense, either, did it?

Like that man Smith, staying with Tom Lindahl. What could possibly have brought those two together? And how had Tom, a man she'd known for probably thirty years, suddenly come up with an "old friend" nobody'd ever heard of before?

No; that was the real world. What she was trying to concentrate on was the world inside this book, and finally, after distracting herself several times, she did succeed, and settled in with these characters and their story. Now she concentrated on the problems of these other relationships and intertwining histories and didn't look up until the room had grown so dark she simply couldn't read any more.

Turning to switch on the floor lamp to her left, she glanced at her watch and saw it was well after seven. Oh, and they hadn't done anything about supper.

Usually, by now, Fred would have come back to tell her the game was over, and sit with her to decide about Sunday supper, which was a much looser arrangement now that Jodie had gone off to Penn State. But today there was no football, no end of game, and no Fred.

Was he going to just sit in there in the living room forever and brood? It had to be much darker in there than out here on the porch, but when she looked toward the doorway, she could see no light at all from inside the house.

Was there something frightening in there, in the dark? Was there something unfamiliar in there, like an unread book, but not one she would enjoy? There was something frightening somewhere, she was sure of that, something she didn't like at all, like a horror movie at the moment when you know something bad is about to happen.

But that was nothing at all, that was just nerves. That was *her* house in there.

Had he fallen asleep? That might even be a blessing, and even more so if he woke feeling better about things. But she should make sure, so she put the bookmark in the book, got to her feet, and moved through the house, switching the lights on along the way.

The living room was empty. She looked toward the bedroom and called, "Fred?" No answer.

Suddenly really frightened, in a more horrible way than any book or horror movie had ever frightened her, she went to the front door to look out. Their garage was full of junk, so the Taurus was always parked in the driveway. It was very dark out there now, and the Taurus was black, so she had to switch on the outside light to be sure the Taurus was not there.

Where was he? What had he done? More and more afraid, almost not wanting the answers to the questions that crowded her mind, she hurried to the bedroom and opened the closet door.

The rifle was gone.

FIVE

"It's night," Tom said, and looked from the window back at the guy he'd grown used to thinking of as Ed, even though he knew that could not possibly in any way be his name. "When do you want to go?"

Ed rose and came over to glance outside. "A little change of plan," he said.

Tom didn't like the sound of that. It was very hard to keep up with what was going on here, with the Pandora's box he'd opened when he'd first seen Ed pulling himself up that hill ahead of the dogs, and when he'd decided to use the man instead of turning him in. That snap decision, born out of frustration and self-contempt, had consequences that just kept echoing, so that Tom almost had the feeling that, without intending to do so, he'd become a rodeo rider, a fellow on a bucking bronco for the first time in his life, where it would be a disaster beyond belief if he were to fall off.

Wondering if his voice was shaking, he said, "Isn't it

late for a new plan? You don't want to do it tonight, after all?"

"No, it's tonight. The change is, you drive down by yourself."

"By myself?" Alarmed, Tom said, "I thought we were doing this together."

"We are. When you get there, that first place you unlocked, you wait. If I'm not there, I'll show up a little later."

"But—" Tom tried to understand what was happening. Ed didn't have a car. He didn't have anybody else here he could ask for help. How was he going to get all the way from here to the track?

"How are you going to get there?"

"I'll get there," Ed said. "You don't have to know what I'm doing."

"I don't get this," Tom said. He didn't just feel confused, he felt very nervous, as though he were at the edge of a cliff or something. A nauseous kind of fear was rising in him, giving him that rotten taste of bile in the back of his throat. "I don't see why you have to change things."

"You'll see when it's over. Listen, Tom."

Reluctantly, Tom said, "I'm listening."

"You leave here, you drive down there. If you see Cory's truck anytime, don't worry about it."

"Why? Are you going to be driving it?"

"No, just don't worry about it. Keep driving. When you get there, wait. If I don't show up in half an hour, you can go do the thing yourself, or you can just turn around and come back, up to you. But I will show up."

"You've got something else going on."

Ed gave him an exasperated look. "We work from different rule books, Tom. You already know that."

"Yes."

Why did I think I could control him? Tom thought, remembering the sight of the man coming up that hill. Because he was on the run? That didn't make him somebody that could be controlled, that made him somebody that could never be controlled.

Ed said, "This'd be a good time for you to go."

Startled, Tom thought, I'm still supposed to go! I'm still supposed to do this. For Christ's sake, Tom, you're not the assistant on this thing, it's *your* theft. You're the one thought of it, you're the one wanted to hurt those bastards at Gro-More with it, and you're the one brought this man into it. And it's still yours.

Very nervous, but knowing there was no choice, Tom looked around his little living room and said, "You'll turn the lights off?"

"Go, Tom."

"All right." Tom looked over at the parrot and saw

the parrot was looking directly back at him. Why didn't I ever name it? he wondered. I'll do it now. When I get back. No, while I'm driving down there, I'll think of a name.

SIX

When it started to turn to night, Jack Riley switched the porch light on. That always brought Suzanne, but tonight it didn't. Where was she?

Four hours. More than four hours ago, she was right here, they were talking about who around here would sneak into a man's house and steal his gun, and she said she'd go off and get some gas and something for them to have supper together, and off she drove.

Jack figured, maybe an hour. He didn't happen to look to see which way she went when she drove off, so she might have gone to Brian Hopwood's gas station here in town, or she might have gone out to the Getty station, the other way, all depending on where she figured to pick up something for their supper. So maybe half an hour, maybe an hour; no more.

A little after six, he woke up in front of the television set – again! . . . and cursed himself for it. He kept promising himself and promising himself, no more sleeping in front of the television set. He'd tell himself what to do: At the first feeling of sleepiness, get up, stand up, walk around. Go outside, maybe. If the lights weren't on, turn them on. Just do anything instead of falling asleep yet again in front of the goddam TV.

Well, he couldn't do it. He'd be sitting there, watching some damn thing, wide awake, and the next he'd know, it would be two or three or four hours later, and he was waking up in front of the set again, mouth dry, head achy, bones stiff.

Damn, how could he stop that? Stand up, maybe? Never watch television sitting down, only stand up in front of the set? Or would he fall asleep standing up and break his nose when he hit the floor?

Women are supposed to outlive you, dammit. They're supposed to be there to give you a poke in the ribs when they see you nodding off. Just another way life was a pain in the butt without Eileen.

Jack Riley was nine years a widower. He'd lived the last seven years in this house, once he'd understood his former home was too much for him to care for on his own, and the money the house had sold for was better off in blue-chip stocks. In the years since his moving here, Suzanne was just about his closest female companion, very different from Eileen, and one of the differences was that it was no way her job description to sit next to him all the time and poke him in the ribs when he started to fall asleep in front of the goddam television set.

Where *was* Suzanne? How far could she have gone in search of gas and food? There hadn't been an accident, had there?

If only he'd been looking out the window when she drove off, so now he'd have some sort of idea where she might be. At Brian Hopwood's station? It was after six, and he knew Brian was long closed by now, but he tried calling the gas station number, anyway, just in case, and, of course, it rang and rang and rang over there in that empty building, where Brian Hopwood would be the last man in the world to install an answering machine.

The other way, maybe? Jack didn't know anybody at the Getty station, and in any case she would have been through there long ago. Back here long ago, if everything was all right.

Jack switched the television off before he sat down again because he didn't want to fall asleep, dammit, he wanted to be wide-awake for when she got home, and in the meantime he wanted to be wide-awake so he could fret.

It had all begun last night, when, having awakened in front of the television set yet again, he'd finally got himself out of his living room chair and into bed. He'd become a creature of many habits since he'd been in this house on his own, and one of those habits, the last thing every night, just as he was getting into bed, was to unlock the drawer in the bedside table and look in at the pistol sitting there.

It was reassuring, when you lived alone in an isolated place like this, to know that little protective device was there. He'd never actually fired the gun; he'd only bought it for the sense of security it gave him, but that sense of security was real – it helped him to sleep soundly every night – and so the ritual was there, at bedtime, to look in for just a second at the gun. Like a pet you're saying good night to.

And last night it was gone. That was a real stomach-churner of a moment. He'd been half-seated on the bed, opening the drawer, and he bolted right up again when he saw that empty space where the gun was supposed to be. Then he stared around wildly, looking for an explanation, trying to remember a moment in which he himself would have moved the gun to some other location – where? – and found no such moment, nor any reason for any such moment.

The next thing he'd done was go through the whole house again, making sure every door and window was shut and locked, and they all were. So had it been sometime during the day that the gun was taken? But who would know he had it, or where to find it, or where to find the key?

He knew the few people who lived in this town, and there wasn't a one of them he could even begin to imagine sneaking into this house and making off with his gun. But who else? Some passing bum? There were no passing bums, no foot traffic at all. Somebody driving by in a car wouldn't suddenly stop and walk into Jack Riley's house and walk out with his gun. It made no sense, no matter how you looked at it.

Feeling totally spooked, he then switched on the front porch light, as though it might attract Suzanne at this late hour, but almost immediately switched it off again, because he knew it wouldn't attract Suzanne in the middle of the night and he didn't want to know who else it *might* attract. Instead, he left lights on in the bathroom and the kitchen, and thus did get some sleep, though not as much as usual, and this morning he called Suzanne to tell her about it.

She was as baffled as he was, of course. She had other things she had to do on Sunday morning, but could come over to see him this afternoon, and did. When she arrived, again he told the story. She double-checked all his doors and windows, helped him look in all the other drawers in the house, then sat down to try to figure out who might have done it.

No suspects came to mind. Eventually Suzanne said she'd go off for gas and supper, and Jack fell asleep in front of the goddam television again, and now what?

Suzanne gone four hours. Night outside. No gun, no Suzanne. Sometime after seven, he accepted the fact that there was no alternative; he had to call the troopers.

He didn't want to. If it turned out there was some simple rational explanation for the disappearance – both disappearances – he'd feel like a fool, some old geezer that's lost his marbles. But the gun is really gone, and Suzanne really hasn't come back, so eventually there was just nothing else to do.

Jack kept all the emergency numbers written on a piece of cardboard tacked to the wall near the kitchen phone, including the nearby state police barracks, because they were the ones responsible for policing this area. Still reluctant, but knowing he just had to do it, he dialed the number, and after a minute a voice came on and said, "Barracks K, Trooper London."

"Hello," Jack said. "I wanna report – well, I wanna report two things."

"Yes, sir. Your name, sir?"

"First I— Oh. Riley. John Edward Riley."

"Your address, sir?"

"Route 34, Pooley," he said, and gave the house number, and then the trooper wanted to know his phone number, and only then did he show any interest in the reason for the call. "You say you want to make a report?"

"A disappearance," Jack said. "Two disappearances."

"Family members, sir?"

"Well, it's— No, wait. The first was last night, was the gun."

"The gun, sir?"

"I've got – I had— When I moved here, I bought this little pistol, it's called a Ranger, I got the permit and all, you know, it's for house defense."

"Yes, sir. And it disappeared?"

"Last night. I keep it locked in a drawer, and last night, before I went to bed, I went to look at it, be sure everything was okay, and it wasn't there."

"Sir, did you have any reason to believe everything was *not* okay?"

"Not till I saw the gun wasn't there."

"Sir, did you have a reason to look for the gun?"

"I always do. Every night, I just double-check."

"Yes, sir, I see. Could you tell me who else resides with you, sir?"

"Just me, I'm on my own."

"Did you have guests, visitors, yesterday, sir?"

"No, it was just me. You see, that's why it doesn't make any sense."

"Did you report the disappearance, sir?"

"Just now. I mean no, not till now. This morning I called my granddaughter, Suzanne, she came over this afternoon, we looked for it, but it's gone. Then, around three o'clock, she went out, she had to get gas and she was gonna get something for our supper, and she never came back."

"This is your granddaughter, sir?"

"Suzanne. Suzanne Gilbert."

So then he had to tell the trooper everything about Suzanne, her looks and her age and her weight and her employment and a whole lot of stuff that didn't seem to Jack as though it mattered, but he figured, it's the trooper's job, let him do it. And after that, there was a lot about Suzanne's car. And after that, he wanted to know everything about Suzanne's personal life; was she married, did she have a boyfriend, was anybody living with her, had she ever gone off on her own before? And through it all, Jack couldn't figure out, from the even, flat way the trooper asked his questions, whether he was being taken seriously or patronized. Because, if there was one hint that he was being patronized, boy, would he start to holler. Never mind the gun; we're talking about *Suzanne* here!

But then at last the trooper said, "We'll dispatch a car, sir. They should be there in less than half an hour."

By God, Jack thought, I hope Suzanne's back by then,

and yet, on the other hand, I hope she isn't. Nothing bad happen to her, just not already here when the troopers show up.

"Thank you," he said. "I'll leave the porch light on."

SEVEN

It wasn't football Fred saw on the blank television screen, it was the cell. The all-purpose cell, sometimes the one he knew he was headed for, sometimes the one George was in right now – what has happened to our family? – but other times the cell/grave in which lay the man he killed, twitching still in death.

He had never seen George's cell, of course, so this cell, constantly shifting, existed only in his imagination, fed mostly by old black-and-white movies watched on nights he couldn't sleep. A small stone room it was, longer than wide, high-ceilinged, with hard iron bars making up one of the short walls and one small high-up window in the opposite wall, showing nothing but gray. The cell smelled of damp and decay. He lay curled on the floor there, or George did, or sometimes that poor man up at Wolf Peak, the last thick dark red blood pulsing out of his back.

It was getting dark outside the living room windows. Imagination had never much bothered Fred before this, but now he was all imagination, screaming nerve ends of imagination, imagining the cell, imagining the shame, and now, as darkness was coming on, imagining the teeth. Destroying the evidence. It gets darker and darker, and all those rustling creatures gather around the body on the forest floor, gnawing at it, snarling at one another, gnawing and gnawing.

His body. The way he sometimes became George, in that Gothic prison cell, now sometimes, too, he became the dead man on Wolf Peak, among all those jaws, all those teeth.

I can't stand this, he thought, I have to get out of this, and what he meant was, he could no longer stand his mind, he had to get away from his mind, and, of course, he understood what he meant by that.

But what stopped him? Not thoughts of his family, his wife, his son, his daughter, they'd get over him after a while, everybody gets over everybody sooner or later. Not cowardice; he had no fear of eating the rifle, he knew the terror would be short and the pain almost nonexistent.

What stopped him was the thought of that man Smith. Ed Smith, or whoever he was. To send that message home with Jane, to play his little psychological games again, the way he'd done up in the woods, the way he'd done on the drive home. Manipulating him.

Sending Jane home with a coded message – don't kill yourself – because the real code under the first code was to put the idea of killing himself into his head.

That's what Smith had in mind, that was so obvious. Pretend sympathy – as though that man knew the meaning of the word "sympathy" – as a way to put that little worm into his brain: Wouldn't it be easier if you were dead?

God, yes, it would. God, he didn't need Ed Smith to tell him that. But with Smith everywhere around him, it was just impossible. No matter how much pain he was in, no matter how hopeless everything was, he couldn't kill himself, he just couldn't, for the one and only reason that he wouldn't give a bastard like Ed Smith the satisfaction.

Time went on, and his thinking circled around the same points, but gradually the angles shifted, gradually he came around to another point of view. If only Ed Smith were gone. It would be possible to become unstuck, to move forward with life, if only Ed Smith were . . .

No. If only Ed Smith didn't exist.

Everything would be different then. The weight of the dead man up on Wolf Peak would bear less heavily on him, the fear of exposure would end. Fred knew that Tom Lindahl would never talk about what had happened up there; Tom wasn't the problem. But how could they trust Ed Smith, how could they be sure what he would or would not do next?

The problem wasn't Fred's imagination, that was just inflamed for now by what had happened. The problem wasn't George, who, of course, would be coming home in a year, less than a year, and, of *course*, Fred would be here to greet him. The problem wasn't Fred or George or Tom or that poor wino up on Wolf Peak.

The only problem was Ed Smith.

After all that thinking, when Fred finally did get to his feet and walk to the bedroom, he did it with almost no conscious thought at all. There was nothing to think about when you were sure, and Fred was sure.

He carried the rifle loosely in his right hand, grasping the warm wood of the stock, pleased as always with the feel of the thing. His memories with that rifle, out hunting, had been very good for a long time, and soon they'd be good again.

He knew that Jane, at the very rear of the house, absorbed in her book, wouldn't hear him drive away, but he coasted backward down the driveway, anyway, and didn't start the engine until he'd backed around onto the empty street. The houses all around him were warmly lit with families together for Sunday evening.

Very soon he'd be back among them. The rifle on the seat beside him, he drove toward Tom Lindahl's house.

EIGHT

The parrot saw things in black and white. He knew about this place of his, that it was very strong, and that he was very strong within it, and that whenever he thought he might be hungry, there was food in his tray. He was clean and preferred to stand on his swinging bar rather than down at the bottom of the world, even at those rare moments when the bottom of the world was made new, almost shining white and black, crisp, noisy if touched, until he began to drop upon it again.

For movement, rather than down there, he preferred to move among the swinging wooden bar and the rigid vertical black metal bars of the cage. Up and over, sometimes, for no reason at all, his strong talons gripping the bars even directly above his head, giving him, when he arched his neck back and stared with one round black and white eye at the world, this world, a whole new perspective.

There wasn't much in this world, but not much was needed. With his strong talons and his strong beak, gripping to the metal bars, a taste like inside your brain on his tongue from the bars, he could move around and control everything he needed.

Outside the cage, enveloping it, was another cage, indifferent to him. Below him, on the one side, dim light glowed upward to suffuse that larger cage with soft auras, constantly shifting. Sometimes grating noises came up from there, too, sometimes not. Beyond, over there, a paler, larger, taller rectangular brightness sometimes briefly appeared, when Creatures entered or departed their world, the one beyond his. At other times they made that rectangle and moved through, but there was no extra light.

He had some curiosity about these Creatures, but not much. He studied them when they were present, usually observing one eye at a time, waiting for them to do something to explain themselves. So far, they had not.

Sometimes the parrot slept. He slept on the swinging bar, talons gripping tight, large button eyes closed, coarse green feathers slightly ruffled upward and forward. When he woke, he always knew he had been asleep, and that nothing had happened, and that, now he was awake, it was time to eat and shit, drink and piss, so he did.

Now it was now. Creatures went out, with not much brightness in their rectangle, and leaving no Creatures behind. The shifting lights from below continued, without the noise. Time went by and the parrot slept, suddenly awakened by a racket.

Another Creature had come in, with banging noises and shouting noises. It crossed in front of the bright square, it went into other darknesses and came back, it yelled and yelled, and then it leaned down to stare at the parrot, to stare at that left eye observing it, and yell and yell the same phrase over and over.

The parrot had never spoken. The parrot had never been in a social situation where it seemed the right thing to do was to speak. The main Creature who lived with him, in his cage outside the cage, almost never spoke. It had never occurred to the parrot to speak.

But now this Creature, some unknown foreign Creature, was yelling the same sounds over and over again, and it came to the parrot that he could make those sounds himself. It might be satisfying to make those sounds. He and the Creature could make those sounds together.

So he opened his beak, for the first time ever not to grip a bar, and the first thing he said was a rusty squawk, which was only natural. But then he got it: "Air izzi? Air izzi? Air izzi?"

The Creature reared back. It shrieked. It yelled many different things, too fast and too many and too jumbled for the parrot to assimilate. Then it jabbed the end of a metal rod into the cage, wanting to poke it against the parrot's chest, but the parrot sidestepped it easily on his swinging bar, then clamped his left talon around the long metal rod.

The Creature had not finished yelling. The parrot joined it: "Air izzi? Air izzi?"

The parrot leaned his head down and swiveled it to the right. His left eye looked down the long round tunnel inside the metal rod. "Air izzi? Air izzi?"

The searing white flame came out so fast.

NINE

Trooper James Duckbundy was a health nut, which was why he liked to drive with the cruiser's window open. Trooper Roger Ellis would have been just as happy with General Motors air, but Duckbundy was at the wheel this time out, so it was his call.

They were driving to Pooley from Barracks K because some old coot had reported mislaying his weapon, a handgun. Both troopers understood the citizens' right to bear arms and all that, but both sincerely believed the world would be a safer place if idiots didn't own guns. They could understand how a person at almost any age could mislay their car keys or watch, but to lose your piece? That was just the sort of individual, in their opinion, who shouldn't be armed in the first place.

Of the sleepy little towns in the world, Pooley had to be one of the sleepiest. They drove in to few lights and no traffic, and Duckbundy parked in front of the address, a small house lit up like a Christmas tree, the only house in town that seemed to have every last light switched on, interior and exterior. Losing his handgun seemed to have made the householder nervous.

Because Duckbundy was a health nut, which meant his window was open, before he even switched off the engine they both heard the flat serious crack of a shot. Up ahead it came from, and on the other side of the road.

They looked at each other. "That was no handgun," Ellis said.

"It wasn't applause, either," Duckbundy said, and put the cruiser back in gear.

There were no further shots as they eased slowly down the road, but there didn't need to be. It is a crime to discharge a firearm within five hundred feet of a dwelling, and one time will do.

They both peered at the houses on the left, inching along, until Ellis said, "Movement back there."

There was a boarded-up empty house at that point, with a driveway next to it and what looked like a garage in back. Duckbundy braked, swiveled the spotlight, and clicked it on. In the sudden glare, a man down there by the garage, with a rifle in his right hand, was just getting into a black Taurus. Something wet glistened on the barrel of the rifle as the man spun around, glaring into the light, clutching the rifle now with both hands.

Ellis had the microphone in his palm and carried it with him as he stepped out to the roadway. *"Police,"* roared the speaker on the cruiser's roof. *"Stop where you are. Lay the weapon down."*

He didn't. He screamed something, gibberish, something, and then he did bring the rifle up.

Between them, the troopers fired eleven shots. Any three would have done the job.

TEN

What do you call a parrot? Does it have to start with "P"? Polly Parrot; Peaches Parrot. Penitentiary Parrot; not good. Greeny Parrot.

There was less traffic tonight, and fewer roadblocks. It seemed to Tom the authorities no longer believed they had the fugitives trapped; they were just going through the motions.

How was Ed going to get there, without a car and without an ally? Or had he somehow phoned someone, while Tom was away from the house, and arranged to meet with another professional like himself, another hard man, who would come with him to Gro-More to help in the robbery? And get what out of it?

Tom's share, of course.

He could still pull over, at any open gas station, and call the state troopers to tell them where they could find one of the men they were looking for. Unless Ed had left the house almost immediately after Tom.

But it didn't matter; he wasn't going to stop. It was

too late to change anything now, too late to decide to do something other than this.

Different cars appeared in his rearview mirror, and some passed him because, with all this fretful thinking inside his head, he couldn't keep up to his normal speed, but poked along at probably ten miles an hour below his regular average. There was a gray Volkswagen Jetta in his mirror for miles, somebody else as poky as he was, but then he came to another of the rare roadblocks, and after that pause, the Jetta was gone, and for some miles his mirror was dark.

He next became aware of other traffic when a different car's lights appeared well behind him, coming on fast. This one was pretty much a speed demon, who tailgated Tom a mile or so and then, at the next passing zone, roared on by him like a freight train. In Tom's headlights, as it raced away, he could see it was a black Infiniti, a faster, more powerful car than his, soon out of sight up ahead.

Perry Parrot? Ed Parrot? Madonna Parrot? William G. Dodd Parrot?

What if he doesn't show up? What if, after all this, I get there and I never see Ed Smith again? What if he's gone from my life just as abruptly as he came into it?

There would be a relief in that, but Tom knew it wasn't the right question. The question was, if Ed

Smith disappeared, could Tom do it himself, come back with *both* duffel bags full, take the whole gate from the track on his own, double the secret inside the boarded-up house?

Tom didn't believe it. If he got there, and waited half an hour and Ed never appeared, he knew damn well what he'd do. He'd turn tail. He was still the same gutless wonder he'd always been. He needed Ed Smith to give him a backbone. He hated that he needed the man, but he knew it was true. Even after all this, he wouldn't be able to take the track's money on his own.

Do I want him to show up? Do I want this thing to happen, or do I want an excuse just to go back to my crappy little house and vegetate in there forever? Which do I want, which do I really want?

Like the parrot's name, he just didn't know.

ELEVEN

Suzanne woke to the patter of pebbles on her window. Annoyed, not wanting to be awake, she thought, Who would be pestering me at this hour? What time is it, anyway?

No, it's not pebbles, it's shooting! Guns, shooting.

Suzanne opened her eyes to utter madness. Instead of the silent dark of her own hushed peaceable room, she was seated upright in some harshly angular place of bands of hard glare that sliced down across full crowded banks of blackness. Light above, dark below, black on all sides – a window?

"Oh! My God, what's—"

"Shut up!"

Another shock. The voice was male, low, intense, guttural, and not at all friendly. It silenced Suzanne like a hand clapped against her mouth, long enough for the sharp bite of the boot lace around her wrists to bring memory crashing back, with all its terror and all its humiliation.

How could she not have realized that it was the bank

robber they'd run into? She had been just so full of her normal assumption, for so many years, that as she moved through the world she was simply going to be mistreated, or ignored, or dealt with unfairly, that when a man suddenly appeared in front of her to wave a gun around and tie people up like political prisoners, then march off without a single word of explanation, it had somehow been *normal,* somehow what she'd expected from the world all along, even though on most days nothing remotely like this had ever happened.

And now that it had happened? She'd been so locked up in her own feelings of mistreatment, expectations fulfilled, that it hadn't even occurred to her to wonder who that man might be or why he would act in such a way.

Bank robbers were being hunted all around the countryside, but when this had happened to Suzanne, did she think, bank robbers? No, she thought, now see what they're doing to me, and it took Brian Hopwood of all people to tell her, not gently, that this time the story wasn't about her, it was about him, about that man, the one who'd tied them up and gone away.

Then, of course, once Brian had explained to her what was actually happening here, she'd felt such belated terror, mixed with such humiliation, that the tension had kept her absolutely silent for hours, afraid to make somehow an even bigger fool of herself. Brian, who never said anything to anybody, anyway, was also silent through all this, until, who knows how much later, the phone had rung, and rung, and rung, and Brian had finally said, "By God, I hope that's Edna, and I hope she's starting to smell a rat."

But then the phone stopped ringing, and Brian said nothing else, and somehow, despite the discomfort, despite the fear, despite the embarrassment, Suzanne had fallen asleep. Asleep! To wake up who knew when, with gunshots somewhere outside.

Finished now. Who was shooting guns? Was the bank robber back, had he decided he should kill them, after all? But it had been so long since he'd gone away; still daylight then. Wouldn't he be miles and miles from here by now, while Suzanne slept like a rag doll on the floor of Brian Hopwood's filthy gas station, wouldn't he be deep into some other badness by now?

She tried a whisper: "Brian."

"Yes." Gruff but not unfriendly.

"Brian, what's going to happen?"

His laugh now was bitter, and not friendly at all. "Well, we're trussed up here like Thanksgiving turkeys. There isn't a thing for either of us to do until somebody decides to look for us."

"But they're shooting out there. Brian? Who's shooting?"

"How would *I* know?" He was getting really irritated now.

Looking as much for some way to appease him as for some way out of their trouble, she said, "Would Edna come here?"

"I don't think that was her, on the phone."

Struck by a sudden thought, she said, "You know, it could have been Jack. You know, my grandfather."

"I know who Jack is," Brian said, very testy. "Why would he call me?"

"Looking for me."

"Oh." Brian considered that, then said, "Will he come looking for you?"

"Not after dark."

"Wonderful."

The silence now outside was worse than the gunshots; in the silence, you didn't know where anybody was. Feeling sudden panic, Suzanne shrilly whispered, "Brian, we have to get out of here!"

"Go ahead." Sardonic, unbelieving, unsympathetic; in other circumstances, rude.

Which she ignored. "No, really," she whispered. "I know you can't move in that chair there—"

"Huh."

"But I can move."

"You're tied hand and foot."

"But I can *move*. Brian, what if I came over there and—"

"How?"

"I don't know, crawled or rolled or something. What difference does it make?"

"All right," he said. "So you're over here."

"I tied that knot on your wrists. I know what I did. I think maybe, I think maybe I could untie it."

"How do you get at it?"

She thought about that. Now that she was awake and oriented, she could see the office more clearly, even though all the illumination came from outside, from the gas pumps and the soda machine and the streetlight. She and Brian were near each other in the front left corner of the room, where no one looking through any window would be able to see them. The chair Brian was in, taped to the floor, was the only furniture near them. Beyond the dark doorway to the service area, Brian's desk hulked like the recently abandoned headquarters of a defeated army. No, not army; a defeated platoon. An armless kitchen chair, a reluctant acknowledgment that there might someday be a customer to accommodate, stood against the wall on the far side of the desk.

She said, "Brian, is that chair on wheels?"

"No, why should it be?"

"I was just wondering."

"Suzanne, let it go. In the morning, they'll find—"

"I can't wait till morning," she said, and realized it was the truth. Now that she was fully awake, she needed a bathroom, and soon. "Let me just try something," she said, though with every movement the need grew more urgent.

"What are you doing?" he asked, testy as ever, as she started hunching herself across the floor toward him.

"Just let me see . . ."

Ankles and wrists tied together, she could only move in strange little lunges, but soon she was where she wanted to be, with her back to Brian, her tied hands down by his ankles, her hunched shoulders against his shins. Exhausted from the effort, she rested her head a minute, until she realized she was resting it against Brian's thigh and that Brian hated that. So she lifted her head, felt around behind her, and at last came to a part of the duct tape holding the screwdrivers as chocks against the floor, to keep the chair from moving.

Now he grew silent again, and she was aware of his head bent as he tried to see what she was doing and whether or not it would get them anywhere. The duct tape clung fiercely to the wooden floor, but finally she felt far enough along it to reach an end, and could yank that upward. Once started, the tape came more readily, and then the screwdriver itself helped, and, out of breath but triumphant, she could whisper, "I got it!"

"It'll take more than one," he said. "But then I'll be able to help."

This shift in him from being testy with her, scornful of her, impatient with her, to someone who could help was instantaneous and unremarked-upon. She simply accepted the offer with a nod and scooted backward a bit more until she could find some duct tape to assault.

The second screwdriver was easier to remove, now that she knew how, and then Brian could move his chair, though only in tiny increments, since his ankles were still tied together and to the chair. "Now what?" he said. "I don't think I can drive this thing through that door."

"Let me bring that other chair over," she said. "If I can get up on it, maybe I can reach the knots on your wrists."

"What good does that do? They're tight, Suzanne, trust me."

"I tied them myself," she said. "Just let me see what I can do."

"Whatever you want," he said, disbelieving her.

She didn't care. Now that she was moving, she was *moving*. She rolled across the floor, making herself dizzy, but at last bumping into that other chair. Her legs tied together with jumper cable made for a blunt instrument, but with them she could kick the chair away from the wall and around the edge of the desk and over toward Brian, who, astonishingly enough, was doing what he could do to help. That is, he kept shifting his body forward while pressing down and back on the floor with his white socked feet, inching the chair on its casters out away from the corner, where she would find him easier to reach.

Maneuvering them into position wasn't hard, with his back turned to her and the other chair so that, if she were sitting sideways on it, Suzanne would be able to reach Brian's wrists. No, the hard part was for her to get up onto the chair. She did manage to lunge herself up so she was lying facedown across the chair seat, but then could do no more, had no traction anywhere. At last, half-muffled in that position, she said, "Brian, I need your help."

"Sure. What?"

"I have to put my foot in your lap, and you have to not let it get away. I can't get *up* on this *chair* unless I can *brace* against something."

"I don't know," he said. "I don't know what you're trying to do here, but all right. Let's try it. *Jesus*, Suzanne, try to be a little careful."

"This will be very fast," she promised.

Well, it wasn't, and she was sorry to have to hear him grit his teeth as her right heel bore into his crotch, but she needed that brace to be able to swivel around on the chair seat, first on her side, then faceup, so that then she could pull herself up with her bound hands behind her against the slats of the chair back.

"There!" she said.

"Jesus."

"I'm sorry, Brian. Can you turn a little more away from me?"

"I certainly can."

There was some fumbling involved, but then, behind her, she could feel his thick-fingered hands, and then the wrists, and then the thin strong shoelace.

Yes, those were the knots she'd made, good strong knots that could be slipped if you knew which part you were pulling. Here's a loop, here's an end, here's—

He jumped as though he'd been electrocuted. "What's that? Wait – wait a minute! My hands are loose!"

"Brian, please, please, untie my wrists, please, please—"

"Yeah, wait, let me see what I'm doing here. He didn't make it easy, that sonofa— There!"

"Oh, thank God!" she said, and bent to tear off the jumper cable pinning her ankles.

He was still struggling with the duct tape on his socks. She jumped to her feet, patting the wall. "Lights."

"We've got to be careful when we go out there, Suzanne, we don't know what's—"

"I don't want to go out there," she said, hurrying through the doorway into the dark interior room. "I want the ladies'!"

He called after her, "You'll need the key!"

TWELVE

Where was Tom going? It didn't make any sense.

Around seven-thirty, Tom Lindahl's Ford SUV had driven away from the little converted garage he lived in and headed south out of Pooley, with Cory and Cal in the Volkswagen Jetta far behind, and an hour later they were all still driving, heading steadily southwest across New York State, away from Pooley and away from Massachusetts, the site of the bank robbery that Ed Smith's money was supposed to be from.

Were Tom and Smith on their way to get the money? What else could they be doing? Cory had more and more questions in his mind about what was going on here, but he didn't want to voice them, afraid Cal would insist on doing something rash, like ramming that vehicle up ahead just to see what would happen. So Cory kept his doubts to himself and just drove, hoping this journey would soon come to an end.

Cory'd had no trouble borrowing the Jetta from his sister. In fact, she'd been so happy at the idea that Cory might get himself a real job – by which she meant white collar, not the factory-floor stuff he and Cal usually did – that he felt guilty lying to her. But he assured himself it was all going to work out fine, and she wouldn't ever have to know the truth, so he wasn't going to worry about it.

What was a little worrying, at least at first, was that, when Cory went back to the diner, Cal had obviously not limited himself to coffee, the way he'd promised. The beer on his breath wasn't as plain as if they'd been in the cab of the pickup together, but you could still smell it. Cory could have said something, but what was the point? Cal would just deny it, that's all, just lie about it and wait for the question to go away.

That was how Cal always handled problems. It wasn't that he was a good liar – in fact, he was a piss-poor liar, unlike Cory, who had a smooth plausibility about himself – but that once Cal took root in a lie, he would never move from it, so why waste your breath?

At first, when they set up in a driveway next to another of Pooley's empty houses, having to keep well away from Tom's place because it was still daylight, Cal had been tensed up and edgy, because of the beer, wanting something to happen right away. His left eye, covered by the black patch, was neutral, but his working eye was staring and agitated, straining to see through walls, around windows. "When are they gonna make their move?"

"We'll just wait and see."

"Maybe I oughta go peek in the window."

"No, we'll just wait here. We'll know when they're going somewhere."

Cal had to get out and pee then, and that kept him calmed down for a while, but not for long. Three more times he wanted to go over and peek in Tom's window to see what was going on over there, and three times Cory had to remind him there was nothing those people could do except, sooner or later, leave the house and come out to the road in this direction. Did Cal want to be halfway down their driveway, on foot, when they came out? Of course not. Did he want them to catch him peeking in the window? Definitely not.

As for what they thought was going on, they'd been over all of that more than once, but restless and bored in the car, waiting for something to happen, Cal had to rehash it just once more. "There's money in it, we know that much for sure," he said. "Only thing that makes sense. Tom wouldn't be hanging out with that guy, giving him cover, pretending he used to work with him, if there wasn't some sort of payoff in there someplace."

Cory nodded. "That's what we're figuring on, anyway."

236

"That's what we're *counting* on," Cal said. "There's got to be some of that bank robbery money still hid somewhere, or Tom just wouldn't be fronting for that guy. I mean, that's a hell of a risk, Cory."

"Yeah, it is."

"So that's the only reason he's gonna do it. For the money." Cal laughed in a sudden burst. "I don't know about you, Cory, but I could use that money. Better than a job over at that college, anyway."

"Well, I wouldn't mind that, either," Cory admitted.

Cal grinned at him and gave his arm a reassuring pat. "You'll come through," he said. "You're the smart one."

"And you're the funny one."

"Damn hysterical. Why don't I find a phone somewhere and give them a call, just to see what they do?"

"Because," Cory said, "I don't want them thinking about us, or thinking there's anybody at all interested in them, that would keep them from what they mean to do."

"Well, maybe."

"Remember, I'm the smart one."

So Cal laughed at that and relaxed a little more, and they waited in companionable silence. Gradually evening came on, and then, just at that tricky twilight moment when it's very hard to see because it's neither day nor night, here came the Ford out of Tom Lindahl's driveway and turned south, away from them.

"There it is!"

"I see it, Cal. Take it easy."

Cory watched the Ford recede almost out of sight before he started the Jetta and followed, keeping well back. Beside him, Cal, breathing loudly through his mouth, pulled up his shirttail in front and reached down inside to come out with a smallish automatic, the High Standard GI model in .45 caliber.

Cory stared. "What are you doing with *that*?"

Cal laughed. "Don't leave home without it." He hadn't seemed drunk before this, but now, hours since he'd had that beer, there was a sudden slurry electricity to him as he sat there holding the automatic with both hands.

"Oh, come on, Cal," Cory said. "You never said you were gonna bring *that*." Up ahead, Tom Lindahl's Ford moved at a slow and steady pace, easy to follow.

"Well, I just knew you'd give me a hard time if I said anything about it," Cal said. "So I figured, I'll just bring it, and then there won't be any argument."

"If we get stopped by a cop—"

"What for? We're doing" – Cal leaned the left side of his head against Cory's upper arm so his right eye could see the dashboard – "forty-five miles per hour. Who's gonna stop us for *that*?"

"Cal, I don't want to see that thing."

"No, no, you're not gonna see it." Cal leaned forward

238

to put the gun on the floor, then sat back and rested his right foot on it. "See? Just sitting there."

"Is the safety on, anyway?"

"Sure it is. Whada you think?"

"When we talk to those guys," Cory said, "please, Cal, don't start waving that goddam gun around."

"*He's* the one talking tough, do you remember that? 'You'd be dead now.' Oh, yeah, would I? We'll just have this little fella down here on the floor here, out of sight, out of mind, and if there *has* to be a little surprise, somewhere down the road, well, guess what, we got one."

"Just leave it there," Cory said.

"It's there."

Somehow the idea of his brother's gun in his sister's car made Cory nervous, as though he'd got himself involved in some kind of serious mistake here somewhere. Cal had bought that goddam thing years ago, in a pawnshop, on a visit to Buffalo, for no reason at all he could ever explain. He'd just seen it and he wanted it, that's all. From time to time, the first year or so, he'd take it out in the woods and practice, shooting at trees or fence posts, but eventually it more or less just stayed in a drawer in his bedroom, barely even thought about. Cory hadn't thought about it for so long it was like something brand-new, a Gila monster or something, when it suddenly appeared in Cal's lap in the car.

All right, let it stay on the floor. If it made Cal feel more secure to have it down there, fine. When it came time, though, to get out of this car, Cory would make damn sure that stupid gun didn't come out with them.

It was a few miles later they saw the bright red and white lights of their first roadblock of the night. Slowing down, Cory said, "Put the damn gun under the seat."

"Right."

Even Cal seemed a little chastened, as he bent down to hide the gun. Cory drove as slowly as he dared, to give Tom a chance to clear the roadblock, then eased to a stop beside the waiting trooper as he reached for his wallet.

The trooper had a long flashlight that he shone first on Cory and then across him on Cal, not quite shining the beam in their eyes. He was the most bored trooper they'd met yet, and he studied Cory's license without saying a word. Cal had the glove compartment open, but the trooper didn't even bother to ask for registration, just handed the license back and used his flashlight to wave them through.

Tom's Ford hadn't gained much ground, was still slowly moving along as though in no hurry to get anywhere in particular tonight. When Cory caught up, and slowed to maintain the same distance as before, Cal said, "What's goin' on, Cory? Is he just out for a drive?"

"I don't know," Cory admitted. "But I just figured out what's out there, down this way."

"Yeah, what?"

"That racetrack where he used to work."

"What? Tom?"

"He worked there for years, and then they fired him for something."

"What the hell would he be going down to that racetrack for?"

"I don't know *what* they're doing," Cory said. "I mean, there they are, they came out tonight, everything like we thought they'd do, but now I don't get it. They aren't leading us to any money."

"Maybe Tom's helping the guy get away from here."

"At forty-five miles an hour? Besides, he could've done that last night. Or today."

"Get up closer," Cal said. "Let's see what they're up to."

"They're driving," Cory said.

"Come on, Cory, close it up."

"You can't see inside a car at night."

"Close it up, goddammit."

So Cory moved up much closer, not quite tailgating the Ford, and they drove like that awhile, trying to figure it out, getting nowhere. Then, way ahead, Cory saw the lights of the next roadblock and said, "I gotta ease back," just as Cal yelled, "Goddammit!"

"What?" Cory's foot was off the gas, the Jetta slowing, the Ford moving toward the distant roadblock, its brake lights not yet on.

"He's alone in there!"

"What?"

"Pull over here, pull over here, goddammit!"

A closed gas station was on the right. Cory pulled in, drifting past the pumps as he said, "What do you mean, he's alone in there?"

"Tom! I could see those lights down there through his windshield, and he's goddammit alone in the goddam car! Stop!"

Cory stopped. "Then where is he? Maybe he's lying down in back."

"For a roadblock? He isn't there," Cal insisted, and a black car suddenly passed them on their left and angled to a stop across the front of the Jetta. Cal's one eye stared. "What *is* this?"

The driver of the other car got out, looking over its roof at them, and, of course, it was Ed Smith. Cory reflexively shifted into reverse as Smith took a step down the other side of his car, as though he wanted to come around and talk to them.

Cal didn't give him the chance. All at once he was lunging out of the Jetta, and when Cory turned to him, he had that automatic in his hand. Cory yelled, "Don't!"

at the same time Cal yelled some damn thing at Smith and lifted the automatic as though to shoot Smith, and in the same instant Smith laid his own hand on the roof of his car, with something small and black in it that coughed a dot of red flame and Cal went reeling backward, the automatic dropping onto the gas station's concrete.

Cory screamed, and tromped on the accelerator, and the Jetta tore backward past the pumps, the open passenger door not quite hitting them but rocking as though it would come off its hinges, until Cory pounded his foot on the brake and the door slammed.

Ahead of him across the gas station, Smith was striding forward, that gun in his hand down at his side. Cory spun the wheel, shifted into drive, and tore away from there northward, leaving Cal and Smith and the Ford and the roadblock and everything else to shrink and disappear in the rearview mirror.

Absolute panic compelled him to drive hard for three or four minutes on a road with no traffic until he overtook a slow-moving pickup and had to decelerate. As he slowed, the panic receded and clear thought came back, and he knew he had to go take care of Cal. He was the younger brother, but he'd always been the one with brains, the one who went along with Cal's stunts but then – sometimes – got them both out of trouble when things went too far.

Cal was hit. Shot. How bad?

Cory made a U-turn and headed south again, and would have missed the gas station this time if he hadn't seen that roadblock far ahead. But there was the station, and Cory pulled in, went past the pumps to where he'd stopped the last time, and stopped again. Smith and the black car were gone.

Afraid of what he would find, Cory got out of the Jetta and looked around on the right side of the car. Cal's automatic lay on the pavement where it had fallen, but there was nothing else there. No Cal.

Cory got back into the car, put the automatic on the passenger seat, and drove this way and that so he could use the headlights to look at every part of the gas station property. He found nothing.

There was a night-light inside the station office. Cory got out of the Jetta again and looked through the windows there. He looked everywhere. Cal was gone.

THIRTEEN

State Police Captain Robert Modale looked at the artist's rendering of the bank robber, crumpled and greasy from having been in a desk drawer in Brian Hopwood's gas station, and now that he knew the truth, he could see it, he could see that face, the same face as the man he'd talked with just yesterday up in the St. Stanislas parking lot. They'd talked about Lyme disease, and who would have ever guessed he was this fellow all along? The felons a man met up with usually weren't that bold.

Captain Modale was a calm man, not given to extremes of temperament, but even for him this was a moment out of the ordinary. A lesser man might have sworn or punched a wall, but Captain Modale merely clenched his lips and flared his nostrils a little and nodded down at that picture he held in his unshaking left hand and thought, I'll know you next time.

At the moment, eight-fifty on this Sunday evening, the captain was standing in the brightly lit living room of an old fellow named Jack Riley, whose report of a stolen revolver, a .22-caliber S&W Ranger, had started the unraveling of tonight's events. Riley, bright-eyed and eager, perched on the forward edge of the easy chair where he obviously usually spent his time watching that television set over there. His granddaughter, Suzanne Gilbert, a good-looking woman if a little peremptory in manner, seeming apparently none the worse for wear after having been knocked around and tied up by the bank robber, sat on the arm of the same chair, her right hand protectively on her grandfather's left shoulder. Brian Hopwood, still in his dirty work clothes, stood beside the sofa, talking on Riley's phone to his wife, explaining to her all that had happened and reassuring her, possibly, that everything was all right now. Trooper Oskott stood at semi-attention over by the front door.

They were all waiting for Captain Modale to sort things out and decide what to do next, but by God, there was a full dossier here of things to sort out. There were too many people in this incident, it seemed to the captain, and too many relationships.

Start with the bank robber, who everyone here had known as Ed Smith, a name that had produced thousands of results upon the captain inputting it into the onboard computer in the cruiser, none of them seeming to be helpful in any way. So start with Mr. Ed Smith, whose name was certainly not Ed Smith, but who, for convenience's sake, would be given that name, at least for now. What were the relationships between Smith and the other people in Pooley – or Fred Thiemann, too, let's not forget the fellow just recently shot down by the captain's own officers just across the road there – and how deep and long-standing might those relationships have been?

On entering this room, after being driven down here by Trooper Oskott from Barracks K, greeting the people already assembled here by the troopers who'd been the first responders to Jack Riley's complaint, the captain had dropped onto the dark wood coffee table in front of the sofa the yellow legal pad he'd brought along with him, so that he could accept the Wanted poster Hopwood insisted on handing him, and now he sat down on the sofa facing that pad, Riley and the Gilbert woman to his right, television set to his left, Hopwood standing at the end of the sofa to his left, and took a retractable pen from his pocket. Clicking it open after putting the Wanted poster under the legal pad, he said, "I'd like first to close with this fellow Smith, and everybody's relationship with him."

Suzanne Gilbert, as though she might become offended, said, "Relationship? None of us had a relationship with that man."

"I never even met him," Jack Riley added.

Brian Hopwood, just off the phone, pulled over the small wooden chair from beside the television set, sat on it as though afraid to make it dirty, and said, "I only saw him that one time in my life, this afternoon, when he came in for gas."

"But you recognized him."

"Not right away. But I thought about it, and when he came back in to get his change – he didn't use up the cash he gave me – I had it doped out who he was, and I went ahead and did one of the dumbest things I've ever done in my life."

"You did exactly what a good citizen should have done, under the circumstances," the captain told him, though he himself didn't believe it even while he was saying it.

Nor did Hopwood. "A good citizen with a death wish," he suggested.

The captain decided to let that drop. Facing the others, he said, "So none of you had had dealings with this man before today."

With seeming reluctance, as though still troubled by that word "relationship," Suzanne Gilbert said, "Well . . . I saw him last night."

"Ah," the captain said, not showing his surprise. "And where was that?"

"Just outside there," she said, nodding at the front

window. "I was driving by, and he was walking along the road. You don't usually see people walking around here."

"No," the captain agreed. "You just happened to be driving by?"

"No, I often drive this way after work," she said, as though he'd accused her of something and she was determined to rise above it. "If Jack wants to talk, he'll have the porch light on."

"Ah. And was the porch light on?"

"No, it wasn't."

"I was asleep in front of the damn TV," Riley said. "Again."

"And you saw this man," the captain said. "Just walking, you say?"

"Yes. I thought it was strange, so I stopped and asked him if I could help with anything, and he said he was staying with Tom Lindahl—"

"The man whose parrot was shot."

She looked blank. "I'm sorry?"

So these people hadn't heard that part of it. "Nothing," the captain said, not wanting a distraction.

But Hopwood said, "Somebody shot a parrot?"

"Tom Lindahl's parrot."

"I never knew he had one," Hopwood said. "Why would anybody shoot a parrot?"

"To keep it from talking," Jack said, and actually cackled.

"Jack!" his granddaughter said, reproving him, and squeezed his shoulder to make him behave.

To her, the captain said, "Let's get back. This man you talked to last night said he was staying with Tom Lindahl."

"Yes." She looked a little confused and said, "So then I thought it was all right."

Hopwood said, "He had Tom's car, at the station, I know that car."

Suzanne Gilbert said, "Did he do something to Tom, too?"

"We don't know, ma'am," the captain said. "He isn't at home, and neither is his car."

Hopwood said, "That fellow stole Jeff Eggleston's car. From my place."

"The black Infiniti," the captain said. "Yes, I know, we've put out a bulletin on it."

"What I mean is," Hopwood said, "if he's got Jeff's car, he can't have Tom's. You can only drive one car."

"Then we have to assume," the captain said, "that Lindahl is driving his own car. Does anybody have any idea where he might go?"

"Nowhere," Hopwood said, and Suzanne Gilbert said, "When I talked to that man last night, he said Tom Lindahl was a hermit. I think that's true."

The captain paused, trying to think of a question that might help him move forward on this problem, and in the little silence the front doorbell rang, startling them all. The captain said, "Trooper Oskott can answer."

The trooper turned, opened the door, and spoke briefly with somebody on the porch. Then he turned back to say, "To see you, Captain."

"Thank you." Rising, he told the others, "I think we're just about finished. Let me see what this is."

"I'd like to get home," Hopwood said.

"I'm sure you would," the captain said, and went out to the porch, where a plainclothes state police inspector named Harrison said, "How's it going?"

"Confusing."

"Well, this may help a little. Mrs. Thiemann gave us a statement."

"Yes?"

"She says her husband was part of the group that went out looking for the fugitives yesterday."

"I saw them there," the captain said. "He was teamed up with the missing householder here, Lindahl, and this fella we've been calling Smith."

"She says, her husband told her, they went up to Wolf Peak—"

"That's right."

"And up there her husband shot and killed a man."

251

Now the captain could not hold his astonishment. "He did *what*?"

"Some old wino, bum, something like that." Harrison shrugged. "He got excited, Thiemann, he thought it was one of the bank robbers, and shot him."

"I swear I don't understand this situation," the captain said. "One of them's a bank robber, another of them suddenly ups and kills a man – *and* a parrot – and the third, an ordinary fellow his entire life, goes missing."

"The thing is," Harrison said, "Thiemann would have turned himself in, but Smith talked him out of it, said it was to protect Thiemann."

"It was to protect Smith."

"Well, sure. But Thiemann couldn't stand it. His wife said it drove him crazy."

The captain looked across the road. "So he came down here to confront Smith. Nobody home."

"Lucky for Lindahl," Harrison said, and corrected himself. "Lucky for somebody."

"This Smith," the captain said, "robs a bank in Massachusetts, escapes, gets this far, hooks up with two other people, ordinary people, everybody starts going nuts."

Harrison said, "You think he did it to them, somehow?"

"I truly don't know," the captain said, and looked out

from the lighted porch at the dark road. "We are not going to know," he said, "what this is really all about until Tom Lindahl tells us. I do wish I could lay my hands on him." He nodded at the darkness. "Yes, Lindahl," he said, "I would really like to know where you are."

FOURTEEN

Around nine-thirty, Bill Henry yawned, stretched, pushed back from the desk where his latest *Field & Stream* had lain open and unread for some time now, and got to his feet. One more yawn and he said, "I think I'll walk around a little."

Max Evanson, his usual partner on the overnight shift, looked up from his *People* magazine in some surprise: "Walk around what?"

"The track. The building. Just around."

Max still didn't get it. A traditional kind of guy, who only believed in, as he'd said more than once, "meat and potatoes," he wouldn't see any reason for Bill or himself or anyone else on night guard duty at Gro-More to get up from his comfortable chair in security unless his shift was over. He said, "You're gonna walk around the *track*? It's, what, it's two miles, mile and a half, something like that."

"I'm not going to walk around the track," Bill said. "That's not what I mean at all. Look, Max, I'm outa here the middle of next month, just in time for Thanksgiving, I'm feeling a little different about the place, okay? You get it?"

"No," Max said.

"I've been working here thirty-seven years," Bill said, "the last five in this dumb security office, and pretty soon I'm not gonna be working here any more."

"I'm fourteen months behind you," Max said, as though it were a prayer.

"Well, fourteen months from now, you'll feel the same way I do," Bill assured him.

"And what's that?" The skepticism twanged in Max's voice.

"Not nostalgic exactly—"

"Nostalgic! For this place? The people running this outfit here—"

"No, not nostalgic," Bill insisted. "It's just— You spend so much of your life at a place, you know you're gonna leave it, you won't really miss it, but still you want to fix it in your mind before you go."

"It's fixed in my mind," Max promised him.

"Well, I'm gonna take a little walk around," Bill said. "Mind the store."

"Huh," Max said.

The way it was set up, because of insurance and getting people bonded and all that, security at Gro-More had been a special set-off company since just after World War Two. The track contracted for security arrangements from that company, everything from staff for crowd control to spy cameras, and the employees of the subcompany shared in the not-very-good health and pension benefits available to the rest of the track's workforce.

For most of his thirty-seven years here, Bill Henry had been assigned crowd control out by the entrance gates, and he'd enjoyed it. It was pleasant out in the air, and more interesting than the occasional stint in front of the betting windows, showing the uniform and the holstered sidearm and looking stern, just as though there was a chance in hell one of these bettors would suddenly up and rob the place. Never happen.

So what they did with the security employees, as they got older, nearer retirement, less intimidating out in public regardless of the brown uniform and the holstered firearm, was move them to the overnight guard detail. A simple, easy life if you liked to read, which most of the guys did. A short workweek, reduced pay, but retirement was right out there at the end of it, so not really a problem.

Parts of the track were kept locked at night, like the money room downstairs and the tellers' cages upstairs, but most of the rest of it inside the security wall was open, illuminated just enough to satisfy the fire code.

Leaving the office now, Bill walked first down the corridor past more offices and then out to the rail near the finish line, down to his right. The main dirt course was a long oval under the dim lights, extending left and right, with the slightly smaller turf course a green river within, and then the interior lawn, a different green, with its ornamental fountain and some perennial flowers that were starting at this time of year to give up the ghost.

At night, empty, the track looked much bigger than in the daytime, as though it could probably be seen from the moon, though he knew that was impossible. Bill liked the size of it at night, and the emptiness of it, and the fact that, in all that big empty space, there was never even one echo. It was as though the track absorbed sound, making the place restful and eternal and also just a little spooky.

He made his way leftward along the rail to the far turn, where a lane would lead down to the paddocks if he felt like going there, but he thought he better not. There were always a few of the grooms and assistant trainers sleeping somewhere near their animals, on cots or in sleeping bags, because this horse or that was having some kind of problem, and those people didn't like other humans around to spook their beasts.

Bill turned away, walking toward the end of the clubhouse and grandstand, all in one building, and as he walked, he saw the reflection of headlights sweep over the white wooden wall that enclosed the entire track area.

Headlights? They were outside, so he couldn't see them directly, only their glow above the wall, and as he stopped to frown at that unexpected aura, the lights switched off.

But what were they doing here? Nobody was supposed to be in that area beyond the wall at night. That would be where the service road came in, at the end of the clubhouse, and there was never any reason for traffic out there after the track shut down.

Unless it was somebody out to harm the horses.

Why that should be, Bill had never understood, but there was a kind of sick human being who just liked to mutilate horses. Attack them with knives, axes, bottles of acid.

Why would people do things like that? They were always caught, drooling and bloody, and they were always put away in a nuthouse somewhere, and there was never any explanation. Whatever went wrong in your life, whatever went wrong in your head, why take it out on a horse?

And is that what he'd happened across tonight? It was those sickos, he knew, who primarily made his job as a night guard here at the track necessary, that and the constant fear of fire. So is that what he'd found, some maniac with a chain saw in his fist? Was he about to become a hero, like it or not?

He thought the thing to do was go back into the clubhouse and walk around to where he could look out one of the windows facing the service road. Let's just see what's out there. Couldn't hurt.

FIFTEEN

Tom Lindahl drove past the main entrance to Gro-More, with its outlined stylized bulls on the gates, then drove on past the dirt road, unmarked except for the Dead End sign, that he should have taken down to the end of the clubhouse. But he just kept driving.

For a mile or two, he didn't even think about what he was doing, but just drove on as though that were his only purpose in being out here, to drive aimlessly, forever. It was easy, and it was comforting, and it didn't make any sense.

After a couple of miles, he came to himself enough to realize this wasn't going to work. He hadn't seen Smith anywhere on the long drive down, he'd come to believe he'd never see Smith again, but that didn't mean he could just drive on and on. Where to? For what?

I can't go back, he thought for the very first time.

That was a chilling thought. He was on a dark country road, and up ahead there was an intersection with a lit-up diner on the right. Refusing to think, clenching his teeth to hold back the floodgates of thought, he waited till he reached the diner, pulled in, stopped in the semidark around at the rear, opened his window, and shut off the engine. Then he slumped and stared at the back of the building, the Dumpster, the screen door closed over the glaringly bright kitchen.

I can't go back there. He meant Pooley, he meant the little converted garage he'd been living in, he meant that whole life.

He didn't think, I can't go home. That wasn't home, he hadn't had a home for years. That was where he'd camped out, waiting for something to happen, although, until Smith had come along, there was never anything going to happen except one day he wouldn't be waiting any more.

But Smith had come along and riled up the waters. Tom had met him, and hooked up with him, and told him about this racetrack opportunity, because he'd thought he wanted revenge and money, but he'd been wrong. He'd wanted a hand grenade to throw into the middle of his empty unbearable life, and boy, he'd sure found one.

He couldn't go back because too many people had seen him with Smith, and, one way or another, who Smith really was would be bound to come out. If somehow they went ahead with this robbery, the police would automatically look at Tom Lindahl, simply because he was a former employee with a grudge, and what would they find? The mysterious Ed Smith, come and gone at just the exact right moment.

But even without the robbery, how long would Smith's identity stay hidden? Fred Thiemann suspected something, though he wasn't sure yet just what it was. Fred's wife, Jane, was smarter and more persistent than Fred, and if she started to wonder about Smith, that would be the end of it. And weren't Cory and Cal Dennison poking their noses in somehow?

So the only thing for Tom to do was what he'd instinctively started to do. Just drive, keep driving south, try to find somebody else to be, somebody else in some other place. Smith had told him it was impossible to disappear like that today, but that couldn't be true. People vanished. And God knows, if there was one thing Tom Lindahl wanted to do, it was vanish.

The only question was, should he go back to the track, just to see if Smith showed up? Without Smith, he knew he wouldn't be doing any robbery here tonight, wouldn't even go into the clubhouse, wouldn't even get out of the car. But at least he should go back, look at Gro-More one last time before closing that part of his life at last. He'd give Smith, say, half an hour, then drive away from here and never be Tom Lindahl again.

Once the decision was made, it was easy, as though it had always been easy; he'd just been too close to it to see the path. Now he could see it. He started the engine, drove back to Dead End, and this time headed on in. He went to where there was the right turn to the chain-link fence, and stopped at the gate there. He didn't get out of the car but looked through the fence at the clubhouse and after a minute switched off the headlights. He didn't need them to know where he was.

Smith, in the dark beside Tom's open window, said, "Time to get started."

PART FOUR

PART FOUR

ONE

Parker saw the gray Volkswagen Jetta start out of Pooley after Tom Lindahl's Ford SUV, and fell in line behind it, in the Infiniti he'd taken from Brian Hopwood's gas station. The best opportunity to deal with the Jetta and the two inside it came just before the second roadblock, when the Jetta pulled off onto the apron of a closed gas station. Parker stopped beside them, planning to talk to them, see what he had to do to get rid of them, maybe shoot their tires out or shoot up their ignition, whatever it would take to scare them off, but before he got close enough to say anything, the idiot Cal was out of the Jetta and waving a handgun around and Parker put him down.

The other one got scared, all right, and skittered away from there like a drop of water on a hot frying pan, but Parker knew he'd be back. Cory'd made it his lifework to stand with his dumber crazier brother, so once the fright wore off, he'd have to come back.

The only problem was the body. Without the body, Cory would have nothing to say to the troopers down there at the roadblock, too far for them to have heard the flat crack of Parker's single shot. The troopers were more bored tonight, less convinced they'd find anything useful out here, and they weren't searching cars, not even cars with two males inside, so Parker threw the body into the trunk, went through the roadblock without a problem, flashing the Infiniti's registration he'd found in the packet with the owner's manual, plus William G. Dodd's driver's license, and a few miles later, at a silent dark empty stretch of road, no buildings in sight, he dumped the body off the road and down a slope toward a chattering little creek he could hear but not see.

Shortly after that, he overtook the SUV, still potting along ten miles below the speed limit. He passed it when he could, and went on to the track, leaving the Infiniti on the scrub ground outside the chain-link fence away to the left of the road, facing back toward the gate. Then he switched off the engine, buttoned the overhead light not to turn on when the door was opened, and waited.

It took longer than it should have for Tom to get there. Had he lost his nerve? If he was running, too spooked to think what best to do for himself, Parker would have no choice but to drive away from here and forget the track. He couldn't get in without Tom's keys and Tom's knowledge.

Without Tom, he'd just drive south through the night. No

profit from the bank in Massachusetts, and now no profit from this racetrack. In the morning, wherever he was, he'd phone Claire to drive out and get him, and that would be the end of it. It had been too long since he'd seen her.

But here was Tom. Parker saw the headlights coming down the dirt road and got out of the Infiniti. Walking toward the gate as the SUV drove to it and stopped, he saw Tom in the amber glow from the dashboard, his window open, Parker coming to him from that side.

Tom just sat there, not aware of Parker, but then at last he switched the ignition off, and in the darkness Parker said, "Time to get started."

TWO

Parker carried the duffel bags, still folded into their plastic wrap, and followed Lindahl through the same routine as last time, first punching the code into the alarm box beside the gate, then keying the gate open so he could drive the Ford in to stop at the closed top of the ramp that led down to the safe room. Getting out of the Ford there, as Parker walked up to him, he looked back at the fence and said, "Do you have a car here?"

"We'll get to it later. We want to be in and out of this."

"Sure. Fine."

Once again Lindahl keyed them into the building and led them among the rooms through the same route around the spy cams. This time there was no leftover food in the accounts department to be knocked over, and no sign of the mess they'd made before. At the end, Lindahl waited for that camera in the corridor to start its sweep away from them, then they strode down to the stairwell door and inside. Down one flight, Lindahl pressed his face to the small window in the door there, to see where this camera was in its cycle, then led them out and to the door at the end of this corridor, the key already in his hand.

Once again, when the door closed behind them, they were in full dark. Parker knew Lindahl was afraid the camera outside would be able to see light through the small window in this door here, so he waited in the darkness, holding the packages of duffel bag and pressing one elbow back against the closed door to keep his orientation.

Out ahead was the sound of Lindahl's scuffing feet as he moved cautiously toward the door they wanted. There was a little silence, then the sound of the key in the lock and the door opening, and at last the ceiling fluorescents clicked on in the safe room off to the right, so Parker could see this outer room with the forklift truck in the corner and the windowless garage door at the far end.

There were two pallets of the money boxes on the floor in here tonight. Lindahl, a nervous grin flickering on his frightened-looking face, said, "Double our money, huh?"

"That's what we're doing. Here."

He handed one of the duffel bags to Lindahl, who took it and said, "How do you want to work this?"

"We open the boxes and put the cash in the bags. Don't bother with singles and fives."

"No, I meant, how do we divide this?"

Parker shook his head. "We aren't gonna divvy it up," he said. "What you put in the bag, you carry home."

"Fine."

They started to strip the plastic off the duffel bags, and a glaring light snapped on in the next room. They stopped, looking at each other, and a voice out there called, "Anybody here?" The voice tried to sound in control, but there was a quaver in it.

Parker handed the duffel to Lindahl and pointed at the corner behind the open door as he started toward that doorway, calling, "Hello? How do I get out of here?"

Behind him, Lindahl moved silently into the corner, his face drained of blood, and Parker stepped through to the outer room, where he saw, over by the door they'd come in, a guy in a brown guard uniform. He was big, maybe six and a half feet, and once brawny, but now out of condition, older and too long comfortable. In the glare of the overhead fluorescents, his eyes and cheekbones showed fear. He was armed with a revolver, but it wasn't in his hand, it was still in its holster on his right hip, and his right hand was still on the light switch just to the right of the door.

Now, seeing Parker, he lowered that hand to the butt of the revolver but didn't unsnap the safety strap that held it in the holster. He patched over the fear with a deep frown and said, "What the hell *you* doing here?"

"Trying to get out." Parker looked back over his shoulder at the safe room. "What kind of place *is* that?"

"What do you mean, trying to get out of here?" The guard, not sensing threat, had settled into the indifferently bullying tactic that would always have been his method with civilians.

Parker spread his hands. "Everything's locked. I can't get out of the goddam place."

"*That's* kept locked," the guard told him, jutting his jaw toward the safe room.

"No, it wasn't," Parker said. "I saw the light in there, maybe it's a way out at last."

"I don't get this," the guard said. "What are you doing in here? The end of the day, every day, there's a sweep, make sure everybody's out."

"I fell asleep," Parker said. "In the men's room, in a stall." He didn't try to act embarrassed, just matter-of-fact. "I didn't have that much to drink. I been working double shifts for a while now . . ." He shrugged it off. "Can you get me out of here?"

The guard was suspicious, but he wasn't sure of what. Nodding at the safe room, he said, "That door's kept locked."

"It was open, just like that," Parker told him, pointing at the doorway. "Door hooked open and the lights on. You think I got keys to this place? Look at the door, I didn't bust in, it was just like that. Listen, I'm sorry. If you wanna call the cops on me, go ahead, but I just gotta get out of here."

The guard considered him. "We'll go to the office," he decided.

"If that's on the way out," Parker said, "fine."

"You lead the way."

"Sure. But you'll have to tell me which way I'm leading."

The guard's right hand went from the revolver butt to the doorknob behind him. Opening the door, stepping to one side, he said, "Just go out and down the hall."

"Sure."

As Parker went by him, the guard frowned at the door he was holding. "Was this unlocked, too?"

"No, it wasn't shut."

"It's always shut."

Parker waited while the guard followed him out and pulled the door closed. "It wasn't like that," he said. "It was almost shut, but not all. I could just push it. And I saw those lights in there."

"Something's funny here," the guard said, and nodded at the corridor. "Just go straight down."

"Right."

They walked past the door on the left leading to the stairwell that Parker and Lindahl had used. Parker didn't look that way but faced straight, and at the end the guard directed him to turn left down a different corridor. This was a completely different route from the one he'd taken before with Lindahl, and it led finally to an elevator. So this guard didn't like climbing stairs.

He also didn't like being in the enclosed space of the metal elevator with Parker. He stood against the back wall, hand on the revolver butt again, this time his fingers toying with the safety strap as he looked sidelong at Parker.

At the top, the corridor was carpeted. "To the left."

They walked down the corridor, Parker in front, and the guard said, "The open door on the right."

"What?" Somebody past that open door had heard the voice.

Parker made the turn, and this was the security room, with banks of television monitors, shotguns locked into racks on the wall, and several desks, only one of them occupied, by a slightly smaller version of the first guard, equally out of shape.

This one started to rise when he saw Parker, then settled back again when his partner came in. Looking at the partner, he said, "Bill? Whatchu got here?"

"He was in the safe room."

"He *what*?" Now he did get up from the desk and frowned at Parker but kept talking to his partner. "What's he doing in there?"

"Says he's trying to find the way out. Says he went asleep in the john." Pointing at the monitors, he said, "You see him on any of the screens?"

"I saw you, that's all." Now he did speak to Parker: "How'd you get in there?"

"Walked."

He didn't like that. "Don't get snotty with *me*, fella."

"I told this guy," Parker said with a gesture at Bill, "I fell asleep, I woke up, I'm trying to get out of here. Everything's locked."

"Except the safe room," said Bill. "How d'ya like that?"

"I don't," the second one said, and to Parker he said, "You got anybody with you?"

"I didn't see anybody," Bill said.

"When I sleep in the men's room," Parker said, "I sleep alone."

The second one was getting steamed. He glared at Parker a long minute, then said, "I may have to tenderize you."

"We'd better call the troopers," Bill said.

"We'll get to that," his partner said. Still glaring at

Parker, he pointed at the top of his desk and said, "Empty your pockets."

"Sure." Parker took the automatic out of his pocket and showed it to them as he stepped to the left, so he could see them both. "Is this good enough?"

"God damn you—" The second one was red-faced now and angrier than ever. He moved as though to come around the desk.

"Max! Jesus, Max, fourteen months, remember?"

That stopped Max, or at least slowed him down. "What a hell of a thing you brought me," he said.

Parker said, "On the floor, both of you, over there. Facedown."

Neither moved. Max said, "There's two of us."

"There could be none of you. You go on the floor without a bullet in you, or you go on the floor *with* a bullet in you. Now."

"Fourteen months, Max," Bill said, and stiffly lowered himself to the floor, having trouble getting down, and then having more trouble rolling onto his stomach.

Max watched him, tense, not wanting the humiliation in front of this armed stranger, but finally realized there was no choice. He tried to be more graceful getting down, but failed, and finally lost his balance and landed on his bottom with a thump. Quickly, then, he scrambled around to lie prone, turning his face away.

Parker said, "Where do you keep the cuffs?"

"Fuck you," Max told the carpet.

Parker said, "I may have to tenderize you, friend."

Bill said, "They're in the desk with the flowerpot on it, bottom side drawer."

Parker found them and tossed them onto the floor between the two guards. "Bill, you put them on Max."

Max was muttering, "Goddammit, goddammit, goddammit," but he stopped when he sensed Bill getting up onto his knees. They all waited to see what Bill would do, which for a few seconds was nothing.

Parker said, "That's far enough up, Bill. Do it."

Bill was sheepish. "Sorry, Max," he said as he clipped the cuffs onto the other man's wrists, behind his back.

"How do we let him do this, goddammit?"

"He's got the gun, Max."

"So do we!"

"His is in his hand."

"Facedown, Bill," Parker said, and quickly cuffed him, then placed two chairs between the men's legs, to keep them from rolling over or moving around. With a last look at all the empty corridors and rooms on the monitor screens, he headed fast for the elevator.

THREE

Lindahl sat on the duffel bags, both of them full. The money trays were scattered around the open boxes, still full of small bills and coins. Lindahl seemed to be thinking hard, and it took him a second to realize Parker had come back. Then, startled, he jumped to his feet and said, "Is it me now?"

Parker looked at him. "Is what you?"

"I knew that guy," Lindahl said. "I recognized the voice. He worked here forever. His name's Bill."

"That's right."

"Big man. I've been trying to remember his last name."

Parker said, "You filled the bags. That's good."

Looking down at them, Lindahl said, "I tried to make it as even as I could, between them. If it matters."

"So now you unlock us out of here."

Lindahl didn't move. He kept gazing at the duffel bags, as though still trying to remember Bill's last name, then looked sidewise at Parker and said, "You killed him, didn't you?"

"No," Parker said. "Why would I have to?"

"I brought you here, I brought you into all this. But you don't belong in this— with these people. I keep thinking about Fred."

Parker needed to get out of here, but Lindahl was going through some sort of crisis and would have to be waited out. "What about Fred?"

"He's going crazy. He killed that man, and it's driving him crazy."

"I think he was a little crazy before that," Parker said. "Maybe because of his son, or I don't know what. He killed a man who wasn't a threat to him or anybody else."

"He should have turned himself in. It was only to save you."

"It would have been bad for him to turn himself in. It wouldn't make him less crazy to wind up doing time."

"It wouldn't be on his conscience now," Lindahl said, "and that man wouldn't be up . . . They'd find his family. He'd get a burial."

"Maybe. Tom, what we have to do now is get these bags out of here, and then it's all over."

"If you killed Bill," Lindahl said, "you'll kill me, too."

"Tom," Parker said, "you don't kill somebody unless you have to. It puts the law on you like nothing else. Worse than what we've been having."

"Where is he?"

Parker frowned at him. This was taking too long. "Bill is handcuffed on the floor in the security office, along with the other one, Max."

"You had handcuffs?"

"The security office had handcuffs. Tom, snap out of this now. We've got to get out of here."

Lindahl looked toward the door, as though he meant to go to the security office, to see for himself if his old friends Bill and Max were alive in there, but then he shook his head and said, "You get to imagine different ways, different ways it can go."

"The way it's going," Parker said, "we get out of here now."

Lindahl took a deep breath. "You're right," he said, and moved toward the doorway, taking keys from his pocket.

FOUR

Parker waited in the safe room doorway as Lindahl carried his keys to the alarm box beside the garage door at the end of the corridor. One key opened the box, and a second switched off the alarm.

This was the alarm that would have made it necessary for them to come back down here after removing the money, shutting the door from the inside and reactivating the alarm, then retracing their route to the other door, so that a light wouldn't flash in security. Now that Parker had had to deal with the guards in security, it didn't matter any more if that light flashed on. A simpler operation but more hurried.

Lindahl, finished with the alarm, opened the garage door, and there was the ramp, leading upward to ground level, where his Ford waited beyond the locked chain-link gate. Parker watched Lindahl start up the ramp to get his car, then he turned back to pick up one of the duffel bags and carry it out of the safe room. When he reached the outer room, Lindahl was back, too soon, without the car and looking worried.

"Something wrong," he said, half a whisper.

Parker put the duffel on the floor. "What?"

"There's another car up there," Lindahl said. "A gray car. It's backed up against the rear bumper of my Ford. I don't see anybody in it."

"No, he's not in it," Parker said. "If he backed his car against yours, that's so he can watch the driver's side. He's up there on the left somewhere, in the dark, in a place where he can watch both the door where we came in and the driver's side of his car. We have to go one way or the other to get out of here, and he knows it."

"But who?" Lindahl peered at Parker as though it had become harder to see him. "Do you know who it is?"

"Cory Dennison."

"Cory! What the hell's *he* doing here?"

"Looking for our money." Parker took a step toward the ramp but didn't go up it.

Lindahl said, "Isn't Cal with him?"

"No, it's just Cory, but that's enough."

Lindahl shook his head. "Cory and Cal are *always* together, they don't do things on their own."

"This time," Parker said, "it's just Cory."

Lindahl stared at him, trying to frame some question.

Parker waited for him, then said, "Is there something you want to know?"

Lindahl thought about it, looking more worried than ever. Then he said, "There was a car behind me, for a while, might have been that one. Was that Cal and Cory?"

"Yes."

"Together then, but just Cory now. Is Cal waiting somewhere else?"

"No."

Lindahl nodded and looked away. Parker said, "What our problem is, he's got us boxed in down here. We can't waste a lot of time on this. If one of those guards has a wife that likes to call him late at night, what happens when she doesn't get an answer?"

Lindahl stopped worrying about Cal and turned to look up the ramp. "You're right. If I go up there and push his car with mine . . ."

"His car is in gear with the emergency brake on. You know that's what he's going to do. The minute you start your engine, he'll shoot you."

"But we have to get out of here."

"We will. The gate's unlocked?"

"Yes, but it's still closed. I was unlocking it when I saw the other car."

"Turn off the lights down here," Parker said, "and sit tight."

284

He started toward the ramp, but Lindahl said, "Wait."

"What is it?"

"What if . . ." Lindahl gestured vaguely at the ramp.

"What if Cory comes down, instead of me?"

"Yes."

Parker nodded at the door to the corridor. "Go that way. You've got keys, lock doors behind you."

"My car."

"The guards have pistols," Parker told him. "Get one and do your best. Lights out."

"Right."

As Lindahl switched off the lights, he was looking at that inner door.

FIVE

Pistol in his hand, Parker went up the ramp in the darkness, stopping by the closed gate to wait for his eyes to adjust. There was no moon right now, but many high stars that gave the world a slight velvet gray illumination. Beyond the chain-link gate, he could see the bulk of Lindahl's black SUV and beyond that the gray Jetta. A number of parked track vehicles were an indistinct mass to the left, along the wall beyond the end of the clubhouse. To left and right, the wall curved away into darkness.

Parker knew this area was a large enclosed trapezoid with this end of the clubhouse as its narrow edge, and eight-foot-high wooden walls curving out from it to meet the main wooden wall that surrounded the property. Inside the wall, there was nothing but grass and dirt, except for those vehicles parked to the left. So that's where Cory would be.

There was no way to be silent when opening the gate. A U-shaped metal bar had to be lifted out of the way. The noise it made was small but sharp; Cory would have heard it.

The gate was built in two sections, hinged at the far sides. Parker pulled open the right side just far enough so he could slip through, then went to the ground in front of the Ford and made his way, prone, leftward past the car, then straight out toward those parked vehicles, crawling forward with the gun out ahead of himself. If he were to move to left or right, there was a chance Cory could see his movements against the white wall or the white end of the clubhouse. As long as he kept that bulk of the two cars and the gate behind him, there'd be nothing to make him a silhouette.

The world was absolutely silent, except for the tiny scuffing sounds he made as he moved across the weedy ground. Then, out ahead, he heard a metallic click, and an instant later a pair of headlights flashed on.

It was some sort of big vehicle, the headlights higher than on a car, pointed at an angle to his right, but with plenty of leftover glare to show him on the ground, midway between the trucks ahead and the gate behind.

Parker shot the nearer headlight, then rolled to his right, closer to the beam, as he heard an answering shot from out in front and the smash of a car window behind him. Prone again, he shot out the second headlight, then rolled back to his left as Cory fired twice more, still shooting too high, the way most people do when they're firing at something below them.

Cory didn't waste any more ammunition. Parker got his elbows underneath himself, then pushed up to his feet and ran forward at a crouch. The headlights had spoiled his night vision for a few seconds, but they would have done the same for Cory.

The rear doors of an ambulance. The vehicle with the headlights had been facing outward and was down to the right. Parker moved around the left side of the ambulance, came to the wall beyond it, and stopped. He looked left and right but saw nothing against the wall. He waited and listened.

Silence. Cory was still in here somewhere, in this collection of vehicles. If he was smart, he'd stay in one place and wait for Parker to move, knowing Parker would have to move, he couldn't still be stuck in here at daybreak.

Cory wouldn't have been inside the vehicle with the lights but would have reached in through an open side window to switch them on. Probably he'd had to stand on an exterior step of the thing, which was why it had been a few seconds before he'd started firing, the time he'd needed to step back down to the ground.

Would he still be over there, near that vehicle? Had he seen Parker's run? Would he have any idea where Parker was now?

Time to move. Keeping his back against the wooden wall, Parker sidled leftward. Next past the ambulance was a pickup truck, also facing this way, then a two-wheeled horse trailer tilted forward, and then a small fire engine, facing out.

Was this the thing with the lights? The next vehicle was another pickup, facing outward, but too small to be the one with those lights.

Parker went down prone behind the fire engine and looked under the vehicles to see if he could find Cory's feet. No; Cory wasn't in the immediate area of the fire engine, and farther away it was impossible to see anything.

He was getting back up on his feet when another set of headlights flashed on, farther to the left. He turned toward them, but almost instantly the lights switched off again, making the darkness darker than before.

So Cory hadn't known where Parker was, and now knew he had to be in here among the vehicles. Parker started toward where the headlights had flashed, and abruptly heard running.

The window in this pickup's driver's door was shut, but the door wasn't locked. Parker pulled it open, causing more light as the interior bulb went on, and switched on the headlights, to see Cory running as fast as he could toward the gate and the ramp. He dove around the far end of the Ford as Parker fired at him, just too late.

Parker slapped off these headlights, slammed the pickup door, and trotted after Cory, calling, "Tom! Get back!"

When he reached the gate, he stopped to listen. Not a sound from down there. Had Lindahl managed to get deeper into the clubhouse, locking doors after himself, or was Cory now moving around inside the building? Or was Cory waiting down there in the darkness for Parker to come after him?

Parker crouched low and slid over in front of the Ford, which would keep him invisible from down below. He waited, and still heard nothing, and gradually became aware that the darkness down there wasn't absolute. The lights were still on in the corridor beyond that room, and they gleamed a faint dark yellow through the thick glass of the small window in the door.

The gate was still slightly open, the way he'd left it. He sidled through, waited, inched forward. Infinitely slow, he traveled in a deep crouch down the ramp, left hand on the tilted concrete floor behind him, right hand holding the pistol out in front, eyes on that dim rectangle of light, hoping to see someone pass across in front of it.

As he advanced, he took shallow silent breaths

through open mouth. He listened for any sound that would tell him where Cory was, but heard nothing.

At the bottom of the ramp, he stayed in the crouch, left hand now on the floor in front of himself. The duffel bag he'd brought in here from the safe room would be ahead and to his left; he moved toward it, always keeping his eye on that dim-lit window.

He had the bag. Turning slowly, bracing himself, he sat on it, knees wide, forearms on legs, hands and gun hanging downward. There was very little time to waste here, but there was time enough for this. He would wait, and Cory would reveal himself, and Parker would kill him. He would wait, and Lindahl would come back and make some sort of disturbance, flushing Cory out, and Parker would kill him.

The small rectangular amber gleam high up in the door was like a window in a castle far up a mountainside. Parker watched it, and breathed evenly, and permitted his body to relax, and waited.

SIX

"Ed! Ed! You down there?"

Maybe ten minutes had gone by, no more than that, the two of them silent in the dark, and all at once this urgent hushed call came down from the top of the ramp. Lindahl, not in the clubhouse, after all, but up there, outside, by the gate and the two cars.

Parker kept his eye on the yellow window in the door as he sat up straighter, gun hand now resting atop his right knee. If Lindahl was outside, he'd made his way all around to that other door, the one they'd come in. If he'd done that, wouldn't he have gone to look at the guards along the way, to see if they were alive or dead, and to take their guns? And if he'd done all that, he must not have left this room when Parker called the warning to him but earlier, the instant Parker had gone up the ramp and out of his sight. And he would have done that because he'd already had plans for the guards' guns.

Defensive plans, or a double cross?

"Ed! Where the hell are you?"

"Come down." It was Cory said that, from the other side of the black room, making his voice sound rough, indistinct.

But he hadn't sounded like Parker, because Lindahl up there at the top of the ramp said, with a quick quaver in his voice, "Who's that? Cory, is that you?"

There was a long pause, and then Cory called, in his own voice, "Yes. Come down."

Parker aimed at that sound, but it didn't go on long enough. If he couldn't be sure of his shot, he wouldn't take it.

Lindahl wasn't coming down. Instead, he was saying, "Where's Ed?"

"He killed my brother." Again too short to home in on.

"I know that," Lindahl said. "Did you kill him, Cory?"

Another long pause. "Yes."

"Cory, listen," Lindahl said. "You don't have any complaint against me, do you?"

"No."

"I didn't have anything to do with him and Cal. It made me sick when he told me about it."

No response from Cory; what response could he make?

Lindahl said, "Cory, come on, turn on the light down there, let's figure out what to do here."

"Where is it?"

"You see the window lit in the door there, to your left? It's just beyond that, on the left side of the door."

"Okay."

Parker raised the gun. Cory was now going to cross that light.

But Lindahl, up there at the top of the ramp, was at an angle to see first when Cory went by the door to block the window light for just an instant, so it was Lindahl who fired one of the guard's pistols. And missed.

Parker rolled to the floor on the far side of the duffel bag as Cory yelled and pulled open the door. He ran out of the room as Lindahl wasted two more shots from above.

There had been just that one instant of light when the door was open, and then dark again. Had Lindahl seen the shape of Parker, on the floor beyond the duffel bag, in that instant? Parker waited, listening, but didn't hear Lindahl coming down, so he got to his feet, crossed over to the door, and looked quickly out through that window to see only the empty corridor. Cory had run fast.

What would Cory do now? Most likely find a place where he could protect his back, hunker down, hope for an opportunity to get to Lindahl before Lindahl could get to him. And why had Lindahl taken those shots? Because he'd understood, just as Parker had, that Cory wanted revenge against both of them for the death of his brother.

So what was Lindahl doing now? Parker walked up the ramp, and at the top he could hear rustling sounds, out ahead. He moved along the side of the Ford and saw that the Jetta was rocking slightly. Lindahl was doing something inside there.

It took him a minute to figure out what had happened. Cory's first shot at Parker had smashed the rear side window of the Jetta on the driver's side. He had, of course, locked the car, but Lindahl had reached through the broken window to unlock that door. From outside, though, he couldn't reach far enough to unlock the driver's door, so he was now inside the Jetta, climbing over from the backseat to the front, grunting with the effort, clumsy in his haste.

Let them play it out. Lindahl was too busy with what he was doing to notice anything else, so Parker turned away, to stride by the clubhouse wall past that door they'd used for entry and along the wooden wall toward the parked vehicles. He stopped when he came to the first of them, a big boxy horse carrier.

By now, Lindahl was getting out of the Jetta, finished with whatever he'd needed to do in there. Cory would have the keys with him, so all Lindahl could have done was put the car in neutral.

Yes. Lindahl's Ford faced the gate and the ramp, its rear bumper against the rear bumper of the Jetta. Now

Lindahl got behind the wheel of the Ford and backed it away from the gate, forcing the Jetta to roll forward. When he had the Jetta well out of his path, he looped around to back up against the gate and get out of the car.

Didn't he plan to do anything about Cory? Or had he understood he wouldn't be able to go back to his old life after this, so it wouldn't matter if somebody from those days wanted to kill him? Did he think the two duffel bags would give him a stronger chance at escape than just the one? Or did he believe Cory that Parker was dead, although Cory had only said so to try to bring Parker into the open, or to convince Lindahl that the shooting was over.

Lindahl got out of the Ford long enough to open the gates wide, then backed the car down the ramp and out of sight. An instant later the lights down there switched on, and an instant after that the near door opened and Cory stepped out.

SEVEN

There wasn't much more light up here than before. It looked as though Lindahl had only switched on the deeper lights, the ones in the safe room. He must have been afraid to draw attention from the outside world. But there was enough added illumination to show Cory come out that door, gun in hand, and pause, first looking over toward that light, then looking at the parked vehicles instead.

Parker could hear Cory's thoughts as though he were saying them out loud. He wasn't sure if any of his bullets had hit Parker. Until he knew where Parker was, or where his body was, he didn't dare turn his back on anything. He knew he didn't have a lot of time before Lindahl would drive up out of there with the money, but first he had to account for Parker.

While Cory was working that out, standing in front of the still-open clubhouse door, as though he might reverse himself and go back inside again, Parker made his own move. The ambulance had ladder rungs bolted to its back, next to the door. Parker went up them and lay flat on the flat roof, facedown, head turned to watch Cory, who finally understood he'd have to come over here and search the vehicles for Parker, and that he'd better be both fast and careful.

All of which was making him nervous, taking some of the steel out of his rage. Down in the darkness, in the waiting time, Cory'd been as silent as Parker, or he wouldn't be alive now. But up here, as he moved in among the vehicles, he was gasping, quick rattle breaths that were like a road map showing his route through the dark.

The time for shooting Cory was gone, because the sound would set Lindahl off in some new scattered direction, and Parker wanted Lindahl, for the moment, just where he was. So he waited, lying on top of the ambulance, and below him Cory moved back and forth among the vehicles, looking inside, looking underneath, always with that gasping noise around him and that pistol hand stuck out front.

Parker waited, and the road map of breath-sounds turned the front of the ambulance, jittered down along its side, and Parker, pistol reversed, swung it down hard onto the back of that shaking head, driving Cory forward and facedown into the ground. He slammed to a stop down there like a broken film projector, frozen on that last frame.

Parker climbed down from the ambulance and didn't bother to check Cory's condition. If dead, he was dead. If alive he wouldn't be any use to anybody for a while.

When Parker reached the open gate at the top of the ramp, Lindahl was just stuffing the second of the duffel bags into the SUV, filling up the storage area behind the backseat. Parker left him to it and loped away to the outer gate in the surrounding wall, which they had left closed but not locked. He stepped through the opening as back there at the clubhouse bright headlights angled upward at the sky from below ground, then leveled out as the Ford appeared. The headlights disappeared for Parker as he moved to his right along the wooden wall.

Lindahl had to stop to open the gate, and when he did, Parker stepped forward into the headlights, saying, "You got our money."

Lindahl staggered. In grabbing the gate to try to brace himself, he made the gate swing instead, and nearly fell down. "Ed! For God's sake!"

Lindahl was not carrying a gun, so Parker put his in his pocket as he came around the end of the gate and said, "Help me carry my duffel out of there."

"Sure— You— He said you were dead."

"He was wrong. Come on, Tom, let's get this over with."

Parker opened the rear cargo door and looked in at

the two long mounds, like body bags. Lindahl came and stood beside him, looking in at the bags. "I did it," he said, his voice quiet but proud. "I know, you and me together did it, but *I* did it. After all this time."

"We'll just put it on the ground outside," Parker said, reaching for the top duffel, "beside the wall."

"You don't want me to see your car."

"You don't need to see my car. Come on, Tom."

They put their arms around the end of the duffel and carried it around the car and through the gate and put it on the ground beside the wall. Looking down at it, Lindahl said, "Half the time, I was sure, if we ever got it, and I never thought we'd get it, but I was sure . . ." His voice trailed off, with a little vague hand gesture.

"You were sure I'd shoot you," Parker said. "I know."

"You could have, anytime."

Parker said, "You brought me the job, you went in on the job with me, that's yours."

Lindahl giggled; a strange sound out here. "You mean," he said, "like, honor among thieves?"

"No," Parker said. "I mean a professional is a professional. Take off, Tom, and stay away from roadblocks. That car might be burned by now."

"I'll be okay," Lindahl said. The giggle had opened some looseness inside him, some confidence, as though he'd suddenly had a drink. "So long," he said, and got behind

300

the wheel of the Ford. His window was open; he looked out and might have said something else, but Parker shook his head, so Lindahl simply put the Ford in gear and drove away from there.

Once Lindahl had made the turn onto the dirt road leading to the county road, Parker went over to bring the Infiniti up close to the duffel. By then, Lindahl was out of sight. Parker wondered how far he'd get.